BuDaYeen Nights

Nights

GEORGE ALEC EFFINGER

*With a Foreword and Story Introductions
by Barbara Hambly*

GOLDEN GRYPHON PRESS • 2003

GEORGE ALEC EFFINGER
1947–2002

"Foreword," copyright © 2003 by Barbara Hambly.

"The City on the Sand," first published in *The Magazine of Fantasy and Science Fiction*, April 1973.

"King of the Cyber Rifles," first published in *Isaac Asimov's Science Fiction Magazine*, Mid-December 1987.

"Marîd and the Trail of Blood," first published in *Sisters of the Night*, edited by Barbara Hambly and Martin H. Greenberg, Warner Aspect, 1995.

"Marîd Changes His Mind," first published in *Isaac Asimov's Science Fiction Magazine*, May 1989.

"Marîd Throws a Party," copyright © 2003 by the Estate of George Alec Effinger. Originally written as the first two chapters of *Word of Night*, the fourth Marîd Audran novel. Previously unpublished.

"The Plastic Pasha," copyright © 2003 by the Estate of George Alec Effinger. Previously unpublished.

"Schrödinger's Kitten," first published in *Omni*, September 1988.

"Slow, Slow Burn," first published in *Playboy*, May 1988.

"The World as We Know It," first published in *Futurecrime*, edited by Cynthia Manson and Charles Ardai, Fine, 1992.

Copyright © 2003 by the Estate of George Alec Effinger. These stories were first published in slightly different form and appear here in the author's preferred text.

Foreword and Story Introductions copyright © 2003 by Barbara Hambly

Cover illustration copyright © 2003 by John Picacio

Edited by Marty Halpern

ISBN: 978-1-930846-19-7

Contents

For Nell, Denise, Helen, Valerie,
and all the others without whom
there would be no Budayeen.

—GAE

Foreword

J T ALWAYS SURPRISED GEORGE WHEN PEOPLE WOULD refer to him as a science fiction writer.

It was a natural perception, of course, of someone who made his debut under the auspices of Damon Knight; and to the end of his days, George used a science-fiction palette to tell fantasy stories. But it wasn't until he began writing the Budayeen novels —*When Gravity Fails, A Fire in the Sun,* and *The Exile Kiss*— that he settled fully into science fiction mode, and reinvented himself as one of the founding fathers of Cyberpunk.

The setting of the Budayeen came about quite naturally, and is intrinsic to the writing of *Gravity*. George had a very dark side to his nature, a fascination with the underworld and the demimonde that came about, I think, because many of his mother's friends were hookers and strippers back in Cleveland: he used to go and watch them dance when he was in his early teens. Maybe this was why he was so comfortable in the shadow-world of New Orleans. (I still remember my first visit to New Orleans, sitting in a bar with George, talking to the barmaid, and watching the dancer on the runway: George leaned over to me and whispered, "You're the only genetically female person in this room.")

He'd hang out in the bars along Chartres and Decatur Streets, nursing a drink, talking to the girls and not-quite-girls, and playing pinball until nearly dawn. He was good friends with a lot of the denizens of that world, including a sexchange named Amber who took the wrong man home one night and ended up being beaten to death and thrown off a balcony.

The New Orleans police being what they were, no investigation was made.

George's outpouring of outrage and helplessness became *When Gravity Fails*. He set it in the nameless Muslim city he'd invented for "The City on the Sand"—which became a pay-the-medical-bills book called *Relatives*—because some of the characters were based on real people, including the local Mafia boss. But when you read it, it's obviously the French Quarter, with maybe a little of the East Village in the sixties where George lived after dropping out of Yale. Being George, he studied Islamic culture extensively, so as not to inadvertently insult those whose world it actually is. He had the manuscript read by Muslim friends, and at one point the office staff of the local Islamic Cooperative Association phoned him up to compliment him on the respect he'd shown for their faith and culture. ("But we're liberal Sunnis," the caller added. "I don't know what the Shi'ites would say about it.")

George intended *Gravity* as a one-shot, but when it took off in popularity and Bantam asked him to do a second book, he found he did have another novel-length tale to tell of that universe, based around the death of his own grandfather, a Cleveland policeman who was killed in the line of duty. He said the Budayeen was the first world he'd created that had depth and richness, whose characters lived lives of their own beyond the boundaries of any individual tale. I think this is the reason the world continues to fascinate: because it is real.

His protagonist, Marîd Audran, fascinates and charms because he, too, is real—or as real as things get in the Budayeen. George said frankly that, like the hapless science-fiction writer Sandor Courane of some of his other tales, Marîd is based on himself. It amused George that many readers take Marîd at Marîd's own evaluation of himself: cool, clever, street-smart, sharp. But in fact, George said, if you look at what Marîd actually *does* rather than what he *says*, he is in fact cowardly, not nearly as clever as he thinks he is, and has a major drug problem which he never quite gets around to addressing.

Like George—dearly as I loved him.

George had a lot of trouble working during the last twelve years of his life. Drugs, chronic pain, alcohol, and depression sapped his energy and his ability to focus: there were days when he'd shove the same three or four words around the computer screen, other days when all he would do was spend hours sending long e-mails to friends, or troll around the Internet in the same fashion that he used to go down to the clubs on Chartres Street. It was heartbreaking to watch, and everyone who knew him tried everything they could think of . . .

And of course, nothing worked. It seldom does.

One of the several tragedies connected with George was how much brilliant potential was wasted: what there could have been.

But what there is, in those three novels and the handful of short stories surrounding them, is unforgettable. Wry and strange and dark, it is a world peopled with folks whose connection with the technological marvels of the twenty-second century are by far the least strange thing about them.

George was above all a very delicate observer of human behavior, fascinated by what people do in their lives and how they do it. The novels tell the main story. These vignettes, these fragments, fill in background to that world—in many ways the most interesting part of the world George created. They are what you see when you sit in the bars and cafés of the Budayeen in the sweltering neon darkness, watching the folks go by on the sidewalk, the way the clueless Ernst Weinraub in "The City on the Sand" watches: the way George would watch folks in the Quarter.

This is the world of *Budayeen Nights*.

Barbara Hambly
Los Angeles
October 2002

Budayeen Nights

Introduction to
Schrödinger's Kitten

This is probably the best known of George's short Budayeen stories. It won the Hugo, Nebula, and Seiun Awards,
and touches deep chords in nearly every reader, for it deals
with—and conquers—deep and universal fears.

Fear of death; fear of change; fear of somehow doing
something wrong that will condemn one's self to a horrible fate. In a way it is every child's fear. It reconstructs
Schrödinger's philosophical image of the cat in the box
—dead or saved only by the opening of the box by an
observer—into an infinity of paths and variations of
hope and destiny. Others have done this—notably Larry
Niven in his story "All the Myriad Ways"—but to different effect.

I think it's what goes on in nearly every writer's mind
when they construct a story. It's certainly how writers look
at their own lives, with a dispassionate infinity of equal
possibilities.

In some worlds George became a doctor.

In some worlds George became a ballplayer.

In some worlds it was possible for George to live happily ever after, as we all hope we will and wish we could.

—Barbara Hambly

+ + +

Schrödinger's Kitten

THE CLEAN CRESCENT MOON THAT BEGAN THE new month hung in the western sky across from the alley. Jehan was barely twelve years old, too young to wear the veil, but she did so anyway. She had never before been out so late alone. She heard the sounds of celebration far away, the three-day festival marking the end of the holy month of Ramadân. Two voices sang drunkenly as they passed the alley; two others loudly and angrily disputed the price of some honey cakes. The laughter and the shouting came to Jehan as if from another world. In the past, she'd always loved the festival of Id-el-Fitr; she took no part in the festivities now, though, and it seemed odd to her that anyone else still could. Soon she gave it all no more of her attention. This year she must keep a meeting more important than any holiday. She sighed, shrugging: The festival would come around again next year. Tonight, with only the silver moon for company, she shivered in her blue-black robe.

Jehan Fatima Ashûfi stepped back a few feet deeper into the alley, farther out of the light. All along the Street, people who would otherwise never be seen in this quarter were determinedly amusing themselves. Jehan shivered again and waited. The moment she longed for would come just at dawn. Even now the sky was just dark enough to reveal the moon and the first impetuous stars. In the Islamic world, night began when one could no longer distinguish a white thread from a black one; it was not yet night. Jehan clutched

3

her robe closely to her with her left hand. In her right hand, hidden by her long sleeve, was the keen-edged, gleaming, curved blade she had taken from her father's room.

She was hungry and she wished she had money to buy something to eat, but she had none. In the Budayeen there were many girls her age who already had ways of getting money of their own; Jehan was not one of them. She glanced about herself and saw only the filth-strewn, damp and muddy paving stones. The reek of the alley disgusted her. She was bored and lonely and afraid. Then, as if her whole sordid world suddenly dissolved into something else, something wholly foreign, she saw more.

Jehan Ashûfi was twenty-six years old. She was dressed in a conservative dark gray woolen suit, cut longer and more severely than fashion dictated, but appropriate for a bright young physicist. She affected no jewelry and wore her black hair in a long braid down her back. She took a little effort each morning to look as plain as possible while she was accompanying her eminent teacher and advisor. That had been Heisenberg's idea. In those days, who believed a beautiful woman could also be a highly talented scientist? Jehan soon learned that her wish of being inconspicuous was in vain. Her dark skin and her accent marked her a foreigner. She was clearly not European. Possibly she had Levantine blood. Most who met her thought she was probably a Jew. This was Göttingen, Germany, and it was 1925.

The brilliant Max Born, who first used the expression "quantum mechanics" in a paper written two years before, was leading a meeting of the university's physicists. They were discussing Max Planck's latest proposals concerning his own theories of radiation. Planck had developed some basic ideas in the emerging field of quantum physics, yet he had used classical Newtonian mechanics to describe the interactions of light and matter. It was clear that this approach was inadequate, but as yet there was no better system. At the Göttingen conference, Pascual Jordan rose to introduce a compromise solution; but before Born, the department chairman, could reply, Werner Heisenberg fell into a violent fit of sneezing.

"Are you all right, Werner?" asked Born.

Heisenberg merely waved a hand. Jordan attempted to continue, but again Heisenberg began sneezing. His eyes were red and tears crept down his face. He was in obvious distress. He turned to his graduate assistant. "Jehan," he said, "please make immediate arrangements, I must get away. It's my damned hay fever. I want to leave at once."

One of the others at the meeting objected. "But the collo-quium—"

Heisenberg was already on his feet. "Tell Planck to go straight to hell, and to take de Broglie and his matter waves with him. The same goes for Bohr and his goddamn jumping electrons. I can't stand any more of this." He took a few shaky steps and left the room. Jehan stayed behind to make a few notations in her journal. Then she followed Heisenberg back to their apartments.

There were no mosques in the Budayeen, but in the city all around the walled quarter there were many mosques. From the tall, ancient towers, strong voices called the faithful to morning devotions. "Come to prayer, come to prayer! Prayer is better than sleep!"

Leaning against a grimy wall, Jehan heard the chanted cries of the muezzins, but she paid them no mind. She stared at the dead body at her feet, the body of a boy a few years older than she, some-one she had seen about the Budayeen but whom she did not know by name. She still held the bloody knife that had killed him.

In a short while, three men pushed their way through a crowd that had formed at the mouth of the alley. The three men looked down solemnly at Jehan. One was a police officer; one was a qadi, who interpreted the ancient Islamic commandments as they applied to modern life; and the third was an imam, a prayer leader who had hurried from a small mosque not far from the east gate of the Budayeen. Within the walls the pickpockets, whores, thieves, and cutthroats could do as they liked to each other. A death in the Budayeen didn't attract much attention in the rest of the city.

The police officer was tall and heavily built, with a thick black mustache and sleepy eyes. He was curious only because he had watched over the Budayeen for fifteen years, and he had never investigated a murder by a girl so young.

The qadi was young, clean-shaven, and quite plainly deferring to the imam. It was not yet clear if this matter should be the respon-sibility of the civil or the religious authorities.

The imam was tall, taller even than the police officer, but thin and narrow-shouldered; yet it was not asceticism that made him so slight. He was well known for two things: his common sense con-cerning the conflicts of everyday affairs, and the high degree of earthly pleasures he permitted himself. He, too, was puzzled and curious. He wore a short, grizzled gray beard, and his soft brown eyes were all but hidden within the reticulation of wrinkles that had slowly etched his face. Like the police officer, the imam had once worn a brave black mustache, but the days of fierceness had long since passed for him. Now he appeared decent and kindly. In truth, he was neither, but he found it useful to cultivate that reputation.

"O my daughter," he said in his hoarse voice. He was very upset. He much preferred explicating obscure passages of the glorious Qur'ân to viewing such tawdry matters as blatant dead bodies in the nearby streets.

Jehan looked up at him, but she said nothing. She looked back down at the unknown boy she had killed.

"O my daughter," said the imam, "tell me, was it thou who hath slain this child?"

Jehan looked back calmly at the old man. She was concealed beneath her kerchief, veil, and robe; all that was visible of her were her dark eyes and the long thin fingers that held the knife. "Yes, O Wise One," she said, "I killed him."

The police officer glanced at the qadi.

"Prayest thou to Allah?" asked the imam. If this hadn't been the Budayeen, he wouldn't have needed to ask.

"Yes," said Jehan. And it was true. She had prayed on several occasions in her lifetime, and she might yet pray again sometime.

"And knowest thou there is a prohibition against taking of human life that Allah hath made sacred?"

"Yes, O Wise One."

"And knowest thou further that Allah hath set a penalty upon those who breaketh this law?"

"Yes, I know."

"Then, O my daughter, tell us why thou hath brought low this poor boy."

Jehan tossed the bloody knife to the stone-paved alley. It rang noisily and then came to rest against one leg of the corpse. "I killed him because he would do me harm in the future," she said.

"He threatened you?" asked the qadi.

"No, O Respected One."

"Then—"

"Then how art thou certain that he would do thee harm?" the imam finished.

Jehan shrugged. "I have seen it many times. He would throw me to the ground and defile me. I have seen the visions."

A murmur grew from the crowd still cluttering the mouth of the alley behind Jehan and the three men. The imam's shoulders slumped. The police officer waited patiently. The qadi looked discouraged. "Then he didst not offer thee harm this morning?" said the imam.

"No."

"Indeed, as thou sayest, he hath *never* offered thee harm?"

"No. I do not know him. I have never spoken with him."

"Yet," said the qadi, clearly unhappy, "you murdered him because of what you have seen? As in a dream?"

"As in a dream, O Respected One, but more truly as in a vision."

"A dream," muttered the imam. "The Prophet, may blessings be on his name and peace, didst offer no absolution for murder provoked only by dreams."

A woman in the crowd cried out, "But she is only twelve years old!"

The imam turned and pushed his way through the rabble.

"Sergeant," said the qadi, "this young girl is now in your custody. The Straight Path makes our duty clear."

The police officer nodded and stepped forward. He bound the young girl's wrists and pushed her forward through the alley. The crowd of fellahîn parted to make way for them. The sergeant led Jehan to a small, dank cell until she might have a hearing. A panel of religious elders would judge her according to Shari'a, the contemporary code of laws derived from the ancient and noble Qur'ân.

Jehan did not suffer in her noxious cell. A lifetime in the Budayeen had made her familiar with deprivation. She waited patiently for whatever outcome Allah intended.

She did not wait long. She was given another brief hearing, during which the council asked her many of the same questions the imam had asked. She answered them all without hesitation. Her judges were saddened but compelled to render their verdict. They gave her an opportunity to change her statement, but she refused. At last the senior member of the panel stood to face her. "O young one," he said in the most reluctant of voices, "The Prophet, blessings be on his name and peace, said, 'Whoso slayeth a believer, his reward is Hell forever.' And elsewhere, 'Who killeth a human being for other than manslaughter or corruption in the earth, it shall be as if he killed all mankind.' Therefore, if he whom you slew had purposed corruption upon you, your act would have been justified. Yet you deny this. You rely on your dreams, your visions. Such insubstantial defense cannot persuade this council otherwise than that you are guilty. You must pay the penalty even as it is written. It shall be exacted tomorrow morning just before sunrise."

Jehan's expression did not change. She said nothing. Of her many visions, she had witnessed this particular scene before also. Sometimes, as now, she was condemned; sometimes she was freed. That evening she ate a good meal, a better meal than most she had taken before in her life of poverty. She slept the night, and she was ready when the civil and religious officials came for her in the morning. An imam of great repute spoke to her at length, but Jehan did not listen carefully. The remaining acts and motions of her life seemed mechanically ordered, and she did not pay great heed to them. She followed where she was led, she responded dully when pressed for a reply, and she climbed the platform set up in the court-yard of the great Shimaal Mosque.

"Dost thou feel regret?" asked the imam, laying a gentle hand on her shoulder.

Jehan was made to kneel with her head on the block. She shrugged. "No," she said.

"Dost thou feel anger, O my daughter?"

"No."

"Then mayest Allah in His mercy grant thee peace." The imam stepped away. Jehan had no view of the headsman, but she heard the collective sigh of the onlookers as the great axe lifted high in the first faint rays of dawn, and then the blade fell.

Jehan shuddered in the alley. Watching her death always made her exceptionally uneasy. The hour wasn't much later; the fifth and final call to prayer had sounded not long before, and now it was night. The celebration continued around her more intensely than before. That her intended deed might end on the headsman's block did not deter her. She grasped the knife tightly, wishing that time would pass more swiftly, and she thought of other things.

By the end of May 1925, they were settled in a hotel on the tiny island of Helgoland some fifty miles from the German coast. Jehan relaxed in a comfortably furnished room. The landlady made her husband put Heisenberg and Jehan's luggage in the best and most expensive room. Heisenberg had every hope of ridding himself of his allergic afflictions. He also intended to make some sense of the opaque melding of theories and counter-theories put forward by his colleagues back in Göttingen. Meanwhile, the landlady gave Jehan a grim and glowering look at their every meeting but said nothing. The Herr Doktor himself was too preoccupied to care for anything as trivial as propriety, morals, the reputation of this Helgoland retreat, or Jehan's peace of mind. If anyone raised eyebrows over the arrangement, Heisenberg certainly was blithely unaware; he walked around as if he were insensible to everything but the pollen count and the occasional sheer cliffs over which he sometimes came close to tumbling.

Jehan was mindful of the old woman's disapproval. Jehan,

however, had lived a full, harsh life in her twenty-six years, and a raised eyebrow rated very low on her list of things to be concerned about. She had seen too many people abandoned to starvation, too many people dispossessed and reduced to beggary, too many outsiders slain in the name of Allah, too many maimed or beheaded through the convoluted workings of Islamic justice. All these years Jehan had kept her father's bloodied dagger, packed now somewhere beneath her Shetland wool sweaters, and still as deadly as ever.

Heisenberg's health improved on the island, and there was a beautiful view of the sea from their room. His mood brightened quickly. One morning, while walking along the shoreline with him, Jehan read a passage from the glorious Qur'ân. "This sûrah is called 'The Earthquake,'" she said. "'In the name of Allah, the Beneficent, the Merciful. When Earth is shaken with her final earthquake, and Earth yields up her burdens and man saith: What aileth her? That day she will relate her chronicles, because thy Lord inspireth her. That day mankind will issue forth in separate groups to be shown their deeds. And whoso doeth good an atom's weight will see it then. And whoso doeth ill an atom's weight will see it then.'"

And Jehan wept, knowing that however much good she might do, it could never outweigh the wrongs she had already performed.

But Heisenberg only stared out over the gray, tumbling waves of the ocean. He did not listen closely to the sacred verses, yet a few of Jehan's words struck him. "'And whoso doeth good an atom's weight will *see* it then,'" he said, emphasizing the single word. There was a small, hesitant smile quivering at the corners of his mouth. Jehan put her arm around him to comfort him because he seemed chilled, and she led him back to the hotel. The weather had turned colder and the air was misty with sea spray; together they listened to the cries of the herring gulls as the birds dived for fish or hovered screeching over the strip of beach. Jehan thought of what she'd read, of the end of the world. Heisenberg thought only of its beginning, and its still closely guarded secrets.

They liked their daily, peaceful walk about the island. Now, more than ever before, Jehan carried with her a copy of the Qur'ân, and she often read short verses to him. So different from the biblical literature he'd heard all his life, Heisenberg let the Islamic scriptures pass without comment. Yet it seemed to him that certain specific images offered their meanings to him alone.

Jehan saw at last that he was feeling well. Heisenberg took up again full time the tangled knot that was the current state of quantum physics. It was both his vocation and his means of relaxation. He told Jehan the best scientific minds in the world were frantically working to cobble together a slipshod mathematical model, one that might account for all the observed data. Whatever approach they tried, the data would not fit together. *He*, however, would find the key; he was that confident. He wasn't quite sure how he'd do it but, of course, he hadn't yet really applied himself thoroughly to the question.

Jehan was not amused. She read to him: "'Hast thou not seen those who pretend that they believe in that which is revealed unto thee and that which was revealed before thee, how they would go for judgment in their disputes to false deities when they have been ordered to abjure them? Satan would lead them all astray.'"

Heisenberg laughed heartily. "Your Allah isn't just talking about Göttingen there," he said. "He's got Bohr in mind, too, and Einstein in Berlin."

Jehan frowned at his impiety. It was the irreverence and ignorant ridicule of the kâfir, the unbeliever. She wondered if the old religion that had never truly had any claim on her was yet still part of her. She wondered how she'd feel after all these years, walking the narrow, crowded, clangorous ways of the Budayeen again. "You mustn't speak that way," she said at last.

"Hmm?" said Heisenberg. He had already forgotten what he'd said to her.

"Look out there," said Jehan. "What do you see?"

"The ocean," said Heisenberg. "Waves."

"Allah created those waves. What do *you* know about that?"

"I could determine their frequency," said the scientist. "I could measure their amplitude."

"Measure!" cried Jehan. Her own long years of scientific study were suddenly overshadowed by an imagined insult to her heritage. "Look here," she demanded. "A handful of sand. Allah created this sand. What do *you* know about it?"

Heisenberg couldn't see what Jehan was trying to tell him. "With the proper instruments," he said, a little afraid of offending her, "in the proper setting, I could take any single grain of sand and tell you—" His words broke off suddenly. He got to his feet slowly, like an old man. He looked first at the sea, then down at the shore, then back out at the water. "Waves," he murmured, "particles, it makes no difference. All that counts is what we can actually measure. We can't measure Bohr's orbits, because they don't really *exist!* So the spectral lines we see are caused by transitions between two states. Pairs of states, yes; but that will mean an entirely new form of mathematical expression just to describe them, referencing tables listing every possible—"

"Werner." Jehan knew that he was now lost to her.

"Just the computations alone will take days, if not weeks."

"Werner, *listen* to me. This island is so small, you can throw a stone from one end to the other. I'm not going to sit on this freezing beach or up on your bleak and dreary cliff while you make your brilliant breakthrough, whatever it is. I'm saying goodbye."

"What? Jehan?" Heisenberg blinked and returned to the tangible world.

She couldn't face him any longer. She was pouring one handful of sand through the fingers of her other hand. It came suddenly to her mind then: If you had no water to perform the necessary ablution before prayer in the direction of Makkah, you were permitted to wash with clean sand instead. She began to weep. She couldn't hear what Heisenberg was saying to her—if indeed he was.

It was a couple hours later in the alley now, and it was getting even colder. Jehan wrapped herself in her robe and paced back and forth. She'd had visions of this particular night for four years, glimpses of the possible ways that it might conclude. Sometimes the young man saw her in the alley shortly after dawn, sometimes he didn't. Sometimes she killed him, sometimes she didn't. And, of course, there was the open question of whether her actions would lead to her freedom or to her execution.

When she'd had the first vision, she hadn't known what was happening or what she was seeing. She knew only the fear and the pain and the terror. The boy threw her roughly to the ground, ripped her clothing, and raped her. Then the vision passed. Jehan told no one about it; her family would have thought her insane. About three months later, the vision returned; only this time it was different in subtle ways. She was in the alley as before, but this time she smiled and gestured to the boy, inviting him. He smiled in return and followed her deeper into the alley. When he put his hand on her shoulder, she drew her father's dagger and plunged it into the boy's belly. That was as much as the vision showed her then. It terrified her even more than had the rape scene.

As time passed, the visions took on other forms. She was certain now that she was not always watching *her* future, *the* future, but rather *a* future, each as likely to come to pass as the others. Not all the visions could possibly be true. In some of them, she saw herself living into her old age in the city, right here in this filthy quarter of the Budayeen. In others, she moved about strange places that didn't seem Islamic at all, and she spoke languages definitely not Arabic. She did not know if these conflicting visions were trying to tell her or warn her of something. Jehan prayed to know which of these versions she must actually live through. Soon after, as if to reward her for her faith, she began to have less violent visions: She could look into the future a short way and find lost objects, or warn against unlucky travel plans, or predict the rise and fall of crop prices. The neighbors, at first amused, began to be afraid of her. Jehan's mother counselled her never to speak of these "dreams" to anyone, or else Jehan might be locked away in some horrible institution. Jehan never told her father about her visions, because Jehan never told her father about anything. In that family, as in the others of the Budayeen—and the rest of the city, for that matter—the father did not concern himself very much with his daughters. His sons were his pride, and he had three strong sons whom he firmly believed would someday vastly increase the Ashûfi prestige and wealth. Jehan knew he was wrong, because she'd already seen what would become of the sons—two would be killed in wars against the Jews; the third would be a coward, a weakling, and a fugitive in the United States. But Jehan said nothing.

A vision: It was just past dawn. The young man—whose name Jehan never learned—was walking down the stone-paved street toward her alley. Jehan knew it without even peering out. She took a deep breath. She walked a few steps toward the street, looked left, and caught his eyes. She made a brief gesture, turned her back, and went deeper into the shadowy seclusion of the alley. She was certain that he would follow her. Her stomach ached and rumbled, and she was shaking with nervous exhaustion. When the young man put his hand on her shoulder, murmuring indecent suggestions, her hand crept toward the concealed knife, but she did not grasp it. He threw her down roughly, clawed off her clothing, and raped her. Then he left her there. She was almost paralyzed, crying and cursing on the wet, foul-smelling stones. She was found some time later by two women who took her to a doctor. Their worst fears were confirmed: Her honor had been ravaged irredeemably. Her life was effectively over, in the sense of becoming a normal adult female in that Islamic community. One of the women returned to Jehan's house with her, to tell the news to Jehan's mother, who must still tell Jehan's father. Jehan hid in the room she shared with her sisters. She heard the violent breaking of furniture and shrill obscenity of her father. There was nothing more to be done. Jehan did not know the name of her assailant. She was ruined, less than worthless. A young woman no longer a virgin could command no bride price. All those years of supporting a worthless daughter in the hopes of recovering the investment in the marriage contract—all vanished now. It was no surprise that Jehan's father felt betrayed and the father of a witless creature. There was no sympathy for Jehan; the actual story, whatever it might be, could not alter the facts. She had only the weeping of her sisters and her mother. From that morning on, Jehan was permanently repudiated and cast out from her house. Jehan's father and three brothers would not even look at her or offer her their farewells.

The years passed ever more quickly. Jehan became a woman of the streets. For a time, because of her youth and beauty, she earned a good living. Then as the decades left their unalterable blemishes upon her, she found it difficult even to earn enough for a meal and a room to sleep in. She grew older, more bitter, and filled with self-loathing. Did she hate her father and the rest of her family? No, her fate had been fixed by the will of Allah, however impossible it was for her to comprehend it, or else by her own timidity in the single moment of choice and destiny in the alley so many years before. She could not say. Whatever the answer, she could not benefit now from either insight or wisdom. Her life was as it was, according to the inscrutable designs of Allah the Merciful. Her understanding was not required.

Eventually she was found dead, haggard and starved, and her corpse was contorted and huddled for warmth coincidentally in the same alley where the young man had so carelessly despoiled any chance Jehan had for happiness in this world. After she died, there was no one to mourn her. Perhaps Allah the Beneficent took pity on her, showing mercy to her who had received little enough mercy from her neighbors while she lived among them. It had always been a cold place for Jehan.

For a while estranged from Heisenberg, Jehan worked with Erwin Schrödinger in Zurich. At first Schrödinger's ideas confused her because they went against many of Heisenberg's basic assumptions. For the time being, Heisenberg rejected any simple picture of what the atom was like, any model at all. Schrödinger, older and more conservative than the Göttingen group, wanted to explain quantum phenomena without new mathematics and elusive imagery. He treated the electron as a wave function, but a different sort of wave than de Broglie's. The properties of waves in the physical world were well known and without ambiguity. Yet when Schrödinger calculated how a change in energy level affected his electron wave, his solutions didn't agree with observed data.

"What am I overlooking?" he asked.

Jehan shook her head. "Where I was born they say, 'Don't pour away the water in your canteen because of a mirage.'"

Schrödinger rubbed his weary eyes. He glanced down at the sheaf of papers he held. "How can I tell if this water is worth keeping or something that belongs in a sewer?"

Jehan had no reply to that, and Schrödinger set his work aside, unsatisfied. A few months later several papers showed that after taking into account the relativistic effects, Schrödinger's calculations agreed remarkably well with experimental results after all.

Schrödinger was pleased. "I hoped all along to find a way to drag Born and Heisenberg back to classical physics," he said. "I knew in my heart that quantum physics would prove to be a sane world, not a realm populated by phantoms and governed by ghost forces."

"It seems unreal to me now," said Jehan. "If you say the electron is a wave, you are saying it is a phantom. In the ocean, it is the water that is the wave. As for sound, it is the air that carries the wave. What exists to be a wave in your equations?"

"It is a wave of probability, Born says. I do not wholly understand that yet myself," he said, "but my equations explain too many things to be illusions."

"Sir," said Jehan, frowning, "it may be that in this case the mirage is in your canteen and not before you in the desert."

Schrödinger laughed. "That might be true. I may yet have to abandon my mental pictures, but I will not abandon my mathematics."

It was a breathless afternoon in the city. The local Arabs didn't seem to be bothered by the heat, but the small party of Europeans was beginning to suffer. Their cruise ship had put ashore at the small port, and a tour had been arranged to the city some fifty miles to the south. Two hours later the travelers concluded that the expedition had been a mistake.

Among them was David Hilbert, the German mathematician, a lecturer at Göttingen since 1895. He was accompanied by his wife, Käthe, and their maid, Clärchen. At first they were quite taken by the strangeness of the city, by the foreign sights and sounds and smells; but after a short time, their senses were glutted with newness, and what had at first been exotic was now only deplorable.

As they moved slowly through the bazaars, shaded ineffectually by awnings or meager arcades of sticks, they longed for the whisper of a single cool breeze. Arab men dressed in long white gallebeyas cried out shrilly, all the while glaring at the Europeans. It was impossible to tell what the Arabs were saying. Some dragged little carts loaded with filthy cups and pots—Water? Tea? Lemonade? It made no difference. Cholera lingered at every stall; every beggar offered typhus as he clutched at sleeves.

Hilbert's wife fanned herself weakly. She was almost overcome and near collapse. Hilbert looked about desperately. "David," murmured the maid, Clärchen, the only one of Hilbert's amours Frau Hilbert could tolerate, "we have come far enough."

"I know," he said, "but I see nothing—nowhere—"

"There are some ladies and gentlemen in that place. I think it's an eating place. Leave Käthe with me there, and find a taxi. Then we shall go back to the boat."

Hilbert hesitated. He couldn't bear to leave the two unprotected women in the midst of this frantic heathen marketplace. Then he saw how pale his wife had become, how her eyelids drooped, how she swayed against Clärchen's shoulder. He nodded. "Let me help," he said. Together they got Frau Hilbert to the restaurant, where it was no cooler but at least the ceiling fans created a fiction of fresh air. Hilbert introduced himself to a well-dressed man who was seated at a table with his family, a wife and four children. The mathematician tried three languages before he was understood. He explained the situation, and the gentleman and his wife both assured Hilbert that he need not worry. Hilbert ran out to find a taxi.

He was soon lost. There were no streets here, not in the European sense of the word. Narrow spaces between buildings became alleys, opened into small squares, closed again; other narrow passages led off in twisting, bewildering directions. Hilbert found himself back at a souk; he thought at first it was where he'd begun and looked for the restaurant, but he was wrong. This was another souk entirely; there were probably hundreds in the city. He was beginning to panic. Even if he managed to find a taxi, how could he direct it back to where his wife and Clärchen waited?

A man's hand plucked at him. Hilbert tried to shrug the long fingers away. He looked into the face of a lean, hollow-cheeked man in a striped robe and a blue knitted cap. The Arab kept repeating a few words, but Hilbert could make no sense of them. The Arab took him by the arm and half-led, half-shoved Hilbert through the crowd. Hilbert let himself be guided. They crossed through two bazaars, one of tinsmiths and one of poultry dressers. They entered a stone-paved street and emerged into an immense square. On the far side of the square was a huge, many-towered mosque, built of pink stone. Hilbert's first impression was awe; it was as lovely an edifice as the Taj. Then his guide was pushing him again through the throng, or hurrying in front to hew a path for Hilbert. The square was jammed and choked with people. Soon Hilbert could see why: a platform had been erected in the center, and on it stood a man with what could only be an executioner's axe. Hilbert felt his stomach sicken. His Arab guide had thrust aside everyone in their way until Hilbert stood at the very foot of the platform. He saw uniformed police and a bearded old man leading out a young girl. The crowd parted to allow them by. The girl was stunningly lovely. Hilbert looked into her huge, dark eyes—"like the eyes of a gazelle," he remembered from reading Omar Khayyám—and glimpsed her slender form undisguised by her modest garments. As she mounted the steps, she looked down directly at him again. Hilbert felt his heart lurch; he felt a tremendous shudder. Then she looked away.

The Arab guide screamed in Hilbert's ear. It meant nothing to the mathematician. He watched in horror as Jehan knelt, as the headsman raised his weapon of office. When the fierce, bellowing cry went up from the crowd, Hilbert noticed that his suit was now spattered with small flecks of red. The Arab screamed at him again and tightened his grip on Hilbert's arm until Hilbert complained. The Arab did not release him. With his other hand, Hilbert took out his wallet. The Arab smiled. Above him, Hilbert watched several men carry away the body of the decapitated girl.

The Arab guide did not let him go until he'd paid an enormous sum.

Perhaps another hour had passed in the alley. Jehan had withdrawn to the darkest part and sat in a damp corner with her legs drawn up, her head against the rough brick wall. If she could sleep, she told herself, the night would pass more quickly; but she would not sleep, she would fight it if drowsiness threatened. What if she should slip into slumber and waken in the late morning, her peril and her opportunity both long since lost? Her only companion, the crescent moon, had abandoned her; she looked up at fragments of constellations, stars familiar enough in their groups but indistinguishable now as individuals. How different from people, where the opposite was true. She sighed; she was not a profound person, and it did not suit her to have profound thoughts. These must not truly be profound thoughts, she decided; she was merely deluded by weariness. Slowly she let her head fall forward. She crossed her arms on her knees and cradled her head. The greater part of the night had already passed, and only silence came from the street. There were perhaps only three more hours until dawn. . . .

Soon Schrödinger's wave mechanics was proved to be equivalent to

Heisenberg's matrix mechanics. It was a validation of both men's work and of the whole field of quantum physics as well. Eventually Schrödinger's simplistic wave picture of the electron was abandoned, but his mathematical laws remained undisputed. Jehan remembered Schrödinger predicting that he might need to take just that step.

Jehan had at last returned to Göttingen and Heisenberg. He had "forgiven her petulance." He welcomed her gladly, because of his genuine feelings for her and because he had much work to do. He had just formally developed what came to be known as the Heisenberg uncertainty principle. This was the first indication that the impartial observer could not help but play an essential, active role in the universe of subatomic particles. Jehan grasped Heisenberg's concept readily. Other scientists thought Heisenberg was making a trivial criticism of the limitations of their experiments or the quality of their observations. It was more profound than that. Heisenberg was saying that one can never hope to know both the position and the momentum of an electron at the same time under *any* circumstances. He had destroyed forever the assumption of the impartial observer.

"To observe is to disturb," said Heisenberg. "Newton wouldn't have liked any of this at all."

"Einstein still doesn't like it right this very minute," said Jehan.

"I wish I had a mark for every time he's made that sour 'God doesn't play dice with the universe' comment."

"That's just the way he sees a 'wave of probability.' The path of the electron can't be known unless you look; but once you look, you change the information."

"So maybe God doesn't play dice with the universe," said Heisenberg. "He plays vingt-et-un, and if He does not have an extra ace up His sleeve, He creates one—first the sleeve, then the ace. And He turns over more natural twenty-ones than is statistically likely. Hold on, Jehan! I'm not being sacrilegious. I'm not saying that God cheats. Rather, He invented the rules of the game, and He *continues* to invent them; and this gives Him a rather large advantage over poor physicists and their lagging understanding. We are like country peasants watching the card tricks of someone who may be either genius or charlatan."

Jehan pondered the metaphor. "At the Solvay conference, Bohr introduced his complementarity idea, that an electron was a wave function until it was detected, and then the wave function collapsed to a point and you knew where the electron was. Then it was a particle. Einstein didn't like that, either."

"That's God's card trick," said Heisenberg, shrugging.

"Well, the noble Qur'ân says, 'They question thee about strong drink and games of chance. Say: In both is great sin, and some usefulness for men; but the sin of them is greater than their usefulness.'"

"Forget dice and cards, then," said Heisenberg with a little smile. "What kind of game *would* it be appropriate for Allah to play against us?"

"Physics," said Jehan, and Heisenberg laughed.

"And knowest thou there is a prohibition against taking of human life that Allah hath made sacred?"

"Yes, O Wise One."

"And knowest thou further that Allah hath set a penalty upon those who breaketh this law?"

"Yes, I know."

"Then, O my daughter, tell us why thou hath brought low this poor boy."

Jehan tossed the bloody knife to the stone-paved alley. It rang noisily and then came to rest against one leg of the corpse. "I was celebrating the Id-el-Fitr," she said. "This boy followed me and I became afraid. He made filthy gestures and called out terrible things. I hurried away, but he ran after me. He grabbed me by the shoulders and pressed me against a wall. I tried to escape, but I could not. He laughed at my fear, then he struck me many times. He dragged me along through the narrowest of streets, where there were not many to witness; and then he pulled me into this vile place. He told me that he intended to defile me, and he described what he would do in foul detail. It was then that I drew my father's dagger and stabbed him. I have spent the night in horror of his intentions and of my deed, and I have prayed to Allah for forgiveness."

The imam put a trembling hand on Jehan's cheek. "Allah is All-Wise and All-Forgiving, O my daughter. Alloweth me to return with thee to thy house, where I may put the hearts of thy father and thy mother at their ease."

Jehan knelt at the imam's feet. "All thanks be to Allah," she murmured.

"Allah be praised," said the imam, the police officer, and the qadi together.

More than a decade later, when Jehan had daughters of her own, she told them this story. But in those latter days children did not heed the warnings of their parents, and the sons and daughters of Jehan and her husband did many foolish things.

*   *   *

Dawn slipped even into the narrow alleyway where Jehan waited. She was very sleepy and hungry, but she stood up and took a few wobbling steps. Her muscles had become cramped, and she could hear her heart beating in her ears. Jehan steadied herself with one hand on the brick wall. She went slowly to the mouth of the alley and peered out. There was no one in sight. The boy was coming neither from the left nor the right. Jehan waited until several other people appeared, going about the business of the new day. Then she hid the dagger in her sleeve once more and departed from the alley. She hurried back to her father's house. Her mother would need her to help make breakfast.

Jehan was in her early forties now, her black hair cut short, her eyes framed by clumsy spectacles, her beauty stolen by care, poor diet, and sleeplessness. She wore a white lab coat and carried a clipboard, as much a part of her as her title, Fräulein Professor Doktor Ashûfi. This was not Göttingen any longer; it was Berlin, and a war was being lost. She was still with Heisenberg. He had protected her until her own scientific credentials became protection of themselves. At that point, the Nazi officials were compelled to make her an "honorary" Aryan, as they had the Jewish physicists and mathematicians whose cooperation they needed. It had been only Jehan's long-standing loyalty to Heisenberg himself that kept her in Germany at all. The war was of little concern to her; these were not her people, but neither were the British, the French, the Russians, or the Americans. Her only interest was in her work, in the refinement of physics, in the unending anticipation of discovery.

She was glad, therefore, when the German atomic bomb project was removed from the control of the German army and given to the Reich Research Council. One of the first things to be done was the calling of a research conference at the Kaiser Wilhelm Institute of Physics in Berlin. The conference would be conducted under the tightest security; no preliminary list of topics would be released in advance, so that no foreign agents might see such terms as "fission cross-sections" and "isotope enrichment," leading to speculation on the long-term goals of these physicists.

At the same time, the Reich Research Council decided to hold a second conference for the benefit of the government's highest officials on the same day. The idea was that the scientists speaking at the Kaiser Wilhelm Institute's meeting could present short, elementary summaries of their work in plain language so that the political and military leaders could be briefed on the progress being made toward a nuclear weapon. Then, following the laymen's presentation, the physicists could gather and discuss the same matters in their more technical jargon.

Heisenberg thought it was a good idea. It was 1942, and material, political support, and funding were getting more difficult to find. The army wanted to put all available research resources into the rocketry program; they argued that the nuclear experiments were not showing sufficient success. Heisenberg was a theoretical physicist, not an engineer; he could not find a way to tell the council that the development of the uranium bomb must necessarily be slow and methodical. Each new step forward in theory had to be tested carefully, and each experiment was expensive in both time and money. The Reich, however, cared only for positive results.

One evening Jehan was alone in an administrative office of the Reich Research Council, typing her proposal for an important test of their isotope-separation technique. She saw on the desk two stacks of papers. One stack listed the simple synopses the physicists had prepared for Göring, Himmler, and the other Reich ministers who had little or no background in science. The second stack was the secret agenda for the physicists' own meeting: "Nuclear Physics as a Weapon," by Professor Dr. Schumann; "The Fission of the Uranium Atom," by Professor Dr. Hahn; "The Theoretical Basis for the Production of Energy from the Fission of Uranium," by Heisenberg; and so on. Each person attending the technical seminar would be given a program after he entered the lecture hall, and he would be required to sign for it.

Jehan thought for a long while in the quiet office. She remembered her wretched childhood. She recalled her arrival in Europe and the people she had come to know, the life she had come to lead here. She thought about how Germany had changed while she hid in her castle of scientific abstractions, uninvolved with the outside world. At last she thought about what this new Germany might do with the uranium bomb. She knew exactly what she must do.

It took her only a few moments to hide the laymen's synopses in her briefcase. She then took the highly technical agendas and dropped them into the already-addressed envelopes to be sent to the Third Reich's highest officials. She had guaranteed that the brief introductory discussion would be attended by no one. Jehan could easily imagine the response the unintelligible scientific papers would get from the political and military leaders—curt, polite regrets that they would not be in Berlin on that day, or that their busy schedules prevented them from attending.

It was all so easy. The Reich's rulers did not hear the talks, and they did not learn how close Germany was to developing an atomic bomb. Never again was there any hope that such a weapon could be built in time to save the Reich—all because the wrong invitations had been slipped into a few envelopes.

Jehan awoke from a dream, and saw that the night had grown very old. It would not be long before the sun began to flood the sky with light. Soon she would have a resolution to her anxiety. She would learn if the boy would come to the alley or stay away. She would learn if he would rape her or if she would find the courage to defend herself. She would learn if she would be judged guilty or innocent of murder. She would be granted a glimpse of the outcome to all things that concerned her.

Nevertheless, she was so tired, hungry, and uncomfortable that she was tempted to give up her vigil. The urge to go home was strong. Yet she had always believed that her visions were gifts granted by Allah, and it might offend Him to ignore the clear warnings. For Allah's sake, as well as her own, she reluctantly chose to wait out the rest of the dying night. She had seen so many visions since last evening—more than on any other day of her life—some new, some familiar from years passed. It was, in a small, human way, almost comparable to the Night of Power that was bestowed upon the Prophet, may Allah's blessing be on him and peace. Then Jehan felt guilty and blasphemous for comparing herself to the Messenger that way.

She got down on her knees and faced toward Makkah and addressed a prayer to Allah, reciting one of the later sûrahs from the glorious Qur'ân, the one called "The Morning Hours," which seemed particularly relevant to her situation. "'In the name of Allah, the Beneficent, the Merciful. By the morning hours, and by the night when it is stillest, thy Lord hath not forsaken thee nor doth He hate thee, and verily the latter portion will be better for thee than the former, and verily thy Lord will give unto thee so that thou wilt be content. Did He not find thee an orphan and protect thee? Did He not find thee wandering and direct thee? Did He not find thee destitute and enrich thee? Therefore the orphan oppresseth not, therefore the beggar driveth not away, therefore of the bounty of thy Lord be thy discourse.'"

When she finished praying, she stood up and leaned against the wall. She wondered if that sûrah prophesied that soon she'd be an orphan. She hoped that Allah understood that she never intended anything awful to happen to her parents. Jehan was willing to suffer whatever consequences Allah willed, but it didn't seem fair for her

mother and father to have to share them with her. She shivered
in the damp, cold air and gazed up to see if there was yet any
brightening of the sky. She pretended that already the stars were
beginning to disappear.

The square was jammed and choked with people. Soon Hilbert
could see why: a platform had been erected in the center, and on it
stood a man with what could only be an executioner's axe. Hilbert
felt his stomach sicken. His Arab guide had thrust aside everyone in
their way until Hilbert stood at the very foot of the platform. He saw
uniformed police and a bearded old man leading out a young girl.
The crowd parted to allow them by. The girl was stunningly lovely.
Hilbert looked into her huge, dark eyes — "like the eyes of a gazelle,"
he remembered from reading Omar Khayyám — and glimpsed her
slender form undisguised by her modest garments. As she mounted
the steps, she looked down directly at him again. Hilbert felt his
heart lurch; he felt a tremendous shudder. Then she looked away.
    The Arab guide screamed in Hilbert's ear. It meant nothing to
the mathematician. He watched in horror as Jehan knelt, as the
headsman raised his weapon of office. Hilbert shouted. His guide
tightened his grip on the outsider's arm, but Hilbert lashed out in
fury and threw the man into a group of veiled women. In the confusion, Hilbert ran up the steps of the scaffold. The imam and the
police officers looked at him angrily. The crowd began to shout
fiercely at this interruption, this desecration by a European kâfir, an
unbeliever. Hilbert ran to the police. "You must stop this!" he cried
in German. They did not understand him and tried to heave him
off the platform. "Stop!" he screamed in English.
    One of the police officers answered him. "It cannot be stopped,"
he said gruffly. "The girl committed murder. She was found guilty,
and she cannot pay the blood price to the victim's family. She must
die instead."
    "Blood price!" cried Hilbert. "That's barbarous! You would kill
a young girl just because she is poor? Blood price! *I'll* pay your goddamn blood price! How much is it?"
    The policeman conferred with the others, and then went to the
imam for guidance. Finally, the English-speaking officer returned.
"Four hundred kiam," he said bluntly.
    Hilbert took out his wallet with shaking hands. He counted out
the money and handed it with obvious disgust to the policeman.
The imam cried a declaration in his weak voice. The words were
passed quickly through the crowd, and the onlookers grew more
enraged at this spoiling of their morning's entertainment. "Take her

and go quickly," said the police officer. "We cannot protect you, and the crowd is becoming furious."

Hilbert nodded. He grasped Jehan's thin wrist and pulled her along after him. She questioned him in Arabic, but he could not reply. As he struggled through the menacing crowd, they were struck again and again by stones. Hilbert wondered what he had done, if he and the girl would get out of the mosque's courtyard alive. His fondness for young women—it was an open joke in Göttingen—had that been all that had motivated him? Had he unconsciously decided to rescue the girl and take her back to Germany? Or was it something more laudable? He would never know. He shocked himself: While he tried to shield himself and the girl from the vicious blows of the crowd, he thought only of how he might explain the girl to his wife, Käthe, and Clärchen, his mistress.

In 1957, Jehan Fatima Ashûfi was fifty-eight years old and living in Princeton, New Jersey. By coincidence, Albert Einstein had come here to live out the end of his life, and before he died in 1955 they had many pleasant afternoons at his house. In the beginning, Jehan wanted to discuss quantum physics with Einstein; she even told him Heisenberg's answer to Einstein's objection to God's playing dice with the universe. Einstein was not very amused, and from then on, their conversation concerned only nostalgic memories of the better days in Germany, before the advent of the National Socialists.

This afternoon, however, Jehan was sitting in a Princeton lecture hall, listening to a young man read a remarkable paper, his Ph.D. thesis. His name was Hugh Everett, and he was saying that there was an explanation for all the paradoxes of the quantum world, a simple but bizarre way of looking at them. His new idea included the Copenhagen interpretation and explained away all the objections that might be raised by less open-minded physicists. He stated first of all that quantum mechanics provided predictions that were invariably correct when measured against experimental data. Quantum physics *had* to be consistent and valid, there was no longer any doubt. The trouble was that quantum theory was beginning to lead to unappetizing alternatives.

Everett's thesis reconciled them. It eliminated Schrödinger's cat paradox, in which the cat in the box was merely a quantum wave function, not alive and not dead, until an observer looked to see which state the cat was in. Everett showed that the cat was no mere ghostly wave function. Everett said that wave functions do not "collapse," choosing one alternative or the other. He said that the process of observation chose one reality, but the other reality existed in its own right, just as "real" as our world. Particles do not choose at random which path to take—they take every path, in a separate, newly branched world for each option. Of course, at the particle level, this meant a huge number of branchings occurring at every moment.

Jehan knew this almost-metaphysical idea would find a chilly reception from most physicists, but she had special reasons to accept it eagerly. It explained her visions. She glimpsed the particular branch that would be "real" for her and also those that would be "real" for other versions of her, her own duplicates living on the countless parallel worlds. Now, as she listened to Everett, she smiled. She saw another young man in the audience, wearing a T-shirt that said, WIGNER: WOULD YOU PLEASE ASK YOUR FRIEND TO FEED MY CAT? THANKS, SCHRÖDINGER. She found that very amusing.

When Everett finished reading, Jehan felt good. It wasn't peace she felt, it was more like the release one feels after an argument that had been brewing for a long while. Jehan thought back over the turns and sidetracks she had taken since that dawn in the alley in the Budayeen. She smiled again, sadly, took a deep breath, and let it out. How many things she had done, how many things had happened to her! They had been long, strange lives. The only question that still remained was: How many uncountable futures did she still have to devise, to fabricate from the immaterial resources of this moment? As she sat there—in some worlds—Jehan knew the futures went on without her willing them to, needing nothing of her permission. She was not cautious of when tomorrow came, but *which* tomorrow came.

Jehan saw them all, but she still understood nothing. She thought, *The Chinese say that a journey of a thousand li begins with a single step. How shortsighted that is! A thousand journeys of a thousand li begin with a single step. Or with each step not taken.* She sat in her chair until everyone else had left the lecture hall. Then she got up slowly, her back and her knees giving her pain, and she took a step. She pictured myriad mirror-Jehans taking that step along with her, and a myriad that didn't. And in all the worlds across time, it was another step into the future.

At last, there was no doubt about it: It was dawn. Jehan fingered her father's dagger and felt a thrill of excitement. Strange words flickered in her mind. "The Heisenty uncertainberg principle," she murmured, already hurrying toward the mouth of the alley. She felt no fear.

Introduction to
Marîd Changes His Mind

This is, of course, the first two chapters of A Fire in the
Sun, the second of the Budayeen novels. George always
said he liked to start a novel with what is essentially an
unrelated (or almost unrelated) short story about the
character, like that first ten-minute sequence of the film
Goldfinger.

George was the first person I knew to write about clip-
in personalities, long before Hollywood explored the idea in
the film Strange Days, and he came back to this device
many times in the Budayeen series. In many ways this story
is an exploration of the Wonderful World of Moddies and
Daddies.

The technology itself, he said, had been designed for
treatment of neurological damage. But like all technology,
it was immediately seized upon and exploited by the entertainment and pornography industries so that its original
intent was almost forgotten.

In this story we also meet some of the Effinger Revolving Cast. George liked to recycle characters from story to
story, sometimes disregarding entirely the fact that they
might have been killed in a previous tale. In "Marîd
Changes His Mind," we encounter the tavern keeper M.
Gargotier and his daughter Maddie, who are prototypical
inhabitants of the Budayeen, having first made their
appearance in "The City on the Sand" and who also
figured in George's caper-novel Felicia—which of course
wasn't set in the Budayeen and hadn't the slightest thing
to do with it.

We also encounter one of the many incarnations of
Sandor Courane, the hapless science fiction writer who gets
killed in so many of George's stories. This is one of
Courane's few appearances where he doesn't die, and in
fact gets to live presumably happily ever after. Courane
(whom we also meet in "The City on the Sand") is, like
Marîd, a version of George himself, so of course Marîd
describes him as looking a little like himself but older,
plumper, and wiser. A poet, allegedly, but not a very good
one.

—Barbara Hambly

✛ ✛ ✛

Marîd Changes His Mind

1

E'D RIDDEN FOR MANY DAYS OUT THE COAST highway toward Mauretania, the part of Algeria where I'd been born. In that time, even at its lethargic pace, the broken-down old bus had carried us from the city to some town forsaken by Allah before it even learned what its name was. Centuries come, centuries go: In the Arab world they arrive and depart loaded on the roofs of shuddering, rattling buses that are more trouble to keep in service than the long parades of camels used to be. I remembered what those bus rides were like from when I was a kid, sitting or standing in the aisle with fifty other boys and men and maybe another two dozen clinging up on the roof. The buses passed by my home then. I saw turbaned heads, heads wearing fezzes or knit caps, heads in white or checked keffiyas. All men. That was something I planned to ask my father about, if I ever met him. "O my father," I would say, "tell me why everyone on the bus is a man. Where are their women?"

And I always imagined that my father—I pictured him tall and lean with a fierce dark beard, a hawk or an eagle of a man; he was, in my vision, Arab, although I had my mother's word that he had been a Frenchman—and I saw my father gazing thoughtfully into the bright sunlight, framing a careful reply to his young son. "O Marîd, my sweet one," he would say—and his voice would be deep and husky, issuing from the back of his throat as if he never used his

27

lips to speak, although my mother said he wasn't like that at all—
"Marîd, the women will come later. The men will send for them
later."

"Ah," I would say. My father could pierce *all* riddles. I could not
pose a question that he did not have a proper answer for. He was
wiser than our village shaykh, more knowledgeable than the man
whose face filled the posters pasted on the wall we were pissing
on. "Father," I would ask him, "why are we pissing on this man's
face?"

"Because it is idolatrous to put his face on such a poster, and it
is fit only for a filthy alley like this, and therefore the Prophet, may
the blessing of Allah be on him and peace, tells us that what we are
doing to these images is just and right."

"And father?" I would always have one more question, and he'd
always be blissfully patient. He would smile down at me, put one
hand fondly behind my head. "Father? I have always wanted to ask
you, what do you do when you are pissing and your bladder is so full
it feels like it will explode before you can relieve it and while you
are pissing, *just then*, the muezzin—"

Saied hit me hard in the left temple with the palm of his hand.
"You sleeping out here?"

I looked up at him. There was glare everywhere. I couldn't
remember where the hell we were. "Where the hell are we?" I asked
him.

He snorted. "*You're* the one from the Maghreb, the great wild
west. You tell me."

"Have we got to Algeria yet?" I didn't think so.

"No, stupid. I've been sitting in that goddamn little coffeehouse
for three hours charming the warts off this fat fool. His name is
Hisham."

"Where are we?

"Just crossed through Carthage. We're on the outskirts of Old
Tunis now. So listen to me. What's the old guy's name?"

"Huh? I don't remember."

He hit me hard in the right temple with the palm of his other
hand. I hadn't slept in two nights. I was a little confused. Anyway,
he got the easy part of the job: Sitting around the bus stops, drinking mint tea with the local ringleaders and gossiping about the
marauding Christians and the marauding Jews and the marauding
heathen niggers and just in general being goddamn smooth; and
I got the piss-soaked alleys and the flies. I couldn't remember why
we divided this business up like that. After all, I was supposed to be
in charge—it was my idea to find this woman, it was my trip, we

were using my money. But Saied took the mint tea and the gossip, and I got—well, I don't have to go into that again.

We waited the appropriate amount of time. The sun was disappearing behind a western wall; it was almost time for the sunset call to prayer. I stared at Saied, who was now dozing. Good, I thought, now I get to hit *him* in the head. I had just gotten up and taken one little step, when he looked up at me. "It's time, I guess," he said, yawning. I nodded, didn't have anything to add. So I sat back down, and Saied the Half-Hajj went into his act.

Saied is a natural-born liar, and it's a pleasure to watch him hustle.

He had the personality module he liked best plugged into his brain—his heavy-duty, steel-belted, mean-mother-of-a-tough-guy moddy. Nobody messed with the Half-Hajj when he was chipping that one in.

Back home in the city, Saied thought it was beneath him to earn money. He liked to sit in the cafés with me and Mahmoud and Jacques, all day and all evening. His little chicken, the American boy everybody called Abdul-Hassan, went out with older men and brought home the rent money. Saied liked to sneer a lot and wear his gallebeya cinched with a wide black leather belt, which was decorated with shiny chrome steel strips and studs. The Half-Hajj was always careful of his appearance.

What he was doing in this vermin-infested roadside slum was what he called fun. I waited a few minutes and followed him around the corner and into the coffeehouse. I shuffled in, unkempt, filthy, and took a chair in a shadowy corner. The proprietor glanced at me, frowned, and turned back to Saied. Nobody ever paid any attention to me. Saied was finishing the tail-end of a joke I'd heard him tell a dozen times since we'd left the city. When he came to the payoff, the shopkeeper and the four other men at the long counter burst into laughter. They liked Saied. He could make people like him whenever he wanted. That talent was programmed into an add-on chip snapped into his bad-ass moddy. With the right moddy and the right daddy chips, it didn't matter where you'd been born or how you'd been raised. You could fit in with any sort of people, you could speak any language, you could handle yourself in any situation. The information was fed directly into your short-term memory. You could literally become another person, Ramses II or Buck Rogers in the 25th Century, until you popped the moddy and daddies out.

Saied was being rough and dangerous, but he was also being charming, if you can imagine that combination. I watched the shop owner reach and grab the teapot. He poured tea into the Half-Hajj's glass, slopping some onto the wooden counter. Nobody moved to mop it up. Saied raised the glass to drink, then slammed it down again. "Yaa salâm!" he roared. He leaped up.

"What is it, O my friend?" asked Hisham, the proprietor.

"My ring!" Saied shouted. He was wearing a large gold ring, and he'd been waving it under the old man's nose for two solid hours. It had had a big, round diamond in its center.

"What's the matter with your ring?"

"Look for yourself! The stone—my diamond—it's gone!"

Hisham caught Saied's flapping arm and saw that, indeed, the diamond was now missing. "Must have fallen out," the old man said, with the sort of folk wisdom you find only in these petrified provincial villages.

"Yes, fallen out," said Saied, not calmed in the least. "But where?"

"Do you see it?"

Saied made a great show of searching the floor around his stool. "No, I'm sure it's not here," he said at last.

"Then it must be out in the alley. You must've lost it the last time you went out to piss."

Saied slammed the bar with his heavy fist. "And now it's getting dark, and I must catch the bus."

"You still have time to search," said Hisham. He didn't sound very confident.

The Half-Hajj laughed without humor. "A stone like that, worth four thousand Tunisian dinars, looks like a tiny pebble among a million others. In the twilight I'd never find it. What am I to do?"

The old man chewed his lip and thought for a moment. "You're determined to leave on the bus when it passes through?" he asked.

"I must, O my brother. I have urgent business."

"I'll help you if I can. Perhaps I can find the stone for you. You must leave your name and address with me; then if I find the diamond, I'll send it to you."

"May the blessings of Allah be on you and on your family!" said Saied. "I have little hope that you'll succeed but it comforts me to know you will do your best for me. I'm in your debt. We must determine a suitable reward for you."

Hisham looked at Saied with narrowed eyes. "I ask no reward," he said slowly.

"No, of course not, but I insist on offering you one."

"No reward is necessary. I consider it my duty to help you, as a Muslim brother."

"Still," Saied went on, "should you find the wretched stone, I'll give you a thousand Tunisian dinars for the sustenance of your children and the ease of your aged parents."

"Let it be as you wish," said Hisham with a small bow.

"Here," said my friend, "let me write my address for you." While Saied was scribbling his name on a scrap of paper, I heard the rumbling of the bus as it lurched to a stop outside the building.

"May Allah grant you a good journey," said the old man.

"And may He grant you prosperity and peace," said Saied, as he hurried out to the bus.

I waited about three minutes. Now it was my turn. I stood up and staggered a couple of steps. I had a lot of trouble walking in a straight line. I could see the shopkeeper glaring at me in disgust. "The hell do you want, you filthy beggar?" he said.

"Some water," I said.

"Water! Buy something or get out!"

"Once a man asked the Messenger of God, may Allah's blessings be on him, what was the noblest thing a man may do. The reply was 'To give water to he who thirsts.' I ask this of you."

"Ask the Prophet. I'm busy."

I nodded. I didn't expect to get anything free to drink out of this crud. I leaned against his counter and stared at a wall. I couldn't seem to make the place stand still.

"*Now* what do you want? I told you to go away."

"Trying to remember," I said peevishly. "I had something to tell you. Ah, yes, I know." I reached into a pocket of my jeans and brought out a glittering round stone. "Is this what that man was looking for? I found this out there. Is this—?"

The old man tried to snatch it out of my hand. "Where'd you get that? The alley, right? *My* alley. Then it's mine."

"No, I found it. It's—"

"He said he wanted me to look for it." The shopkeeper was already gazing into the distance, spending the reward money.

"He said he'd pay you money for it."

"That's right. Listen, I've got his address. Stone's no good to you without the address."

I thought about that for a second or two. "Yes, O Shaykh."

"And the address is no good to me without the stone. So here's my offer: I'll give you two hundred dinars for it."

"Two hundred? But he said—"

"He said he'd give me a thousand. *Me*, you drunken fool. It's worthless to you. Take the two hundred. When was the last time you had two hundred dinars to spend?"

"A long time."

"I'll bet. So?"

"Let me have the money first."

"Let me have the stone."

"The money."

The old man growled something and turned away. He brought a rusty coffee can up from under the counter. There was a thick wad of money in it, and he fished out two hundred dinars in old, worn bills. "Here you are, and damn your mother for a whore."

I took the money and stuffed it into my pocket. Then I gave the stone to Hisham. "If you hurry," I said, slurring my words despite the fact that I hadn't had a drink or any drugs all day, "you'll catch up with him. The bus hasn't left yet."

The man grinned at me. "Let me give you a lesson in shrewd business. The esteemed gentleman offered me a thousand dinars for a four-thousand-dinar stone. Should I take the reward, or sell the stone for its full value?"

"Selling the stone will bring trouble," I said.

"Let me worry about that. Now you go to hell. I don't ever want to see you around here again."

He needn't worry about that. As I left the decrepit coffeehouse, I popped out the moddy I was wearing. I don't know where the Half-Hajj had gotten it; it had a Malaccan label on it, but I didn't think it was an over-the-counter piece of hardware. It was a dumbing-down moddy; when I chipped it in, it ate about half of my intellect and left me shambling, stupid, and just barely able to carry out my half of the plan. With it out, the world suddenly poured back into my consciousness, and it was like waking from a bleary, drugged sleep. I was always angry for half an hour after I popped that moddy. I hated myself for agreeing to wear it, I hated Saied for conning me into doing it. He wouldn't wear it, not the Half-Hajj and his precious self-image. So I wore it, even though I'm gifted with twice the intracranial modifications as anybody else around, enough daddy capacity to make me the most talented son of a bitch in creation. And still Saied persuaded me to damp myself out to the point of near vegetability.

On the bus, I sat next to him, but I didn't want to talk to him or listen to him gloat.

"What'd we get for that chunk of glass?" he wanted to know. He'd already replaced the real diamond in his ring.

I just handed the money to him. It was his game, it was his score. I couldn't have cared less. I don't even know why I went along with him, except that he'd said he wouldn't come to Algeria with me unless I did.

He counted the bills. "Two hundred? That's all? We got more the last two times. Oh, well, what the hell—that's two hundred dinars more we can blow in Algiers. 'Come with me to the Kasbah.' Little do those gazelle-eyed boys know what's stealing toward them even now, through the lemon-scented night."

"This stinking bus, that's what, Saied."

He looked at me with wide eyes, then laughed. "You got no romance in you, Marîd. Ever since you had your brain wired, you been no fun at all."

"How about that." I didn't want to talk anymore. I pretended that I was going to sleep. I just closed my eyes and listened to the bus thumping and thudding over the broken pavement, with the unending arguments and laughter of the other passengers all around me. It was crowded and hot on that reeking bus, but it was carrying me hour by hour nearer to the solution of my own mystery. I had come to a point in my life where I needed to find out who I really was.

The bus stopped in the Barbary town of Annaba, and an old man with a grizzled gray beard came aboard selling apricot nectar. I got some for myself and some for the Half-Hajj. Apricots are the pride of Mauretania, and the juice was the first real sign that I was getting close to home. I closed my eyes and inhaled that delicate apricot aroma, then swallowed a mouthful of juice and savored the thick sweetness. Saied just gulped his down with a grunt and gave me a blunt "Thanks." The guy's got all the refinement of a dead bat.

The road angled south, away from the dark, invisible coast toward the city of Constantine. Although it was getting late, almost midnight, I told Saied that I wanted to get off the bus and grab some supper. I hadn't eaten anything since noon. Constantine is built on a high limestone bluff, the only ancient town in eastern Algeria to survive through centuries of foreign invasions. The only thing I cared about, though, was food. There is a local dish in Constantine called *chorba beida bel kefta*, a meatball soup made with onions, pepper, chickpeas, almonds, and cinnamon. I hadn't tasted it in at least fifteen years, and I didn't care if it meant missing the bus and having to wait until tomorrow for another, I was going to have some. Saied thought I was crazy.

I had my soup, and it was wonderful. Saied just watched me wordlessly and sipped a glass of tea. We got back on the bus in time. I felt good now, comfortably full, and warmed by a nostalgic glow. I took the window seat, hoping that I'd be able to see some familiar landscape as we passed through Jijel and Mansouria. Of course, it was as black as the inside of my pocket beyond the glass, and I saw nothing but the moon and the fiercely twinkling stars. Still, I pretended to myself that I could make out landmarks that meant I was drawing closer to Algiers, the city where I had spent a lot of my childhood.

When at last we pulled into Algiers sometime after sunrise, the Half-Hajj shook me awake. I didn't remember falling asleep. I felt terrible. My head felt like it had been crammed full of sharp-edged broken glass, and I had a pinched nerve in my neck, too. I took out my pill case and stared into it for a while. Did I prefer to make my entrance into Algiers hallucinating, narcotized, or somnambulant? It was a difficult decision. I went for pain-free but conscious, so I fished out eight tabs of Sonneine. The sunnies obliterated my head-ache—and every other mildly unpleasant sensation—and I more or less floated from the bus station in Mustapha to a cab.

"You're stoned," said Saied when we got in the back of the taxi. I told the driver to take us to a public data library.

"Me? Stoned? When have you ever known me to be stoned so early in the morning?"

"Yesterday. The day before yesterday. The day before that."

"I mean except for then. I function better with a ton of opiates in me than most people do straight."

"Sure you do."

I stared out the taxi's window. "Anyway," I said, "I've got a rack of daddies that can compensate."

"Marîd Audran, Silicon Superman."

"Look," I said, annoyed by Saied's attitude, "for a long time I was terrified of getting wired, but now I don't know how I ever got along without it."

"Then why the hell are you still decimating your brain cells with drugs?" asked the Half-Hajj.

"Call me old-fashioned. Besides, when I pop the daddies out, I feel terrible. All that suppressed fatigue and pain hits me at once."

"And you don't get paybacks with your sunnies and beauties, right? That what you're saying?"

"Shut up, Saied. Why the hell are you so concerned all of a sudden?"

He looked at me sideways and smiled. "The religion has this ban on liquor and hard drugs, you know." And this coming from the Half-Hajj who, if he'd ever been inside a mosque in his life, was there only to check out the boys' school.

So in ten or fifteen minutes the cab driver let us out at the library. I felt a peculiar nervous excitement, although I didn't understand why. All I was doing was climbing the granite steps of a public building; why should I be so wound up? I tried to occupy my mind with more pleasant thoughts.

Inside, there were a number of terminals vacant. I sat down at the gray screen of a battered Bab el-Marifi. It asked me what sort of search I wanted to conduct. The machine's voice synthesizer had been designed in one of the North American republics, and it was having a lot of trouble pronouncing Arabic. I said, "Name," then "Enter." When the cursor appeared again, I said, "Monroe comma Angel." The data deck thought about that for a while, then white letters began flicking across its bright face:

> Angel Monroe
> 16, Rue du Sahara
> (Upper) Kasbah
> Algiers
> Mauretania
> 04–B–28

I had the machine print out the address. The Half-Hajj raised his eyebrows at me and I nodded. "Looks like I'm gonna get some answers."

"Inshallah," murmured Saied. If God wills.

We went back out into the hot, steamy morning to find another taxi. It didn't take long to get from the library to the Kasbah. There wasn't as much traffic as I remembered from my childhood—not vehicular traffic, anyway; but there were still the slow, unavoidable battalions of heavily laden donkeys being cajoled through the narrow streets.

Number 16 was an exhausted, crumbling brick pile with two bulging upper stories that hung out over the cobbled street. The apartment house across the way did the same, and the two buildings almost kissed above my head, like two dowdy old matrons leaning across a back fence. There was a jumble of mail slots, and I found Angel Monroe's name scrawled on a card in fading ink. I jammed my thumb on her buzzer. There was no lock on the front door, so I went in and climbed the first flight of stairs. Saied was right behind me.

Her apartment turned out to be on the third floor, in the rear. The hallway was carpeted, if that's the right word, with a dull, gritty fabric that had at one time been maroon. The traffic of uncountable feet had completely worn through the material in many places, so that the dry gray wood of the floor was visible through the holes. The walls were covered with a filthy tan wallpaper, hanging down here and there in forlorn strips. The air had an odd, sour tang to it, as if the building were occupied by people who had come there to die, or who were certainly sick enough to die but instead hung on in lonely misery. From behind one door I could hear a family battle, complete with bellowed threats and crashing crockery, while from another apartment came insane, high-pitched laughter and the sound of flesh loudly smacking flesh. I didn't want to know about it.

I stood outside the shabby door to Angel Monroe's flat and took a deep breath. I glanced at the Half-Hajj, but he just gave me a shrug and pointedly looked away. Some friend. I was on my own. I told myself that nothing weird was going to happen—a lie just to get myself to take the next step—and then I knocked on the door. There was no response. I waited a few seconds and knocked again, louder. This time I heard the rattle and squeak of bedsprings and the sound of someone coming slowly to the door. The door swung open. Angel Monroe stared out, trying very hard to focus her eyes.

She was a full head shorter than me, with bleached blonde hair curled tightly into an arrangement I would call "ratty." Her black roots looked as if no one had given them much attention since the Prophet's birthday. Her eyes were banded with dark blue and black makeup, in a manner that brought to mind the more colorful Mediterranean saltwater fish. The rouge she wore was applied liberally, but not quite in the right places, so she didn't look so much wantonly sexy as she did feverishly ill. Her lipstick, for reasons best known to Allah and Angel Monroe, was a kind of pulpy purple color; her lips looked like she'd bought them first and forgot to put them in the refrigerator while she shopped for the rest of her face.

Her body led me to believe that she was too old to be dressed in anything but the long white Algerian haik, with a veil conservatively and firmly in place. The problem was that this body had never seen the inside of a haik. She was clad now in shorts so small that her well-rounded belly was bending the waistband over. Her sagging breasts were not quite clothed in a kind of gauzy vest. I knew for certain that if she sat in a chair, you could safely hide the world's most valuable gem in her navel and it would be completely invisible. Her legs were patterned with broken veins like the dry chebka valleys of the Mzab. On her broad, flat feet she wore tattered slippers with the remains of pink fuzzy bows dangling loose.

To tell the truth, I felt a certain disgust. "Angel Monroe?" I asked. Of course, that wasn't her real name. She was at least half Berber, as I am. Her skin was darker than mine, her eyes as black and dull as eroded asphalt.

"Uh huh," she said. "Kind of early, ain't it?" Her voice was sharp and shrill. She was already very drunk. "Who sent you? Did Khalid send you? I told that goddamn bastard I was sick. I ain't supposed to be working today, I told him last night. He said it was all right. And then he sends you. *Two* of you, yet. Who the hell does he think I am? And it ain't like he don't have no other girls, either. He could have sent you to Efra, that whore, with her plug-in talent. If I ain't feeling good, it don't bother me if he sends you to her. Hell, I don't care. How much you give him, anyway?"

I stood there, looking at her. Saied gave me a jab in the side. "Well, uh, Miss Monroe," I said, but then she started chattering again.

"The hell with it. Come on in. I guess I can use the money. But you tell that son of a bitch Khalid that—" She paused to take a long gulp from the tall glass of whiskey she was holding. "You tell him if he don't care enough about my health, I mean, making me work when I already told him I was sick, then hell, you tell him there are plenty of others I can go work for. Anytime I want to, you can believe that."

I tried twice to interrupt her, but I didn't have any success. I waited until she stopped to take another drink. While she had her mouth full of the cheap liquor, I said, "Mother?"

She just stared at me for a moment, her filmy eyes wide. "No," she said at last, in a small voice. She looked closer. Then she dropped her whiskey glass to the floor.

2

Later, after the return trip from Algiers and Mauretania, when I got back home to the city, the first place I headed was the Budayeen. I used to live right in the heart of the walled quarter, but events and fate and Friedlander Bey had made that impossible now. I used to have a lot of friends in the Budayeen, too, and I was welcome anywhere; but now there were really only two people who were generally glad to see me: Saied the Half-Hajj, and Chiriga, who ran a club on the Street halfway between the big stone arch and the cemetery. Chiri's place had always been my home-away-from-home, where I could sit and have a few drinks in peace, hear the gossip, and not get threatened or hustled by the working girls. Chiri's a hard-working woman, a tall black African with ritual facial scars and sharply filed cannibal teeth. To be honest, I don't really know if those canines of hers are mere decoration, like the patterns on her forehead and cheeks, or a sign that dinner at her house was composed of delicacies implicitly and explicitly forbidden by the noble Qur'ân. Chiri's a moddy, but she thinks of herself as a smart moddy. At work, she's always herself. She chips in her fantasies at home, where she won't bother anyone else. I respect that.

When I came through the club's door, I was struck first by a welcome wave of cool air. Her air conditioning, as undependable as all old Russian-made hardware, was working for a change. I felt better already. Chiri was deep in conversation with a customer, some bald guy with a bare chest. He was wearing black vinyl pants with the look of real leather, and his left hand was handcuffed behind him to his belt. He had a corymbic implant on the crest of his skull, and a pale green plastic moddy was feeding him somebody else's personality. If Chiri was giving him the time of day, then he couldn't have been dangerous, and probably he wasn't even all that obnoxious.

Chiri didn't have much patience with the crowd she caters to. Her philosophy is that *somebody* has to sell them liquor and drugs, but that doesn't mean she has to socialize with them.

"*Jambo*, Bwana Marîd!" Chiriga called to me when she noticed that I was sitting nearby. She left the handcuffed moddy and drifted slowly down her bar, plopping a cork coaster in front of me. "You come to share your wealth with this poor savage. In my native land, my people have nothing to eat and wander many miles in search of water. Here I have found peace and plenty. I have learned what friendship is. I have found disgusting men who would touch the hidden parts of my body. You will buy me drinks and leave me a huge tip. You will tell all your new friends about my place, and they will come in and want to touch the hidden parts of my body. I will own many shiny, cheap things. It is all as God wills."

I stared at her for a few seconds. Sometimes it's hard to figure what kind of mood Chiri's in. "Big nigger girl talk dumb," I said at last.

She grinned and dropped her ignorant Dinka act. "Yeah, you right," she said. "What is it today?"

"Gin and bingara," I said. I usually have that over ice with a little Rose's lime juice. The drink is my own invention, but I've never gotten around to naming it. Other times I have vodka gimlets, because that's what Philip Marlowe drinks in *The Long Goodbye*. Then on those occasions when I just really want to get loaded fast, I drink from Chiri's private stock of *tende*, a truly loathsome African liquor from the Sudan or the Congo or someplace, made, I think, from fermented yams and spadefoot toads. If you are ever offered *tende*, DO NOT TASTE IT. You *will* be sorry. Allah knows that I am.

Indihar was dancing on stage. She was a real girl with a real personality, a rarity in that club. Chiri seemed to prefer in her employees the high-velocity prettiness of a sexchange. Chiri told me once that changes take better care of their appearance. Their prefab beauty is their whole life. Allah forbid that a single hair of their eyebrows should be out of place.

By her own standards, Indihar was a good Muslim woman. She didn't have the head-wiring that most dancers had. The more conservative imams taught that the implants fell under the same prohibition as intoxicants, because some people got their pleasure centers wired and spent the remainder of their short lives amp-addicted. Even if, as in my case, the pleasure center is left alone, the use of a moddy submerges your own personality, and that is interpreted as insobriety. Needless to say, while I have nothing but the warmest affection for Allah and His Messenger, I stop short of being a fanatic about it. I'm with that twentieth century King Saud who demanded that the Islamic leaders of his country stop dragging their feet when it came to technological progress. I don't see any essential conflict between modern science and a thoughtful approach to religion.

"So," said Chiri, trying to make conversation, "how did your trip turn out? Did you find whatever you were looking for?"

I looked at her, but didn't say anything. I wondered if I *had* found it. When I saw my mother again in Algiers, her appearance had shocked me. In my imagination, I'd pictured her as a respectable, moderately well-to-do matron living in a comfortable neighborhood. I hadn't seen or spoken to her in years, but I just figured she'd managed to lift herself out of the poverty and degradation. Now I thought maybe she was happy as she was, a haggard, strident old whore. I spent an hour with her, hoping to hear what I'd come to learn, trying to decide how to behave toward her, and being embarrassed by her in front of the Half-Hajj. She didn't want to be troubled by her past. She didn't like me dropping back into her life after all those years.

"Believe me," I told her, "I didn't like hunting you up either. I only did it because I have to."

"Why do you have to?" she wanted to know. She reclined on a musty smelling, torn, old sofa that was covered with cat hair. She'd made herself another drink, but had neglected to offer me or Saied anything.

"It's important to me," I said. I told her about my life in the faraway city, how I'd lived as a subsonic hustler until Friedlander Bey had chosen me as the instrument of his will.

"You live in the city now?" She said that with a nostalgic longing. I never knew she'd been to the city.

"I lived in the Budayeen," I said, "but Friedlander Bey moved me into his palace."

"You work for him?"

"I had no choice." I shrugged. She nodded. It surprised me that she knew who Papa was, too.

"So what did you come for?"

That was going to be hard to explain. "I wanted to find out everything I could about my father."

She looked at me over the rim of her whiskey glass. "You already heard everything," she said.

"I don't think so. How sure are you that this French sailor was my dad?"

She took a deep breath and let it out slowly. "His name was Bernard Audran. We met in a coffee shop. I was living in Sidi Bel Abbes then. He took me to dinner, we liked each other. I moved in with him. We came to live in Algiers after that, and we were together for a year and a half. Then after you was born, one day he just left. I never heard from him again. I don't know where he went."

"I do. Into the ground, that's where. Took me a long time, but I traced Algerian computer records back far enough. There was a Bernard Audran in the navy of Provence, and he was in Mauretania when the French Confederate Union tried to regain control over us. The problem is that his brains were bashed out by some unidentified noraf more than a year before I was born. Maybe you could think back and see if you can get a clearer picture of those events."

That made her furious. She jumped up and flung her half-full glass of liquor at me. It smashed into the already stained and streaked wall to my right. I could smell the pungent, undiluted sharpness of the Irish whiskey. I heard Saied murmuring something beside me, maybe a prayer. My mother took a couple of steps toward me, her face ugly with rage. "You calling me a *liar?*" she shrieked.

Well, I was. "I'm just telling you that the official records say something different."

"Fuck the official records!"

"The records also say that you were married seven times in two years. No mention of any divorces."

My mother's anger faltered a bit. "How did that get in the computers? I never got officially married, not with no license or nothing."

"I think you underestimate the government's talent for keeping track of people. It's all there for anybody to see."

Now she looked frightened. "What else'd you find out?"

I let her off her own hook. "Nothing else. There wasn't anything more. You want something else to stay buried, you don't have to worry." That was a lie; I had learned plenty more about my mom.

"Good," she said, relieved. "I don't like you prying into what I done. It don't show respect."

I had an answer to that, but I didn't use it. "What started all this nostalgic research," I said in a quiet voice, "was some business I was taking care of for Papa." Everybody in the Budayeen calls Friedlander Bey "Papa." It's an affectionate token of terror. "This police lieutenant who handled matters in the Budayeen died, so Papa decided that we needed a kind of public affairs officer, somebody to keep communications open between him and the police department. He asked me to take the job."

Her mouth twisted. "Oh yeah? You got a gun now? You got a badge?" It was from my mother that I learned my dislike for cops.

"Yeah," I said, "I got a gun *and* a badge."

"Your badge ain't any good in Algiers, salaud."

"They give me professional courtesy wherever I go." I didn't even know if that was true here. "The point is, while I was deep in the cop comp, I took the opportunity to read my own file, and a few others. The funny thing was, my name and Friedlander Bey's kept popping up together. And not just in the records of the last few years. I counted at least eight entries—hints, you understand, but nothing definite—that suggested the two of us were blood kin." That got a loud reaction from the Half-Hajj; maybe I should have told him about all this before.

"So?" said my mother.

"The hell kind of answer is that? So what does it mean? You ever jam Friedlander Bey, back in your golden youth?"

She looked raving mad again. "Hell, I jammed *lots* of guys. You expect me to remember all of them? I didn't even remember what they looked like while I was jamming them."

"You didn't want to get involved, right? You just wanted to be good friends. Were you ever friends enough to give credit? Or did you always ask for the cash up front?"

"Maghrebi," cried Saied, "this is your *mother!*" I didn't think it was possible to shock him.

"Yeah, it's my mother. Look at her."

She crossed the room in three steps, reached back, and gave me a hard slap across the face. It made me fall back a step. "Get the fuck *out* of here!" she yelled.

I put my hand to my cheek and glared at her. "You answer one thing first: Could Friedlander Bey be my real father?"

Her hand was poised to deliver another clout. "Yeah, he could

be, the way practically *any* man could be. Go back to the city and
climb up on his knee, sonny boy. I don't ever want to see you
around here again."

She could rest easy on that score. I turned my back on her and
left that repulsive hole in the wall. I didn't bother to shut the door
on the way out. The Half-Hajj did, and then he hurried to catch up
with me. I was storming down the stairs. "Listen, Marîd," he said.
Until he spoke, I didn't realize how wild I was. "I guess all this is a
big surprise to you—"

"You do? You're very perceptive today, Saied."

"—but you can't act that way toward your mother. Remember
what it says—"

"In the Qur'ân? Yeah, I know. Well, what does the Straight Path
have to say about prostitution? What does it have to say about the
kind of degenerate my holy mother has turned into?"

"You've got a lot of room to talk. If there was a cheaper hustler
in the Budayeen, I never met him."

I smiled coldly. "Thanks a lot, Saied, but I don't live in the
Budayeen anymore. You forget? And I don't hustle anybody or anything. I got a steady job."

He spat at my feet. "You used to do nearly anything to make a
few kiam."

"Anyway, just because I used to be the scum of the earth, it
doesn't make it all right for my mother to be scum, too."

"Why don't you just shut up about her? I don't want to hear
about it."

"Your empathy just grows and grows, Saied," I said. "You don't
know everything I know. My alma mater back there was into rent-
ing herself to strangers long before she had to support the two of us.
She wasn't the forlorn heroine she always said she was. She glossed
over a lot of the truth."

The Half-Hajj looked me hard in the eye for a few seconds.
"Yeah?" he said. "Half the girls, changes, and debs we know do the
same thing, and you don't have any problem treating *them* like
human beings."

I was about to say "Sure, but none of them is my mother." I
stopped myself. He would have jumped on that sentiment, too, and
besides, it was starting to sound foolish even to me. The edge of my
anger had vanished. I think I was just greatly annoyed to have to
learn these things after so many years. It was hard for me to accept.
I mean, now I had to forget almost everything I thought I knew
about myself. For one thing, I'd always been proud of the fact that I
was half-Berber and half-French. I dressed in European style most

of the time—boots and jeans and work shirts. I suppose I'd always felt a little superior to the Arabs I lived among. Now I had to get used to the thought that I could very well be half-Berber and half-Arab.

The raucous, thumping sound of mid-twenty-first-century hispo roc from Chiri's jukebox broke into my daydream. Some forgotten band was growling an ugly chant about some damn thing or other. I've never gotten around to learning any Spanish dialects, and I don't own a Spanish-language daddy. If I ever run into any Colombian industrialists, they can just damn well speak Arabic. I have a soft spot in my liver for them because of their production of narcotics, but outside of that I don't see what South America is for. The world doesn't need an overpopulated, starving, Spanish-speaking India in the Western Hemisphere. Spain, their mother country, tried Islam and said a polite no-thank-you, and their national character sublimed right off into nothingness. That's Allah punishing them.

I was bored as hell. I knocked back the rest of my drink. Chiri looked at me and raised her eyebrows. "No thanks, Chiri," I said. "I got to go."

She leaned over and kissed me on the cheek. "Well, don't be a stranger now that you're a fascist swine cop."

"Right," I said. I got up from my stool. It was time to go to work. I left the rest of my change for Chiri's hungry register and went back outside.

3

There was always a crowd of young children outside the station house on Walid al-Akbar Street. I don't know if they were hoping to see some shackled criminal dragged in, or waiting for their own parents to be released from custody, or just loitering in the hopes of begging loose change. I'd been one of them myself not so very long ago in Algiers, and it didn't hurt me any to throw a few kiam into the air and watch them scramble for it. I reached into my pocket and grabbed a clutch of coins. The older, bigger kids caught the easy money, and the smaller ones clung to my legs and wailed, "Baksheesh!" Every day it was a challenge to shake my young passengers loose before I got to the revolving door.

I had a desk in a small cubicle on the third floor of the station house. My cubicle was separated from its neighbors by pale green plasterboard walls only a little taller than I was. There was always a sour smell in the air, a mixture of stale sweat, tobacco smoke, and disinfectant. Above my desk was a shelf that held plastic boxes filled with dated files on cobalt-alloy cell-memories. On the floor was a big cardboard box crammed with bound printouts. I had a grimy Annamese data deck on my desk that gave me trouble-free operation on two out of every three jobs. Of course, my work wasn't very important, not according to Lieutenant Hajjar. We both knew I was there just to keep an eye on things for Friedlander Bey. It amounted to Papa having his own private police precinct devoted to protecting his interests in the Budayeen.

Hajjar came into my cubicle and dropped another heavy box on my desk. He was a Jordanian who'd had a lengthy arrest record of his own before he came to the city. I suppose he'd been an athlete ten years ago, but he hadn't stayed in shape. He had thinning brown hair and lately he'd tried to grow a beard. It looked terrible, like the skin of a kiwi fruit. He looked like a mother's bad dream of a drug dealer, which is what he was when he wasn't administering the affairs of the nearby walled quarter.

"How you doin', Audran?" he said.

"Okay," I said. "What's all this?"

"Found something useful for you to do." Hajjar was about two years younger than me, and it gave him a kick to boss me around.

I looked in the box. There were a couple hundred blue cobalt-alloy plates. It looked like another really tedious job. "You want me to sort these?"

"I want you to log 'em all into the daily record."

I swore under my breath. Every cop carries an electronic log book to make notes on the day's tour: where he went, what he saw, what he said, what he did. At the end of the day, he turns in the book's cell-memory plate to his sergeant. Now Hajjar wanted me to collate all the plates from the station's roster. "This isn't the kind of work Papa had in mind for me," I said.

"What the hell. You got any complaints, take 'em to Friedlander Bey. In the meantime, do what I tell you."

"Yeah, you right," I said. I glared at Hajjar's back as he walked out.

"By the way," he said, turning toward me again, "I got someone for you to meet later. It may be a nice surprise."

I doubted that. "Uh huh," I said.

"Yeah, well, get movin' on those plates. I want 'em finished by lunchtime."

I turned back to my desk, shaking my head. Hajjar annoyed the hell out of me. What was worse, he knew it. I didn't like giving him the satisfaction of seeing me irked.

I selected a productivity moddy from my rack and chipped it onto my posterior plug. The rear implant functions the same as everybody else's. It lets me chip in a moddy and six daddies. The anterior plug, however, is my own little claim to fame. This is the one that taps into my hypothalamus and lets me chip in my special daddies. As far as I know, no one else has ever been given a second implant. I'm glad I hadn't known that Friedlander Bey told my doctors to try something experimental and insanely dangerous. I guess he didn't want me to worry. Now that the frightening part is over, though, I'm glad I went through it. It's made me a more productive member of society and all that.

When I had boring police work to do, which was almost every day, I chipped in an orange moddy that Hajjar had given me. It had a label that said it was manufactured in Helvetia. The Swiss, I suppose, have a high regard for efficiency. Their moddy could take the most energetic, inspired person in the world and transform him instantly into a drudge.

Not into a stupid drudge, like what the Half-Hajj's dumbing-down hardware did to me, but into a mindless worker who isn't aware enough to be distracted before the whole assignment is in the Out box. It's the greatest gift to the office menial since conjugal coffee breaks.

I sighed and took the moddy, then reached up and chipped it in.

The immediate sensation was as if the whole world had lurched and then caught its balance. There was an odd, metallic taste in Audran's mouth and a high-pitched ringing in his ears. He felt a touch of nausea, but he tried to ignore it because it wouldn't go away until he popped the moddy out. The moddy had trimmed down his personality, like the wick of a lamp, until there was only a vague and ineffectual vestige of his true self left.

Audran wasn't conscious enough even to be resentful. He remembered only that he had work to do, and he pulled a double handful of cobalt-alloy plates out of the box. He slotted six of them into the adit ports beneath the battered data deck's comp screen. Audran touched the control pad and said, "Copy ports one, two, three, four, five, six." Then he stared blankly while the deck recorded the contents of the plates. When the run was finished, he removed the plates, stacked them on one side of the desk, and loaded in six more. He barely noticed the morning pass as he logged in the records.

"Audran." Someone was saying his name.

He stopped what he was doing and glanced over his shoulder. Lieutenant Hajjar and a uniformed patrolman were standing in the

entrance to his cubicle. Audran turned slowly back to the data deck.
He reached into the box, but it was empty.
    "Unplug that goddamn thing."
    Audran faced Hajjar again and nodded. It was time to pop the
moddy.

There was a dizzy swirl of disorientation, and then I was sitting
at my desk, staring stupidly at the Helvetian moddy in my hand.
"Jeez," I murmured. It was a relief to be fully conscious again.
    "Tell you a secret about Audran," Hajjar said to the cop. "We
didn't hire him because of his wonderful qualities. He really don't
have any. But he makes a great spindle for hardware. Audran's just
a moddy's way of gettin' its daily workout." The cop smiled.
    "Hey, you gave me this goddamn moddy in the first place," I said.
Hajjar shrugged. "Audran, this is Officer Shaknahyi."
    "Where you at?" I said.
    "All right," said the cop.
    "You got to watch out for Audran," Hajjar said. "He's got one of
those addictive personalities. He used to make a big deal out of not
havin' his brain wired. Now you never see him without some kind
of moddy stuck in his head."
    That shocked me. I hadn't realized I'd been using my moddies
so much. I was surprised anyone else had noticed.
    "Try to overlook his frailties, Jirji, 'cause you and him are gonna
be workin' together."
    Shaknahyi gave him a sharp look. I did the same. "What do you
mean, 'working together'?" said the cop.
    "I mean what I said. I got a little assignment for you two. You're
gonna be workin' very closely for a while."
    "You taking me off the street?" asked Shaknahyi.
    Hajjar shook his head. "I never said that. I'm pairin' Audran with
you on patrol."
    Shaknahyi was so outraged, I thought he was going to split down
the middle. "Shaitan take my kids first!" he said. "You think you're
teaming me up with a guy with no training and no experience,
you're goddamn crazy!"
    I didn't like the idea of going out on the street. I didn't want
to make myself a target for every loon in the Budayeen who owned
a cheap needle gun. "I'm supposed to stay here in the station
house," I said. "Friedlander Bey never said anything about real cop
work."
    "Be good for you, Audran," said Hajjar. "You can ride around
and see all your old buddies again. They'll be impressed when you
flash your badge at them."

"They'll hate my guts," I said.

"You're both overlooking one small detail," said Shaknahyi. "As my partner, he's supposed to guard my back every time we walk into some dangerous situation. To be honest, I don't have a lick of faith in him. You can't expect me to work with a partner I don't trust."

"I don't blame you," said Hajjar. He looked amused by the cop's opinion of me. My first impression of Shaknahyi wasn't so good, either. He didn't have his brain wired, and that meant he was one of two kinds of cop: Either he was a strict Muslim, or else he was one of those guys who thought his own naked, unaugmented brain was more than a match for the evildoers. That's the way I used to be, but I learned better. Either way, I wouldn't get along with him.

"And I don't want the responsibility of watching his back," I said. "I don't need that kind of pressure."

Shaknahyi didn't want any part of it. "I wanted to be a cop because I thought I could help people," he said. "I don't make a lot of money, I don't get enough sleep, and every day I mix into one goddamn crisis after another. I never know when somebody's gonna pull a gun on me and use it. I do it because I believe I can make a difference. I didn't sign on to baby-sit Friedlander Bey's protégé." He glowered at Hajjar until the lieutenant had to look away.

"Listen," I said to Shaknahyi, "what's your problem with me?"

"You're not a cop, for one thing," he said. "You're worse than a rookie. You'll hang back and let some creep nail me, or else you'll get itchy and shoot a little old lady. I don't want to be teamed with somebody unless I think I can count on him."

I nodded. "Yeah, you right, but I can wear a moddy. I've seen plenty of rookies wearing police officer moddies to help them through the routines."

Shaknahyi threw up his hands. "He just makes it worse," he muttered.

"Get used to it," said Hajjar, " 'cause you don't have a choice."

Shaknahyi rubbed his forehead and sighed. "All right, all right. I just wanted to have my objection on the record."

"Okay," said Hajjar, "it's been noted."

"Want us to start right away?" I asked.

Hajjar gave me a wry look. "If you can fit it into your busy social calendar."

"Fine," I said.

"Right," said Shaknahyi, walking out of my cubicle.

"You two didn't hit it off real well," said Hajjar.

"We just have to get the job done," I said. "We don't have to go dancing together."

"Yeah, you right." And then he turned and left me alone, too.

4

A few days later, Friedlander Bey sent a message that he'd like to speak with me, and he invited me to have supper with him afterward. I went into my bedroom and undressed. Then I took a quick shower and thought about what I wanted to say to Friedlander Bey. I wanted to let him know that I wasn't happy about being teamed with Officer Shaknahyi.

I got out of the shower and toweled myself dry. Then I stared into a closet for a while, deciding what to wear. Papa liked it when I wore Arab dress. I figured what the hell and picked a simple maroon gallebeya. I decided that the knitted skullcap of my homeland wasn't appropriate, and I'm not the turban type. I settled on a plain white keffiya and fixed it in place with a simple black rope akal. I tied a corded belt around my waist, supporting a ceremonial dagger Papa'd given me. Also on the belt, pulled around behind my back, was a holster with my seizure gun. I hid that by wearing an expensive tan-colored cloak over the gallebeya. I felt I was ready for anything: a feast, a debate, or an attempted assassination. Papa's offices were on the ground floor in the main part of the house connecting the two wings. When I got there, one of the Stones That Speak, Friedlander Bey's twin giants, was in the corridor, guarding the door. He glanced at me and nodded, and bowed his head slightly as I went past him into Papa's waiting room. Then he closed the door behind me. Friedlander Bey was in his inner office. He was sitting behind his gigantic desk. He didn't look well. His elbows were on the desktop, and his head was in his hands. He was massaging his forehead. He stood up when I came in. "I am pleased," he said. He didn't sound pleased. He sounded exhausted.

"It's my honor to wish you good evening, O Shaykh," I said. He was wearing an open-necked white shirt with the sleeves rolled up and a pair of baggy gray trousers. He probably wouldn't even notice the trouble I'd taken to dress conservatively. You can't win, right?

"We will dine soon, my son. In the meantime, sit with me. There are matters that need our attention."

I sat in a comfortable chair beside his desk. Papa took his seat again and fiddled with some papers, frowning. It wasn't my place to question him. He'd begin when he was ready.

He shut his eyes for a moment and then opened them, sighing. His sparse white hair was rumpled, and he hadn't shaved that morning. I guessed he had a lot on his mind. I was a little afraid of what he was going to order me to do this time.

"We must speak," he said. "There is the matter of alms-giving."

Okay, I'll admit it: Of all the possible problems he could have chosen, alms-giving was pretty low on my list of what I expected to hear. How foolish of me to think he wanted to discuss something more to the point. Like murder.

"I'm afraid I've had more important things on my mind, O Shaykh," I said.

Friedlander Bey nodded wearily. "No doubt, my son, you truly believe these other things are more important, but you are wrong. You and I share an existence of luxury and comfort, and that gives us a responsibility to our brothers."

Jacques, my infidel friend, would've had trouble grasping his precise point. Sure, other religions are all in favor of charity, too. It's just good sense to take care of the poor and needy, because you never know when you're going to end up poor and needy yourself. The Muslim attitude goes further, though. Alms-giving is one of the five pillars of the religion, as fundamental an obligation as the profession of faith, the daily prayer, the fast of Ramadân, and the pilgrimage to Makkah.

I gave the same attention to alms-giving that I gave the other duties. That is, I had profound respect for them in an intellectual sort of way, and I told myself that I'd begin practicing in earnest real soon now.

"Evidently you've been considering this for some time," I said.

"We have been neglecting our duty to the poor and the way-farers, and the widows and orphans among our neighbors."

Some of my friends—my old friends, my former friends—think Papa is nothing but a murderous monster, but that's not true. He's a shrewd businessman who also maintains strong ties to the faith that created our culture. I'm sorry if that seems like a contradiction. He could be harsh, even cruel, at times; but I knew no one else as sincere in his beliefs or as glad to meet the many obligations of the noble Qur'ân.

"What do you wish me to do, O my uncle?"

Friedlander Bey shrugged. "Do I not reward you well for your services?"

"You are unfailingly gracious, O Shaykh," I said.

"Then it would not be a hardship for you to set aside a fifth part of your substance, as is suggested in the Straight Path. Indeed, I desire to make a gift to you that will swell your purse and, at the same time, give you a source of income independent of this house."

That caught my attention. Freedom was what I hungered for every night as I drifted off to sleep. It was what I thought of first when I woke in the morning. And the first step toward freedom was financial independence.

"You are the father of generosity, O Shaykh," I said, "but I am unworthy." Believe me, I was panting to hear what he was going to say. Proper form, however, required me to pretend that I couldn't possibly accept his gift.

He raised one thin, trembling hand. "I prefer that my associates have outside sources of income, sources that they manage themselves and whose profits they need not share with me."

"That is a wise policy," I said. I've known a lot of Papa's "associates," and I know what kind of sources they had. I was sure he was about to cut me into some shady vice deal. Not that I had scruples, you understand. I wouldn't mind getting my drugs wholesale. I've just never had much of a mind for commerce.

"Until recently the Budayeen was your whole world. You know it well, my son, and you understand its people. I have a great deal of influence there, and I thought it best to acquire for you some small commercial concern in that quarter." He extended to me a document laminated in plastic.

I reached forward and took it from him. "What is this, O Shaykh?" I asked.

"It is a title deed. You are now the owner of the property described upon it. From this day forward it is your business to operate. It is a profitable enterprise, my nephew. Manage it well and it will reward you, inshallah."

I looked at the deed. "You're—" My voice choked. Papa had bought Chiriga's club and was giving it to me. I looked up at him. "But—"

He waved his hand at me. "No thanks are necessary," he said. "You are my dutiful son."

"But this is Chiri's place. I can't take her club. What will she do?"

Friedlander Bey shrugged. "Business is business," he said simply.

I just stared at him. He had a remarkable habit of giving me things I would have been happier without: my career as a cop, for instance. It wouldn't do any good at all to refuse. "I'm quite unable to express my thanks," I said in a dull voice. I had only two good friends left, Saied the Half-Hajj and Chiri. She was really going to hate this. I was already dreading her reaction.

"Come," said Friedlander Bey, "let us go in to dinner." He stood up behind his desk and held out his hand to me. I followed him, still astonished. It wasn't until later that I realized I hadn't spoken to him about my job with Hajjar.

Chiri's club was crowded that night. The air was still and warm inside, sweet with a dozen different perfumes, sour with sweat and spilled beer. The sexchanges and pre-op debs chatted with the customers with false cheerfulness, and their laughter broke through the shrill music as they called for more champagne cocktails. Bright bolts of red and blue neon slashed down slantwise behind the bar, and brilliant points of light from spinning mirrorballs sparkled on the walls and ceiling. In one corner there was a hologram of Honey Pílar, writhing alone upon a blond mink coat spread on the white sands of some romantic beach. It was an ad for her new sex moddy, *Slow, Slow Burn*. I stared at it for a moment, almost hypnotized.

"Audran," came Chiriga's hoarse voice. She didn't sound happy to see me. "Mr. Boss."

"Listen, Chiri," I said. "Let me—"

"Lily," she called to one of the changes, "get the new owner a drink. Gin and bingara with a hit of Rose's." She looked at me fiercely. "The *tende* is mine, Audran. Private stock. It doesn't go with the club, and I'm taking it with me."

She was making it hard for me. I could only imagine how she felt. "Wait a minute, Chiri. I had nothing to do with—"

"These are the keys. This one's for the register. The money in there's all yours. The girls are yours, the hassles are yours from now on, too. You got any problems, you can go to Papa with 'em." She snatched her bottle of *tende* from under the bar. "*Kwa heri*, motherfucker," she snarled at me. Then she stormed out of the club.

Everything got real quiet then. Whatever song had been playing came to an end and nobody put on another one. A deb named Kandy was on stage, and she just stood there and stared at me like I might start slavering and shrieking at any moment. People got up from their stools near me and edged away. I looked into their faces and I saw hostility and contempt.

Friedlander Bey wanted to divorce me from all my connections to the Budayeen. Making me a cop had been a great start, but even so I still had a few loyal friends. Forcing Chiri to sell her club had been another brilliant stroke. Soon I'd be just as lonely and friendless as Papa himself, except I wouldn't have the consolation of his wealth and power.

"Look," I said, "this is all a mistake. I got to settle this with Chiri. Indihar, take charge, okay? I'll be right back."

Indihar just gave me a disdainful look. She didn't say anything. I couldn't stand to be in there another minute. I grabbed the keys Chiri'd dropped on the bar and I went outside. She wasn't anywhere in sight on the Street. She might have gone straight home, but she'd probably gone to another club. In a way, I was relieved that I hadn't found her, but I knew that there were surely more ugly scenes to come.

The next morning I left my car on the Boulevard and walked from there to Laila's modshop on Fourth Street. Laila's was small, but it had character, crammed between a dark, grim gambling den and a noisy bar that catered to teenage sexchanges. The moddies and daddies in Laila's bins were covered with dust and fine grit, and generations of small insects had met their Maker among her wares. It wasn't pretty, but what you got from her most of the time was good old honest value. The rest of the time you got damaged, worthless, even dangerous merchandise. You always felt a little rush of adrenalin before you chipped one of Laila's ancient and shopworn moddies directly into your brain.

She was always—*always*—chipped in, and she never stopped whining. She whined hello, she whined goodbye, she whined in pleasure and in pain. When she prayed, she whined to Allah. She had dry black skin as wrinkled as a raisin, and straggly white hair. Laila was not someone I liked to spend a lot of time with. She was wearing a moddy this morning, of course, but I couldn't tell yet which one. Sometimes she was a famous Eur-Am film or holo star, or a character from a forgotten novel, or Honey Pílar herself. Whoever she was, she'd yammer. That was all I could count on.

"How you doing, Laila?" I said. There was the acrid bite of ammonia in her shop that morning. She was squirting some ugly pink liquid from a plastic bottle up into the corners of the room. Don't ask me why.

She glanced at me and gave me a slow, rapturous smile. It was the look you get only from complete sexual satisfaction or from a large dose of Sonneine. "Marîd," she said serenely. She still whined, but now it was a serene whine.

"Got to go out on patrol today, and I thought you might have—"

"Marîd, a young girl came to me this morning and said, 'Mother, the eyes of the narcissus are open, and the cheeks of the roses are red with blushing! Why don't you come outside and see how beautifully Nature has adorned the world!'"

"Laila, if you'll just give me a minute—"

"And I said to her, 'Daughter, that which delights you will fade in an hour, and what profit will you then have in it? Instead, come inside and find with me the far greater beauty of Allah, who created the spring.'" Laila finished her little homily and looked at me expectantly, as if she were waiting for me either to applaud or collapse from enlightenment.

I'd forgotten religious ecstasy. Sex, drugs, and religious ecstasy.

Those were the big sellers in Laila's shop, and she tested them all out personally. You had her personal Seal of Approval on every moddy.

"Can I talk now, Laila?"

She stared at me, swaying unsteadily. Slowly she reached one scrawny arm up and popped the moddy out. She blinked a couple of times, and her gentle smile disappeared. "Get you something, Marîd?" she said in her shrill voice.

Laila had been around so long, there was a rumor that as a child she'd watched the imams lay the foundation of the Budayeen's walls. But she knew her moddies. She knew more about old, out-of-print moddies than anyone else I've ever met. I think Laila must have had one of the world's first experimental implants, because her brain had never worked quite right afterward. And the way she still abused the technology, she should have burnt out her last gray cells years ago. She'd withstood cerebral torture that would have turned anyone else into a drooling zombie. Laila probably had a tough protective callus on her brain that prevented anything from penetrating. Anything at all.

I started over from the beginning. "I'm going out on patrol today, and I was wondering if you had a basic cop moddy."

"Sure, I got everything." She hobbled to a bin near the back of the store and dug around in it for a moment. The bin was marked "Prussia/Poland/Breulandy." That didn't have anything to do with which moddies were actually in there; Laila'd bought the battered dividers and scuffed labels from some other kind of shop that was going out of business.

She straightened up after a few seconds, holding a shrink-wrapped moddy in her hand. "This is what you want," she said.

It was the pale blue Complete Guardian moddy I'd seen other rookie cops wearing. It was a good, basic piece of procedure programming that covered almost every conceivable situation. I figured that between the Half-Hajj's mean-mother moddy and the Guardian, I was covered. I wasn't in a position to turn down any kind of help, friend or fantasy. For someone who once hated the idea of having his skull amped, I was sure building up a good collection of other people's psyches. I paid Laila for Complete Guardian and put it in my pocket.

She gave me that tranquil smile. It was toothless, of course, and it made me shiver. "Go in safety," she said in her nasal wail.

"Peace be upon you." I hurried out of her shop, walked back down the Street, and passed through the gate to where the car was parked. It wasn't far from there to the station house. I worked at my desk for a little while until Officer Shaknahyi ducked his head into my cubicle. "Time to roll," he said.

It didn't bother me in the least to tell my data deck to quit. I followed Shaknahyi downstairs to the garage. "That's mine," he said, pointing to a patrol car coming in from the previous shift. He greeted the two tired-looking cops who got out, then slid behind the steering wheel. "Well?" he said, looking up at me.

I wasn't in a hurry to start this. In the first place, I'd be stuck in the narrow confines of the cop car with Shaknahyi for the duration of the shift, and that prospect didn't excite me at all. Second, I'd really rather sit upstairs and read boring files in perfect safety than follow this battle-hardened veteran out into the mean streets. Finally, though, I climbed into the front seat. Sometimes there's only so much stalling you can do. He looked straight out the windshield while he drove.

We cruised around the streets of the city for about an hour. Then, suddenly, a shrill alarm went off, and the synthesized voice of the patrol car's comp deck crackled. "Badge Number 374, respond immediately to bomb threat and hostage situation, Café de la Fée Blanche, Ninth Street North."

"Gargotier's place," said Shaknahyi. "We'll take care of it." The comp deck fell silent.

And Hajjar had promised me I wouldn't have to worry about anything like this. "Bismillah ar-Rahman ar-Raheem," I murmured. In the name of Allah, the Compassionate, the Merciful.

5

A crowd had gathered outside the low railing of the Café de la Fée Blanche's patio. "Get these people out of here," Shaknahyi growled at me. "I don't know what's happening in there, but we got to treat it like the guy has a real bomb. And when you got everybody moved back, go sit in the car."

"But—"

"I don't want to have to worry about you, too." He ran around the corner of the café to the north, heading for the building's rear entrance.

I hesitated. I knew backup units would be getting here soon, and I decided to let them handle the crowd control. At the moment, there were more important things to worry about. I still had Complete Guardian, and I tore open the shrink-wrap with my teeth. Then I chipped the moddy in.

Audran was sitting at a table in the dimly lighted San Saberio salon in Florence, listening to a group of musicians playing a demure Schubert quartet. Across from him sat a beautiful blonde woman named Costanzia. She raised a cup to her lips, and her china-blue eyes looked at him over the rim. She was wearing a subtle, fascinating fragrance that made Audran think of romantic evenings and soft-spoken promises.

"This must be the best coffee in Tuscany," she murmured. Her voice was sweet and gentle. She gave him a warm smile.

"We didn't come here to drink coffee, my darling," he said. "We came here to see the season's new styles."

She waved a hand. "There is time enough for that. For now, let's just relax."

Audran smiled fondly at her and picked up his delicate cup. The coffee was the beautiful color of polished mahogany, and the wisps of steam that rose from it carried a heavenly, enticing aroma. The first taste overwhelmed Audran with its richness. As the coffee, hot and wonderfully delicious, went down his throat, he realized that Costanzia had been perfectly correct. He had never before been so satisfied by a cup of coffee.

"I'll always remember this coffee," he said.

"Let's come back here again next year, darling," said Costanzia.

Audran laughed indulgently. "For San Saberio's new fashions?"

Costanzia lifted her cup and smiled. "For the coffee," she said.

After the advertisement, there was a blackout during which Audran couldn't see a thing. He wondered briefly who Costanzia was, but he put her out of his mind. Just as he began to panic, his vision cleared. He felt a ripple of dizziness, and then it was as if he'd awakened from a dream. He was rational and cool and he had a job to do. He had become the Complete Guardian.

He couldn't see or hear anything that was happening inside. He assumed that Shaknahyi was making his way quietly through the café's back room. It was up to Audran to give his partner as much support as possible. He jumped the iron railing into the patio, then walked decisively into the interior of the bar.

The scene inside didn't look very threatening. Monsieur Gargotier was standing behind the bar, beneath the huge, cracked mirror. His daughter, Maddie, was sitting at a table near the back wall. A young man sat at a table against the west wall, under Gargotier's collection of faded prints of the Mars colony. The young man's hands rested on a small box. His head swung to look at Audran. "Get the fuck out," he shouted, "or this whole place goes up in a big bright bang!"

"I'm sure he means it, monsieur," said Gargotier. He sounded terrified.

"Bet your ass I mean it!" said the young man.

Being a police officer meant sizing up dangerous situations and being able to make quick, sure judgments. Complete Guardian suggested that in dealing with a mentally disturbed individual, Audran should try to find out why he was upset and then try to calm him. Complete Guardian recommended that Audran not make fun of the individual, show anger, or dare him to carry out his threat. Audran raised his hands and spoke calmly. "I'm not going to threaten you," Audran said.

The young man just laughed. He had dirty long hair and a patchy growth of beard, and he was wearing a faded pair of blue jeans and a plaid cotton shirt with its sleeves torn off. He looked a little like Audran had, before Friedlander Bey had raised his standard of living.

"Mind if I sit and talk with you?" asked Audran.

"I can set this off any time I want," said the young man. "You got the guts, sit down. But keep your hands flat on the table."

"Sure." Audran pulled out a chair and sat down. He had his back to the barkeeper, but out of the corner of his eye he could see Maddie Gargotier. She was quietly weeping.

"You ain't gonna talk me out of this," said the young man.

Audran shrugged. "I just want to find out what this is all about. What's your name?"

"The hell's that got to do with anything?"

"My name is Marîd. I was born in Mauretania."

"You can call me Al-Muntaqim." The kid with the bomb had appropriated one of the Ninety-Nine Beautiful Names of God. It meant "The Avenger."

"You always lived in the city?" Audran asked him.

"Hell no. Misr."

"That's the local name for Cairo, isn't it?" asked Audran.

Al-Muntaqim jumped to his feet, furious. He jabbed a finger toward Gargotier behind the bar and screamed, "See? See what I mean? That's just what I'm talkin' about! Well, I'm gonna stop it once and for all!" He grabbed the box and ripped open the lid.

Audran felt a horrible pain all through his body. It was as if all his joints had been yanked and twisted until his bones pulled apart. Every muscle in his body felt torn, and the surface of his skin stung as if it had been sandpapered. The agony went on for a few seconds, and then Audran lost consciousness.

"You all right?"

No, I didn't feel all right. On the outside I felt red-hot and glowing, as if I'd been staked out under the desert sun for a couple of days. Inside, my muscles felt quivery. I had lots of uncontrollable little spasms in my arms, legs, trunk, and face. I had a splitting headache and there was a horrible, sour taste in my mouth. I was having a lot of trouble focusing my eyes, as if someone had spread a thick translucent gunk over them.

I strained to make out who was talking to me. I could barely make out the voice because my ears were ringing so loud. It turned out to be Shaknahyi, and that indicated that I was still alive. For an awful moment after I came to, I thought I might be in Allah's greenroom or somewhere. Not that being alive was any big thrill just then. "What—" I croaked. My throat was so dry I could barely speak.

"Here." Shaknahyi handed a glass of cold water down to me. I realized that I was lying flat on my back on the floor, and Shaknahyi and M. Gargotier were standing over me, frowning and shaking their heads.

I took the water and drank it gratefully. When I finished, I tried talking again. "What happened?" I said.

"You fucked up," Shaknahyi said.

"Right," I said.

A narrow smile crossed Shaknahyi's face. He reached down and offered me a hand. "Get up off the floor."

I stood up wobbily and made my way to the nearest chair. "Gin and bingara," I said to Gargotier. "Put a hit of Rose's lime in it." The barkeep grimaced, but he turned away to get my drink. I took out my pill case and dug out maybe eight or nine Sonneine.

"I heard about you and your drugs," said Shaknahyi.

"It's all true," I said. When Gargotier brought my drink, I swallowed the opiates. I couldn't wait for them to start fixing me up. Everything would be just fine in a couple of minutes.

"You could've gotten everybody killed, trying to talk that guy down," Shaknahyi said. I was feeling bad enough already, I didn't want to listen to his little lecture right then. He went ahead with it anyway. "What the hell were you trying to do? Establish rapport or something? We don't work that way when people's lives are in danger."

"Yeah?" I said. "What do you do?"

He spread his hands like the answer should have been perfectly obvious. "You get around where he can't see you, and you ice the motherfucker."

"Did you ice me before or after you iced Al-Muntaqim?"

"That what he was calling himself? Hell, Audran, you got to expect a little beam diffusion with these static pistols. I'm real sorry I had to drop you, too, but there's no permanent damage, inshallah. He jumped up with that box, and I wasn't gonna wait around for you to give me a clear shot. I had to take what I could get."

"It's all right," I said. "Where's The Avenger now?"

"The meat wagon came while you were napping. Took him off to the lock ward at the hospital."

That made me a little angry. "The mad bomber gets shipped to a nice bed in the hospital, but I got to lie around on the filthy floor of this goddamn saloon?"

Shaknahyi shrugged. "He's in a lot worse shape than you are. You only got hit by the fuzzy edge of the charge. He took it full."

It sounded like Al-Muntaqim was going to feel pretty rotten for a while. Didn't bother me none.

"No percentage in debating morality with a loon," said Shaknahyi. "You go in looking for the first opportunity to stabilize the sucker." He made a trigger-pulling motion with his right index finger.

"That's not what Complete Guardian was telling me," I said. "By the way, did you pop the moddy for me? What did you do with it?"

"Yeah," said Shaknahyi, "here it is." He took the moddy out of a shirt pocket and tossed it down on the floor beside me. Then he raised his heavy black boot and stamped the plastic module into jagged pieces. Brightly colored fragments of the webwork circuitry skittered across the floor. "Wear another one of those, I do the same to your face and then I kick the remnants out of my patrol car."

So much for Marîd Audran, Ideal Law Enforcement Officer.

I stood up feeling a lot better, and followed Shaknahyi out of the dimly lighted bar. M. Gargotier and his daughter, Maddie, went with us. The bartender tried to thank us, but Shaknahyi just raised a hand and looked modest. "No thanks are necessary for performing a duty," he said.

"Come in for free drinks any time," Gargotier said gratefully.

"Maybe we will." Shaknahyi turned to me. "Let's ride," he said.

We went out through the patio gate. On the way back to the car I said, "It makes me feel kind of good to be welcome somewhere again."

Shaknahyi looked at me. "Accepting free drinks is a major infraction."

"I didn't know they *had* infractions in the Budayeen," I said. Shaknahyi smiled. It seemed that things had thawed a little between us.

Shaknahyi cruised back down the Street and out of the Buda-yeen. Curiously, I was no longer wary of being spotted in the cop car by any of my old friends. In the first place, the way they'd been treating me, I figured the hell with 'em. In the second place, I felt a little different now that I'd been fried in the line of duty. The experience at the Fée Blanche had changed my thinking. Now I appreciated the risks a cop has to take day after day.

Shaknahyi surprised me. "You want to stop somewhere?" he asked.

"Sounds good." I was still pretty weak and the sunnies had left me a little lightheaded, so I was glad to agree.

I unclipped the phone from my belt and spoke Chiri's comm-code into it. I heard it ring eight or nine times before she answered it. "Talk to me," she said. She sounded irked.

"Chiri? It's Marîd."

"What do *you* want, motherfucker?"

"Look, you haven't given me any chance to explain. It's not my fault."

"You said that before." She gave a contemptuous laugh. "Famous last words, honey: 'It's not my fault.' That's what my uncle said when he sold my mama to some goddamn Arab slaver."

"I never knew—"

"Forget it, it ain't even true. You wanted a chance to explain, so explain."

Well, it was show time, but suddenly I didn't have any idea what to say to her. "I'm real sorry, Chiri," I said.

She just laughed again. It wasn't a friendly sound.

I plunged ahead. "One morning I woke up and Papa said, 'Here, now you own Chiriga's club, isn't that wonderful?' What did you expect me to say to him?"

"I know you, honey. I don't expect you to say *anything* to Papa. He didn't have to cut off your balls. You sold 'em."

"Chiri, we been friends a long time. Try to understand. Papa got this idea to buy your club and give it to me. I didn't know a thing about it in advance. I didn't want it when he gave it to me. I tried to tell him, but—"

"I'll bet. I'll just bet you told him."

I closed my eyes and took a deep breath. I think she was en-joying this a lot. "I told him about as much as anyone can tell Papa anything."

"Why *my* place, Marîd? The Budayeen's full of crummy bars. Why did he pick mine?"

I knew the answer to that: Friedlander Bey was prying me loose from the few remaining connections to my old life. Making me a cop had alienated most of my friends. Forcing Chiriga to sell her club had turned her against me. Next, Papa'd find a way to make Saied the Half-Hajj hate my guts, too. "Just his sense of humor, Chiri," I said hopelessly. "Just Papa proving that he's always around, always watching, ready to hit us with his lightning bolts when we least expect it."

There was a long silence from her. "And you're gutless, too."

My mouth opened and closed. I didn't know what she was talking about. "Huh?"

"I said you're a gutless *panya*."

She's always slinging Swahili at me. "What's a *panya*, Chiri?" I asked.

"It's like a big rat, only stupider and uglier. You didn't dare do this in person, did you, motherfucker? You'd rather whine to me over the phone. Well, you're gonna have to face me. That's all there is to it."

I squeezed my eyes shut and grimaced. "Okay, Chiri, whatever you want. Can you come by the club?"

"*The* club, you say? You mean, *my* club? The club I used to own?"

"Yeah," I said. "Your club."

She grunted. "Not on your life, you diseased jackass. I'm not setting foot in there unless things change the way I want 'em. But I'll meet you somewhere else. I'll be in Courane's place in half an hour. That's not in the Budayeen, honey, but I'm sure you can find it. Show up if you think you can handle it." There was a sharp click, and then I was listening to the burr of the dial tone.

"Dragged you through it, didn't she?" said Shaknahyi. He'd enjoyed every moment of my discomfort. I was starting to like the guy, but he was still a bastard sometimes.

I clipped the phone back on my belt. "Ever hear of a bar called Courane's?"

He snorted. "This Christian chump shows up in the city a few years ago." He was wheeling the patrol car through Rasmiyya, a neighborhood east of the Budayeen that I'd never been in before. "Guy named Courane. Called himself a poet, but nobody ever saw much proof of that. Somehow he got to be a big hit with the European community. One day he opens what he calls a salon, see. Just a quiet, dark bar where everything's made out of wicker and glass and stainless steel. Lots of potted plastic plants. Nowadays he ain't the darling of the brunch crowd anymore, but he still pulls this melancholy expatriate routine. That where you're gonna meet Chiri?"

I looked at him and shrugged. "It was her choice."

He grinned at me. "Want to attract a lot of attention when you show up?"

I sighed. "Please no," I muttered. That Jirji, he was some kidder.

6

Twenty minutes later we were in a middle-class district of two- and three-story houses. The streets were broader than in the Budayeen, and the whitewashed buildings had strips of open land around them, planted with small bushes and flowering shrubs. Tall date palms leaned drunkenly along the verges of the pavement. The neighborhood seemed deserted, if only because there were no shouting children wrestling on the sidewalks or chasing each other around the corners of the houses. It was a very settled, very sedate part of town. It was so peaceful, it made me uncomfortable.

"Courane's is just up here," said Shaknahyi. He turned onto a poorer street that was little more than an alley. One side was hemmed in by the back walls of the same flat-roofed houses. There were small balconies on the second floor, and bright, lamplit windows obscured by lattices made of narrow wooden strips. On the other side of the alley were boarded-up buildings and a few businesses: a leather-worker's shop, a bakery, a restaurant that specialized in bean dishes, a bookstall.

There was also Courane's, out of place in that constricted avenue. The proprietor had set out a few tables, but no one lingered in the white-painted wicker chairs beneath the Cinzano umbrellas. Shaknahyi tapped off the engine, and we got out of the patrol car. I supposed that Chiri hadn't arrived yet, or that she was waiting for me inside. My stomach hurt.

"Officer Shaknahyi!" A middle-aged man came toward us, a welcoming smile on his face. He was about my height, maybe fifteen or twenty pounds heavier, with receding brown hair brushed straight back. He shook hands with Shaknahyi, then turned to me.

"Sandor," said Shaknahyi, "this is my partner, Marîd Audran."

"Glad to meet you," said Courane.

"May Allah increase your honor," I said.

Courane's look was amused. "Right," he said. "Can I get you boys something to drink?"

I glanced at Shaknahyi. "Are we on duty?" I asked.

"Nah," he said. I asked for my usual, and Shaknahyi got a soft drink. We followed Courane into his establishment. It was just as I'd pictured it: shiny chrome and glass tables, white wicker chairs, a beautiful antique bar of polished dark wood, chrome ceiling fans, and, as Shaknahyi had mentioned, lots of dusty artificial plants stuck in corners and hanging in baskets from the ceiling.

Chiriga was sitting at a table near the back. "Where you at, Jirji? Marîd?" she said.

"Aw right," I said. "Can I buy you a drink?"

"Never in my life turned one down." She held up her glass. "Sandy?" Courane nodded and went to make our drinks.

I sat down beside Chiri. "Anyway," I said uncomfortably, "I want to talk to you about coming to work in the club."

"Kind of a ballsy thing for you to ask, isn't it?" Chiri said.

"Hey, look, I told you what the situation was. How much longer you gonna keep this up?"

Chiri gave me a little smile. "I don't know," she said. "I'm getting a big kick out of it."

I'd reached my limit. I can only feel so guilty. "Fine," I said. "Go get another job someplace else. I'm sure a big, strong kâfir like you won't have any trouble at all finding somebody who's interested."

Chiri looked hurt. "Okay, Marîd," she said softly, "let's stop." She opened her bag and took out a long white envelope, and pushed it across the table toward me.

"What's this?" I asked.

"Yesterday's take from your goddamn club. You're supposed to show up around closing time, you know, to count out the register and pay the girls. Or don't you care?"

"I don't really care," I said, peeking at the cash. There was a lot of money in the envelope. "That's why I want to hire you."

"To do what?"

I spread my hands. "I want you to keep the girls in line. And I need you to separate the customers from their money. You're famous for that. Just do exactly what you used to."

Her brow furrowed. "I used to go home every night with all of this." She tapped the envelope. "Now I'm just gonna get a few kiam here and there, whatever you decide to spill. I don't like that."

Courane arrived with our drinks and I paid for them. "I was gonna offer you a lot more than what the debs and changes get," I said to Chiri.

"I should hope so." She nodded her head emphatically. "Bet your ass, honey, you want me to run your club for you, you're gonna have to pay up front. Business is business, and action is action. I want fifty percent."

"Making yourself a partner?" I'd expected something like that.

Chiri smiled slowly, showing those long, filed canines. She was worth more than fifty percent to me. "All right," I said.

She looked startled, as if she hadn't expected me to give in so easily. "Should've asked for more," she said bitterly. "And I don't want to dance unless I feel like it."

"Fine."

"And the name of the club stays 'Chiriga's.'"

"All right."

"And you let me do my own hiring and firing. I don't want to get stuck with Floor-Show Fanya if she tickles you into giving her a job. Bitch gets so loaded, she throws up on customers."

"You expect a hell of a lot, Chiri."

She gave me a wolfish grin. "Paybacks are a bitch, ain't they?" she said.

Chiri was wringing every last bit of advantage out of this situation. "Okay, you pick your own crew."

She paused to drink again. "By the way," she said, "that's fifty percent of the *gross* I'm getting, isn't it?"

Chiri was terrific. "Uh, yeah," I said, laughing. "Why don't you let me give you a ride back to the Budayeen? You can start working this afternoon."

"I already passed by there. I left Indihar in charge." She noticed that her glass was empty again, and she held it up and waved it at Courane. "Want to play a game, Marîd?" She jerked a thumb toward the back of the bar, where Courane had a Transpex unit.

It's a game that lets two people with corymbic implants sit across from each other and chip into the machine's CPU. The first player imagines a bizarre scenario in detail, and it becomes a wholly realistic environment for the second player, who's scored on how well he adapts—or survives. Then in turn the second player does the same for the first.

It's a great game to bet money on. It scared the hell out of me at first, though, because while you're playing, you forget it's only a game. It seems absolutely real. The players exercise almost godlike power on each other. Courane's model looked old, a version whose safety features could be bypassed by a clever mechanic. There were rumors of people actually having massive strokes and coronaries while they were chipped into a jiggered Transpex.

"Go ahead, Audran," said Shaknahyi, "let's see what you got."

"All right, Chiri," I said, "let's play."

She stood up and walked back to the Transpex booth. I followed her, and both Shaknahyi and Courane came along, too. "Want to bet the other fifty percent of my club?" she said. Her eyes glittered over the rim of her cocktail glass.

"Can't do that. Papa wouldn't approve." I felt pretty confident, because I could read the record of the machine's previous high games. A perfect Transpex score was 1,000 points, and I averaged in the upper 800s. The top scores on this machine were in the lower 700s. Maybe the scores were low because Courane's bar didn't attract many borderline nutso types. Like me. "I'll bet what's inside this envelope, though."

That sounded good to her. "I can cover it," she said. I didn't doubt that Chiri could lay her hands on quite a lot of cash when she needed it.

Courane set fresh drinks down for all of us. Shaknahyi dragged a wicker chair near enough to watch the computer-modeled images of the illusions Chiri and I would create. I fed five kiam into the Transpex machine. "You can go first, if you want," I said.

"Yeah," said Chiri. "It's gonna be fun, making you sweat." She took one of the Transpex's moddy links and socketed it on her corymbic plug, then touched Player One on the console. I took the second link, murmured "Bismillah," and chipped in Player Two.

At first there was only a kind of warm, flickering fog, veined with iridescence like shimmery mother-of-pearl. Audran was lost in a cloud, but he didn't feel anxious about it. It was absolutely silent and still, not even a whisper of breeze. He was aware of a mild scent surrounding him, the fragrance of fresh sea air. Then things began to change.

Now he was floating in the cloud, no longer sitting or standing, but somehow drifting through space easily and peacefully. Audran still wasn't concerned; it was a perfectly comfortable sensation. Only gradually did the fog begin to dissipate. With a shock Audran realized that he wasn't floating, but swimming in a warm, sun-dappled sea.

Below him waved long tendrils of algae that clung to hillocks of brightly colored coral. Anemones of many hues and many shapes reached their grasping tentacles toward him, but he cut smartly through the water well out of their reach.

Audran's eyesight was poor, but his other senses let him know what was happening around him. The smell of the salt air had been replaced by many subtle aromas that he couldn't name but were all achingly familiar. Sounds came to him, sibilant, rushing noises that echoed in hollow tones.

He was a fish. He felt free and strong, and he was hungry. Audran dived down close to the rolling sea bottom, near the stinging anemones where tiny fishes schooled for protection. He flashed among them, gobbling down mouthfuls of the scarlet and yellow creatures. His hunger was appeased, at least for now. The scent of others of his species wafted by him on the current, and he turned toward its source.

He swam for a long while until he realized that he'd lost the trace. Audran couldn't tell how much time had passed. It didn't matter. Nothing mattered here in the sparkling, sunny sea. He browsed over a gorgeous reef, worrying the delicate featherdusters, sending the scarlet banded shrimps and the porcelain crabs scuttling.

Above him, the ocean darkened. A shadow passed over him, and Audran felt a ripple of alarm. He could not look up, but compression waves told him that something huge was circling nearby. Audran remembered that he was not alone in this ocean: It was now his turn to flee. He darted down over the reef and cut a zigzag path only a few inches above the sandy floor.

The ravenous shadow trailed close behind. Audran looked for somewhere to hide, but there was nothing, no sunken wrecks or rocks or hidden caves. He made a sharp evasive turn and raced back the way he'd come. The thing that stalked him followed lazily, easily.

Suddenly it dived on him, a voracious, mad engine of murder, all dead black eyes and gleaming chrome-steel teeth. Flushed from the sea bottom, Audran knifed up through the green water toward the surface, though he knew there was no shelter there. The great beast raged close behind him. In a froth of boiling sea foam, Audran broke through the waves into the fearfully thin air, and—flew. He glided over the whitecapped water until, at last, he fell back into the welcoming element, exhausted.

And the nightmare creature was there, its ghastly mouth yawning wide to rend him. The daggered jaws closed slowly, victoriously, until for Audran there was only blackness and the knowledge of the agony to come.

"Jeez," I murmured, when the Transpex returned my consciousness.

"Some game," said Shaknahyi.

"How'd I do?" asked Chiri. She sounded exhilarated.

"Pretty good," said Courane. "623. It was a promising scenario, but you never got him to panic."

"I sure as hell tried," she said. "I want another drink." She gave me a quirky grin.

I took out my pill case and swallowed eight Paxium with a mouthful of gin. Maybe as a fish I hadn't been paralyzed with fear, but I was feeling a strong nervous reaction now. "I want another drink, too," I said. "I'll stand a round for everybody."

"Bigshot," said Shaknahyi.

Both Chiri and I waited until our heartbeats slowed down to normal. Courane brought a tray with the fresh drinks, and I watched Chiri throw hers down in two long gulps. She was fortifying herself for whatever evil things I was going to do to her mind. She was going to need it.

Chiri touched Player Two on the game's console, and I saw her eyes slowly close. She looked as if she were napping placidly. That was going to end in a hell of a hurry. On the holoscreen was the same opalescent haze I'd wandered through until Chiri'd decided it was the ocean. I reached out and touched the Player One panel.

Audran gazed down upon the ball of mist, like Allah in the highest of the heavens. He concentrated on building a richly detailed illusion, and he was pleased with his progress. Instead of letting it take on form and reality gradually, Audran loosed an explosion of sensory information. The woman far below was stunned by the purity of color in this world, the clarity of sound, the intensity of the tastes and textures and smells. She cried out and her voice pealed in the cool, clean air like a carillon. She fell to her knees, her eyes shut tightly and her hands over her ears.

Audran was patient. He wanted the woman to explore his creation. He wasn't going to hide behind a tree, jump out, and frighten her. There was time enough for terror later.

After a while the woman lowered her hands and stood up. She looked around uncertainly. "Marîd?" she called. Once again the sound of her own voice rang with unnatural sharpness. She glanced behind her, toward the misty purple mountains in the west. Then she turned back to the east, toward the shore of a marshy lake that reflected the impossible azure of the sky. Audran didn't care which direction she chose; it would all be the same in the end.

The woman decided to follow the swampy shoreline to the southeast. She walked for hours, listening to the liquid trilling of songbirds and inhaling the poignant perfume of unknown blossoms. After a while the sun rested on the shoulders of the purple hills behind her, and then slipped away, leaving Audran's illusion in darkness. He provided a full moon, huge and gleaming silver like a serving platter. The woman grew weary, and at last she decided to lie down in the sweet-smelling grass and sleep.

Audran woke her in the morning with a gentle rain shower. "Marîd?" she cried again. He would not answer her. "How long you gonna leave me here?" She shivered.

The golden sun mounted higher, and while it warmed the

morning, the heat never became stifling. Just after noon, when the woman had walked almost halfway around the lake, she came upon a pavilion made of crimson and sapphire-blue silk. "What the hell is all this, Marîd?" the woman shouted. "Just get it over with, all right?"

The woman approached the pavilion anxiously. "Hello?" she called.

A moment later a young woman in a white gown came out of the pavilion. Her feet were bare and her pale blonde hair was thrown carelessly over one shoulder. She was smiling and carrying a wooden tray. "Hungry?" she asked in a friendly voice.

"Yes," said the woman.

"My name is Maryam. I've been waiting for you. I'm sorry, all I've got is bread and fresh milk." She poured from a silver pitcher into a silver goblet.

"Thanks." The woman ate and drank greedily.

Maryam shaded her eyes with one hand. "Are you going to the fair?"

The woman shook her head. "I don't know about any fair."

Maryam laughed. "Everybody goes to the fair. Come on, I'll take you."

The woman waited while Maryam disappeared into the pavilion again with the breakfast things. She came back out a moment later. "We're all set now," she said gaily. "We can get to know each other while we walk."

They continued around the lake until the woman saw a scattering of large, peaked tents of striped canvas, all with colorful pennants snapping in the breeze. She heard many people laughing and shouting; and the sound of axes biting wood, and metal ringing on metal. She could smell bread baking, and cinnamon buns, and lamb roasting on spits turning slowly over glowing coals. Her mouth began to water and she felt her excitement growing despite herself.

"I don't have any money to spend," she said.

"Money?" Maryam asked, laughing. "What is money?"

The woman spent the afternoon going from tent to tent, seeing the strange exhibits and miraculous entertainments. She sampled exotic foods and drank concoctions of unknown liquors. Now and then she remembered to be afraid. She looked over her shoulder, wondering when the pleasant face of this fantasy would fall away. "Marîd," she called, "what are you doing?"

"Who are you calling?" asked Maryam.

"I'm not sure," said the woman.

Maryam laughed. "Look over here," she said, pulling on the

woman's sleeve, showing her a booth where a heavily muscled woman was shaping a disturbing collage from the claws, teeth, and eyes of lizards.

They listened to children playing strange music on instruments made from the carcasses of small animals, and then they watched several old women spin their own white hair into thread, and then weave it into napkins and scarves.

One of the toothless hags leered at Maryam and the woman. "Take," she said in a gravelly voice.

"Thank you, grandmother," said Maryam. She selected a pair of human-hair handkerchiefs.

The hours wore on, and at last the sun began to set. The moon rose as full as yestereve. "Is this going to go on all night?" the woman asked.

"All night and all day tomorrow," said Maryam. "Forever."

The woman shuddered.

From that moment she couldn't shake a growing dread, a sense that she'd been lured to this place and abandoned. She remembered nothing of who she'd been before she'd awakened beside the lake, but she felt she'd been horribly tricked. She prayed to someone called Marîd. She wondered if that was God.

"Marîd," she murmured fearfully, "I wish you'd just end this already."

But Audran was not ready to end it. He watched as the woman and Maryam grew sleepy and found a large tent filled with comfortable cushions and sheets of satin and fine linen. They laid themselves down and slept.

In the morning the woman arose, dismayed to be still trapped at the eternal fair. Maryam found them a good breakfast of sausage, fried bread, broiled tomatoes, and hot tea. Maryam's enthusiasm was undiminished, and she led the woman toward still more disquieting entertainments. The woman, however, felt only a crazily mounting dread.

"You've had me here for two days, Marîd," she pleaded. "Please kill me and let me go." Audran gave her no sign, no answer.

They passed the third day examining one dismaying thing after another: teenage girls who seemed to have living roses in place of breasts; a candle maker whose wares would not provide light in the presence of an infidel; staged combat between a blind man and two maddened dragons; a family hammering together a scale model of the fair out of iron, a project that had occupied them for generations and that might never be completed; a cage of crickets that had been taught to chirp the Shahada, the Islamic testament of faith.

The afternoon passed, and once again night began to fall. All through the fair, men jammed blazing torches into iron sconces on tall poles. Still Maryam led the woman from tent to tent, but the woman no longer enjoyed the spectacles. She was filled with a sense of impending catastrophe. She felt an urgent need to escape, but she knew she couldn't even find her way out of the infinite fairgrounds.

And then a shrill, buzzing alarm sounded. "What's that?" she asked, startled. All around her, people had begun to flee.

"Yallah!" cried Maryam, her face stricken with horror. "Run! Run and save your life!"

"What is it?" the woman shouted. "Tell me what it is!"

Maryam had collapsed to the ground, weeping and moaning. "In the name of Allah, the Beneficent, the Merciful," she muttered over and over again. The woman could get nothing more sensible from her.

The woman left her there and followed the stream of terrified people as they ran among the tents. And then the woman saw them: Two immense giants, impossibly huge, hundreds of feet tall, crushing the landscape as they came nearer. They waded among the distant mountains, and then the shocks from their jolting footsteps began to churn the water in the lake. The ground heaved as they came nearer. The woman raised a hand to her breast, then staggered backward a few steps.

One of the giants turned his head slowly and looked straight at her. He was horribly ugly, with a great scar across one empty eye socket and a mouthful of rotten, snaggled fangs. He lifted an arm and pointed to her.

"No," she said, her voice hoarse with fear, "not me!" She wanted to run but she couldn't move. The giant stooped toward her, fierce and glowering. He bent to capture her in his enormous hand.

"Marîd!" the woman screamed. "Please!" Nothing happened. The giant's fist began to close around her.

The woman tried to reach up and unplug the moddy link, but her arms were frozen. She wouldn't escape that easily. The woman shrieked as she realized she couldn't even jack out.

The disfigured giant lifted her off the ground and drew her close to his single eye. His horrid grin spread and he laughed at her terror. His stinking breath sickened the woman. She struggled again to lift her hands, to pull the moddy link free. Her arms were held fast. She screamed and screamed, and then at last she fainted.

My eyes were bleary for a moment, and I could hear Chiri panting for breath beside me. I didn't think she'd be so upset. After all, it was only a Transpex game, and it wasn't the first time she'd ever played. She knew what to expect.

"You're a sick motherfucker, Marîd," she said at last.

"Listen, Chiri, I was just—"

She waved a hand at me. "I know, I know. You won the game and the bet. I'm still just a little shook, that's all. I'll have your money for you tonight."

"Forget the money, Chiri, I—"

I shouldn't have said that. "Hey, you son of a bitch, when I lose a bet I pay up. You're gonna take the money or I'm gonna cram it down your throat. But, God, you've got some kind of twisted imagination."

"That last part," said Courane, "where she couldn't raise her hands to pop the moddy link, that was real cold." He said it approvingly.

"Hell of a sadistic thing to do," said Chiri, shivering. "Last time I ever touch a Transpex with *you*."

"A few extra points, that's all, Chiri. I didn't know what my score was. I might have needed a couple more points."

"You finished with 941," said Shaknahyi. He was looking at me oddly, as if he were impressed by my score and repelled at the same time. "We got to go." He stood up and tossed down the last slug of his soft drink.

I stood up, too. "You all right now, Chiri?" I put my hand on her shoulder.

"I'm fine. I'm still shaking off the game. It was like a nightmare." She took a deep breath and let it out. "I got to get back to the club so Indihar can go home."

"Give you a ride?" asked Shaknahyi.

"Thanks," said Chiri, "but I got my own transportation."

"See you later then," I said.

"*Kwa heri*, you bastard." At least she was smiling when she called me that. I thought maybe things were okay between us again. I was real glad about that.

Outside, Shaknahyi shook his head and grinned. "She was right, you know. That was a hell of a sadistic thing. Like unnecessary torture. You *are* a sick son of a bitch."

Maybe, I thought as we headed back to the station house. But if ever I decided that I no longer liked my true personality, there was an almost unlimited supply of artificial ones I could chip in.

I leaned back in my seat and stared out the window. I'd managed to heal the bad feelings between Chiri and me, and I was getting a handle on this cop business. All that remained was Angel Monroe, and a solution to that problem would occur to me soon. I was sure that Laila had a Perfect Mother moddy in her shop. Of course, my mom's skull wasn't amped like mine, but I could take care of that for her, even if I had to wire her brain myself with a jackknife and a coat hanger.

See? Life is hard, all right, so you've got to take help wherever you can find it. I thought about that as I scratched my scalp around my corymbic implant. As Shaknahyi swung the patrol car into the garage, I thought, what's the point of sexy new technology if you can't find some way to pervert it?

Introduction to
Slow, Slow Burn

One of George's best stories, it was one of a number that he sold to Playboy magazine over the years. The version printed here, from his own file copy of the story, differs slightly from the way it originally appeared in Playboy, and is his preferred version.

In a way the whole story is a logical extrapolation of George's theory about the relationship of technology and pornography: If sex moddies do exist, there has to be someone who makes the best—and what does the use of sex moddies do and mean to the consumer, the producer, and the artist. And at the back of all the technology there's still someone, some single human being, whom everyone in the world now fantasizes about.

From start to finish of the story, Honey Pílar remains as opaque as the image in the moddy: look at me, touch me, have sex with me, BE ME WHILE I'M HAVING SEX . . . marry me . . . But you still don't know one single solitary thing about me.

A capsule version of how women appear to men?

And the beauty of the story is that by its end, we know that Honey Pílar is more than a match for any of the men who think they know who she is and what she's about. Did she get rid of Husband #4 because of the quarrel, or because after five years' trial she decided his control of her career is what's causing her sales to decline? Is it Kit (as in, "put together from a—") who's having the slow, slow burn, or is it Honey, the real woman observing from behind that sweet and stupid facade?

George both loved women and liked them, and was, I think, fascinated by them: Honey is a marvelous creation.

—Barbara Hambly

+ + +

Slow, Slow Burn

"ALL RIGHT, THIS IS THE WAY I PICTURE IT: WE'RE IN a busy midtown brass and fern bar, okay? Maybe at a table on the sidewalk, under an umbrella says Cinzano on it, we'll see. Two women poking at salads, glasses of white wine. They're dressed very nice, expensive but not flashy, they pay attention to details, they accessorize, you know what I mean? Maybe a bag or something in the shot with a very exclusive name on it, sets these women up as fashion-conscious, upscale, the best taste in everything. One's older, see, she's the younger woman's mother, though there's no real noticeable age difference. They could be sisters. Make 'em both blondes. The older one's got kind of a suit on, she's the dynamic woman-on-the-go. The daughter sort of mirrors that, a subtle thing, she's got a nice blouse or shirt on with a jacket that says she's shopping the right stores and she's never more than fifteen minutes out of style. Whatever these women talk about, the people at home are gonna know they could make their own croissants from scratch if they felt like it, and they don't live in no trailer park, either. This is like 'Beauty Hints of the Idle Rich' or something. The older woman smiles and says something like, 'I'm glad you enjoyed the villa. I knew you and Ramon would find it pleasant.'

"So the girl is toying with her radicchio, see, and she puts her fork down and goes, 'Mother, may I ask you a personal question?'

"Mom says, 'Of course, darling.'

73

"Daughter looks down at her plate, she's just a little bit embarrassed. That's good, that makes her human. Audience will relate to that. She looks back up and goes, 'Mother, have you ever used—' pause for effect '—modular marital aids?'

"Big smile from the understanding old bitch. Maybe she, you know, reaches out and pats the kid's hand. Like: There, there. She says, 'Let me tell you a secret, dear. Your father and I have the biggest collection of sex moddies in the diocese.' She laughs. The daughter laughs. Then Mom reaches into her bag, see, and what do you think she takes out? Take a guess."

Two account executives have flown all the way from America to talk with Honey Pílar, who everyone agrees is the most desirable woman in the world. Even account executives want her, though their motives are mixed, and that's why these two anxious men have come from New York to Honey's walled estate in the south of France. She is sitting at a long table made of polished limba, an exotic hardwood from the Congo Basin that not even the architectural magazines know about yet. Beside her is her husband, Kit, who likes to think of himself as her manager. One of the admen is speaking; his throat is very dry because he is desperate that Honey Pílar likes his proposal, yet he is too self-conscious to sip from the fluted glass of Perrier-Jouet in front of him. He glances quickly at his associate, but it is easy to see that he can expect no help from that quarter.

Kit stares at the account executive, but he's not going to say anything. The silence goes on and on. The hopeful smile the adman is wearing begins to vanish. He looks at his associate, who is still no help whatsoever.

"On the phone, I think we discussed the kids' market," says Kit wearily. He purses his lips and turns to Honey, who is sipping Campari and soda through a straw. "She doesn't like it. I don't like it. Come back with something else."

The adman lays his sweating hands on the beautiful, glossy tabletop. "Miss Pílar?" he says hopelessly.

"Kit like doing business," she says, and shrugs. When she smiles, both account executives are inspired with possible new approaches. The sound of her voice, they tell themselves, is enough reward for their failed labor. The opportunity to meet with her again will motivate them to find just the pitch she and Kit are looking for. "You have nice flight," she says.

Kit is in the control room watching his wife on the bed with a seventeen-year-old Italian boy. Kit watches them through the grimy glass, wishing he'd worn a shirt because he is sweating heavily in the hot, stale air of the studio, and his naked back is sticking to the black vinyl padding of the chair. He peels himself away and leans forward, checking meters and digital readouts that don't really need checking. Honey is a consummate performer. It's as if she has an accurate internal clock ticking behind her forehead, cuing her: 00:00 initiate encounter, 00:30 initiate foreplay with passionate kiss, 00:45 experience preliminary arousal. . . . They are seven minutes, ten seconds into the thirty-minute recording. By the outline on Kit's clipboard, Honey is supposed to begin oral stimulation at 07:15, and goddamn if she isn't already sliding down the boy's tanned body. No cue cards, she doesn't even need hand signals. Kit pretends to check the levels again, then turns away from the big glass window.

Kit had his own brain wired long before he met Honey Pílar. If he wanted, he could jack into a socket on the board and feel just what the Italian boy is feeling, or he could jack into another socket and eavesdrop on Honey. Kit doesn't need to peek on the boy's responses because he's been married to Honey for five years, and she's every bit as good live-in-person as she is on a module. Honey Pílar is still, at the age of forty-five, the most desired woman in the world. One out of every eight moddies—of all kinds—sold through the big modshop chains is a Honey Pílar sex moddy. Kit has never been her partner on any of them.

At 14:20, Honey and the boy curl together on their sides. Honey's eyes are closed, her face flushed. She is only wearing some kind of white cotton peasant-looking blouse and rope sandals. The boy is naked except for a pair of black matte-finish sunglasses. Drops of sweat glisten on his hairless chest. Kit stands up and turns away again. He leaves the control room, sure that nothing out of the ordinary will happen. He wanders down the long hall. He kicks off his deck shoes and feels the pile carpet warm on the soles of his feet. There is the strong odor of stale beer in the hall, as if several cans had soaked the floor recently and no one had cared to do anything about it. None of the windows are open, and it is even hotter in the hall than in the control room. Kit pushes open the scarred blond wood door at the end of the hall. He is in another control room. He chases a green lizard the size of his hand from the padded chair and sits behind the board. He stares at meters and digital readouts. They are all flickering at safe levels.

Beyond the glass, a young woman in a torn T-shirt and a bikini bottom sits at a microphone, clutching a sheaf of printed pages. Kit knows that she works for some revolutionary organization, but there are too many even to begin to guess which one. She reads the pages in a slow, husky voice. Kit thinks her voice is pretty damn sexy. He likes everything about this girl, what little he knows. He likes her bikini bottom, her torn shirt, her rumpled black hair, and the way she talks. After a moment, Kit hears what she is reading. "Achtung, Achtung," she says. Her voice has no accent, neither German nor otherwise. She herself has brown skin, pale full lips, and Oriental eyes. "Achtung, drei hundert neun-und-siebzig. Fünf-und-zwanzig." Then she begins reading a list of five-digit numbers. "39502, 95372, 01814, 66589." She reads twenty-five groups of digits, meaningful only to the certain audience listening to her frequency, reading the key to her code. "Ende," she says. A moment later, after shifting to another frequency, she begins again in Spanish. "Atención, atención." More numbers, more signals. Kit would like to buy the brown-skinned girl a drink, look into her black eyes, ask her if she herself knows who might be listening to her broadcast.

Kit leaves her control room. She has never looked up, never known for an instant that he was there. Kit walks back down the stifling hallway. As he enters the small room, he sees Honey Pílar astride the Italian boy. Kit checks the clock on the board, checks the script. The recording is still precisely on schedule. He hasn't been missed. Just as the girl at the microphone did not know he was there, Honey does not know he has been gone.

Kit sits in the black vinyl chair. He takes a moddy from a stack on the control board. He doesn't care which moddy it is. He reaches up and chips it in. There is a moment of disorientation, and then Kit's vision clears. He is Cary Grant as Roger Thornhill in *North by Northwest*, suave, well-dressed, and certainly in command of his feelings. He allows himself a moment of sadness for Honey Pílar, whose life could never be as interesting as his. After all, he is Cary Grant. His future will be better than good: It will be amusing.

"Twenty-six years ago, I was a young feature reporter for EuroUrban Holo on my first assignment, to interview Honey Pílar. I was sitting cross-legged on the rough wooden pier down the hill and across the beach from her walled estate. The sparkling Mediterranean waves lapped rhythmically at the pilings. I remember the bright morning sun making me squint a little into the camera. The ragged cries of sea birds punctuated my lead-in. 'Here in her palatial estate,' I said, 'Honey Pílar reigns as the superstar of the sex moddies. In five years she has risen from talented newcomer to both critical acclaim and commercial supremacy. Let's take a quick look behind the scenes and find out what Honey Pílar is like in her unguarded moments.'

My cameraman and I went to the main gate but we were not allowed in, although my news service had confirmed our appointment for that morning. Honey had changed her mind.

"Fifteen years later I was working for Visions/Rumelia, and once again I stood by the high, gilded gate. 'What secrets does this young beauty know,' I said on that occasion, 'that maintain her position as the world's premier moddy star?' My story didn't go on to reveal any actual secrets, of course. Honey Pílar never tells her secrets. But she did make a rare personal appearance and answered some mild questions about her favorite foods and her thoughts on the world situation. She was tanned and smiling and, well, perfect. A week before that interview, a poll had announced that sixty-eight percent of the seven billion people on earth could identify her face. Eighteen percent could identify her naked, unaugmented breasts.

"Today, Rio Home Data has asked me to begin this series it calls *Honey Pílar: A Quarter Century of Fascination*. Never in the history of the personality module industry has one performer so dominated the charts. Since her now-classic first moddy, *A Life in Lace*, she has turned out thirty-eight full-length recordings and nine of the 'quickies' that ABT experimented with and then abandoned. Her total sales top one hundred and twenty million units, and every one of her recordings remains in print. As of last week, she has eight titles on the Brainwaves Hot 100 Chart, with two in the Top Ten.

"The question always arises, what has this remarkable success cost the young woman who became Honey Pílar? *A Life in Lace* was recorded when she was only fourteen years old. Has her career been at the expense of her happiness? She's been married four times, and she lives a private, almost reclusive existence. She rarely grants interviews, and in keeping with that, she refused to appear with us on Rio Home Data. Her legions of fans want to know: Just what kind of woman invites the whole world to listen in on her private sexual experiences? Is Honey Pílar providing surrogate passion to millions of people dissatisfied with their own love lives, or is she merely pandering to an emerging taste for high-tech titillation? We can only speculate, of course, but next time, in a highly personal way, I'll tell you how this reporter sees it."

Kit and Honey are having dinner in a small, dimly lighted café near the ocean. There is a tall white taper burning on their table and, shining through their wineglasses, it is casting soft burgundy shimmers on the linen tablecloth. Across the narrow room there is a stage made of scuffed green tiles. Lively North African music, distorted and shrill, is playing too loudly through invisible speakers;

hovering just an inch or two above the stage is the holographic figure of a demure-eyed, big-hipped belly dancer. There are streaks and scratches on the woman's face and body, as if this recording has been played many times over many years.

Honey Pílar sips some of the wine and makes a little grimace. "How are you thinking?" she asks in a soft voice.

"It was all right," says Kit. He looks down at his broiled fish. "What do you want me to say? It's always all right. It'll sell a million; you outdid yourself. Your climaxes made the dials go crazy. Okay?"

"I never know you telling me truth." She frowns at him, then picks up a delicate forkful of couscous and eats it thoughtfully.

Kit tears a chunk of the flat bread and puts it in his mouth, then takes a gulp of wine. Communion, he thinks, I'm absolved. Time for new sins. "You don't believe me when I tell you it was all right? You don't take my word for it? If you didn't believe me a minute ago, what can I say or do that will make you believe me now?"

Honey looks hurt. She puts her fork down carefully beside her plate. Kit wishes the shrieking Arab music would die away forever. The café smells of cinnamon, as if teams of bakers have been making sweet rolls all day long and then hidden them away, because nothing on their plates or on the menu contains the least hint of cinnamon. Kit knows that Honey wants desperately to go back to the house in Provence. She's not comfortable in strange places.

Kit finishes his glass of wine. He reaches for the bottle, tops up Honey's glass, then fills his own. He takes out a beige pill case from his shirt pocket, finds four yellow Paxium, and drinks them down with a Chateau L'Angelus that deserves better. "What next?" he says.

"What next now?" asks Honey. "What next tonight, what next tomorrow, or what next we make another moddy?"

Kit squeezes his eyes shut and lets his head fall back. He opens his eyes and sees black beams made of structural plastic crossing the space overhead. He wishes that something, anything, with Honey Pílar could be simple, even dinner, even conversation. So she's the most desirable woman in the world, he thinks. So she makes more money in one year than the CEOs of any ten major corporations you'd care to name. So what. His private opinion is that she has the intelligence of three sticks and a stone. He lowers his gaze and forces himself to smile back at her. "What do you want to do, sweetheart? Stay here, go back home, take a trip? You've earned a vacation, baby. We've got your next blockbuster in the can. The world is at your feet. You name it, chiquita. Someplace exotic. Someplace you've always wanted to go."

He knows, as well as he knows anything in the world, exactly what she will say next.

She says it. "I rather only go home."

"Home," he repeats quietly. He finishes the wine in one long swallow, and signals the waiter.

"Kit," she says, "I was in happy mood. You always do that. You always make me feel I choose wrong."

I was in a happy mood, thinks Kit. Then I woke up, and we were married. But don't let me kid you, sweetie. It's been great.

"It is very early in the morning, and the haggard winter sun is rising over the red-tiled roofs of Santa Coloma. Wrapped in scarves, packaged in parkas, slapping their mittened hands together to fend off frostbite, Fawn and Dawn huddle against the fogged plate-glass window of the Instant Memories Modshop on Bridger Parkway. Fawn and Dawn are standing in a long line of people waiting for the manager to open the store. They've been waiting all night in the cold and wind and sleet, because today's the day Honey Pílar's new moddy, *Slow, Slow Burn*, goes on sale. Fawn and Dawn want to be the first in their neighborhood to own the new Honey Pílar. They want to get it as soon as the shop opens, and take it to school with them. Fawn and Dawn are in the ninth grade; these days in Santa Coloma, ninth graders all have their skulls amped, except for the trolls and feebs.

"'My God,' mutters Fawn, shivering, 'I haven't felt my toes since midnight.'

"'I haven't felt my lips,' says Dawn. 'Or my nose, or my ears, or my fingers.'

"'But if we leave now, I'm going to feel like a total fool.'

"'We can't leave now. These jerk-offs behind us will get our place.'

"Fawn makes a face. 'If only the wind would stop blowing.'

"'Oh, sure, the wind. If only the wind stopped blowing, it would still be, like, ten degrees below zero or something.'

"Fawn rubs her cheeks. 'Hey!' she cries. She points through the display window. 'Here he comes!'

"'Let us in now,' Dawn prays to the store manager, 'and you can have me right on top of the cash register.'

"The manager is, in fact, opening the front door. He's smiling in anticipation; the store is going to make a fortune today. *Slow, Slow Burn* is stacked up four feet high in the front window, piled up beside every register, and loaded into cardboard dumps scattered all around the selling floor. You can't turn around inside the store without staring into the liquid green eyes of Honey herself. Her holographic likeness is more than just inviting; if the mythical sirens had looked like Honey Pílar, they wouldn't have needed to sing.

"When the door opens, of course, what disappears is any respect for the length of time Fawn and Dawn have been waiting in the freezing night air. They are pushed aside by the jerk-offs behind them, and by the jerk-offs behind *them*. Fawn and Dawn are cast aside by the charging throng of people. They announce that this is truly unfair and rude, that they'd stood in line longer, that they are going to complain, but no one listens. The flood of bakebrains shoves the two girls this way and that, until they are afraid of being trampled. At last, however, first Fawn and then Dawn are pitched up like driftwood at the front cash register, each with credit card in one hand, moddy in the other.

"'Wow,' says Fawn, as she clutches her package and fights her way out of the shop.

"On the street again, with the air so cold it shocks nose and throat, the two girls wait for the bus to take them to school. 'Are you and Adam going to use it tonight?' asks Dawn.

"Fawn's eyes open wider and she smiles. She taps the crown of her head, the corymbic plug invisible now beneath her hair. 'I've got it all down on this moddy,' she says, her smile becoming sly. 'Who needs him anymore?'

"Think what study period will be like, to be Honey Pílar in the throes of ecstasy, instead of Fawn and Dawn in the grip of homework."

The two account executives sit on a couch in the north parlor. "Nice, huh?" says one of the admen. Kit thinks that "nervous" doesn't begin to do the man's condition justice.

"I think—" says Honey.

"She doesn't like it, either," says Kit. He has to be tough, and quick, or else she'll say something and these Madison Avenue guys will think they're doing her a favor. And then it will make it that much harder to deal with them the next time. Kit wonders why Honey hasn't learned this by now.

"I think it work fine," says Honey.

Kit gives her a stern glance, but she ignores it.

"Good," says the adman, tremendously relieved. "We think we've put together a nice spot here."

"I'm not sure," says Kit. He doesn't want these men to get too self-congratulatory.

"Kit," says Honey, "be quiet. I like it. It's for my moddy, I like it."

Kit realizes that he's going to have to have a serious talk with Miss Honey Pílar, International Star. He doesn't tell her how to do *her* job, he doesn't want her telling him how to do *his*.

"The girls, they pretty," she says.

The account executive's smile grows wider. "My daughters," he says in a proud voice.

Later that evening, after the account executives have had dinner and gone back to their hotel, Kit watches what he has come to call Moodswing by Candlelight.

Honey Pílar marches, dressed in tight zebraskin pants—not zebra-stripe, but the genuine pelt of a former zebra, which is becoming less obtainable all the time—and a gauzy moiré tunic created by the actual hands of Lenci Urban of Prague – not by one of his underling designers but by Lenci himself, making the item even dearer than the zebraskin – back and forth in front of the long, high picture window. Kit watches her eclipse first the lighthouse beyond, then the strings of lights marking the marina, then the sallow moon maundering over the ocean. Honey reaches the far end of the room and turns, blocking out the moon again. In the air is the heavy scent of incense, church incense, the fragrance Honey Pílar loves best because she thinks it reminds her of her childhood, but she's not sure. Tonight Kit hates it, and he's panting in shallow breaths, feeling an obscure panic begin. In a corner of the room is the largest commercial datalink money can buy, where Honey can keep an eye on it while she's stalking first east and then west. Kit sits at the keyboard and calls up the first reactions to *Slow, Slow Burn*. Honey watches it indict her.

Total sales for the first seven hours of release: 825,000 units.

"Eight hundred thousand," says Honey Pílar. She is carrying half a melon in one hand, hacking at it with a knife she holds in the other, and flicking seeds across the dusty rose carpet.

"Eight hundred thousand," says Kit noncommittally.

"In one day, I sell eight hundred thousand. Eight hundred thousand people come out of their house all over the world, they just to get the new moddy. You don't know what can be happening, the rain, the bombs in the airport, the police, all these people come out to pay money for me."

Kit presses a key and columns of figures begin to scroll up the screen. "Sales are up in Provence and Aragon," he says. "They love you here."

"I see that, I see," says Honey. She tosses the bulk of the melon into a corner of the white-on-white brocade couch. "I see also I have no million sales today, first day. I thought a million sales. You told me a million sales, so I don't worry."

Kit glances up at the ceiling, hoping for courage. "A million sales, eight hundred thousand, what difference does it make?"

"Sales up at home," she says, turning her back on him, looking out the window. Far below, the crisp thin line of surf wrinkles toward the beach. "Sales down in England, Burgundy, Catalonia. That list get longer." She faces the screen again, and the sales reports are like the incessant waves, each one weak by itself, but in their sum they are victorious, devastating. "Turn it off," she pleads.

Kit is glad to kill the data. He watches Honey Pílar misplace her manic energy. How quickly she is drained and empty. She will not pace for another day, perhaps longer if this is a bad spell. Kit feels a peculiar thrill, knowing that none of the eight hundred thousand who have bought the new moddy could even imagine their dream lover in such a mood, that he alone is privileged with this intimacy. She lowers herself into a black leather chair and draws her small feet up on the cushion. She hugs her knees. Kit knows that she wants him to tell her the sales figures mean nothing; he does not say anything. He knows she wants him to come over and rub her neck and shoulders. She always does. He will not. It is a way for him to assert himself, to establish that he, too, has a life and an identity. He watches her massage her temples with trembling fingers. On the first day of sales, Honey Pílar's latest moddy has sold eight hundred twenty-five thousand copies. Her previous moddy, on its first day, sold nine hundred seventy-two thousand. The one before that, one million, two hundred thousand. Is this a trend?

Goddamn right, it's a trend, Kit thinks. If it weren't, why have computers track the numbers? Honey and Kit respond differently, however. Kit doesn't see any practical point in mourning a hundred thousand sales one way or the other.

Still, Honey Pílar weeps quietly. In the silence, in the candle-light, in the cloud of burning incense, there is a peculiarly sup-plicatory feeling in the house. Honey herself seems wrapped in a fragile innocence. Kit thinks that, for him, this was once one of her chief attractions.

"This is Jerome Nkoro for *New York Comm Net Morning Magazine*, and have I got a moddy for you. Today I'm going to be talking about *Slow, Slow Burn*, Honey Pílar's new moddy from ABT.

"In these days, when, thanks to surgical and biological wonders we've all come to take for granted, men and women routinely maintain their youthful looks well past their seventieth or eightieth birthdays, it probably shouldn't be too unusual that our number one fantasy girl has just celebrated her forty-fifth. Honey Pílar is forty-five. Does that make you feel old? It makes me feel like the last of the dinosaurs.

"I can remember having holos of Honey Pílar in my bedroom when I was twelve, alongside my Death to Argentina football and my scale model of the Mars colony. My first sexual experience was a dream in which Honey Pílar couldn't remember her locker combination. And now they tell me this is her thirty-ninth moddy, and she's old enough to be a grandmother.

"But don't get me wrong, I still think Honey Pílar is the most exciting woman in the world. I've left word with my secretary that, if Honey calls, she can have my home phone number anytime. The problem with *Slow, Slow Burn* is not Honey, or the fact that she's no pouting teenager anymore. The problem is that my moddy library has two full shelves devoted to her, and I'm beginning to ask myself, 'Do I really need another Honey Pílar moddy?'

"I've never had a complaint yet from anyone when I've suggested we use one of Honey's moddies. My partners agree with me that they're likely to get more pleasure from Honey than from anyone else's moddy (or from me, either, for that matter. Sometimes, when we explore the limits of the bizarre, we do it with no moddies chipped in, with our own unembellished brains. I don't recommend this to you beginners out there). I use the moddies myself now and then, to see what it's like from the Honey Pílar point of view, and it's always an incendiary experience. So whether the moddy is turning my partner into a hungry, writhing Honey Pílar, or consuming me in one of Honey's recorded sexual firestorms, there's never any chance that she will fail to perform.

"The question is simply this: How will she continue to keep our interest? Her partner on *Slow, Slow Burn* is an uncredited seventeen-year-old. As she gets older, must her partners get younger? I am horrified by the vision of Honey Pílar offering the kids ten-speed bikes to entice them. And doesn't a lifelong relationship with three-dozen plastic moddies begin to resemble (I hate to suggest this) a marriage? I mean, if for the sake of variety you decide not to use the Honey Pílar moddy tonight, what are you left with? You're left with the person whose sexual performance led you to use the moddy in the first place.

"I realize that so far I haven't said anything terribly cogent about *Slow, Slow Burn* itself. I'm not being fair to Honey Pílar, because her new moddy is right up to the standard she's set throughout her long and dazzling career. I guess it's just that after all these years,

I'm beginning to realize that although I've been to bed with Honey Pílar a million times, I'm never actually going to have her, not in any real sense at all. All I'm going to have is two shelves of plastic with her name on it, and an exquisitely detailed knowledge of what she's like in the sack.

"I wonder what Honey Pílar likes to talk about afterward. I guess I'm getting wistful in my old age. But don't mind me, go out and buy *Slow, Slow Burn*. Like always, it does what it's supposed to do."

Kit and Honey are throwing a party in their hotel suite. This was the night of the annual Pammie Awards, and Honey is still clutching the special Lifetime Achievement statuette she was given. It has been a wonderful, satisfying evening for Honey Pílar. Reporters and fans and fellow artists come up to her and tell her again and again that the honor is long overdue. Honey knew well in advance that the Association was presenting her with the Lifetime Achievement, so her acceptance speech was gracious and tearful and as nearly grammatically correct as she could manage. She looks beautiful in her silver Lenci sheath.

Kit stands looking out across a city that seems to live for the night, toward a black harbor streaked with the pale green lights of bridges. He imagines that he's on board one of the slowly moving ships creasing the dark water, going away, sailing off toward some useful existence. Beyond the window the world seems cold and clean. People are hurrying according to unknown but vital reasons, they are not . . . wandering. The stars are hard, white, not dimmed and hazy with smoke. Kit turns and gazes at the room, at the men and women talking and laughing. The hotel has catered this party, and the champagne is cheap and sweet. Kit sets his plastic champagne glass on the holoset for the maid to clear away. He looks for Honey.

He finds her in a corner, talking with her agent and a representative from ABT. He brings her a fresh glass of the awful champagne. Honey looks up quickly and smiles at him. Her eye makeup looks terrible. The agent indicates the Lifetime Achievement Award in her hand. "They wouldn't have given that to you if they didn't love you, you know," he says.

"I owe you, too," says Honey. Kit thinks that he wound her up too much earlier in the evening, and now she just can't stop being gracious.

The agent smiles. "You did all the work, Honey."

Kit thinks of the seventeen-year-old boy from the beach.

The woman from ABT swallows the last of her potato salad. "Are you giving any thought yet to retiring?" she asks.

The agent glares at her. Honey's eyes open wide, and then she runs across the room. Kit follows her. He hears the agent say, "There isn't any air in here anymore."

Half an hour later the party is over. Kit and the agent are trying to make Honey feel better. "That woman was a fool," says the agent. Honey shakes her head. "They give me the Lifetime Award. They do when your career is over."

"That's not what it meant at all," says the agent. "They were telling you that you're the best, that you've always been the best."

Kit takes a deep breath and lets it out. "I think we'd better call it a night," he says.

The agent stands up. "Well, anyway, it's time for me to run. Thanks for all the free drinks." He bends to kiss Honey on the cheek. "Congratulations, baby," he says. "Don't worry about that ABT woman. She'll be out of a job tomorrow."

When they're alone, Honey puts her head on Kit's shoulder and sobs. He pushes her away. "Don't start that on me now," he says. "Don't get into this sad and insecure business again. I don't want to put up with it right now, I'm too tired."

Honey stares at him. "How do you talk to me like that?"

Kit turns away. "It's easy," he says. "We have this same conversation about three times a week. I've learned my part. You're still trying to get it right because in your line of work you don't have to worry about learning lines."

Honey turns him around and slaps his face. Kit gives her a thin smile. "You want me to pat your shoulder for you, is that it? You want me to tell you that you're not getting old?"

Honey slams her fist into his chest. He flinches, but says nothing. "I tell you I hate you like this," she says, tears falling down her lovely cheeks. She runs into their bedroom and slams the door behind her.

Kit stares after her. "You're still my wife, you know," he calls after her. "Get undressed, and get ready." He knows that will make her even angrier.

This is the only part of their relationship that is all his, that exists only between the two of them. As long as there is this small domain that no one else shares, he will stay with her. Kit becomes aroused at last. "I want you," he says.

She opens the bedroom door and looks at him blankly.

"I want you," he says. "But tonight I want you to use this." He offers her a pink plastic moddy. He's never asked her to be anyone else before.

Her eyes narrow. She looks at the moddy. "But this is me," she says, not understanding.

He laughs. "Yes, it's you. Only younger." Kit wants to make love to her tonight. He will hold her in his arms and let himself be carried away by her passion, but already he is thinking of someone else, a young woman with Oriental eyes, leaning close to a microphone and murmuring cryptic messages in other languages.

"Here on Venezia Affascinante tonight, we're going to get you excited, and we're going to tell you everything there is to tell about the people you love and the people you'd rather hate.

"There are a billion people in this world right now who don't like Honey Pílar, and there are a billion people who don't care. The other five billion, though, absolutely adore her, and we're wondering tonight how they'll take the news that her fourth marriage has come to a shattering, devastating conclusion. Shattering and devastating to her fourth husband, Kit, because after you've been married to Honey Pílar, the rest of the women in the world must suddenly look a little on the drab side. And poor Kit will be hearing a lot of cheeky questions from his friends from now on, like, 'Say, Kit, how could you have screwed up such a fantastic situation? What's wrong with you?'

"Venezia Affascinante conducted its own scientific poll of Honey Pílar admirers, and then compared the results with Kit's own personal reactions, which we gathered via an exclusive long-distance interview. Our question to one hundred average moddy users was this: 'Which aspect of their relationship will Kit miss the most, now that, thanks to his own stupidity, he's been abruptly shown the way out of Honey Pílar's life?' The most popular reply was her quick starts, low maintenance, and high performance, if you take our meaning. The second most popular answer was Honey's bank account, because, after all, a good deal of her irresistible attraction lies in her wealth, her extravagant lifestyle, and her association with the most stimulating celebrities in the world. The third answer was, unaccountably, her nose, which we must admit is certainly cute enough.

"It took us several hours to get in touch with Honey's most recent ex-husband. When he finally accepted our call, we put our question to him for his definitive reply. He said, and this is a direct quote, 'You can goddamn go to hell!' And you'll hear that nowhere else but Venezia Affascinante.

"Some unanswered questions remain: How long will it be before Honey Pílar marries again? Does she already have a candidate in mind? Could this be what led to the divorce? No one particularly cares what happens to Kit, of course, but every detail of

Honey's personal life is of absorbing interest to her vast army of fans. Will she continue to record new moddies, or does this alteration in her life signal a desire to make a fundamental change in her professional career as well? And if she does continue to turn out award-winning moddies, will she take over the reins of her huge financial empire, or will she look for a new business manager as well? Will that business manager be her new husband, or did her experience with Kit teach her a sad lesson about combining her emotional and business interests in one person?

"Whatever she decides, it will be impossible for Honey Pílar to keep her feelings secret for long. Not while Venezia Affascinante is on the job to bring you twenty-four-hour-a-day coverage of the world you like best, the world you wished you lived in. We'll be back after this word."

The two account executives are sitting in the smaller of the two dining rooms in Honey Pílar's home in Provence. They've finished lunch and are sipping brandy and beaming down at Honey at the far end of the long table. Both men feel very good, first because the meal they've just enjoyed was one of the finest in their memory, and second because this is the only time they've come to the walled estate with any real confidence that they'd be able to bring their business to a satisfactory conclusion.

"That was truly marvelous, Miss Pílar," says the first adman.

"Was good, no?" Honey smiles with innocent pleasure. "Kit gone now, I have what I like to eat. Hire new cook."

"Well," says the account executive, letting his expression become gradually more serious. "Perhaps it's time to turn our attention to business."

"Go ahead," says Honey. "You shoot."

"Yes, well . . . Slow, Slow Burn has been in the stores now for a little more than six months. I trust you've had the chance to look over the compilation of figures we sent you."

"Yes, I see them."

"And I suppose you'd like me to go over them with you. They're a little difficult to understand, even after you've been in the business as long as I have."

"No, okay, I understand them fine."

The adman frowns. "That is, I know you've been without a business manager ever since, uh—"

Honey gives him a reassuring smile. "Ever since I kick Kit his ass for him."

The man from the agency looks a little uncomfortable. "And

since then, as I say, you've been without a business manager. Well, we want you to know that we value your account very highly. We've represented you for almost twenty years. I've been sent to tell you that you may continue to rely on us during these troubled months."

"No trouble," says Honey.

The adman opens his briefcase and takes out a report. "We've taken the liberty of drawing up a plan for you, a preliminary schedule of promotional opportunities for *Slow, Slow Burn* and a suggested scenario for your next personality module. *Slow, Slow Burn* is doing rather well, although, of course, it doesn't appear to be as great a success as we hoped at first. Our consultants have made some valuable suggestions relevant to regaining the market support you enjoyed on some of your previous releases."

Honey gives him her brightest smile. The account executive smiles back. "May I have?" she asks, holding out her slender hand for the report.

"Certainly," says the adman. "I'll be happy to—"

Honey rips the papers in half while she looks directly into the man's eyes. Her smile never wavers. "I tell you what I do—*if* I do promotion, and *when* I make new moddy."

"Miss Pílar," says the adman unhappily, "we have some of the best market analysts in the business studying current trends in the personality module industry, and your own standing as a recording artist. While your reputation is greater now than ever, your impact at what we call point-of-sale seems to be softening somewhat. Our proposals are designed to make the best use of what our agency considers your chief strengths—"

"In twenty years," says Honey Pílar, "I earn much money for your agency, no?"

"Why, yes, of course."

"We call New York. We tell your boss to do it my way. Your boss is good friend. He do what *I* tell him, you do what *he* tell you."

The man takes out a handkerchief and mops at the perspiration on his upper lip. "I don't think that will be necessary," he says. "We'll simply go back and give them your views. Later, if you should find that handling your career on your own is too much for you, we can always—"

"I handle my career thirty years," Honey says. "Husbands, managers, or no. I handle my career. I think you go now."

The two men from New York glance at each other nervously and stand up. "As always, Miss Pílar," says the first adman, "it's been a pleasure."

"You bet," she says.

As the men are retreating from her home, the second account executive pauses to murmur something to her. This is the first time he's actually summoned the nerve to speak. "Miss Pílar," he says, looking down at the tiled floor, "I was wondering if I might invite you to dinner tonight."

Honey laughs. "You Americans!" she says, truly amused. "No, Kit was American too, and next husband will be tall blond, Swedish maybe, Dutch."

The second adman is terribly disappointed. He hurries after his colleague, not even looking back at their client. Honey watches them for a moment, then closes the door. She is still holding the ad agency's torn report. She goes back into the house, where she can find a wastebasket.

Introduction to
Marîd and the Trail of Blood

This story is one I commissioned, and gave George the idea for. I had been asked to edit an anthology of stories about lady vampires, and I went to several science fiction and fantasy writers (as opposed to horror writers), to get a science fictional take on what vampires are or might be. (Another story that appeared in the same anthology was Larry Niven's "Song of the Night People," which expanded into The Ringworld Throne.*)*

This also is one of my favorite Budayeen stories, mostly because it spotlights one of my favorite characters in that world, Bill the Cab Driver. Bill is a minor character in all three of the novels: Having won the lottery, he spent all the money to have one of his lungs removed and replaced with a sac containing a lifetime supply of the most powerful hallucinogen known to the underworld, time-released into his bloodstream so that Bill can be permanently, blissfully, and devastatingly stoned for the rest of his days, a condition which doesn't improve his cab driving any.

Bill is, in his way, a very New Orleans character—like Safiyya the Lamb Lady, who also figures in the story, and Laila who runs the moddy shop. Certainly there are enough dented fenders in New Orleans to attest to the fact that, for a long time, Louisiana had no open-container law. Maybe they still don't. George was fascinated by the strange New Orleans street-people who wandered around the French Quarter for years.

"Trail of Blood" is also one of the few Budayeen stories in which Marîd acts from an almost unselfish motive —that is, without being backed against a wall and put in peril of his own life.

Just one of those things you see on the Street on those long hot Budayeen nights.

—Barbara Hambly

✝ ✝ ✝

Marîd and the Trail of Blood

T HERE IS A SAYING: "THE BUDAYEEN HIDES FROM the light." You can interpret that any way you like, but I'm dissolute enough to know exactly what it means. There's a certain time of day that always makes me feel as if my blackened soul were just then under the special scrutiny of Allah in Paradise.

It happens in the gray winter mornings just at dawn, when I've spent the entire night drinking in some awful hellhole. When I finally decide it's time to go home and I step outside, instead of the cloaking forgiveness of darkness, there is bright, merciless sun shining on my aching head.

It makes me feel filthy and a little sick, as if I'd been wallowing in a dismal gutter all night. I know I can get pretty goddamn wiped out, but I don't believe I've ever sunk to wallowing; at least, I don't remember it if I did. And all the merchants setting up their stalls in the souks, all the men and women rising for morning prayers, they all glare at me with that special expression: They know exactly where I've been. They know I'm drunk and irredeemable. They give freely of contempt that they've been saving for a long time for someone as depraved and worthless as me.

This is not even to mention the disapproving expression on Youssef's face last Tuesday, when he opened the great wooden front door at home. Or my slave, Kmuzu. Both of them knew enough not to say a word out loud, but I got the full treatment from their attitudes, particularly when Kmuzu started slamming down the breakfast things half an hour later. As if I could stand to eat. All I wanted to do was collapse and sleep, but no one in the household would allow it. It was part of my punishment.

So that's how this adventure began. I reluctantly ate a little breakfast, ignored the large quantity of orders, receipts, ledgers, and other correspondence on my desk, and sat back in a padded leather chair wishing my mortal headache would go away.

Now, when I first had my brain wired, I was given a few experimental features. I can chip in a device that makes my body burn alcohol faster than the normal ounce an hour; last night had been a contest between me and my hardware. The liquor won. I could also chip in a pain-blocking daddy, but it wouldn't make me any more sober. For now, in the real world, I was as sick as a plague-stricken wharf rat.

I watched a holoshow about a sub-Saharan reforestation program, with the sound turned off. Before it was over, I lied to myself that I felt just a tiny bit better. I even pretended to act friendly toward Kmuzu. I forgave him, and I forgave myself for what I'd done the night before. I promised both of us that I'd never do it again.

I laughed; Kmuzu didn't. He turned his back and walked out of the room without saying a word.

It was obvious to me that it wasn't a good day to spend around the house. I decided to go back to the Budayeen and open my night-club at noon, a little early for the day shift. Even if I had to sit there by myself for a couple of hours, it would be better company than I had at home.

About 12:15, Pualani, the beautiful *real* girl, came in. She was early for work, but she had always been one of the most dependable of the five dancers on the day shift. I said hello, and before she went to the dressing room she sat down beside me at the bar. "You hear what happened to crazy Vi, who works by Big Al's Old Chicago?"

"No," I said. I can't keep up with what goes on with every girl, deb, and sexchange in the Budayeen.

"She turned up dead yesterday. They say they found her body all drained of blood, and she had two small puncture marks on her neck. It looks like some kind of vampire jumped on her or something." Pualani shuddered.

I closed my eyes and rubbed my throbbing temples. "There are no such things as vampires," I said. "There are no afrits, no djinn, no werewolves, no succubae, and no trolls. There has to be some other explanation for Vi." I recognized the woman's name, but I couldn't picture her face.

"Like what?"

"I don't know, a murderer with an elaborate scheme to throw suspicion on a supernatural suspect, maybe."

"I don't think so," Pualani said. "I mean, everything just fits."

"Uh-huh," I said.

Pualani went into the back to change into her working outfit. I reached over the bar and filled a tall glass with ice, then poured myself a carbonated soft drink.

Chiriga, my partner, arrived not long after. She owned half the club and acted as daytime barmaid. I was glad to see her because it meant that I didn't have to watch the place anymore. I rested my head on my arms and let the hangover headache do its throbbing worst.

Nothing felt fatal until someone shook my shoulder. I tried to ignore it, but it wouldn't go away. I sat up and saw Yasmin, one of the dancers. She was brushing her glistening black hair. "You hear about Vi?" she said.

"Uh-huh."

"You know I warned Vi about staying out of that alley. She used to go home that way every night. That's what she gets for working at the Old Chicago and going home that way. I must've told her a dozen times."

I took a deep breath and let it out. "Yasmin, the poor girl didn't deserve to die just because she walked home through an alley."

Yasmin cocked her head to one side and looked at me. "Yeah, I know, but still. You hear they think it was Sheba who killed her?"

That was news to me. "Sheba?" I asked. "She worked here maybe eight or nine months ago? That Sheba?"

Yasmin nodded. "She's over by Fatima and Nassir's these days, and she belongs there."

Chiri wiped the bar beside me and tossed a coaster in front of Yasmin. "Why do you think it was Sheba who killed crazy Vi?" Chiri asked.

" 'Cause," Yasmin said in a loud whisper. "Vi was killed by a vampire, right? And you never see Sheba in the daytime. Never. Have you? Think about it. Let me have some peppermint schnapps, Chiri."

I glanced at Chiri, but she only shrugged. I turned back to Yasmin. "First everybody's sure Vi was killed by a vampire, and now you're sure that the vampire is Sheba."

Yasmin raised both hands and tried to look innocent. "I'm not making any of this up," she said. She scooped up her peppermint schnapps and went to sit beside Pualani. No customers had come in yet.

"Well," I said to Chiri, "what do you think?"

Chiri's expression didn't change. "I don't think anything. Do I have to?" Chiri's the only person in the Budayeen with any sense. And that includes me.

The afternoon passed slowly. The other three dancers, Lily, Kitty, and Baby, came in when they felt like it. We made a little money, sold a few drinks, the girls hustled some champagne cock-tails. I listened to the same damn Sikh propaganda songs on the holo system and watched my employees parade their talents.

It was getting on toward dinnertime when Lily and Yasmin got into an argument with two poor European marks. I strolled over toward their table, not because I care anything for marks—I gener-ally don't—but because a bad enough argument might send the two guys out into the Street and into somebody else's club.

"Marîd, listen—" Lily said.

I held up a hand, interrupting her. "Are you two gentlemen enjoying yourselves?" I asked.

They had puzzled looks on their faces, but they nodded. Some people are born marks, others achieve markdom, and some people have markdom thrust upon them.

"What's the problem?" I said in a warning voice. "I can hear you all the way across the bar."

"We were talking about Vi," Lily said. "We were warning Lazaro and Karoly to stay out of that alley."

"We were going to suggest a nice, safe place where we could go," Yasmin said. She tried to look innocent again. Yasmin hasn't been innocent since her baby teeth fell out.

"Look, you two," I said, meaning my two fun-loving hustlers, "let me clear this up right now. I'll call the morgue and find out what they know about crazy Vi."

"You're gonna call the morgue?" Lily said. She was suddenly very interested.

"Get back to work," I said. I went back to my seat at the bar. I unclipped the phone from my belt and murmured the commcode of the Budayeen's morgue. The medical examiner there, Dr. Besharati, had helped me with a couple of other matters over the years. He was normal enough for a guy who worked surrounded by dead bodies all day. He liked to tootle a jazz trumpet in between autopsies. That was his kick.

I got one of his assistants. The coroner was busy putting brains into jars or something. "Yeah? Medical examiner's office."

"I wanted to get some information about one of the, ah, deceased currently in your custody."

"You a family member?"

I blinked. "Sure," I said.

"Okay, then. What you want?"

"Young woman, killed last night in an alley in the Budayeen. Her name was Vi."

"Yeah?" He wasn't making it any easier for me.

"We were just wondering if you have determined the cause of death yet."

There was a long pause while the assistant went off to investigate. When he returned he said, "Well, we ain't got to her yet, but she died on account she was murdered. Slashed throat, heavy loss of blood. That'll do it every time."

I grimaced. I could only hope they'd be a little gentler with Vi's real family. "Could you tell me, were there any puncture wounds on the throat?"

"Told you we ain't got to her yet. Don't know. Call again tomorrow maybe. We ought to have her on the slab by then. Do you need to come watch?"

I just hung up after leaving my commcode. I was sure that Lily would have happily viewed the autopsy, but even if I couldn't quite remember who Vi was, she probably deserved better treatment than that.

The two European marks got up and left the club about a half hour later. Yasmin came and leaned against the bar near me. She was brushing her hair again. "What jerks," she said.

They're all jerks, is the general opinion.

"I called about Vi," I said. "No vampire. She was just murdered in the alley."

"Huh," Lily said dubiously. "Like she could bite herself in her own neck."

I spread my hands. "They haven't confirmed the business about the puncture wounds. You're just exaggerating all of this way out of proportion."

Yasmin looked at me knowingly. "You'll see," she said. She turned to Lily, who nodded her agreement. Dealing with my employees is sometimes very hard on my nerves. I thought about having my first drink of the day, but I didn't. I went out to get something to eat instead.

Now, Chiriga's is about halfway between the eastern gate of the Budayeen and the western end—the cemetery. There are plenty of places to eat along the Street, and on this particular occasion I decided to head toward Kiyoshi's. I hadn't walked far before I saw the Lamb Lady.

"Oh boy," I muttered. Safiyya the Lamb Lady is a regular feature of the Budayeen, one of our favorite odd characters. She's harmless, but she can talk at you so long you're sure you'll never get away. She lives on money people give her and she sleeps wherever anybody will let her. I've let her stay in my club a few times. She's completely honest, just addled a bit. That's why I was surprised to see her wearing a lot of expensive-looking jewelry. She had on eight or ten silver rings, two silver necklaces, silver earrings, and silver bracelets and bangles from her wrists halfway to her elbows.

"Where'd you get all that, Safiyya?" I asked.

"Watch out for the lamb," she said in a hoarse voice. She used to have a lamb that followed her around the Budayeen, but it was accidentally killed. Now Safiyya has an imaginary lamb. I'd almost bumped into it.

"Sorry," I said.

"Isn't this nice stuff?" she said. She jingled her bracelets. "I found it all in the trash."

"In the trash?" The silver she was wearing must have been worth four or five hundred kiam. "Where?"

"Oh, it's all gone now," Safiyya said. "I took it. I'll show you, though, if you want to see." I followed her because I was curious. She led me to the back of a whitewashed, two-story apartment building, where four trash cans had been upended. Garbage was strewn all over the narrow passageway between buildings, but we didn't find any more jewelry.

When Safiyya started showing off all this silver, she would make herself a target for robbery, or worse. I decided to mention this to one of my connections in the police department; they'd keep an eye on Safiyya. With crazy Vi's unsolved murder the night before, I guessed there'd be a stronger police presence in the Budayeen tonight. I'd hate to see the Lamb Lady become the killer's second victim.

However, the rest of the day passed quietly. Nothing happened to Safiyya, and nothing happened to me. I went home, trimmed my beard, took a long shower, and sat down at my desk to get some of my paperwork done. After a while, Kmuzu interrupted me.

"The master of the house wishes you to meet with him in an hour, yaa Sidi," he said.

I nodded. The master of the house was my great-grandfather, Friedlander Bey, who controlled much of the illicit activities in the city. He was a very powerful man, so powerful that he also found it profitable to control the rise and fall of certain nearby nations. It was like a hobby with him.

Forty-five minutes later I was dressed the way Papa liked me to dress, standing at the door to his office. It was guarded by Habib and Labib, Papa's huge, silent bodyguards. I wasn't going in until they felt like letting me go in.

Tariq, Friedlander Bey's secretary and valet, came out and noticed me. "I hope you haven't been waiting long," he said.

I shrugged. "I've just been watching these two guys. You know, they don't move at all. They don't even breathe. How do they manage that?"

Tariq did the smart thing and ignored me. He ushered me into Papa's inner office. Friedlander Bey reclined on a lacquered divan. He indicated that I should seat myself across from him. Between us was a table loaded down with trays of food and fruit, juices and silver coffee things. We chatted informally while we drank the customary cups of coffee. Then, suddenly, Papa was all business.

"You are spending too much time in the Budayeen," he said.

"But O Shaykh, you gave me the nightclub—"

He raised a hand. I shut up. "There are more important matters. Representatives from the Empire of Parthia will be arriving tomorrow. They wish our support in their expansion into Kush."

"I didn't even know they—"

"I do not believe we will give them what they desire. Indeed, I think it is time that Parthia be, shall we say, disunited."

What could I do but agree? We discussed these weighty affairs for some time. At last, Papa relaxed. He took an apple and a small paring knife. "You called the medical examiner today, my darling," he said.

I was astonished. "Yes, O Shaykh."

"You are interested in the death of the young dancer. It is of no importance."

Maybe it's because I used to be a poor street kid myself, but the lives and deaths of the people of the Budayeen matter more to me.

Friedlander Bey went on. "Your employees believe in vampires." He was amused. "Lieutenant Giragosian of the police does not." Here his amusement ended. "You will not pursue this further. It is a waste of time, and it is unseemly for you to concern yourself with what is, after all, chiefly a Christian myth."

Crazy Vi's body in the morgue was no myth. And in the Maghreb, the far western part of North Africa where I'd grown up, there are still stories of the Gôla. She is a female djinn, very big and strong, sometimes with goat's feet and covered with hair like an unshorn sheep. Her trick is that she speaks sweetly and gently to people, and then kills them and drinks their blood. The Gôla is usually described as having those familiar long, fierce, canine teeth and eyes like blazing fire. Still, I wasn't about to mention any of this to my benefactor.

"You and I will share luncheon tomorrow with the Parthians," Papa said. "Forget about the murdered woman, your nightclub, and the Budayeen for a while."

"As you wish, O Shaykh," I said. Yeah, sure, I thought.

I returned to my suite and relaxed with a detective novel by Lutfy Gad, my favorite Palestinian mystery writer. He'd been dead for decades, so there were no new Gad books, but the old ones were so good I could enjoy them again and again. This one was called *The Deep Cradle*, and if I remembered correctly, it was the one in which Gad's dark and dangerous detective, al-Qaddani, ended up in Breulandy with almost every bone in his body broken.

It's amazing, sometimes, how resilient those paperback detectives are. I wish I knew how they did it.

The phone on my belt rang. That meant the call was probably from one of my disreputable friends and associates; otherwise, the desk phone would have rung. I unclipped it and murmured, "Marhaba."

"Marîd? It's Yasmin, and guess what?"

She actually waited for me to guess. I didn't bother.

"You know that boys' club of yours?" she said. I have a small army of kids who look out for me in the Budayeen, watch me and make sure I'm not being followed by the cops or anything. I throw them a few kiam now and then.

"What about them?" I asked.

"One of 'em's dead and it looks like Sheba all over again. Kid's throat is torn open and before you say anything, I saw the goddamn puncture marks this time, like from fangs. So you're wrong."

It bothered me that her notion about Sheba was more important to her than the death of that poor boy. "Who was it?" I asked. "Anybody you know?"

"Yeah, stupid. Sheba, like I been telling you."

I took in a deep breath and let it out slowly. "No, not her. The boy. Who was it?"

I could almost hear her shrug. "They have names, Marîd? I mean, how would I know?"

I closed my eyes. "Call the police, Yasmin."

"Chiri already did."

"All right. I've got to go now."

"Something else, Marîd. Lily and me and this girl you don't know, Natka, and Sheba were all going to have supper after work tonight. At Martyrs of Democracy. Anyway, Sheba comes in real late with this lame excuse about having this admiral or something buy her one bottle of champagne after another even though the night shift had come in. What's an admiral doing in the Budayeen in the first place? And I know Sheba's no dayshift girl. So she's all out of breath and she seems really nervous, not just to me, you can ask Lily about it. And you know what? When we ordered the food, she asked me please not to get the pork strings in garlic sauce. That's what I always order. So I asked her why, and she said her stomach was bothering her, like maybe she was pregnant or had the flu or something, and the smell of the garlic would make her sick. Garlic, Marîd, get it?"

I opened my eyes. "Maybe it wasn't the garlic, sweetheart. Maybe she just remembered that none of you good Muslim women ought to be eating pork, in strings or anyhow."

There was a pause while Yasmin figured if I was kidding her or not. She let it go. "How much more proof do you need, Marîd?" she asked angrily. "You're really being a jackass about this." I heard her slam the phone down. I put mine back on my belt and shook my head.

Behind me, I heard Kmuzu say, "If I may say so, yaa Sidi, I have noticed a tendency on your part to hesitate to get involved in such matters until you yourself are personally threatened. In the meantime, innocent lives can be lost. If you think back, I'm sure you'll recall other—"

"The voice of my conscience," I said wearily, turning to face him. "Thank you so much. Are you telling me I should take this vampire stuff seriously? Especially after Papa specifically told me to ignore it?" You see, Kmuzu wasn't merely my slave; he'd been a "gift" from Friedlander Bey, someone to spy on me and report back to Papa.

He shrugged. "The people of the Budayeen have no one to turn to but you."

"So if I pursued this, you'd help me?"

Kmuzu spread his hands. "Oh no. The master of the house has made his feelings clear. Nevertheless, you could telephone Lieutenant Giragosian and learn what he knows."

I did just that. I called the copshop. "Lieutenant Giragosian's office," a man said.

"I'd like to speak to the lieutenant, please. This is Marîd Audran."

"Audran, son of a bitch. The lieutenant isn't, uh, available right now."

"Who's this, then?"

"This is his executive assistant, Sergeant Catavina." Jeez, the laziest, most easily bought cop in the city. How his star had risen.

"Look, Catavina," I said, "there've been two murders in the Budayeen in the last couple of days. One was a dancer, a real girl named Vi, and the other was a boy. Both had their throats torn out. Know anything about them?"

A pause. "Sure we do." He was playing it cagey. Dumb cagey.

"Look, pal, you want me to have Friedlander Bey send over a couple of guys to question you personally?"

"Take it easy, Audran." There was a gratifying hint of anxiety in Catavina's voice. "What are you looking for?"

"First, what's the ID on the boy?"

"Kid named Mahdi il-Mallah. Eleven years old."

I knew him. He was one of my friends. I felt a familiar coldness in my gut. "What about puncture wounds on the neck?"

"How'd you know? Yeah, that's in the report. Now, I got to tell the lieutenant you called. What you want me to tell him when he asks me what you're up to?"

I sighed. I wasn't happy about this. "Tell him I'm going to catch his vampire for him."

"Vampire! Audran, what are you, crazy?"

I hung up instead of replying.

Kmuzu's expression was difficult to read. I didn't know if he approved or not. I don't know why I cared. "One piece of advice, yaa Sidi, if you'll permit me: It would be a mistake to begin your investigation of this woman Sheba tonight."

"Uh-huh. Why do you say that?"

He shrugged again. "If I had to hunt a vampire, I'd do it during the daylight."

Good point. The next day I arose at dawn, made my ritual ablutions and prayed, then set out to begin serious investigations. If Kmuzu wasn't planning to offer any direct assistance—meaning that he wouldn't even drive me over to the Budayeen—then I'd have to rely on Bill the cab driver. Now, if you know Bill, you know how amusing the concept of relying on him is. He's as dependable as a two-legged footstool.

I phoned him from the bathroom because I didn't want Kmuzu to overhear me. I told Bill to pick me up just outside the high walls that surrounded Friedlander Bey's estate. Bill didn't remember who I was for a while, but that's usual. Bill's about as aware as a sleeping skink. He chose that for himself years ago, buying an expensive bodmod that constantly braised his brain in a very frightening high-tech hallucinogen. It would have driven most people to suicide within a handful of days; in Bill's case, I understand it sort of settled him down.

On the way from Papa's mansion to the eastern gate of the Budayeen, Bill and I had a disjointed conversation about the imminent war with the state of Gadsden. I eventually figured out that he was having some kind of flashback. Before he came to the city he'd lived in America, in the part now called Sovereign Deseret. His skink brain let him believe he was still there.

It was all right because he found the Budayeen easily enough. I gave him enough money so that he'd wait for me and drive me home after I finished the morning's legwork. I started up the Street in the direction of the cemetery. I didn't know yet what I wanted to do first. What did I have to go on? Two homicide victims, that's all, with nothing tangible connecting them except the similarity of method. I had, on one hand, my employees' overheated warning that a vampire was loose around here, and, on the other hand, my absolute disbelief in the supernatural.

There was nothing to do but call Chiri. I knew I'd be waking her up. I heard her pick up her phone and say, "Uh. Yeah?"

"Chiri, it's Marîd. I'm not waking you up, am I?"

"No." Her voice was real damn cold.

"Sorry. Listen, do you know where Sheba lives?"

"No, and I don't care, either."

"Then who do we know who could give me the address? I think I need to just drop by and ask Sheba a couple of things."

There was a pause: Chiri was being angry. "Yasmin would know. Or Lily."

"Yasmin or Lily. I probably should've called them first."

Another pause. "Probably."

I grimaced. "Sorry, Chiri. Go back to sleep. I'll see you later." She didn't say anything before she slammed the phone down.

I called Yasmin next, but I didn't get an answer. That didn't surprise me. I remembered from the days when Yasmin and I lived together that she was one of the best little sleepers that Allah ever invented. She could sleep through any major catastrophe except a missed meal. I gave up after listening to the phone ring a dozen and a half times, and then I called Lily. She was just as unhappy to be roused as Chiri, but her tone changed when she found out it was me. Lily has been waiting for me to call for a long time. She's a gorgeous sexchange, and she was well aware that I've never had much success with real women.

She was less happy when I told her I just wanted another girl's address and commcode. I heard ice through the ether again, but she finally gave me the information. It turned out that Sheba didn't live too far from my club.

"And one other thing," Lily said. "We checked by the Red Light Lounge. Sheba couldn't have been late to supper on account of some guy buying her drinks. She doesn't work daytimes, she's never worked daytimes—just like we said. So she lied. You just don't see her around when the sun is up."

"I'll keep that in mind," I said.

"So why you want to get next to that for? If you're spending too much time all by yourself, honey, I'll help you out."

I didn't need this now. "Yasmin would scratch your eyes out, Lily. I've only been protecting you."

"Huh, Yasmin don't remember how to spell your name, Marîd." She slammed the phone down, too. I decided it wouldn't be a good idea to set foot in my own business today. I'd probably be slashed to ribbons.

I found Sheba's apartment building and went up to the second floor. It was an old place with a thin, worn carpet runner on the stairs. The paint on the walls hung down in grimy, blowzy strips. Sheba's front door was painted a dark reddish brown, the color of a bloodstain on clothing. I knocked. There was no response. Well, Sheba was a Budayeen hustler, she was probably asleep. I knocked louder and called her name. Finally I unclipped my phone again and murmured her commcode into it; I could hear the ringing from within the apartment.

It took me perhaps a minute and a half to get past her lock. The first thing I learned was that Sheba wasn't home. The second was that it appeared she hadn't been around for a while—several envelopes had been pushed beneath her door. One had been closed only with a rubber band. I opened it; it contained a hundred kiam in ten-kiam bills, and a note from some admirer. Clothes, jewelry, stuffed animals, all sorts of things were strewn across the floor of the apartment's large room.

There was a mattress with a single sheet lying tipped up against a wall. The room's only window was standing open, water-stained yellow curtains blowing in on a warm breeze. Below the window was another heap of clothing and personal articles. I brushed the curtains aside and looked out. Below me was a narrow alley leading crookedly in the direction of Ninth Street.

A light was on in the bathroom; when I looked in there, it was as much a mess as the other room. It seemed to me that Sheba had been in a hell of a hurry, had grabbed up a few things, and had gotten out of the apartment as fast as she could. I couldn't guess why.

I looked more closely at what she'd left behind. Near the bathroom was a pile of cellophane and cardboard scraps that Sheba had kicked together. I sorted through the stuff and saw quickly that it was mostly packaging material ripped from several personality modules. I was familiar enough with the blazebrain field to know that some of the moddies Sheba had collected were not your regular commercial releases.

Sheba fancied black-market titles, and very dangerous ones, too. She liked illegal underground moddies that fed her feelings of superiority and power; while she was wearing them she'd become these programmed people, and her behavior could range from the merely vicious to the downright sinister and deadly. She could almost certainly become capable of murder.

I recalled that months ago, when she worked for me at Chiri's, she was almost always chipped in to some moddy or other. That wasn't unusual among the dancers though. I was sure that Sheba wasn't using these hardcore moddies back then, at least not at work. Something had happened in the meantime, something that had drastically changed her, and not for the better.

I put some of the wrappers in my pocket and went back to the window. A niggling thought had been bothering me, and I looked outside again. My attention was drawn to the four trash cans below. They weren't just any trash cans. Safiyya the Lamb Lady had brought me here. She had found all her silver jewelry in Sheba's alley.

I took another look around Sheba's shabby apartment. There were dead flowers shoved into one corner, several books thrown together on the floor, and shattered glass everywhere. I found another double handful of abandoned jewelry, a heap of pendants and necklaces, cheap stuff. Most were decorated with familiar symbols, all jumbled together—there were a couple of Christian crosses; Islamic crescents and items with Qur'ânic inscriptions; a Star of David; an ankh; Buddhist, Hindu, and other Asiatic religious tokens; occult designs; Native American figures; and others I wasn't able to identify. These were the only things I saw that might have had some connection to the vampire mythology, but I still discounted them—the things might just have been left behind like the rest of the jewelry. I couldn't be sure there was any particular significance to them.

Nothing else set off a bell in my highly perceptive crime-solving mind. The moddies were the best clue, and so my next stop was Laila's modshop on Fourth Street. I was surprised that Laila herself wasn't in when I got there, but I was relieved, too. Laila is almost impossible to deal with. Instead, there was a young woman standing behind the counter.

She smiled at me. She didn't seem crazy at all. She was either wearing a moddy that force-fed her a pleasant personality, or something was definitely not right here. This was not a shop where you met people under the control of their own unaugmented selves.

"Can I help you?" she asked me in English. I don't speak much English, but I have an electronic add-on that takes care of that for me. I kept the language daddy chipped in almost all the time, because there are a lot of important English-speaking people in the city.

I took the wrappers from my pocket. "Sell any of these lately?"

She shuffled the cellophane around on the counter for a few seconds. "Nope," she said brightly. I was positive now that I wasn't dealing with her real personality. She was just too goddamn perky.

"How do you know?" I asked.

She shrugged. "This shop and its owner are much too concerned about upholding local ordinances to sell illegal bootleg moddies."

I almost choked. "Yeah, you right," was all I said.

"Anything else I can help you with?" She was deeply concerned, I could tell. That was some moddy Laila had found for her.

"I'll just browse a bit." I went toward the bins of moddies based on characters from old books and holoshows. For some dumb reason, I couldn't come up with the name of the villain I was looking for. "You know what a vampire is?"

"Sure," she said. "We had to watch that movie in a class in high school." She made a scornful expression. "Twentieth Century Literature."

"What was the vampire's name again?"

"Lestat. They made us watch that movie and another classic. *Airport*, it was. None of us could figure out what they had to do with the real world. I like modern literature better."

I'll bet she did. Lestat wasn't who I was searching for. I browsed through the bins for half an hour before I came across a set of vampire-character moddies. The package had been torn open. I took it to the counter and showed it to the young woman. "Know anything about this?" I asked.

She was upset. "We don't break sets open," she said. "We wouldn't have done that." The Dracula moddy was missing, leaving the Jonathan Harker, Lucy Westenra, Dr. Van Helsing, and

Renfield moddies. I gave a little involuntary shudder. I didn't want to meet the person who'd be eager to chip in Renfield.

"Do you suppose someone could have shoplifted the missing moddy?" I asked.

I almost wished I hadn't said it. The young woman paled. I could see how abhorrent the entire idea was to her. "Perhaps," she murmured. The word she used was "perhaps," not "maybe." That had to be the software talking.

"Forget it," I said, coming to a decision. "I'll buy the rest of the package."

"Even though part of it's been stolen? You know I'm not authorized to offer you a discount."

It took me a little while longer to persuade her to sell me the things, and I was already chipping in Dr. Van Helsing, that fearless old vampire hunter, as I left the shop and headed back toward the eastern gate.

The first thing Audran noticed was that he was somewhat taller and a good deal older. There was a painful twinge in his left shoulder, but he decided it wouldn't hinder him too much. He also felt very Dutch; he—Van Helsing—was from Amsterdam, after all.

Audran's own consciousness lurked in a tiny, hidden-away area submerged beneath the overlay of Van Helsing. There he wondered what "feeling Dutch" meant. It was probably just some programmer's laziness. That person had known that Van Helsing was Dutch, but had not bothered to include specific dutchnesses. It was a weakness that Audran despised in poorly written commercial moddies.

It did not take long for Audran's muscles and nerves to compensate for the differences between his own physical body and the one the moddy's manufacturer imagined. As long as the moddy was chipped in, Audran would move, feel, and respond as Van Helsing. There was also an annoying nervous flutter in his right eyelid, and Audran sincerely hoped it would go away as soon as he popped the moddy out.

Van Helsing was still heading east, on the sidewalk; Audran preferred walking in the middle of the street. As he approached the arched gate of the Budayeen, Van Helsing considered the things they had found in Sheba's apartment. Now, with his special knowledge, the evidence took on new significance.

How could Audran be expected to appreciate the absolute horror of what he'd discovered in the abandoned apartment? How could Audran know that the dead flowers, roses, were shunned by all vampires; that the broken glass came from shattered mirrors around the room; *that the sacred symbols were powerful weapons against the Undead?*

More compelling yet were the books and papers left with seeming carelessness on the floor. They had looked harmless enough to Audran, but Van Helsing knew that within their pages were terrible, evil passages describing rituals through which a living human being could become a vampire, and others that gave instructions for inviting demons to invade and possess one's immortal soul.

Through Audran's inaction, the situation had become dire and deadly; more than human lives were at stake now. An unholy monster was loose among the unsuspecting people of the Budayeen. Once again, it was left to Dr. Van Helsing to restore peace and sanctity, if he could.

Cursing Audran for a fool, Van Helsing quickened his pace. Audran should've guessed the truth when the young boy had been attacked. Dracula's victim, Lucy, had preyed largely upon children. Van Helsing felt an uncomfortable stirring of his emotions. Although he'd never admit the fact to anyone, he was aware of his barely sublimated lust toward female vampires. And now he'd been called upon to battle a new one. He shook his head; at the ultimate moment, he knew, he would be strong enough. He passed through the arch and onto the beautiful Boulevard il-Jameel.

Bill the cab driver was still waiting for him. He tapped Van Helsing on the shoulder. "Ready to go?" he asked.

"Gott im Himmel!" Van Helsing exclaimed.

"That's easy for you to say," Bill said. "Get in."

Van Helsing and Audran glanced at the taxi. Together they reached up and popped the moddy out.

"The guy's a total loon," I muttered as I slid into the cab's backseat.

"Got a complaint about me, pal?" Bill asked.

"No," I said, "I'm talking about this Van Helsing jerk. He sees deadly gruesome creatures everywhere he looks."

Bill shrugged. "Well, hell, so do I, but I just steer around 'em." I thought that was a pretty sensible attitude.

Bill delivered me to the front gate of Friedlander Bey's estate. I hurried inside and up to my suite just in time for Kmuzu to remind me about the important luncheon meeting scheduled with Papa and the political representatives of some damn place. I showered again, feeling just a little sullied after letting that repressed Van Helsing character occupy my mind and body. I put on my best gallebeya and keffiya, going so far as to belt a gorgeous jeweled ceremonial dagger in front at the waist. I looked good, and I knew Papa would be pleased.

The luncheon itself was fine, just fine. I don't even remember what we ate, but there was tons of it and the delegation from Parthia was appropriately impressed. More important, though, was that they were appropriately intimidated. I sat in my chair and looked thoughtful, while Friedlander Bey explained to them the facts of life here in the early years of the twenty-third century of the Christian Era.

What it all amounted to was that the Parthians pretended to be grateful after being denied the help they'd come for. They even tried to bribe Papa further by guaranteeing him exclusive influence with the victorious side in the brand-new Silesian revolt. Since no one at that moment could predict which party would end up in power, and since Papa had little interest in nations beyond the Islamic realm, and since everyone in the room including Habib and Labib knew that the Parthians couldn't deliver on their promise in the first place, we acted as if they hadn't said a word. It was an embarrassing blunder on their part, but Friedlander Bey handled it all with grace and assurance. He just waved to have the coffee and kataifi brought in. Papa's extremely fond of kataifi, a Greek dessert something like baklava, except it looks like shredded wheat. It may be his only worldly weakness.

With all the formal greetings and salutations and invitations and flatteries and thank-yous and blessings and leave-takings, it was about five o'clock before I was able to return to my rooms. I started to tell Kmuzu what had gone on, but naturally he already knew all about it. He even had a little advice for me concerning the people of Kush, who no doubt would soon strike back against the weakened Parthians.

"Fine," I said impatiently. "Thank you, Kmuzu, I don't know what I'd do without you. If you'll just excuse me—"

"The family of the young murdered boy said they were sorry you couldn't come to the funeral. They know how fond of you he'd been. I explained that you'd been detained by the master of the house."

I regretted missing the service. I wished I could have at least been at the cemetery to offer my condolences.

"I think I'll just relax now," I said. "I'm going to rest for a while, and then I'm going to see how my nightclub is doing without me. That is all right, isn't it? I mean, I'm allowed to go down there this evening, aren't I?"

Kmuzu gave me a blank stare for a second or two. "I have been advised otherwise, yaa Sidi," he said.

"Oh. Too bad. Then—"

I was looking at his back. "You have two visitors waiting to speak with you, a man and a boy. They've been here since two o'clock."

"In the anteroom? All this time?" I didn't want to see anyone else, but I couldn't just tell these people to go home and come back tomorrow. "All right, I'll—" Kmuzu wasn't paying any attention. He was already going toward my office. I followed, trying not to let all this power go to my head.

When I saw who was waiting for me, I was startled. It was Bill the cab driver and a boy from the Budayeen. Bill was standing up with his back to the room, his hands stretched up as high against the wall as he could reach. Don't ask me why. The kid's name was Musa Ali, and his dirty face was streaked with tears. He was sitting quietly in a chair. I felt sorry for him, having to spend all those hours alone with Bill. I wouldn't have done it.

When I came in, they both began speaking at once. They talked fast and furiously. I couldn't make any sense out of it. I signaled Bill to shut up, and then I let Musa Ali explain things. "My sister," he said, his eyes wide with fear, "she's taken her."

I looked at Bill. "The vampire," he said. Suddenly he was very calm and matter-of-fact. His hands were still raised high, but I didn't hold that against him. You took what you could get with Bill.

Between the two of them, I got an idea of the story. Not the truth, necessarily, but the story. Apparently, just at noon, Sheba, in her vampire form, had stolen another child, Musa Ali's six-year-old sister. Bill had tried to interfere, and a tremendous fight had erupted. On one side was this burly full-grown man, and on the other was a short nightclub dancer burdened with a struggling child in her arms. Bill was covered with dark bruises and bloody cuts and scratches, so I didn't really have to ask which way the conflict had gone.

"She turned into a bunch of mist," Bill said, shrugging. He sounded apologetic. "I couldn't fight a bunch of mist, could I? She just floated away on the breeze. Reminded me of that time this guy from Tunis tried to cheat me out of my fare, and just then I heard this music from Heaven that was too high-pitched for normal humans to hear, see, so I turned around as fast as I could, but he was trying to get out of the cab, so then—"

I stopped listening to Bill. "Mist?" I asked Musa Ali.

"Uh-huh," the boy said.

So now I was tracking down a fog lady. A murderous vampire fog lady. Suddenly I really wanted another piece of kataifi. . . .

It was getting late. I returned quickly to my apartment, to change clothes again and pick up a few items I thought might be useful. One of those things was the Van Helsing moddy—after all, the excitable Dutch fanatic knew more about hunting vampires than I ever would. I just had to try to maintain a little rational control, to offset Van Helsing's own serious hang-ups.

I avoided Kmuzu and hurried back to Bill and Musa Ali, still waiting in my office. With some difficulty, we managed to slip out of the house without any direct interference from Friedlander Bey's staff, and I gave Bill the order to drive us back to the Budayeen. "First I take you over there," Bill complained, "then I bring you back, then I go home, then I come back here, now we go over there again. Maybe I'll be lucky and we'll all get killed tonight. I don't do this driving thing because I enjoy it, you know."

Bill can trap you that way, by fooling you into asking the next obvious question. That always leads into an even more bizarre rant, and I've promised myself not to get suckered in anymore. I didn't ask him what he wanted me to ask.

"Are you taking me home?" Musa Ali asked. "I can't go home until I find my sister."

He was a brave kid. "You go home," I said. "We'll find your sister."

"Okay," he said. He was brave, but he wasn't a fool.

"We're going to the cemetery, Bill," I said. "It's the only logical place to look for Sheba."

"They won't let me into the cemetery, pal," he said.

"Who won't?"

"The dead people. They won't let me into the cemetery because I'm American."

"They don't have dead people in America?" I asked. I had already forgotten my promise to myself.

"Oh, sure they do," Bill said. "But the dead people here in the city still hold it against Americans that they have the wrong unlucky number. It's not thirteen, see, like Americans believe, because—" I stopped listening. I reached up and chipped in the Van Helsing moddy instead.

There was another moment of disorientation, but it passed quickly. "Stakes!" Van Helsing said loudly. "We need sharp wooden stakes! How could Audran have forgotten them? We have to stop and find some!"

"Don't worry about stakes," Bill said calmly. "Got 'em in the trunk. I got some in case I ever get a tent." Van Helsing was wise enough not to pursue it any further.

Because Van Helsing wasn't as familiar with the city as Audran, he didn't notice immediately that Bill, for all his many years of experience, was getting pretty damn lost. The probable explanation *was that his invisible evil temptresses were leading him astray. Both Van Helsing and Audran would have understood that. Instead, though, the vampire hunter stared out the taxi's window, watching the neighborhoods slide by.*

Time passed, and the sun dropped silently toward the horizon. It was almost dark when Bill finally drove past the Budayeen's eastern gate. He jammed on the brakes, and Van Helsing and he jumped out of the car. More time was spent as Bill searched for the trunk key. At last they armed themselves with the stakes; they couldn't find a hammer, but Bill carried an old, dead battery that could be used for pounding purposes.

"We'll need something to cut off Sheba's head, too," Van Helsing said in a worried voice. "We'll need to get a large cleaver. And garlic to stuff into her mouth."

Bill nodded. "There's an all-night convenience store on our way."

Van Helsing still seemed apprehensive. "Sheba will be at her full powers soon."

"Well," Bill said, smiling broadly, "so am I." That didn't do very much to reassure his companion.

There are sixteen blocks between the eastern gate and the cemetery, the length of the Street, the width of the Budayeen. They hurried as fast as they could, but Bill had never been very agile, and Van Helsing was not a young man anymore. They pushed through the crowds of local folk and foreign tourists with growing desperation, but by the time they arrived at their goal, the sun had set. It was night. They would have to face the full fury of the vampire's power.

"Have no fear," Van Helsing said. "This isn't the first time I've challenged the Undead on their own territory. You have nothing to worry about."

"That's easy for you to say," Bill said. "You don't have to worry about the ground opening up in horrible fissures right in front of you."

Van Helsing paused. "Bill," he said at last, "the ground isn't opening up."

Bill put a finger alongside his nose. "No, you're right," he confided, "but that doesn't mean I'm not going to worry about it."

Van Helsing looked up to Heaven, where God was watching. "Come on," he told Bill. "We mustn't be too late to save the little girl."

They arrived at the cemetery. No one else was nearby. Van Helsing saw the flowers and other offerings on the ground near where Mahdi il-Mallah had been laid to rest. The boy's parents couldn't afford an above-ground tomb, so he'd been interred in a small, oven-like vault built into one of the cemetery's red brick walls.

"Oh my God," Bill cried. He motioned toward the back of the graveyard.

Van Helsing turned and looked where Bill was pointing. He saw Sheba, dressed in a long, filthy black shift. Her hair was wildly disheveled and matted with leaves and twigs. There were streaks of dirt on her face and bare arms. She stared at Van Helsing and snarled. Even from that distance, the Dutchman could see the great, long canine teeth, the mark of the vampire.

"It's her," Van Helsing said in a quiet voice.

"You mean, 'It's she,'" Bill said.

"Or what remains of her earthly body, now inhabited by something of unspeakable foulness. Take warning: Remember that she has the strength of a dozen or more normal people." Beneath Van Helsing's overwhelming presence, Audran realized that the vampire moddy was constructed with an endocrine controller, letting a flood of adrenalin loose in Sheba's bloodstream. Whoever was correct —Audran or Van Helsing, believer in natural law or in evil magic—it made no difference. The ultimate effect was the same.

"You know," Bill said thoughtfully, "she wouldn't be half-bad looking if she'd just fix herself up a little."

Van Helsing did not deign to reply. He moved toward Sheba, feeling terror, determination, and an odd longing mixed together. Sheba stood before a large whitewashed tomb, its marble front panel removed and cast aside. This was where she'd taken up residence after leaving behind her human dwelling place. There was a vile stench emanating from the tomb. Nevertheless, Van Helsing summoned his courage and stepped nearer.

He heard small rustling noises, and behind Sheba he saw movement. It had to be Musa Ali's sister, still alive, but bound and made captive by this loathsome creature. "Thanks be to all the angels that we are yet in time," he said.

Sheba did not cry out or utter any verbal challenges; it was as if she'd lost the power of speech. Instead, she made harsh, guttural, animal noises deep in her throat.

"Unbind the child and let her go free," Van Helsing demanded.

Once again Sheba bared her perilous fangs and hissed at them, not like a snake, but like a great feral cat. Then she rushed forward more swiftly than even Van Helsing had anticipated and leaped on him, reaching for his unprotected throat with her clawed fingers and savaging him with her demon teeth.

Bill hurried to Van Helsing's defense. "Not again," he said. "Not another one."

"What?" Van Helsing asked.

"Another, what you call, an abomination. Yeah. Bloodthirsty, too. Bad luck always comes in threes, you know. So the third one is going to be a real showstopper."

Bill attacked first, clouting the hideous thing with all the strength he had. The blow had little effect. Bill lurched backward, shaking his injured hand. His enemy was very tall, towering over him in a confident slouch. Despite his mental and physical handicaps, Bill was a better boxer than his opponent; he had a quicker punch, and his bob-and-weave was deft by comparison. Again and again Bill struck, but for all the pain he was causing himself, and for the complete lack of results he was achieving against his foe, Bill might as well have been beating up the brick wall.

Meanwhile, Van Helsing had as much as he could handle with Sheba. She fought like a cornered beast, ripping and tearing and biting at him. He ordered her again to release the young girl. Then he tried to reason with Sheba. Finally, he resorted to threats. Nothing worked. She was no longer human, no longer susceptible to his powers of persuasion.

He was covered with his own blood when he finally managed to throw Sheba to the ground. He'd put a foot behind one of hers, then shoved her shoulder heavily. She toppled backward, shrieking in incoherent rage. Van Helsing wasted no time congratulating himself. He reached for one of the sharpened stakes and a loose brick.

Sheba glared up at him, her lips drawn back in an animal growl. She was completely in the power of the vampire now, no longer human in any respect, yet there was also a frightened pleading in her eyes—or so Van Helsing chose to believe. Audran saw it, too.

"She's as moddy-driven as Van Helsing," Audran thought. "He's a self-righteous, demented maniac, as murderous as she is. Maybe she deserves some compassion." With an exhausting effort of will, Audran and Van Helsing reached up and popped the moddy out.

"Jeez," I muttered, dropping the plastic moddy to the ground. It was a great relief again to be rid of Van Helsing's monomania. Meanwhile, I had little time to think. I was still trying to control the enraged Sheba, who struggled and bucked in my grasp.

Bill had evidently vanquished his enemy. "That's right, pal," he said, reaching for one of the fire-hardened stakes. "You hold her and I'll ostracize her."

The first thing I did, while I ignored Bill, was to pop out Sheba's vampire moddy. The transformation was immediate and dramatic. The knowledge of what she'd done while under its influence flooded in, horrifying her. "I just couldn't take it out," she gasped between loud sobs. "Other moddies I can take or leave alone, but this one was different. I couldn't control myself."

"Some irresponsible programmer wrote that into the moddy," I said. I tried to speak in a soothing voice. I no longer feared or hated Sheba; I felt only immense sadness. She just collapsed in tears as if she hadn't heard me.

"Hey," Bill said proudly, "you notice that I took care of my guy all right?"

"Bill," I explained wearily, "you were savagely going ten rounds with a date palm."

He stared at me. "A date palm? Well, hell, who knows what afrit was inside it when it hit me. Maybe we should get somebody up here to exorcise that tree."

"It didn't hit you, Bill. I saw the whole thing from the beginning."

Bill scratched uneasily with one foot in the black soil. "Anyway, I think I killed it. Now I'm sorry, if it's only a date palm."

I gave him a reassuring smile, although I didn't really feel like it. "Don't worry, Bill. I'm sure it's only stunned."

He brightened considerably. "That's easy for you to say," he said.

I smashed both the Dracula and Van Helsing moddies with the brick. Who can say how much good that did, because the next homicidal blazebrain still had plenty of murderous moddies to choose from, at Laila's store or any of the other modshops in the Budayeen. I let out a deep sigh. I'd worry about those killers when the time came.

I helped Sheba to her feet. She was still hysterical, but now she clung to me for comfort. Her violent sobbing subsided. I saw that her vampire's elongated canine teeth were fake, a bodily modification that Sheba had paid for at one of the Budayeen store-front surgical clinics. I reached up slowly and gently pulled the fangs free.

I knew Sheba had an addictive personality—there was a lot of that going around the Budayeen these days—and although she wouldn't wear the vampire moddy again, she was more than likely going to become something just as dangerous to herself and to other people in the near future.

Still, I thought, I could hope that the sudden awareness of what she'd done would get her to seek help. There was nothing more that I could do for her now. The rest was up to Sheba herself.

In the same way, my own future would be shaped in part by the moddies I bought and wore. Hell, I'd just come very close to killing a seriously troubled young woman while I was under the influence of the Van Helsing moddy. I was certainly in no position to judge her.

That gave me an awful lot to think about, but I could put that off until later, or tomorrow, or some other time. Right then I turned my attention to Musa Ali's little sister. I untied her and satisfied myself that although she was exhausted and terrified, she was otherwise unharmed. Bill bent down and picked her up in his arms. He always got along well with children.

As the Budayeen characters began to arrive at the cemetery, drawn by the shouting and racket of our small battle with the Undead, I took Sheba's arm and led her out of the graveyard, back down the Street to her long-unused apartment. As of that moment, all she had was hope.

Introduction to
King of the Cyber Rifles

A number of people asked George why he never mentioned anything that was going on in the rest of the world during When Gravity Fails. *This would be a little like having Jane Austen mention the Napoleonic Wars during* Pride and Prejudice—*which she never does*—*or Raymond Chandler take a break during* The Big Sleep *to discuss the conquest of Poland by Nazi Germany.*

The Budayeen is the only world its inhabitants care about.

Even as personality-transfer technology was assimilated by prostitutes and pornographers, so it has been incorporated into modern warfare. Like the denizens of the Budayeen, the hero of this tale doesn't know much of what's going on in the rest of the world, and doesn't care. All he knows is where he is, and what he has to do for the rest of the day. With the amount of lies—propaganda and electronic—going around, it's all he CAN know, and sometimes not even that.

The story is almost surrealist, but has a horrifyingly genuine feel. Its hero doesn't really know why he's there or how his technology works, any more than the folks in the far-off Budayeen do. They're quite clearly in the same world, and haven't the faintest idea of each other's existence.

Like the heroes of many of George's stories, the soldier Jân Muhammad is agonizingly isolated, a reflection, I think, of George's own perception of himself. For a man as gregarious as George was, and as good at dealing with all kinds of people, he was in fact half-afraid of people, seeking solitude while simultaneously dreading it.

And, like the heroes of so many of George's stories, Jân Muhammad is simply trying to do his job in the best way that he knows how, taking what pride he can in the miniscule, mindless, and insignificant tasks he's been given.

And getting absolutely no thanks from anybody.

—Barbara Hambly

King of the Cyber Rifles

JÂN MUHAMMAD STOPPED HALFWAY UP THE STONY hill and put down his double armload of dry sticks. By the Persian calendar, it was the second week of Mordaad, the hottest part of the summer. What little grass grew on his hillside was already burnt brown for lack of rain. The dust was thick and the tumbled red rocks gave off an arid, baked smell. Jân Muhammad mopped the perspiration from his forehead with the sleeve of his uniform tunic. Flies buzzed all around his head, but he had long ago given up trying to chase them away. High overhead, the sun was a plate of brass hanging motionless. Jân Muhammad looked down reluctantly at his burden of firewood, then opened the catch at the throat of his tunic. Sand and grit had worked down under his collar and had begun to rub his neck raw. He wished he had enough water to rinse his sweat-streaked skin.

He carried the wood up the rest of the way to the observation post. He had a box for the fuel inside the small bunker, so he wouldn't need to step outside again to fetch it. If he were under attack and the broken branches were outside, he would have to suffer in the icy night of the wasteland, or do without hot soup and tea. It was still too early in the day to think of lighting the stove, though. He had a lot of work to do before evening.

The narrow room where he ate, slept, kept watch, and fought was solidly built of roughly dressed stone and cement. He had a cot and a chair he had lashed together himself out of tree limbs, a blanket, a jug of water and a basin, another basin for evacuation, a small stove, and his data deck. He did not understand how the power source worked. It was buried in the hillside beside the observation post, and supplied current to the data deck, the weapons systems, the portable communications equipment, and two bare light bulbs that glared starkly through the long, empty nights. The army had not seen fit to give him an electric stove or any other conveniences. Jân Muhammad supposed they didn't want him to get too comfortable. He could have reassured them on that point.

Like a crack of thunder from a clear sky, a mortar shell ripped a hole in the thin soil two hundred yards downslope. Jân Muhammad stood in the center of his small room, cursing softly. He'd just been thinking about a Mohâjerân raid, and now their deafening shell-bursts were walking slowly up toward his observation post, leaving craters like the devastating footprints of an invisible giant. The armed refugees had tried many times in the last year to pry the lonely soldier from his defensive position. Although they had stolen grenades, machine guns, and small arms, they had no leadership, no discipline, no strategies, and no definite goals. They were just a large mob in possession of some sophisticated weapons. They were poorly matched against Jân Muhammad and his data deck.

He sat down calmly at his work space. "Diagnostics," he murmured. The autotest lights came on, all burning green; he grabbed the red plastic command module and chipped it onto the anterior implant plug at the crown of his skull. He gasped as the hot, stale-smelling observation post melted away. His brain began to receive information only through the data deck. He saw a panoramic view of his hilltop, the rugged pass to the west, and the cracked, dry plain to the east. The view was assembled from input from many holocameras hidden in the surrounding area, processed through the data deck, and presented to Jân Muhammad in a view he might have if he were hovering peacefully some fifty feet in the air. It took him a moment to let go of his body's senses and surrender to the deck. As much as he liked chipping in, he resisted for an instant each time, with a tingling, absurd fear that on this occasion he wouldn't be able to disengage.

Jân Muhammad chipped the black personality module onto his posterior implant plug. Now it wasn't his physical environment that vanished, but Jân Muhammad himself. His own anxious, impetuous identity faded beneath an artificial construct wired into the black moddy. A fictional soldier usurped his brain, as perfect a warrior as the military programmers could make him: competent, cool, fiercely loyal, and absolutely fearless. With his distant sensors, Jân Muhammad watched the mortar shells blasting all around him, searching with terrible fingers for the stone bunker. The explosions didn't concern him. He spoke a few words to the data deck and called up a magnified scan of the eastern perimeter. He caught the glitter of sunlight on metal at six hundred yards, near a tall shoulder of rock. Without needing to put his request into words, he got the precise coordinates of the target from the data deck. He fired a salvo of demolition rockets, waited fifteen seconds, and fired a second round. He watched twenty or thirty people, men and women, young and old, all dressed in rags and carrying rifles, sprint from the blasted rocks toward new shelter across fifty yards of open plain. Jân Muhammad put down a blaze of heavy machine gun fire; none of the rebels reached their cover alive.

He turned his attention to the Mohâjerân mortars. The attackers didn't know how to use the weapons. Instead of making patterned searches, the mortar shells seemed to wobble all over the landscape. It would be only luck if one happened to find its target. Jân Muhammad was now conscious of the fact that sooner or later, the Mohâjerân might get lucky. He deduced that there couldn't be more than two mortars in operation. He analyzed the parabolic paths of a dozen shells and calculated where each mortar was hidden. He fired three explosive rockets and two fragmentation shells at the targets. A moment later, stillness settled over the hillside, broken only by the occasional racket of Mohâjerân rifle fire.

Jân Muhammad relaxed a little, knowing that he had eliminated the chief danger. Through his amplifiers he heard the shrill, trilling war cry, "Allahu akbar!" Two squads of refugees charged up the hillside, one on the north slope, the other a quarter of the way around on the western side. It was suicide. Jân Muhammad's machine guns opened up on both detachments; it took only a few seconds to dispose of them all. He would have to go out later and throw all the corpses into the defile. That irritated him more than anything else.

The rest of the Mohâjerân fled now, some shrieking and wailing for their dead comrades. Jân Muhammad watched them go, letting them escape. He didn't feel like cutting them down with machine gun bullets or rockets. He didn't feel like dealing with any more dead bodies around his post than he had to. They'd come back, they'd definitely come back; he'd kill them all another day. He popped the personality moddy out first, then the command moddy. He gasped again as his heightened senses and abilities fell away. He was once again limited to his own mortal body. The fatigue, fear, hunger, and thirst that had been obscured by the moddies flooded through him. He leaned forward and rested his head wearily on his arms. He still had his chores to finish.

By the time he'd finished breaking up the firewood and stowing it in the box, he heard a man's voice calling to him from down on the hill. "Yaa sarbaaz!" came the high-pitched, wavering cry. It was Rostam, who traveled out from the village of Ashnistan twice a week with supplies.

Jân Muhammad grunted. He was looking forward to the goat cheese and fresh bread the old man was bringing. Quickly he threw a handful of sticks onto the crumbling coals in the stove and blew the fire into life. He poured water from a hanging goatskin into a small teapot and put it on to boil.

"Yaa sarbaaz! Soldier! Turn off your guns!"

Jân Muhammad made sure that the scrawny, bearded trader was alone, then slapped off the automatic ranging and firing mechanisms. Then he went outside. "It's all right, O my uncle. Come on up." He watched Rostam pick his way slowly among the rocks, leading his raw-boned, red-eyed mule.

When Rostam came close enough so that he didn't need to shout, he gave Jân Muhammad a nod. "Salâm alêkom," he said hoarsely.

"Alêkom-os-salâm," said Jân Muhammad. "Come inside, I'm making tea."

"Thank you, my son." The old man lifted a coarse sack from the mule's back and followed the soldier into the stone strongpoint.

Jân Muhammad checked the water, but it wasn't hot yet. He turned back and offered Rostam the single chair in the bunker; he himself sat down on the edge of the cot. After a moment, he realized that the old man was staring at him. Jân Muhammad had forgotten to put his cap back on. Rostam was looking at the two chrome-steel plugs in the young man's skull. The soldier leaned forward, grabbed his tan forage cap from where it lay on his data monitor, and jammed it low over his brow.

The old man pushed his lips out, then in, then out again. "Aga, I've brought you flour, lard, cheese, tea, and a little dried meat," he said. "I've also brought you what we talked about a week ago."

Jân Muhammad raised his eyebrows.

Rostam looked around nervously, as if there were listening devices hidden in the bare stone room. As a matter of fact, the comm unit in the military data deck could transmit everything that was said in the observation post, but Jân Muhammad had learned how to cut himself out of the net. He preferred to use the portable equipment. If he ever needed to use the deck's link—if, for instance, the portable unit was disabled—he knew how to patch himself back in. "Don't worry, O my uncle, we may talk."

Rostam let out his breath in a rattling sigh. "I have brought you tobacco and some white liquor. I've brought magazines, too, aga. They're printed in some language, I don't know which, but they have good pictures. You know what I mean? Good pictures?"

Jân Muhammad nodded wearily. Rostam was his one connection to the village, to the world beyond his observation post. The soldier was not permitted to leave his small stony domain. From what his superiors said, this one hill guarding an unused pass through the Persian mountains was the key to the future of the Mahdi's army, a vital position that guaranteed the inevitable Islamic conquest. Jân Muhammad didn't believe all that, of course. He only knew that the post and the rocky defile below were his responsibility, and he was doomed—"honored," in the words of his sergeant—to remain there like a mad hermit saint until he was killed by Mohâjerân raiders or until the rest of the world acknowledged the supremacy of the young savior, whichever came first.

The young soldier jingled his few remaining coins in his pocket. The payroll officer wouldn't be coming by for at least another two weeks. Jân Muhammad guessed that before then, as usual, he would have to go a week or ten days without meat and tobacco. "How much do you want?" he asked.

"Twenty tumân, aga," said Rostam.

The soldier gave him a sharp look. The price was twice what the supplies were worth.

"Eighteen tumân," said Rostam. "It is getting difficult for me to bring these to you, my son. The shopkeeper in the village has sympathies with the Mohâjerân, he does not like selling me these things, knowing that they come to you. He charges me more than his other customers. And I am not as strong as I used to be, aga. The long journey from the village—"

"All right, I'll give you sixteen."

"You are the soul of your father," murmured Rostam, catching the coins.

"You had better go now," said Jân Muhammad. He was suddenly in a hurry to see the old man on his way back down the hill. "If the Mohâjerân should return while you're here, I can't guarantee that you'll be safe."

Rostam's eyes opened wide. He got slowly to his feet. "You are right, my son. Thank you. Praise be to Allah for your kindness."

"May you go in peace, O my uncle." He watched as the old

man hurried as fast as he could out of the bunker and down the hill. Rostam picked up a heavy stick and began beating his mule, which didn't seem to pay any attention to the blows; it neither quickened its pace nor strayed from its path. Jân Muhammad waited until both man and animal were out of sight, then he took the water off the stove and dropped a healthy pinch of tea into the pot.

When he'd finished his refreshment and began stowing his supplies, the data deck interrupted him with a recorded call of a muezzin. Jân Muhammad immediately let a bag of flour he held fall onto his cot. He went to the deck and made a quick security check of the area outside. Then he went to the goatskin and let out a little water into his hands. He thought, "I perform the ablutions to prepare myself for prayer and seeking the nearness of Allah." He drew his moist right hand briskly down from his hairline to his chin. He removed a ring on his right hand and quickly washed his right arm from elbow to fingertips. He did the same with his left arm. He drew the wet fingers of his right hand from the middle of his head forward to the hairline. He put the heel of his right hand on the toes of his right foot, and brought his fingers up to the ankle, then washed his left foot. He took his prayer rug and went outside, where he stood facing the southwest, toward the Kaaba in Makkah. While he prayed, all thoughts of his bloody battle that morning vanished. As usual, he murmured a prayer for the health of the Mahdi, and for his quick victory over the unbelievers. Jân Muhammad also added a prayer for the Muslims—like those he fought now in Mazanderan—who were in error, who had gone astray and did not recognize the Messiah who had come out of what had once been Algeria.

After his devotions, he couldn't put off the unpleasant task of tending to the slain Mohâjerân any longer. He returned the prayer rug to its place, made another security check, then decided to chip in a personality module to take his mind off his work. He chose a blue plastic moddy manufactured in Riyadh, and settled it in place on his posterior plug. He chipped in three add-ons as well, one that would override his fatigue, one to override thirst, and a third that contained the entire text of the noble Qur'ân.

The moddy took possession of his consciousness and transported him from the barren Persian landscape to a fully-realized fantasy of Paradise. He wasn't aware of the morbid labor he was performing. It was as if Jân Muhammad's soul had left his body, or as if he had been lifted physically, still alive, into Heaven. Wonder and reverence enthralled him. Here was his reward for a lifetime of faithfulness. Here was ample payment for all the hardships he had endured for the sake of his love of Allah. He was refreshed, and the pleasures of Paradise were far greater than any his earthly imagination could have invented. What he had forsaken in life was now his to enjoy. The most delicious wine gurgled from exquisite fountains. Houris more beautiful than any mortal woman smiled at him and made him welcome. Above everything else, though, was the joy of his union with God. He felt a terrible sadness when he thought of the unbelievers, how they had scorned the Straight Path and would never know this peace.

Still marveling at everything he witnessed, Jân Muhammad slowly lifted a hand to his head and popped the moddy out. He stood squinting in the bright glare of the sun for a few seconds, confused, as the real world claimed him once again. He let out a deep sigh. It was good to be able to carry a bit of Paradise with him, but it was always a painful jolt to be thrust back into his own mind, faced again with his worldly troubles. The lingering effect of the moddy was that he knew that Paradise, when he was accepted into it in truth, would be inexpressibly more blessed than what the moddy designers had offered him. "Praise be to the Lord of the Worlds," said Jân Muhammad.

He stood a few yards from his observation post, looking down into the Tang-e-Kuffâr, the Pass of the Infidels; many feet below, the broken bodies of the Mohâjerân men and women lay on the craggy floor of the defile. Their worthless automatic rifles, pistols, and grenades were now piled in a heap at the edge of the cliff. Jân Muhammad frowned, then turned and went back into the bunker.

Toward nightfall, while making another scheduled security check, he noticed movement at the northeast end of the pass. He called for greater magnification. Now he was certain; a small party, maybe twenty-five or thirty people, was moving slowly and carefully among the rocks. He watched as they stopped and knelt beside the corpses. Some of the Mohâjerân glanced upward. Jân Muhammad could see the hatred on their faces. A few of them unslung their rifles and held them ready, as if Jân Muhammad might suddenly appear, alone and vulnerable, from behind a pile of red boulders. At last the refugees left their dead fellows and continued their cautious way through the pass. Through the data deck, Jân Muhammad could hear their low murmurs, but could not make out any of their words.

He trained his guns on the rebels in the front of the column, fed the position and distance information from the data deck to the firing control, and watched as the Mohâjerân crept silently out of his field of vision. One by one, they disappeared from view through the ragged southern cut of the Tang-e-Kuffâr.

He felt a helpless rage build in him, then a swift, cold fear. He
hadn't fired a shot. He'd permitted every one of the enemy to escape
unscathed. How could that be? "By the life of my eyes," he swore.
He was no traitor, no coward. He knew the significance of what
had happened: The Mohâjerân had slipped through his guard to
the desolate valley beyond. They were free now to join others of the
growing refugee mob, to attack the Mahdi's Persian Conciliatory
Army where it was weakest. Every rebel that got by Jân Muhammad
meant injury to the Mahdi, an obstacle to the victory of orthodox
Islam.

Jân Muhammad slammed the data deck with a fist in frustration. He had to find out what had prevented him from destroying
these Mohâjerân.

He tapped the diagnostic key on the data deck. Again all the test
lights lit green. His deck was in perfect condition, both hardware
and software. The problem was not with the deck or the weapons
systems; it was with himself. That would be more difficult to deal
with. He popped the military personality moddy. His anger and
dread intensified, for Jân Muhammad was less able to confront this
crisis than the electronic mind built into the moddy. With the
command moddy still chipped in, he picked a spot high on the
walls of the mountain pass and swung his machine guns and rocket
launchers to bear on it. He wanted to let loose a few shots, but somehow the desire to fire wasn't translated into a mental command.
Nothing happened. No sound disturbed the chilly stillness of the
twilight.

With a trembling hand, Jân Muhammad popped the command
moddy out. The terrible truth was that he was now helpless and
defenseless. He had a mighty arsenal linked to his data deck; but
if he was somehow blocked from using it, he might as well be sitting on the hilltop with nothing more deadly than a slingshot. If
the Mohâjerân learned the truth, he could be overwhelmed and
murdered before the next day was out.

The thing to do now was contact his platoon sergeant. He used
the portable transmitter. It took a few minutes to calculate the
proper frequency for the day, tune the scrambler, identify himself
to his headquarters and be recognized, and get patched through to
Sergeant Abadani. He had to wait a long while. Finally, he heard
the sergeant's grumbling, cheerless voice. "Listen, sarbaaz, I'm
going to tell you why you called me. Let me know if I'm right. You
saw some goddamn Mohâjerân mucks and you proceeded to set up
your attack by the numbers. Everything was fine until it was time to
fire. Then you couldn't. You didn't stop a single one of the bastards.
Right?"

Jân Muhammad was startled. "Right, Sarge. How—?"

"You're not the only one that's happened to today. Now, where are you?"

"The Tang-e-Kuffâr."

"Yeah. Well, seven of your buddies have called in with the same story. What we've figured is that somebody has entered your station and fed a baggie to your data deck. That's what happened to the other seven posts."

"But nobody has access to my deck but me."

"That's what they all said. But in every case, they could think of some Persian who had been permitted inside the bunker."

Jân Muhammad opened his mouth to protest, then closed it again. "There's an old man from Ashnistan who brings me my food. He's such a feeble old son of a bitch that I usually make him tea and let him rest inside my bunker."

"And you like talking to him, too, right? Against orders?"

"Yes," Jân Muhammad admitted. "I don't get to see anyone else."

"Is he your likely suspect?"

"He's the *only* suspect, Sarge."

"Good. Well, then, the next time you see him, you're going to have to neutralize him."

Jân Muhammad stared at the transmitter for a moment. "Maybe it would be better to let him live," he said.

"The orders are to get rid of these saboteurs."

"But, Sarge, the Mohâjerân are behind all this. When they know their agent has done what he's supposed to, they're sure they're safe. They can just sneak through the pass whenever they want. I can't use my guns or rockets. But if I kill old Rostam, they'll know something's up. They'll know we're on to them. If I just act normally and let Rostam think he's safe, I may be able to account for a few refugee patrols before they catch on and start their frontal attacks again. That's if I can get my weapons systems operational again."

"Don't worry about that. We'll have a tech team out to you tomorrow as soon as we can." Now it was the sergeant's turn to fall silent for a few seconds. "You might have an idea there, sarbaaz. I'll mention it to the lieutenant."

"So what's wrong with my data deck, then?"

Sergeant Abadani gave a humorless laugh. "You don't know what a baggie is?"

"I'm a gunner, Sarge, I'm not a deck expert."

"You're supposed to be both. Your Persian slipped a bubble microplate into your deck, just long enough for your deck to copy it and add it to its memory. It wasn't an assassin program, but it was a crippler. Your deck won't respond to certain orders now, not through your cyberlink. It'll feed you sensory input and perform harmless functions, but it won't take any sort of offensive or defensive action. It's like your spy tied a little invisible bag around a part of your deck's operating system, isolating it and making it inaccessible to you. Until tomorrow, when we can slice out the baggie."

"Well, what the hell am I supposed to do until then? What if I'm attacked?"

"You probably won't be. Like you said, the rebels figure you're more useful the way you are, with your teeth pulled. They don't want to give the show away. They'll just parade a few more units through the pass."

Jân Muhammad frowned. "Is there any way I can operate the weapons systems the hard way? Bypassing the cyberlink?"

"Sure," said Sergeant Abadani, "but you said you weren't an expert. There's a sequence of options that will let you fire any of your guns and rockets by selecting from a series of menus. It takes a lot of time. If you've never worked with it, it probably won't be any use to you."

"But it's better than letting those bastards get by me. I hate the idea of watching them troop past like a gang of schoolchildren on a holiday."

"Your attitude's all right, sarbaaz, but you don't know what you're talking about." Then the sergeant told his gunner how to request the firing control menus from the data deck.

"That won't be bagged, too?" asked Jân Muhammad.

"It wasn't on the other seven decks."

"All right, Sarge."

"Report back if you see any action. We'll be there sometime tomorrow. Now, clear the air."

Jân Muhammad signed off. He tapped in the commands that called up the first of the attack menus.

> *Do you wish to activate automatic rifles?*
> *Enter 1=yes, 0=no*
> *Do you wish to activate submachine guns?*
> *Enter 1=yes, 0=no*
> *Do you wish to activate heavy machine guns?*
> *Enter 1=yes, 0=no*
> *Do you wish to activate 40 millimeter cannons?*
> *Enter 1=yes, 0=no*
> *Do you wish to activate trench mortars?*

Enter 1=yes, 0=no
Do you wish to activate light artillery?
Enter 1=yes, 0=no
Do you wish to activate antitank guns?
Enter 1=yes, 0=no
Do you wish to activate antiaircraft guns?
Enter 1=yes, 0=no

A second menu presented him choices of rockets and bombs. A third menu let him activate the antipersonnel and antitank mines buried on the hillside and in the defile. It took Jân Muhammad a quarter of an hour to go through the entire sequence. If he had initiated the selection process just when he'd spotted a party of Mohâjerân, they would have run safely through the pass before he was finished. And he hadn't even begun the targeting and firing procedures. The sergeant had been right; this was worse than useless.

He chipped in the command moddy and let his deck-enhanced senses make certain there were no Mohâjerân nearby. He chose a flat place on the floor of the Tang-e-Kuffâr that the rebels would have to cross in order to flee into the valley beyond. Caught for a moment in the open, they would have to choose between running a hopeless race through a storm of machine gun bullets or giving up and retracing the way they had come.

Through the cyberlink, Jân Muhammad knew the coordinates, in three dimensions, of every point within range of the cameras. With the link, he experienced the weapons systems as extensions of his augmented mind. He tried firing a few shots, willing the guns to open up on the target. When they remained silent, he sighed and called up the attack menu, then began running through the time-consuming manual procedures.

Do you wish to fire submachine guns?
Enter 1=yes, 0=no

Jân Muhammad typed 1.

Do you wish continuous fire?
Enter 1=yes, 0=no

Jân Muhammad typed 0.

How many rounds do you wish to fire?

Jân Muhammad typed 5.

To commence firing on your mark, type 1.

When he typed 1, each submachine gun that could bear on the target spat five rounds into the hard-packed earth. Although it was a dark, moonless night, the data deck let him see the clouds of flying rock chips and dust. He felt better knowing that he could still operate his weapons, even in this clumsy way. He relaxed for the first time since early in the day, when he'd failed to stop the Mohâjerân party from making their defiant escape.

Just before dawn, after Jân Muhammad had succumbed to fatigue and was suffering through an uneasy dream of childhood and poverty, an alarm woke him. He swung groggily off his cot and leaned over the data deck, fumbling the command moddy and the military personality moddy into place. He felt a familiar elation as the confining bunker dissolved, replaced by an immediate awareness of every movement, every scent, every sound around his post.

Another small unit of Mohâjerân was picking its way through the mountain pass. They were moving boldly, confidently, knowing that Jân Muhammad's armaments were disabled. He had an unpleasant surprise waiting for them.

When the first of the refugees reached the target, he jabbed his finger down on the 1 key. The shrill scream of the machine gun bullets ricocheting off rocks filled the narrow pass. Three unfortunate people at the head of the column howled and fell wounded to the red dirt. After a short while, however, the Mohâjerân realized that all the machine gun fire was aimed at one place. They began to move cautiously around that area, giving it as much room as they could. One by one, they gathered courage and slipped by to one side.

Jân Muhammad cursed. Of course, he could retarget the machine guns to another point, but the same thing would happen again. The enemy would realize they were safe elsewhere in the defile. And it was pointless to aim the guns by tapping information into the data deck. The refugees would all be gone long before he got the next position set up.

Jân Muhammad hurried outside. The deep blue sky of the false dawn and a cool breeze gave the morning an innocence that was pure illusion. Jân Muhammad knelt briefly on the edge of the cliff, glaring down in frustration, until a few shots from below made him scuttle back. That gave him an idea. Not far away, the weapons of the Mohâjerân he had killed were stacked together until headquarters sent someone to collect them. Jân Muhammad grabbed a plastic and alloy-steel automatic rifle. He examined it quickly; it was in disgraceful condition, but with luck it wouldn't blow up in his face. He lay down with his head raised just high enough to see over the edge.

Jân Muhammad waited for a chance to avenge the insult they had paid him. When he saw a flicker of motion, he squeezed off a few rounds and was gratified to hear a shrill cry of pain. He still had his command moddy chipped in, so he was getting an unbroken view of the pass from one end to the other. He could see where each rebel had concealed himself. They had neutralized his data deck and his heavy weapons, but they were wrong if they thought he was going to admit defeat. He would fight even if he were reduced to throwing rocks and stones. He grinned as he looked down patiently from the cyberlink, down at his enemy. They didn't realize how exposed they were.

Besides the rifles, Jân Muhammad had captured a number of grenades as well. He began tossing them down into the Tang-e-Kuffâr, flushing some of the refugees from hiding. The Mohâjerân decided to chance a break, and as they sprinted through the pass, Jân Muhammad picked them off in their panic. He had been trained to use cyberlinked guns, not conventional infantry weapons; but now the refugees were learning how badly they had underestimated him. When the sun first edged over the broad, parched plain, he had accounted for half the Mohâjerân in the party.

As the morning stretched on, he got a few more as they attempted to rush by him, and the rest when they withdrew up the winding, unprotected path. He stood up at last, his neck muscles aching and stiff. He hadn't given up, although the refugees had taken away his advantage. Even if the Mohâjerân tried storming his bunker again, he wasn't afraid. Without the cyber weapons, he was still confident that he could keep them from overrunning his position. He wondered what Sergeant Abadani would say when he heard that Jân Muhammad, using antique guns and toy rifles, had beaten a unit of Mohâjerân.

Hours later, while he was frying some flour in lard and chewing on a greasy stick of dried mutton, Rostam's voice called to him from the bottom of the hill. The old man sounded frightened. That made Jân Muhammad laugh, but it was a somber and dangerous laugh. Jân Muhammad was curious if Rostam had been sent to try another scheme of some kind. The old man was a fool, and Jân Muhammad might have been amused, except he understood clearly that if Rostam had been successful, Jân Muhammad might well be dead now.

"Yaa sarbaaz!" Rostam's voice quavered in the hot, still air. "Yaa sarbaaz, we must talk!"

Jân Muhammad kept scraping the browning flour in the pan. He added another spoonful of lard and watched it melt. "Rostam?" he called.

"We must talk!" The spy was terrified.

"Why do you say that? What do we have to talk about?"

"Don't act that way, aga. Please let me explain. Let me come up."

"Explain if you want to, but do it from out there. This bunker stinks enough as it is."

"I can't just stand here and shout at you, aga."

"Why the hell not?"

There was a pause. Jân Muhammad glanced out and saw Rostam shifting nervously from one foot to the other. He held his large stick, but the mule was nowhere to be seen. "Listen, O worthy one: It is true that I did as the Mohâjerân ordered, but I was forced to do it. They threatened me. I'm many times a grandfather, I'm all used up. I can't stand up to strong young men when they force their way into my home."

"They gave you something to put into my data deck?"

"Yes, aga."

Jân Muhammad muttered a curse. "Did you think you were helping me, when you did what they told you?"

Another pause. "No, aga, but I had no choice! The shopkeeper in the village, he was with them, and he said that I'd die slowly in front of everyone if I did not cooperate. He said that he'd never sell me another loaf of bread, another bottle of wine for solace in my old age."

"But you never thought to warn me. You were more afraid of this shopkeeper and the refugees than all of the Mahdi's army. You are *worse* than the Mohâjerân; you have refused the service of the blessed Mahdi. You think only of your worthless belly, when you were given an opportunity to benefit the deputy of Allah."

"I was afraid, aga!"

Jân Muhammad spat in disgust. "You've made that very clear, old man. You threw in your lot with the Mohâjerân, so now you'll have to ask for protection from them. I wish you luck."

"But, sarbaaz, the entire village . . . when they heard, they drove me out, into the desert—"

"And what do you want from me? Sympathy?"

Rostam began to weep. "I can't live without food, without water. Where will I go?"

Jân Muhammad had stopped paying attention. He tapped a few keys on the data deck.

Do you wish to fire submachine guns?
Enter 1=yes, 0=no

Jân Muhammad typed 1.

"Sarbaaz! *Help* me! I beg you, as one servant of Allah to another!"

"You submit when it serves your purpose," shouted the soldier. "And when it doesn't serve your purpose, you break every law of the Prophet, may blessings be upon his name and peace."

Do you wish continuous fire?
Enter 1=yes, 0=no

Jân Muhammad typed 1.

"Pity me!" Rostam was hysterical. He had fallen to his knees in the stony soil, and now he raised his arms in supplication. "Think of your own father. Would you treat *him* this way?"

"My own father would not have left me weak and vulnerable to my enemies, and he wouldn't have taken sides with the haters of Allah."

To commence firing on your mark, type 1.

"Bismillah!" screamed Rostam. He fell forward, laying his forehead in the dust, trembling with terror.

Jân Muhammad's finger descended over the keys, hesitated, then hung motionless in the air. He could not bring himself to murder this wretched old man. "Go!" he called. "Get off my hill! Go starve to death in the wilderness! Walk to Jerusalem and ask the forgiveness of the Mahdi!"

"'Whoever forgives and amends, he shall have his just reward from Allah,'" quoted Rostam. He staggered off, away from the young man he had betrayed, away from the village that had turned him out.

Jân Muhammad closed his eyes tightly, wondering at his sudden change of heart. "In the profane mouth of an unbeliever," he murmured, "even the words of the Prophet can lose their beauty." Behind him, unheeded, his poor midday meal burned and was ruined. With his augmented vision, Jân Muhammad watched the old man until he was out of sight, swallowed up by the seared and withered expanse of waste.

Introduction to
Marîd Throws a Party

This was the first portion—two chapters—of the fourth Budayeen book, Word of Night, *and the only part to actually have been written. When I met George in 1990 (not counting the several times we'd been in the same room and HADN'T met, but that's another story), he was working on these.* The Exile Kiss *had just been published, and the editors asked him for an outline of* Word of Night *(untitled, then) so they could get a cover-painting done. George didn't have an outline, but since they needed to know SOMETHING that happened in the book, he said it started out with a party at Marîd's club, which was all he knew about what happened in the book at the time. Later he and I worked out an outline for it, a wonderful story which I had hoped, in the fullness of time, to see through to fruition.*

When he died in 2002, these first two chapters were still all he had written.

Brilliant chapters, and what promised to be a wonderful book.

—*Barb Hambly*

✝ ✝ ✝

Marîd Throws a Party

I KNOW THE MOST FRIGHTENING WORDS IN THE world.

Imagine waking up and having someone say, "Do you know what you *did* last night?" I shiver just thinking about it. I've heard those words before, and I pray to Allah I never hear them again.

It was Kmuzu who murmured that horrible question to me one morning. Kmuzu was a black African given to me by Friedlander Bey. I had not wanted a slave, just as I hadn't wanted any of the other things Friedlander Bey had given me. Still, it just wasn't good policy to turn Papa down. Everyone in the Budayeen—hell, everyone in the entire *city*—knew that.

Over the last few years, however, Kmuzu had become quite a lot more than a slave to me. He was someone I'd come to depend on; God well knew that I couldn't always depend on myself. I needed someone like Kmuzu to look out for me from time to time. He was loyal and honest, a good man for a Christian.

Despite that, I could've done without the disapproval in his voice when he woke me up. I looked at him, my eyes bleary and my mouth tasting like I'd French-kissed a pigeon coop. "Yallah," I groaned, feeling a booming throb in my head just behind my eyes.

"You need some breakfast, yaa Sidi," Kmuzu said.

That was an infidel's answer for everything: food. I didn't want food, not ever again. The whole idea of breakfast was already nauseating me. "All right, you're going to tell me anyway," I said. "I'm a tough guy, I can take it. What'd I do last night?"

"There was a party." He watched me trying to maneuver myself out of bed.

Yes, there had been a party, all right. It had been at my nightclub —well, the club I own with my partner, Chiriga. It had been a going-away party in my honor, because in a few days Papa and I were embarking on the pilgrimage to the holy city of Makkah.

This is one of the Five Pillars of Islam, something required of every Muslim at least once during his lifetime. Neither Friedlander Bey nor I had fulfilled that obligation, although we had spoken of making the hajj every year as the month of Dhul-Hijjah approached. Now this year, 1632 on the Islamic calendar, 2205 of the Christian era, we'd decided that we were at last both healthy enough and able. There was no way of knowing, of course, how many dead bodies would accumulate during our sacred and spiritual quest.

Anyway, to celebrate this holy undertaking, my friends had turned my place of business into an even more raucous den of licentiousness. I guess it seemed reasonable at the time. I only wished I could recall more of what had gone on.

I didn't have any problem remembering what I'd done earlier in the day. I'd conspired with a Damascene whore to revenge myself on a man, someone who had betrayed my trust and stolen some money from me. The financial loss had been insignificant; it was the insult that had to be dealt with.

The man was Fuad, whom the people of the Budayeen called il-Manhous, which means something like "the Universally Despised." When the Greek philosopher Plato sat down to consider the Ideal Form of "loser," it was Fuad he imagined.

No one really liked Fuad. He whined, he begged, and he couldn't carry out the simplest tasks without finding humiliating new ways to screw up. Still, his reputation was that he was a pitiful guy but basically harmless. I never would've believed him clever enough to scam me for twenty-four-hundred kiam, yet he had. I couldn't let him get away with that, of course, but I could afford to be patient enough to work out a satisfying counter-sting.

Friedlander Bey, my great-grandfather and the most powerful man in the city, hears of everything that happens. I hear *almost* everything, because I'm Papa's trusted right-hand man and because a lot gets said in my nightclub when the liquor's flowing.

It was a little after two o'clock in the afternoon, about eight hours before the party was due to begin. I was sitting in my usual spot at the bar, where it curved in the back. Chiriga had thrown together my first white death of the day—gin, bingara, and a little Rose's lime juice. I had a chipzine plugged into one of my two corymbic implants, and I was hearing a speech by the new amir of Mauretania, the country where I'd been born. As for all the seminaked women, sexchanges, and debs in the club, they were no distraction. After the first hundred thousand twirling tassels, the industry begins to lose some of its raw fascination.

The lovely young Yasmin sat beside me, sipping peppermint schnapps. She was a gorgeous, black-haired sexchange with whom I'd been having an on-again, off-again affair for the last few years. I was glad to have her back working for me. She put down her glass and stretched her lithe body. "Never guess what I heard," she said, yawning.

Yasmin hears almost as much gossip as I do, but her problem is she *believes* all of it. I reached up and popped out my chipzine. "You heard that they're going to build a replica of the Budayeen out in the desert so the tourists won't bother us local residents around here."

Yasmin's dark eyes grew larger. "No! *Are* they? For real?"

"Forget it, Yasmin, I just made that up. What did you hear?"

She lifted her peppermint schnapps again and sucked up the rest of it noisily through a straw. "Fuad, that's what."

I raised my eyebrows. "What about Fuad?"

"Oh, just that he's back in town. I heard it from Floor-Show Fanya who works over by the Red Light."

I nodded. The Red Light had always been Fuad's favorite club. Dumb criminals really *do* return to the scene of the crime, as if the Felons Federation had given him a copy of their pamphlet *Common Sense: Why Bother?* Here he was back in the city and probably believing that I'd never find out about it.

"I praise Allah for your good news," I said. "That's Fuad's idea of laying low, huh?"

"You heard how he's got this weird thing about going out with the black working girls. They know they can rob him all day and all night long. It gets him hot or something. Now he's got himself a job as an itinerant crumber."

I closed my eyes and rubbed my forehead. It was only two in the afternoon, and already things were getting a little strange. "The hell is an itinerant crumber, Yasmin?"

"Oh, a guy who travels from town to town, friendless and alone, living on his wits, with his stainless steel implement. He scrapes away the bread crumbs and stuff between courses in good restaurants."

"You mean like a busboy?"

"Sure," she said, nodding. Then she shook her head. "No, not really. Crumbing is one step below busboy. He's working over by Anna's restaurant in the Hotel Palazzo di Marco Aurelio, you want to go see."

Didn't interest me. "What, he wears a white shirt and a bow tie and all that waiter drag?"

Yasmin nodded again. "Yeah, but he's so starved-looking, he's no great advertisement for the restaurant."

"Shukran," I said. Thanks. "Very interesting, sweetheart."

"Thought you'd like to hear it." She squeezed my arm, slipped off her stool, and casually made her way down the bar toward the three customers who'd just come into the club. There were worse ways to get hustled than by buying Yasmin drinks for an hour.

Chiriga, my good friend, partner, and barmaid, rested her elbows on a clean bar towel. She noticed that I'd already knocked back about half my white death. "You take it easy with those," she said, frowning. "I think Papa and Kmuzu are right. You're more fun to have around when you're not drunk or taking pills."

I didn't even answer. This was one of those black-pot kettle-calling times. Instead, I looked around our club. There were five dancers working for us in the daytime. One was Yasmin; one was the beautifully restructured real girl, Pualani; the third was Lily, a sexchange who had a crush on me; and two new dancers named Baby and Kitty. I hadn't yet read them: Were they real girls, debs, changes? I didn't really need to know, but everyone else on the Street hung on the day the truth would come out.

"Slow shift so far," I said.

"Always slow in the daytime. The really kinky girls make more money at night."

"So why don't you work nights again and make more money?"

Chiri looked at me as if I were stupid. "Didn't I just say? 'Cause the really kinky girls are there." She gave a little shudder, as if she herself hadn't seen everything and done it all twice.

"Depends on your definition of kinky," I said. I was twisting my thin little red straw into an equilateral triangle.

Chiri grinned at me. Her strong white teeth were filed to points, the ancient fashion among the old cannibals back home. "*I'm* kinky, Marîd. *You're* kinky. Every girl, deb, and change here in the afternoon is kinky. But those bitches at night, though—wow, kinky is what they did *last* summer. They're into whole new realms by now. I don't even want to think about it."

"Another drink, Chiri, please." She took my tumbler and scooped some ice cubes into it, then went to the back bar for the bingara.

I thought some more about Fuad. I suppose that with my connections I could've gotten even with him with less expensive preparations, but I didn't care at all about the money. Papa had made me wealthier than I'd ever dreamed, although I never let anyone know the details. As far as my interest in Fuad was concerned, it was the principle of the thing. And after all, I was planning to get back my twenty-four-hundred kiam, as well as every copper fiq that I would invest in the scheme to make it work.

Now, what did I know for sure? Only that Fuad was back in the city, working at the Ristorante Maximo, and still courting trouble nightly at Fatima and Nassir's Red Light Lounge. Good enough. It was time to set my scheme in motion.

I unclipped my phone from my belt and whispered Sulome's name into it. The phone found her stored commcode and began ringing. After a few moments, I heard her voice, husky with sleep. "Marhaba," she said.

"Il-hamdu lillaah!" I said. Praise be to God. "I'm sorry I woke you up, Sulome. It's Marîd Audran." Chiri brought my second white death, and served it to me with a decided lack of graciousness.

"You couldn't have waited another couple of hours?" Sulome sounded grumpy. "It was a long night."

"I said I was sorry. Anyway, the guy I told you about came back to the city a few weeks ago, and he's just lately started showing up in all his old haunts. I think it's a good time to take him down, if you're not too busy, of course."

There was a pause from Sulome. "Well, I've got nothing important lined up. What do you want me to do?"

I looked at my watch. "You go back to sleep. I'll send one of my associates—"

"One of your murdering thugs, you mean."

I smiled. "Bin Turki's reliable. I'll send him on a suborbital with your ticket and half the money we agreed on. You'll both be back in the city by sunset prayers tonight. I'll have my man Kmuzu meet your flight and take you to our house. We'll sort out all the small details in the morning."

"Fine," Sulome said in a bored voice.

"And keep your hands off bin Turki. He's a good kid."

Sulome laughed. "Sure, except he kills people. Whatever you say, Audran. See you later." And then I was listening to empty dial tone.

I returned the phone to my belt and felt good. Business is business, and action is action—and I liked action better.

I slammed back the second drink and stood up. Yasmin was being shyly courted by a quiet Eur-Am guy. Lily had taken up conversation with a dark Mediterranean gentleman. Pualani was busily describing something chest-high to a man with Asian features. And Baby and Kitty were, as usual, brushing each other's hair. There were other customers for them to try, men who would probably fall all over themselves buying champagne cocktails just to hear their low, purring voices, yet they only had eyes for each other.

"Going home early," I announced to Chiri.

"When you get there," she said, "tell that fine young man, Kmuzu, to come park his ass in here for a while. I think I could teach him a thing or two."

"You and I both know you could teach him plenty. You've heard him, though. Won't mess with a woman while he's still my slave, he says."

Chiri grinned slowly. "And that gets me so *crazy*. I think about him a lot, you know."

"I know you do."

"I think about him a *lot*." She waved the bar towel at me, and I went out into the bright, hot, afternoon sun.

I didn't want to wait for Kmuzu to come pick me up in my car, so I walked along the Street to get something to eat. It seemed as if every kind of flower in the world was in bloom, hanging in pots from balconies in a shower of pink, purple, white, red, and blue; it was like daytime neon. The air was still except for the lazy buzzing of insects—and the signals of the boys and men who watched over me while I was in the Budayeen. They whistled an old children's tune that told me all was clear, I wasn't being followed.

I bought a stick of broiled meat, onions, and peppers from the sidewalk window at Vast Foods. The kebab wasn't really all that huge; "vast" had been only a sign painter's error. The lamb and beef were coated in a rich, sticky sauce and I savored every succulent bite. It was one of those days when I realized again how much I'd given up, to move from the street life into the magnificent mansion of Friedlander Bey.

Beyond the eastern gate was the gorgeous Boulevard il-Jameel, with towering palm trees and carefully tended flowerbeds planted on the median strip. I walked to the cabstand and, yes, Bill was there. I was feeling confident and content, so much so that I was almost positive I would live through another ride with him.

"Bill," I said, "you want to take me home?"

"Sorry, pal, but I only go home with girls."

In any conversation with Bill, you had to give him a good head start because he's generally slower on the uptake than most people.

That's because most people haven't traded one of their lungs for an artificial sac dripping measured amounts of lightspeed hallucinogen into their bloodstream. That's what Bill did, and that's what's made him into the barrel-of-fun, hold-onto-your-hat kind of driver that he was. Much of the time he's crashing his cab through monstrous threatening paisleys that only he can see.

I ride with him because few other people will, and because I've seen those paisleys often enough myself.

"What I meant, Bill, was will you take me to Friedlander Bey's house?"

"Papa, huh? Why didn't he come down and get you himself?"

"Told him I'd rather ride with you. It's faster."

Bill snorted. "Sure as hell is that. I can make it even faster if you want. We can try for the land speed record, you know. As long as the streets are clear of bugs. They got bugs now, you know. *Big* bugs. Bugs as big as . . . as big as *things*." He shivered.

"Won't be any bugs around with me in the car," I said calmly.

"No? You sure? You promise? Okay then, get in."

"Oh, and Bill? We don't have to try for the land speed record. Maybe next time."

"Next time," he muttered. "Son of a bitch, it's *always* next time."

We careened through narrow, twisting lanes, depending solely on Bill's shrill horn and good karma to keep us from smashing into a jutting building or a recalcitrant pack animal. There was no direct route from the Budayeen to Papa's estate near the Christian quarter, so Bill tried to make one. All in all, though, it was a good ride: Once again I'd survived, which was what counted most.

I paid Bill his fare and added a generous tip in the hope that he'd spend it on something sensible, such as food or shelter, instead of anti-bug-and-paisley weapons. The expatriate from the American republic of Sovereign Deseret backed out of the white-pebbled driveway. I heard the small stones crunching and then the burring sound of Bill's electric taxi heading back toward the Budayeen.

Papa's house—and now my home, as his legitimate though reluctant heir—was hidden behind half a jungle of tall, slender trees, well-kept shrubbery, and masses of flowering plants. It must have cost Friedlander Bey a small fortune to coax that floral effusion from the dry, sandy soil of the city. I hoped he enjoyed the beautiful result, although I'd never once heard him remark on it.

I looked up at the towers built at the corners of the walled estate. When I'd first come here, my suspicions were that they housed armed guards. They did, of course, all except the minaret, up which

Papa's personal muezzin climbed five times daily to call him to prayer. Papa would have nothing to do with the electronic recordings that called almost everyone else in the city through loudspeakers.

I went slowly up the broad, smooth marble stairs to the house's entrance. Before I reached the carved front door, Youssef, our butler, opened it. "I pray to God that the day is pleasant to you, Shaykh Marîd."

"Salâm alêkom," I said. Peace be with you.

"Alêkom-os-salâm," Youssef murmured.

"Thanks, Youssef," I said. I walked by him. I wanted to go straight to my apartments in the west wing. When I got there, I found Kmuzu, my slave and watchdog, busily straightening my already achingly clean and neat rooms.

"You are home before we expected you," Kmuzu said. "Are you not feeling well?"

"I'm just fine."

"Can I get you something to eat, then? It's well past lunch time."

I sighed. "No, I grabbed something in the Budayeen. Please find bin Turki and send him to my office."

"I must tell you that the master of the house wishes to see you at your earliest convenience."

"I'll be having dinner with him later. For now, send bin Turki to me."

Kmuzu nodded. "Immediately, yaa Sidi." Kmuzu was a *very* good slave.

I had been seated at my desk for only a few minutes, making flight reservations through one of the data decks, when Kmuzu announced bin Turki. The young man came from a nomadic Bedu tribe called the Bani Salim. He had returned with me to the city because he had a great hunger to see and learn new things. He was becoming a very useful helper; he merely shrugged and did what I asked, and showed no hesitation about the more "difficult" tasks I assigned him.

"God grant you peace, O Shaykh, inshallah," he said. You hear the word inshallah a lot around the city; it means "if Allah wills."

"May your day be happy, bin Turki,"

"You sent for me, Shaykh Marîd?"

"Yes, O Clever One. I've just purchased your ticket on the next suborbital to Ash-Shâm. Damascus. It will be a good experience for you to visit that ancient place."

"Ash-Shâm!" bin Turki said with wonder. "The mother city of them all! I've dreamt of going there. What must I do for you?"

"A simple task. Here, the data deck is finished printing. Two round-trip tickets, one for you to and from Ash-Shâm, a second round-trip from there to this city and back. You are to fetch a woman called Sulome el-Khabbâz. Here is her address and comm-code. She'll be expecting you."

"If Allah grants it, there will be no difficulty."

"Please bring her directly to this house," I said. "Make her comfortable if I'm not home to receive her. I will tell Kmuzu to attend to her needs. Tell no one about her—as impossible as it sounds, try to keep her secret even from Youssef, Tariq, the Stones That Speak, and especially the master of the house. May you go and come in safety."

"I understand, O Shaykh," bin Turki said. "Salâm alêkom." He took the suborbital tickets and Sulome's address and left my office. When you gave that young Bedu a job, he just went ahead and did it, and he never complained. I liked bin Turki and trusted him. He reminded me of myself at a certain age.

I spent the rest of the afternoon going over ledgers, reports, and financial accounts. Reconciling the daily figures wasn't nearly as enjoyable as people-watching in Chiri's, but I hadn't been elevated from punkhood merely to have fun. I'd guessed early on that I was in training for . . . something.

I worked at my data deck until Kmuzu came up behind me and murmured that it was almost time for dinner. I wasn't unhappy to close the books for another day.

Dining with Friedlander Bey meant changing into more traditional Arab clothing. Kmuzu had laid out a clean white gallebeya with a light tan cloak to wear over it, a black-and-white-checked keffiya—the Arab headdress—with a simple black rope akal to hold it in place, as well as sandals instead of my dusty black boots. This was all to keep Friedlander Bey happy; he was almost two hundred years old, and he was getting a little conservative in his old age.

Even after all this time, I was still a little unnerved by our meetings. I had never gotten over my awe of Papa's kinglike power. When he was pleased with me and my activities, he was like a loving father. Just as often, however, his eyes would narrow and grow stern with unvoiced displeasure.

I'd purchased a gift for Papa, and I brought it along as Kmuzu and I walked toward the smaller dining room. When we arrived, we were confronted by Papa's huge, grim-faced bodyguards, the Stones That Speak. "Habib," I greeted one. "Labib," I greeted the other. I never knew if I attached the correct name to the right individual, they were so alike. Fortunately, they never responded, however offended they might have been.

"Wait," Habib or Labib said from above my head.

We waited.

It did not take long for the other Stone to discover that we were, after all, expected. "Go in," he said. His voice was like the sound of granite being scraped by a blunt stone chisel.

We went in. Papa reclined on one of his elegant, expensive divans. There was a second divan facing him, and between us was a table spread with all sorts of meat, vegetables, and fruit dishes. Friedlander Bey raised a glass of sweet mint tea, "Ahlan wa sahlan," he said, welcoming me.

I rested comfortably on the second divan. Kmuzu stood silently behind me. I raised my glass of mint tea toward Papa and said, "May your table last forever."

He smiled and replied, "May Allah lengthen your life."

We continued through a series of formalized Arab niceties until I announced, "I have brought you a gift, O Shaykh."

Papa was pleased. "And I have one for you, as well, my nephew."

By Almighty God, this was the last thing I wanted to hear— that Friedlander Bey had yet another one of his gifts for me. All the others had changed my life in unexpected and generally unwelcome ways. Of course, everywhere else in the world it's considered impolite to refuse a present. Here in the city, in the midst of a land of Arab customs and Muslim traditions, such a show of ingratitude toward Papa could easily prove harmful to my well being.

"You are the Father of Generosity, O Shaykh," I said. I had a tense, uncomfortable feeling in my belly, but I said it anyway.

Papa smiled at me indulgently. He enjoyed these occasions, principally because he was almost always the one in control. Few people caught Papa by surprise; if they did, they were usually instructed by Habib or Labib not to let it happen again. "It's nothing," Friedlander Bey said. "A mere trifle, really, yet I'm sure that you'll find my gift profitable and rewarding."

Papa had given me Chiriga's, once upon a time. The nightclub had also proven to be profitable and rewarding. Of course, for a long while I lost the friendship of Chiriga herself, because she hadn't really wanted to sell her establishment. Friedlander Bey had "persuaded" her. I wondered if his new present would have similar effects.

"May the Prophet of Allah—peace be upon him—bless you for your kindness," I said. "I'm sure that I'll be greatly surprised and pleased." Well, surprised, anyway.

"It gives me great satisfaction to make this small gesture," he said. He waved a hand to show how negligible his effort had been. I didn't buy it for a minute.

"Please, my uncle," I said, "allow me to show you what I've done. First, may I offer you this special edition of the noble Qur'ân?" According to common practice, you're not supposed to buy or sell the holy book—a willing student of the Straight Path shouldn't be prevented by poverty from learning the wisdom of the Qur'ân. The clever local way around this decree is that the contents of the book are always free of charge, but the merchant may sell the *binding* for whatever he can get. In this particular case, I'd had some of the best artists and craftsmen in the city create a beautiful, one-of-a-kind copy of the scriptures for Friedlander Bey, to take with him on the holy pilgrimage.

"This volume is truly lovely," he said, as he turned the gold-edged pages. "Of course, even the plainest edition would be more than good enough for me. All that really matters is that I have the solace and guidance of the inspired words of the Disciple of God, may the blessings of Allah be on him and peace." His words were modest, but the tone of his voice and his expression said something else. I could tell that he was very happy with my gift.

"There is still more, O Shaykh," I said.

His eyes opened wider. "More?"

"Yes, if you will permit it. I've taken the liberty of making all the necessary bookings for our pilgrimage. You've told me your father's story often, about his own journey to Makkah. Well, I've done a little research, and I've arranged for us to follow exactly in his footsteps. We will hire the same means of transportation and stop at the same lodgings along the way. We will find our guides through the same agencies, and conduct our pilgrimage as much like your father's as is possible in this day and age." After all, a century and a half had passed since my twice-great-grandfather had made his trip to the holy city.

I don't believe I'd ever seen Friedlander Bey completely astonished before. He started to say something, closed his mouth, opened it again, then gave up. He raised a hand to his forehead and shut his eyes for a moment. If it hadn't been Papa—if he had been, say, an *ordinary* person—I might have thought he was about to show some strong emotion.

Instead, he quickly regained his composure and gave me only the briefest of smiles. Friedlander Bey had not climbed to the summit of wealth and power in the city by letting just anyone know his true thoughts and feelings. He put the copy of the Qur'ân aside and said quietly, "You've given me great happiness, my nephew. Now I will tell you what I've planned in return."

I couldn't imagine what Papa had done for me. A new car would've been nice, I guess; I just hoped I wasn't getting another slave or some valuable treasure that had been grabbed away from one of my dearest friends.

"A few years ago," Friedlander Bey said, picking up a sugared, nut-stuffed date and examining it carefully, "I arranged for you to have the finest experimental brain implants available. I was very gratified by the results. Now, however, surgical procedures have advanced further. Your brain-wiring is no longer unique. In fact, in some ways you are at a disadvantage compared to the present state of the art."

Oh jeez, I thought. I knew for sure that I wasn't going to like this.

Papa went on, still not looking directly at me. "I've made plans with the neurosurgery staff at al-Amir Hospital to upgrade you before we begin our pilgrimage. We decided to augment your cerebral functions by enclosing your brain in a reticule of delicate gold mesh."

"Yes, O Shaykh, but—"

"Also, today's implants are much smaller and can easily be hidden at the base of the skull. The new personality modules and data add-ons are now only a small fraction the size of your older ones. The hospital will fit you out with a new set. I know you'll be as pleased as I am."

"Yes, O Shaykh, but—"

Friedlander Bey raised a hand in dismissal. "No thanks are needed, my nephew. You will have the surgery tomorrow morning, and there will be enough time to recuperate before our departure." He put the stuffed date in his mouth. There was nothing more to be said—by either of us.

So now I had plenty to think about while I got ready for the party.

Kmuzu tiptoed heavily around my suite of rooms. He wasn't saying anything, but he was shooting me hard-eyed glances that were more reproachful than I thought the situation called for. All right, so I'd gone to a party the night before, so I'd stayed out Allah-only-knew how late and came in so damaged that I couldn't even remember how I'd gotten home. I mean, I'm an adult—maybe not a completely *responsible* adult, but that's my business.

Or so I thought that morning. I liked to cherish the fantasy that there was still a little liberty in my life. I won't say that I didn't enjoy living in Papa's palace and having more money than I ever dreamed possible; it's just that I got good and tired of having to account for every minute of my day, and that almost everything I *really* wanted to do was against the wishes of the master of the house. It didn't help that everyone I knew in the Budayeen would've gladly traded places with me in a Marrakesh minute.

I caught Kmuzu staring at me again. He was trying to look impassive, but his lips were pressed together and his teeth were clenched so tightly that I could see his jaw muscles jumping. I wondered how long this was going to go on. "You reminded me about the party, Kmuzu," I said. "What is it that you're not telling me?"

"Do you recall that you are scheduled for surgery today, yaa Sidi?"

I closed my eyes and rubbed them. I nodded. "I remember. And that's why I can't have breakfast. I wasn't supposed to eat anything after midnight."

"You weren't supposed to drink anything, either."

I opened my eyes and tried to look innocent. "As far as I can remember, I didn't."

Well, that one didn't get by Kmuzu. He didn't say anything, but his expression was as disgusted as I've ever seen him. I told myself it didn't matter to me *what* he was thinking.

In my mind I went over what had happened at the party. In the early stages it had been just fine—but no one ever cares about the early stages of a party. That's why so many people always show up late. Now, what had gone on that could have put Kmuzu in such a snit?

Suddenly I remembered. My eyes opened wider. "Mary and Jesus!" I said in a low voice. "Somebody turned up dead in my club. In one of the booths."

"Yes, yaa Sidi."

"I don't even know who it was, just some guy. I can't remember anything after that. Yallah, I really don't need this, not today."

Kmuzu looked me directly in the eye and let two or three heartbeats pass. Then he said, "It gets worse."

Fateful things were said and done at the party, despite my long-standing policy against that happening in my club. I didn't ask for any of it—I usually don't have to—but because of it my life would be a nonstop nightmare in the weeks to come.

In Chiriga's, as in most of the Budayeen bars, the day shift runs from noon until eight in the evening, and the night shift from eight until four in the morning. Some owners even have a late, late shift from 4 A.M. until noon. You wouldn't think there'd be enough trade to make it worthwhile to stay open then, but evidently there is. I personally don't care. I'm not that hard up for money.

I told my gang that we'd be closing Chiri's early because of the party. I shut the place down about two hours before midnight. Of course, Brandi, Kandy, and the other night girls complained about losing six hours of prime money-making time—and they weren't talking about wages, either. I paid them for the whole shift; they were upset over the lost tips. I guess "tips" is one way of describing their supplemental income.

"It's not fair, Marîd," Brandi said. "The day girls got to work their whole shift and then they get to come to the party, too."

I nodded sympathetically. "Life is like that sometimes. Listen, you don't have to stay here, you know. I'm sure if you went down the Street to Frenchy's, he'd let you work the rest of the night. But who knows? Maybe you'll meet the love of your life here at the party. I mean, it could happen."

Brandi grunted, her expression of supreme irony. "The love of my life lives in a drawer of my nightstand."

"Well, the love of your evening, then. Or at least a solid twenty minutes."

She shook her head and turned to Kandy. "What do you want to do?"

"I want to go to Frenchy's," Kandy said. "Or maybe the Red Light. We can always come back here if we don't find anything better."

All the night-crew dancers left, but I was paying Rocky, the late-shift barmaid, to stay and help out during the party. Rocky was a sturdy, broad-shouldered woman with short, brushy black hair. I'd hired her when Jo-Mama, her previous employer, had gone off to spend a year meditating in the amir's women's prison. As crazy as the night girls were, none of them wanted to mix with Rocky. She kept order in my place when I wasn't around, and I was glad I could count on her.

For the first half hour, it wasn't much of a party. It was Rocky and me, and Pualani, Lily, and Yasmin. I didn't want to get too drunk too fast, so I chipped in an experimental add-on that caused my body to get rid of alcohol at faster than the usual ounce-an-hour rate. I was prepared for a night of grueling fun, so I had Rocky build me a white death. Her version didn't taste as good as Chiri's, but it did what it was supposed to do.

The five of us sat at the bar and gossiped about people who

weren't there to defend themselves. "Hey," Lily said, "this is just like being at work, only we're not getting paid."

"You don't have to listen to some stupid mark's boring life story, either," Rocky said.

"That's true," Pualani said. "Wait 'til I tell you what happened today. I'm sitting right here at the bar, okay? And this guy comes in wearing a James Bond moddy."

"Yeah?" Rocky didn't sound very interested.

The Bond story caught *my* attention, though, because three years ago another creep wearing a similar James Bond moddy had actually *shot* somebody in my club. Killed the poor bastard.

Pualani went on. "And he comes up to me and he goes, 'My name is Bond. *James* Bond.' So I look at him and I'm like, 'Off. *Fuck* off.'"

Yasmin snickered. "Cut him *down*, girlfriend," she said. She raised her nearly empty glass. "After hours we don't have to drink that lousy cheap champagne. Rocky, can I have another one of these, please?"

Rocky nodded and poured a peppermint schnapps for Yasmin. Nobody said anything else for a while. It wasn't starting out to be much of a party.

And then Kmuzu came in with Indihar, my wife. They were carrying several large packages. Rocky and Pualani were glad to see them; both Lily and Yasmin gave Indihar some sour looks. Neither of them had been pleased when Friedlander Bey had, in his usual manner, provided me with a wife. It didn't make any difference to Lily or Yasmin that Indihar and I hadn't been pleased, either.

"What's all that?" I asked.

"Put it down on the bar, Kmuzu," Indihar said. She set her packages down and came up to me. "I thought I'd help get the party started. Looks like it *needs* starting."

"Wow!" Yasmin said, investigating one of the packages. "Fried chicken! Where's this from?"

"NOSFFF," Indihar said. That was the New Orleans Soul and Fast Food Franchise, not far from the club. "I only got extra spicy."

"That's okay by me," Yasmin said. If anything could take her mind off her semisecret jealousy, it was free food.

"What else is there?" Pualani asked.

"Well, I have about fifteen kinds of sushi and sashimi from Kiyoshi's, and about a ton of couscous from Meloul's, and a hundred fried dumplings from Martyrs of Democracy."

"That's perfect," I said. I really love pot stickers.

Indihar glanced at me. "I got a hundred fried dumplings. Fifty of them are for Marîd, the other fifty are for everybody else. And there's meze from that new Turkish place on Sixth Street."

"What's meze?" Rocky asked.

"Lots of different kinds of dishes that you're supposed to sample while drinking," I said.

"Like appetizers?" Yasmin said. "Sometimes I go into Martyrs of Democracy and have like six different appetizers for supper."

"Then you should like this," Indihar said. "There are another few packages still outside. Kmuzu, would you bring them in for me, please?"

"Yes, immediately, yaa Sitti."

Indihar gave me a kiss on the cheek. "Enjoy yourself, Marîd, but don't have too much fun. You have a busy day tomorrow."

"I know, I remember." I wasn't happy about her talking to me that way. We were married, but we weren't *that* married.

"I'm going to go now. Have a good time. It was nice seeing all of you again."

"Indihar," Rocky said, "you're not going to stay?"

She shook her head. "I've got to get home to the kids."

"The kids should be asleep already," I said. "Anyway, I'm paying Senalda to give you a hand with them. Let her watch the kids tonight. Stay a little while."

"I'll go with you to the hospital tomorrow, Marîd. Good night, everybody."

After she and Kmuzu left the club, Yasmin turned and said, "Well, that just means more fried chicken for the rest of us."

"Son of a bitch, Yasmin," Rocky said, "that's cold." Yasmin just laughed and flung her long black hair over her shoulder.

I'm sure it wasn't a coincidence that the first guests to show up — right after the food arrived — were Jacques, Mahmoud, and Saied the Half-Hajj. These guys had been my best friends in the Budayeen, although in recent times events had reduced them from three to a total of no more than one-half of a best friend among them.

Jacques was three-quarters European and he made sure everyone knew it. He was a snob, and I didn't like to be around him very much, but I'd put him to work in one of Friedlander Bey's commercial ventures. Thanks to me, Jacques was making some good money and getting a little influence of his own, so now he showed me more respect. That was very generous of him, as he still found ways to remind me that I'd always be a full twenty-five percent less French than he.

Mahmoud had not been born a man. As a matter of fact, I can remember him as a slender, rather pretty girl with big, dark eyes, dancing at Jo-Mama's Greek club some years ago. Now he weighed a lot more, had developed a mean, cruel personality, and still thought no one knew he worked for Friedlander Bey's rival and enemy, Shaykh Reda Abu Adil. It was okay with me if Mahmoud believed he was fooling me. It was that much easier to keep a close watch on him.

Saied was actually a friend, but the kind of friend you wished lived in, say, Transoxiana—the kind of friend who sent you a letter every ten years or so, and you never had to deal with up close and personal. We called him the Half-Hajj because he had once set out on the holy pilgrimage to Makkah, got a brilliant idea for making a ton of money in a short amount of time, quit the pilgrimage and headed back home, and forgot the brilliant idea before he got back here. He's so scatterbrained that I rarely saw him when he wasn't wearing a personality module with a better short-term memory built in.

These three hung out together all the time. In simpler days— when I was still living on the street and my time was my own— I hung out with them, too. We used to sit in the Café Solace and play cards and gossip. I don't get to do that much anymore.

The Half-Hajj had brought a date—some guy with light brown hair and blue eyes, tall but not very muscular, and good-looking enough, I suppose. My eyebrows raised, because I knew that Saied had been keeping time with the American kid everyone called Abdul-Hassan, whom he'd inherited when the boy's previous pro- tector was killed.

I knew better than to say a word, though. In the Budayeen, you never ask personal questions, not even something as innocent as "How's the wife and kids?" Since the last time you saw them, they could have been sold into slavery or traded for a nice Esmeraldas holo system.

I went to greet them. "You just missed Indihar," I said. "She brought the food and left."

"Marîd," Jacques said, "the drinks are on the house, right?"

That was so goddamn typical. "Yes, Jacques," I said, "the drinks are free." He smiled and went to the bar. I glanced at Saied, who just gave me a little shrug.

"It's good that you're making the hajj," Mahmoud said.

"As if the religion means a copper fîq to you," Saied said.

"Well," I said, "it's mostly Friedlander Bey's idea."

"It usually is," Jacques said. He had come back carrying what looked like a tequila mockingbird. He'd probably had to tell Rocky how to make one.

"Papa's starting to hear the calendar pages whisper," I said. "He wants to go on the pilgrimage before he gets too old."

"Ha," Mahmoud said, "he'll outlive us all."

"He'll certainly outlive *some* of us, I'm sure." I tried to look completely innocent when I said that. I don't even know if Mahmoud understood what I meant.

Saied reached out and tapped me on the shoulder with a forefinger. "I really should introduce you. Marîd, darling, this is my new friend, Ratomir. He's in the city on business."

"It's Radomil, actually." He gave me a brief, empty smile. "Good to meet you. You own this club?" He was obviously European, but he was speaking perfect Arabic. I took it for granted that he had an Arabic-language daddy chipped in.

"I own half of it," I said. "Get a drink, have some food."

"Let me get you something, sweetheart," the Half-Hajj said. "What are we drinking?"

"Beer is fine," Radomil said. Saied nodded and went to get the beer. A couple of things startled me: First, I don't believe I'd ever heard Saied use any term of endearment on any occasion whatsoever; and second, he *never* fetched for anyone. That wasn't his image, and he cared a lot about his image.

"It's his new moddy," Mahmoud said, knowing what I was thinking.

"Has to be," I said.

"It's a niceness moddy," Jacques said. He was having trouble stifling his laughter.

I shook my head in wonder. Until now, the Half-Hajj's favorite moddy had been Rex, the Butch Brute.

Radomil looked puzzled. "I rather prefer this personality to the one he was wearing when I first met him."

Saied returned, and while he was handing Radomil a glass of beer and a plate of sushi, Jacques whispered in my ear, "Ain't love grand?"

"I'm not going to say a single word," I said. It was none of my business. It would just take me a little while to get used to a "nice" Saied, that's all.

"Marîd," Yasmin said, "don't look now, but here come the Bucket-of-Mud Girls."

"Who?" Mahmoud asked.

"As in 'dumb as a bucket of mud,' " Lily explained.

"We're *back!*" It was the triumphant return of Baby and Kitty, staggering drunkenly on either side of an obese bearded black man wearing a blue robe and sandals. He had a carefully trimmed beard, eyes like anthracite chips, and a small, bemused smile on his lips. There was something wrong with this picture. He didn't look like he belonged in Chiriga's, and he didn't look like he belonged with Baby and Kitty, either.

They walked a crooked line to one of the booths in the back, near the rest rooms. As they passed me, I said softly, "Where'd you find this guy?"

Baby laughed. "We were in Frenchy's, and he was buying bottles. He wanted to see Chiri's. We told him we'd rather stay in Frenchy's, but he *wanted* to see *Chiri's.*" Baby shrugged. "So here we are. See if he wants to buy us another bottle."

They squeezed into the booth, all three of them on one side. It looked like Kitty was getting crushed on the inside, but I didn't hear her complain. "Would you like to buy these young ladies a drink, sir?" I asked.

"Whatever they want," he said. His voice was low and solemn. He wasn't drunk.

"A bottle!" Baby said.

I glanced at the man. Bottles went for a hundred sixty kiam. If he was looking for sex, he could get it a lot cheaper almost anywhere else in the Budayeen. I didn't think he was looking for sex. I didn't know what his angle was, or even if he *had* an angle.

"A bottle," he said. "And for me, just coffee, please."

I nodded. We didn't have coffee in the club, but if the gentleman was going to spill cash for a bottle, I could send out for his coffee.

"See?" Baby said. "What did I tell you?"

"I don't remember what you told me," I said.

"You asked me before why we don't like to dance when it's our turn. Where we worked before, our boss told us that there were like two kinds of girls in these clubs. There are front-room girls and back-room girls. We're like back-room girls."

I mulled that one over for a few seconds. "Baby," I said at last, "how long have you worked for me?"

She looked puzzled. "A couple of weeks, I think. How come?"

"In that couple of weeks, haven't you noticed that we don't have a back room?"

"You *don't?*" She looked across the heavyset mark at Kitty, who seemed even more bewildered.

"Just take it easy," I said. "I'll have Rocky bring your bottle."

"Happy birthday, Mr. Boss!" Baby called after me. Okay, let her think it was my birthday. Close enough.

I headed back toward the front of the club, and I saw Chiri come in. That cheered me up, because she was sensible enough to cancel out Baby and Kitty, with the Half-Hajj thrown in. "Hey, Chiri," I said.

"Say, Bwana. I was expecting more of an actual *party*, you know what I mean? It's too quiet in here. Play some *music*, for God's sake."

"I don't know. I kind of like it like this. I get real tired of hearing the same songs all day."

Chiri nodded. "I brought some different stuff from home. You mind if I play it?"

I shrugged. "Hey, the club's half yours, isn't it?"

"Yes," she said, giving me a smile with absolutely no humor in it. "Half of it."

"You missed Kmuzu. He and Indihar came in a little while ago. They brought all that food."

"*Choo,*" Chiri said. "I wish I'd known they were passing by. They didn't stay very long, did they?"

I shook my head. "You might've been able to talk them into hanging around."

"I sure as hell would've tried with Kmuzu," she said. "Nothing against Indihar, of course." She went toward the club's holo system. For the rest of the night we'd all learn more about Chiri's taste in music.

About the time her first selection started playing—it was one of those goddamn Sikh propaganda songs, and Chiri *knows* how much I hate them—I decided it was time to grab myself a few pot stickers. I took a paper plate, plopped six fried dumplings on it, and spooned on the black soy sauce and vinegar combination that Martyrs of Democracy had packaged in a plastic cup. I closed my eyes and murmured "Bismillah"—in the name of God; then I gulped down all six of the pot stickers and took six more. Even though the dumplings had cooled a little by now, they were still great. I told myself I should savor them more slowly. I didn't.

"Here, Marîd," Rocky said. She put a white death in front of me. "Thanks, Rocky. Come on, eat something!"

"Oh," she said, "I'll pass. I don't like the way NOSFFF makes their chicken, and you couldn't pay me to eat that raw fish stuff."

"Have some pot stickers then."

Her eyebrows went up a little. "You mean it, Marîd? I thought they were all for you."

I laughed. "I can't eat a *hundred* of 'em, Rocky."

"Bet you could. I'll try a little of that couscous. The guy who runs the restaurant, he's a Maghrebi like you, isn't he?"

"Meloul? Yeah, we're both from Algeria. I mean, Mauretania. I think he's a Berber from Oran, though. I grew up in Algiers."

Rocky shrugged. "Same difference," she said. In this city, far from the Maghreb—the "sunset" or western lands—it didn't matter very much. People didn't care where you came from or what you'd done there. The city—the Budayeen in particular—was a perfect place to lose your past and start over. I'd done just that, and most of the people I knew had done it, too. That made me wonder for a moment: Did I know anyone who'd actually been born and raised here?

"Trouble," Rocky murmured.

I turned and looked. The *'ricain* kid, Abdul-Hassan, had come in. He shot a black look at Saied and his friend for the night, Radomil. The Half-Hajj hadn't yet noticed that the kid had joined the party. I hoped Rocky's prediction didn't come true, but in a worst-case scenario I could handle Abdul-Hassan. I had proved that before.

Of course, the first thing the boy did was walk right toward me. "May you go and come in safety, Shaykh Marîd," he said. Hooray, I thought, Saied had finally given the kid an Arabic-language daddy. Then Abdul-Hassan raised himself on his toes and gave me a kiss on the mouth. It was over in about two seconds, but it was a *very good* kiss.

That caught me off-guard. I glanced at Saied, but his expression was empty of resentment or anger. I didn't know if the Half-Hajj truly didn't care, or if his attitude was a function of the niceness moddy. Yasmin, however, was glowering. She was already fiercely jealous of Indihar; I *knew* she didn't want to see anything develop between me and the American kid.

"Thank you for your good wishes, O Clever One," I said. I tried to put a little more distance between us, but as I backed away, the kid followed.

At that moment, Yasmin decided to join the tableau. "Marîd," she said in a chilly voice, "I really need to talk to you. Privately."

"Sure," I said. "Let's go sit down at the bar."

Abdul-Hassan put a hand on my arm and slowly scratched downward with his fingernails. "My heart will be empty until you get back from the hajj," he said. I'd never noticed how long his eyelashes were. He gave my arm a little squeeze.

"Right *now*, Marîd," Yasmin said.

"All right, Yasmin." I said to the boy, "Enjoy the party. May it be pleasant to you."

He said, "All who see you, live, O Shaykh. Maybe we can talk again later." I had no trouble reading his expression, and I understood that talking was very low on the list of things he'd like to do with me later.

Yasmin and I took seats at the bar. "What is it?" I asked.

"I don't have anything to say to you," Yasmin said. "I just thought you needed someone to rescue you from that American slut. I didn't think you were a chicken hawk, Marîd."

"Are you serious?"

"Serious as a heart attack."

I was amazed. "Believe me, you've got nothing to worry about."

She tilted her head and looked at me for a few seconds. "You forget that I *know* you, honey. I think you'd jam anything that held still long enough. In the right situation."

"He's pretty, Yasmin, but he's too young and he belongs to the Half-Hajj."

"Tell that to Saied, if you can get his attention away from that trick he brought in here."

I got up from the stool. "You should listen to yourself. You're jumping to all kinds of wrong conclusions."

"What I said, Marîd." She stood up and headed toward the plate of fried chicken.

The party lurched on toward midnight. I got pretty drunk despite the daddy I was wearing. More people came in, and I was very gracious and charming. At least, that's how I remember it. I greeted Frenchy Benoit, who ran his own club on the Street, and Frenchy's friendly barmaid, Dalia; we had a drink together.

Heidi, the beautiful blue-eyed German barmaid from the Silver Palm came in and wished me well; we had a drink together. Old Ibrahim, who owned the Café Solace, and Monsieur Gargotier, who owned the Fée Blanche, each had a drink with me. They stayed just long enough to mutter a few words in my ear and load up on free food. I thought Ferrari, who lived above his club, the Blue Parrot, might come by, but either he didn't or he arrived after I'd stopped remembering things.

Safiyya the Lamb Lady dropped by for a little while. She was what other people on the Street called a "character." She was harmless, though, as long as you didn't threaten her imaginary lamb. She didn't even realize there was a party going on. I gave her some food and a glass of beer, and she thanked me. She was the only person in Chiri's all night long who thanked me for anything.

I do recall Kenneth being there for part of the evening. He was a tall, slender European with wire-rimmed spectacles. He had thin lips, always pressed tightly together; his expression showed that he was cursed to go through life surrounded by people and objects he dreaded to touch. The most notable thing about Kenneth, however, was that he was Shaykh Reda Abu Adil's lieutenant and current fuck-buddy. Just as Abu Adil hated Friedlander Bey, so Kenneth hated me. The feeling was mutual.

"Shaykh Reda sent me," Kenneth said. "He wanted me to convey his best wishes to you and to Friedlander Bey for your journey to Makkah."

"Thank Shaykh Reda for me," I said. I stared at him. I wasn't going to say anything more. I wanted to see what he was really up to.

He stared back at me, and the silence got longer and more ridiculous. "I will have a glass of beer," he said at last.

"Knock yourself out, Kenny," I said.

His mouth twisted, but he didn't say anything. A couple of minutes later I saw him, holding his glass of beer, in some kind of intense conference with Mahmoud. I didn't know what they were discussing, but whatever it was it wouldn't be good news for Papa and me.

Things began to get blurry soon after that. I have a vague memory of dropping my glass and spilling liquor and ice cubes on the floor. The glass shattered, and when I bent down clumsily, I overturned my plateful of couscous and meze on somebody. The American kid helped me to a chair at a table, and I sat down heavily. The room was making sickening circles with me at its center, and I told myself it might be a good idea to skip a couple of drinks until I was steady again.

Then Baby and Kitty were bending down, kissing me goodbye. The way I was feeling, it was too much effort to raise my eyes to their faces. Instead, I just stared at their remarkable tits. I gathered that Baby and Kitty were abandoning the bearded black man because he'd stopped spending money on them. Sure, okay. I guess they went to another club. The large gentleman himself called out to Rocky to bring him another cup of coffee.

I crossed my arms on the table and put my head down. The room spun even faster. I knew that if I did anything drastic, such as move or breathe, I was in danger of throwing up. I didn't move or breathe.

The next thing I remember was someone shaking me by the shoulder. I supposed it was Abdul-Hassan, until I opened my eyes.

I was wrong. It was Sulome, the working girl from Damascus. She was *not* supposed to be there. As drunk as I was, I knew that for a fact. "What?" I said. I hoped she understood what I meant, because I didn't think I could say it any more plainly than that.

Sulome laughed. "*This* is the Marîd Audran I remember," she said. She dragged another chair to my table and sat down. "Are you still promising everybody that you're going to give up getting wasted?"

"Sulome?" I said. What I actually wanted to say was much more comprehensive than that, but I heard myself speak just the one word.

"So this is your bar. It's okay, I guess. Some of these girls aren't *girls*, Marîd, but I suppose you know that, and it probably doesn't make any difference to you. Listen, I can see you're not in very good shape right now. I'll just get myself something to munch on. Don't worry about me, I'll be fine."

"Sulome?" I said. I sat up a little straighter. I was not happy to see her in Chiri's. Nobody was supposed to know that she was even in town, and nobody was *ever* supposed to know that she and I knew each other. I didn't want anything to spoil my scheme to get even with Fuad.

I saw her walk to the bar and fill a plate with fried dumplings. I admired how well she walked; I used to be able to walk just that easily, but that was many ounces of gin and bingara ago. I was about to find out how well I could navigate in this condition. I stood up—no problem, although I had to lean on my chair for a moment until my head stopped reeling. Then I set out on a generally north-westerly course, tacking across the floor in the hope of intersecting Sulome's path somewhere.

Lily stopped me. "Listen, Marîd," she said, "you're in pretty bad shape. You really ought to go sleep it off. Rocky can close up here for you. Why don't you let me take you home? I don't live very far from here. I know you have to get up early tomorrow to go to the hospital. Just—"

I raised a hand, hoping Lily would understand what the gesture meant. I brushed by her, still following Sulome.

Then it was Jacques. "Marîd, is it my imagination, or is that moddy Saied's wearing making him behave just a little on the *nelly* side of nice, know what I mean? If he could see and hear himself, he'd rip that moddy out and stomp it into tiny plastic pieces."

I raised my hand again and kept moving. Sulome seemed to be getting farther away. I didn't understand how that could be.

Frenchy grabbed me by the arm. "Listen, cap," he said, "before you leave town—"

I raised my hand.

I'd almost caught up to Sulome. She was collecting a triple Johnny Walker Red with a Coke back from Rocky. I was too drunk to be aware of much that was going on around me, but somehow I can remember what she was drinking. Don't ask me why. Anyway, she couldn't have been more than six feet away. I took a step, then another. I reached out toward her.

Yasmin put herself between us. "This time I've *had* it, you *noraf* son of a bitch." I didn't know what the hell she was talking about.

"Sulome," I said. I put my hand on her shoulder, and she turned around so fast she nearly knocked me down.

"Don't *ever* grab at me again," she snarled.

"Sorry," I said. She and I weren't getting off on the right foot here. "You're supposed to be—"

"Back at Friedlander Bey's house," she said. "Fuck that. I didn't want to sit in a room all night. Bin Turki and this Kmuzu guy made sure I had everything I needed, and when they left me alone I snuck out. What you gonna do, *fine* me?"

I looked around helplessly. "Nobody's supposed to know—"

"Yeah, yeah. Who knows me here, except you? If anybody connects us later on, it's because they're watching us talking right now. So *go away.*"

"I think we both should go back to the house. Grab some food and let's go. I'll kick you an extra hundred if that'll get you out of here right now."

She shrugged. "A hundred. *Cash.* Forget the food, I can't stand that sushi stuff. What are we going to do, get a cab? Or you gonna call one of your thugs?"

"Stop calling them—" I was urging Sulome toward the door. We'd almost reached it, when Fuad came into the club. I pulled Sulome back.

"*Goddamn*, Marîd, didn't I just warn you about that?"

"We can't let that guy see us together." This had to be one of the worst nights of my life. I wondered how many of my past sins I was paying for all at once.

"Who? That ugly scrawny guy? Hey, that's not—"

"That's Fuad, all right. That's your mark. Oh, hell, he's seen us. You don't know me, all right?"

"What do you want me to do?" she asked in a hoarse whisper.

"The hell do *I* know? Fake it."

She grunted. "*That* I know how to do."

I couldn't believe that Fuad had crashed my party. Coming back to the city at all was pretty dumb; showing up at his old hangouts was plain stupid; but walking right into my nightclub was the kind of mistake that usually removed you permanently from the common gene pool. He was heading straight for me—and he was *grinning!*

"Marîd!" he said cheerfully, as if I'd be overjoyed to see him. I nodded. "Fuad," I said. He held his hand out, but I didn't shake it.

After a few seconds he glanced down at his hand and put it in his pocket. He looked at Sulome, who was pretending to be interested in something happening behind Fuad's head. I could see that he was immediately interested in her. Well, I'd known he would be; I just hadn't planned for them to meet this way, or this soon. "Where y'at, Marîd?" he said.

"I'll be right back," I said. "I got to hit the john." That was the truth. I turned and staggered to the back of the club, steadying myself on every piece of furniture along the way. I went into the men's toilet, leaned my head against the dirty green wall, and closed my eyes. I paid back most of what I'd had to drink that night. I just hoped that my master plan for Fuad hadn't been totally screwed up before it even started.

I threw a little water in my face—I wanted it to be cold, but during the summer months in the city there's no such thing as cold water—and I told myself I felt better. I took a quick glance at my reflection in the mirror, and I did not look good at all. I left the toilet, trying to decide whether to get Sulome out of the club, or let her make a first impression on our victim.

As I walked by, I saw the big bearded guy who'd come in with Baby and Kitty. He was still sitting in the same booth with a cup of coffee in front of him. He'd fallen asleep; I figured I'd do him a favor, so I shook him by the shoulder. "Not a good idea to nap in here," I said. "You could lose your wallet. Or something. I can call for a cab if you like."

I shook him twice more before I realized that this man was *not* going to wake up. Ever. "Yaa âlam, yaa nâs!" I muttered. That was "O world, O people!" a phrase I saved for those times when every force under Heaven was conspiring against me.

I must've been at least partly sober, because I did something right for a change. I sat in the booth beside the poor dead guy, and I unclipped my phone from my belt. I called Friedlander Bey's house and spoke to Tariq, Papa's valet. I told him exactly what had happened. He instructed me to do just what I was doing, not let anyone else know about the situation, and wait twenty minutes before calling the police.

It was the better part of an hour before the cops actually arrived.

If I'd been smart, I would've laid off the white deaths, at least until after they'd taken my statement. Well, sure, it's easy enough to say that now. That night I figured another drink or two couldn't make things any worse.

So it had to be almost two in the morning when a softclothes guy and a uniform came in. I recognized the uniform—it was Sergeant Catavina, who had taken corruption to such a high level, he might as well have been honest. I mean, with Catavina you knew exactly how he'd react to any situation, so in an odd sort of way he was completely dependable. He was easier to deal with than someone who changed the rules as he went along.

Catavina didn't have much to do though. He was along to make sure no one left before Detective ibn Tali said they could leave. I'd never met ibn Tali before, but I knew there'd been a big shakeup in the police department, particularly in the copshop that oversaw activities in the Budayeen. The previous man in charge there, a real motherfucker by the name of Hajjar, had come to a bad end at the hands of an unruly mob. I'd had a little to do with that, and I hoped the current lieutenant, whoever he was, didn't hold it against me.

Because I'd discovered the body and because I'd phoned the police, ibn Tali wanted to talk with me first. That was just fine, because by then I really wanted to get out of the club and go home. I told the detective everything I could remember about the party from the time we closed Chiriga's at ten o'clock. I mentioned that I'd never seen the victim before, that he'd come in with Baby and Kitty, that the two girls had left to seek their fortune elsewhere before he'd turned stiff, and that I couldn't imagine anyone at the party had any sort of motive to kill the poor bastard in the first place.

Ibn Tali jotted that all down in his notebook. "I'm gonna listen to everybody else's story," he said. "Then I'm gonna come back to you, and you're gonna tell me yours all over again. That'll give you a chance to put in the little bits you forgot about the first time through."

"Excuse me, officer." A very sleepy looking man in a pale yellow gallebeya and plain white checked keffiya had come up to the booth where we were sitting. I wondered how he'd gotten past Sergeant Catavina.

"It's detective," ibn Tali said, "not officer. And wait your turn. We're all gonna be here for a long time, so just make yourself comfortable."

The newcomer shoved a sheet of paper at ibn Tali. It must've been a magic sheet of paper, because as he read it, the detective's face became more and more unhappy. Ibn Tali stood up, and the two men moved away a few feet and conferred in low voices. The detective shook his head, the yellow gallebeya insisted. This went on for a minute or two. At last, ibn Tali looked disgusted, muttered something under his breath, and turned back to me.

"Audran," he said, "this guy's from the city. *High up* in the city, one of the amir's special assistants. He's tellin' me you can go home now. Thank Friedlander Bey for that when you see him; but look, I ain't done with you. I hear you're goin' into the hospital today, so I'll probably be there waitin' when the anesthetic wears off."

"I'll be looking forward to it, detective." I stood up, and I almost passed out right in front of everybody. That was the last thing I remembered about last night.

No wonder Kmuzu was treating me with such badly concealed disdain. I had been pathetic last night, and it was my bad luck to be in that shape during a moment of crisis. Now, sober again, I was frankly humiliated, and I didn't need any more of Kmuzu's silent disregard. I felt like standing under the shower and letting the hot water beat down on me for half an hour.

"Yaa Sidi," he said, "before you—"

I waved at him. "Later, Kmuzu. Let me get cleaned up."

"Wait, yaa Sidi! There's—"

I went into the bathroom and caught sight of myself in the mirror. I was going to have to stop doing that; I looked as terrible as I felt. Then I saw that I couldn't take a shower, because the bathtub was already filled, with steaming warm water and bubbles.

And in the bubbles, relaxing luxuriously, was Abdul-Hassan, the American kid. When he saw me, he gave me a slow, languorous smile.

Kmuzu had warned me—"It gets worse." I wished it would *stop* getting worse pretty goddamn soon.

Introduction to
The World as We Know It

*George wrote this one for an anthology of future crime
stories, attempting to devise a kind of crime that wouldn't
even have been thought of in earlier days and ages. He
had the idea for Consensual Realities long before; the
Futurecrime anthology just gave him a way to play with
it, to link it to something.*

When he wrote The Exile Kiss, *George planned out
two more Budayeen novels to complete the character arcs
of Marîd, Friedlander Bey, Indihar, and the complex net-
work of friendships, rivalries, and enmities in which they
exist. Though the narrator of this story never says it, he is,
of course, Marîd Audran—Marîd after the end of the
unwritten, untitled fifth book, when he is an outcast
hiding from Friedlander Bey's victorious enemies.*

*An older, tireder, and less cocky Marîd, simultane-
ously looked down upon and looked up to by the newcomer punks of a crime scene that is as far beyond Marîd's
own street-punk days as the science fiction of the nineties
was beyond that of the seventies, when George first burst
upon the scene in the forefront of the so-called New Wave.*

The Grand Master as Has-Been.

But still able—marginally—to hold his own.

—Barbara Hambly

✛   ✛   ✛

The World as We Know It

THE SETUP COULD HAVE BEEN PRETTY CLEVER with a little more thought, I have to admit. Using some of the newest-generation cerebral hardware, an ambitious but dangerously young man, a recent parolee—you know, a low-level street punk, much as I'd been once upon a time—had stolen a small crate from Mahmoud's warehouse. The punk hadn't even known what was in the crate. It turned out, if I can trust Mahmoud, that the crate contained a shipment of recently developed biological agents.

These bios had two major uses: They could promote the healing of traumatic wounds while making the attendant pain disappear for a while, without subjecting the patient to the well-documented narcotic disadvantages we've all come to know and love; or what was contained in the many disposable vials could easily be reconfigured to wipe out entire cities, using very small doses—thus becoming the most powerful neurological weapons ever devised. The small crate was labeled to be shipped to Holland, where the Dutch revolution was still at its full, vicious, inhuman peak.

Of course, Mahmoud was frantic to get his crate back. He and a few of my old friends, from the good old days when I had power and could move through the city without fear of being dusted by my many enemies, knew where I was now living. I'd left the Budayeen and adopted a new identity. Mahmoud had come to me and offered me money, which I didn't need—I'd lost just about everything, but

163

I'd carefully protected the cash I'd acquired—or contacts and agents, which I did need, and desperately. I agreed to look into the matter for Mahmoud.

It wasn't very difficult. The thief was such a beginner that I almost felt like taking him aside and giving him a few pointers. I restrained that impulse, however.

The kid, who told me his name was Musa, had left a trail through the city that had been easy as hell for a predator like me to follow. I know the kid's name wasn't Musa, just as he knew my name wasn't the one I gave him when I finally caught up to him. Names and histories were not important information to either of us at the time. All that mattered was the small crate.

I dragged him back to my office, far from the Budayeen, in a neighborhood called Iffatiyya. This part of the city, east beyond the canal, had been reduced to rubble in the last century, the fifteenth after the Hegira, the twenty-second of the Christian era. It was now about a hundred years later than that, and at last some of the bombed-out buildings were being reclaimed. My office was in one of them.

I was there because most of my former friends and associates had leaped to the other side, to the protection of Shaykh Reda Abu Adil. There were very few places that were safe for me back in the walled quarter, and few people I could trust. Hell, I didn't really trust Mahmoud—never had—except he was reliably, scrupulously straightforward when large sums of money were involved.

I opened the outer door of my office, the one with the glass panel on which some frustrated portrait artist had lettered my new name, in both Arabic and Roman alphabets. Inside the door was a waiting room with a sagging couch, three wooden chairs, and a few items to help my few anxious clients pass the time: a scattering of newspapers and magazines, and chipzines for my more technologically advanced visitors, to be chipped directly into a moddy or daddy socket located in the hollow at the base of the skull.

I had a good grasp of the material of Musa's gallebeya, which I used to propel him through the open inner door. He fell sprawling on the bare, shabby, wooden floor. I slouched in the comfortable chair behind my beat-up old desk. I let a sarcastic smile have its way for a second or two, and then I put on my grim expression. "I want to clear this up fast," I said.

Musa had gotten to his feet and was glaring at me with all the defiance of youth and ignorance. "No problem," he said, in what he no doubt imagined was a tough voice. "All you gotta do is come across."

"By fast," I said, deliberately not responding to his words, "I mean superluminal. Light-speed. And I'm not coming across. I don't do that. Grab a seat while I make a phone call, O Young One."

Musa maintained the rebellious expression, but some worry had crept into it, too. He didn't know who I planned to call. "You ain't gonna turn me over to the rats, are you?" he asked. "I just got out. Yallah, another fall and I think they'll cut off my right hand."

I nodded, murmuring Mahmoud's commcode into my desk phone. Musa was right about one thing: Islamic justice as currently interpreted in the city would demand the loss of his hand, possibly the entire arm, in front of a huge, cheering crowd in the courtyard of the Shimaal Mosque. Musa would have no opportunity to appeal, either, and he'd probably end up back in prison afterward, as well.

"Marhaba," said Mahmoud when he answered his phone. He wasn't the kind of guy to identify himself until he knew who was on the other end of the line. I remembered him before he had his sex change, as a slender, doe-eyed sylph, dancing at Jo-Mama's. Since then, he'd put on a lot of weight, toughness, and something much more alarming.

"Yeah, you right," I replied. "Good news, Mahmoud. This is your investigator calling. Got the thief, and he hasn't had time to do anything with the product. He'll take you to it. What becomes of him afterward is up to you. Come take charge of him at your convenience."

"You are still a marvel, O Wise One," said Mahmoud. His praise counted about as much as a broken Bedu camel stick. "You have lost much, but it is as Allah wills. Yet you have not lost your native wit and ability. I will be there very soon, inshallah, with some news that might interest you." Inshallah means "if God wills." Nobody but He was too sure about anything of late.

"The news is the payment, right, O Father of Generosity?" I said, shaking my head. Mahmoud had been a cheap stiff as a woman, and he was a cheap stiff now as a man.

"Yes, my friend," said Mahmoud. "But it includes a potential new client for you, and I'll throw in a little cash, too. Business is business."

"And action is action," I said, not that I was seeing much action these days. "You know how much I charge for this sort of thing."

"Salâm alêkom, my friend," he said hurriedly, and he hung up his phone before I could salâm him back.

Musa looked relieved that I hadn't turned him over to the

police, although I'm sure he was just as anxious about the treatment
he could expect from Mahmoud. He had every reason in the world
to be concerned. He maintained a surly silence, but he finally took
my advice and sat down in the battered red-leather chair opposite
my desk.

"Piece of advice," I said, not even bothering to look at him.
"When Mahmoud gets here—and he'll get here fast—take him
directly to his property. No excuses, no bargains. If you try holding
Mahmoud up for so much as a lousy copper fiq, you'll end up
breathing hot sand for the remainder of your brief life. Understand?"

I never learned if the punk understood or not. I wasn't looking
at him, and he wasn't saying anything. I opened the bottom drawer
of my desk and took out the office bottle. Apparently a slow leak had
settled in, because the level of gin was much lower than I expected.
It was something that would bear investigating during my long
hours of solitude.

I built myself a white death—gin and bingara with a hit of
Rose's lime juice—and took a quick gulp. Then I drank the rest
of the tumblerful slowly. I wasn't savoring anything; I was just
proving to myself again that I could be civilized about my drinking habits.

Time passed in this way—Musa sitting in the red-leather chair,
sampling emotions; me sitting in my chair, sipping white death.
I'd been correct about one thing: It didn't take Mahmoud long to
make the drive from the Budayeen. He didn't bother to knock on
the outer door. He came through, into my inner office, accompanied by three large men. Now, even I thought three armed chunks
were a bit much to handle ragged, little old Musa there. I said
nothing. It wasn't my business any longer.

Now, Mahmoud was dressed as I was, that is, in keffiya, the
traditional Arab headdress, gallebeya, and sandals; the men with
Mahmoud were all wearing very nice, tailored European-style
business suits. Two of the suit jackets had bulges just where you'd
expect. Mahmoud turned to those two and didn't utter a word. The
two moved forward and took pretty damn physical charge of Musa,
getting him out of my office the quickest way possible. Just before
he passed through the inner door, Musa jerked his head around
toward me and said, "Rat's puppet." That was all.

That left Mahmoud and the third suit.

"Where you at, Mahmoud?" I asked.

"I see you've taken to dyeing your beard, O Wise One," said
Mahmoud by way of thanks. "You no longer look like a Maghrebi.
You look like any common citizen of Asir or the Hejaz, for instance.
Good."

I was so glad he approved. I was born part Berber, part Arab, and part French, in the part of Algeria that now called itself Maure-tania. I'd left that part of the world far, far behind, and arrived in this city a few years ago, with reddish hair and beard that made me stand out among the locals. Now all my hair was as black as my prospects.

Mahmoud tossed an envelope on the desk in front of me. I glanced at it but didn't count the kiam inside, then dropped the envelope in a desk drawer and locked it.

"I cannot adequately express my thanks, O Wise One," he said in a flat voice. It was a required social formula.

"No thanks are needed, O Benefactor," I said, completing the obligatory niceties. "Helping a friend is a duty."

"All thanks be to Allah."

"Praise Allah."

"Good," said Mahmoud with some satisfaction. I could see him relax a little, now that the show was over. He turned to the re-maining suit and said, "Shaykh Ishaq ibn Muhammad il-Qurawi, O Great Sir, you've seen how reliable my friend is. May Allah grant that he solve your problem as promptly as he solved mine." Then Mahmoud nodded to me, turned, and left. Evidently, I wasn't high enough on the social ladder to be actually introduced to Ishaq ibn Muhammad il-Qurawi.

I motioned to the leather chair. Il-Qurawi made a slight wince of distaste, then sat down.

I put on my professional smile and uttered another formulaic phrase that meant, roughly, "You have come to your people and level ground." In other words, "Welcome."

"Thank you, I—"

I raised a hand, cutting him off. "You must allow me to offer you coffee, O Sir. The journey from the Budayeen must have been tiring, O Shaykh."

"I was hoping we could dispense with—"

I raised my hand again. The old me would've been more than happy to dispense with the hospitality song-and-dance, but the new me was playing a part, and the ritual three tiny cups of coffee was part of it. Still, we hurried through them as rapidly as social graces permitted. Il-Qurawi wore a sour expression the whole time.

When I offered him a fourth, he waggled his cup from side to side, indicating that he'd had enough. "May your table always be prosperous," he said, because he had to.

I shrugged. "Allah yisallimak." May God bless you.

"Praise Allah."

"Praise Allah."

"Now," said my visitor emphatically, "you have been recommended to me as someone who might be able to help with a slight difficulty."

I nodded reassuringly. Slight difficulty, my Algerian ass. People didn't come to me with slight difficulties.

As usual, the person in the leather chair didn't know how to begin. I waited patiently, letting my smile evaporate bit by bit. I found myself thinking about the office bottle, but it was impossible to bring it out again until I was alone. Strict Muslims looked upon alcoholic beverages with the same fury that they maintained for the infidel, and I knew nothing about il-Qurawi's attitudes about such things.

"If you have an hour or two free this afternoon," he said, "I wonder if you'd come with me to my office. It's not far from here, actually. On the eastern side of the canal, but quite a bit north of here. We've restored a thirty-six-story office building, but recently there's been more than the usual amount of vandalism. I'd like to hire you to stop it."

I took a deep breath and let it out again. "Not my usual sort of assignment, O Sir," I said, shrugging, "but I don't foresee any problem. I get a hundred kiam a day plus expenses. I need a minimum of five hundred right now to pique my interest."

Il-Qurawi frowned at the discussion of money and waved his hand. "Will you accept a check?" he asked.

"No," I said. I'd noticed that the man was stingy with honorifics, so I'd decided to hold my own to the minimum.

He grunted. He was clearly annoyed and doubtful about my ability to do what he wanted. Still, he removed a moderate stack of bills from a black leather wallet, and sliced off five for me. He leaned forward and put the money on my desk. I pretended to ignore it.

I made no pretense of checking an appointment book. "I'm certain, O Shaykh, that I can spare a few hours for you."

"Very good." Il-Qurawi stood up and spent a few moments vitally absorbed in the wrinkles in his business suit. I took the time to slide the five hundred kiam into the pocket of my gallebeya.

"I can spare a few hours, O Shaykh," I said, "but first I'd like some more information. Such as who you are and whom you represent."

He didn't say a word. He merely slid a business card to the spot where the money had been.

I picked up the card. It said:

Ishaq ibn Muhammad il-Qurawi
Chief of Security
CRCorp

Below that was a street address that meant nothing to me, and a commcode. I didn't have a business card to give him, but I didn't think he cared. "CRCorp?" I asked.

He was still standing. He indicated that we should begin moving toward the door. It was fine by me. "Yes, we deal in consensual realities."

"Uh huh," I said. "I know you people." By this time, we were standing in the hallway and he was watching me lock the outer door.

We went downstairs to his car. He owned a long, black, chauffeur-driven, restored, gasoline-powered limousine. I wasn't impressed. I'd ridden in a few of those. We got in and he murmured something to the driver. The car began gliding through the rubble-strewn streets, toward the headquarters of CRCorp.

"Can you be more exact about the nature of this vandalism, O Sir?" I said.

"You'll see. I believe it's being caused by one person. I have no idea why; I just want it stopped. There are too many clients in the building beginning to complain."

And it's beyond the capabilities of the Chief of Security, I thought. That spoke something ominous to me.

After about half an hour of weaving north and east, then back west toward the canal, then farther north, we arrived at the CRCorp building. Allah only knew what it had been before this entire part of the city had been destroyed, but now it stood looking newly built among its broken and blasted neighbors. One fixed-up building in all that desolation seemed pretty lonely and conspicuous, I thought, but I guess you had to start someplace.

Il-Qurawi and I got out of the limousine and walked across the freshly surfaced parking area. There were no other cars in it. "The executive offices are on the seventeenth floor, about halfway up, but there's nothing interesting to see there. You'll want to visit one or two of the consensual realities, and then look at the vandalism I mentioned."

Well, sure, as soon as he said there wasn't anything interesting on the seventeenth floor, I immediately wanted to go there. I hate it when other people tell me what I want to do, but it was il-Qurawi's five hundred kiam, so I kept my mouth shut, nodded, and followed him inside to the elevators.

"Give you a taste of one of the consensual realities," he said. "We just call them CRs around here. We'll stop off first on twenty-six. It's functioning just fine, and there's been no sign of vandalism as yet."

Still nothing for me to say. We rode up quickly, silently in the mirrored elevator. I glanced at my reflection. I wasn't happy with the appearance I'd had to adopt, but I was stuck with it.

We got off at twenty-six. The elevator doors opened, we stepped out, and passed through a small, well-constructed airlock. When I turned to look, the elevator and airlock had disappeared. I mean, there was no sign that elevator doors could possibly exist for hundreds of miles. I felt for them and there was nothing but air. Rather thin, cold air. If I'd been pressed to make a guess, I'd have said that we were on the surface of Mars. I knew that was impossible, but I'd seen holo shots of the Martian surface, and this is just what they looked like.

"Here," said il-Qurawi, handing me a mask and a small tank, "this should help you somewhat."

"I am in your debt, O Great One." I used the tight-grip straps to hold the mask in place, but the tank was made to be worn on a belt. I had a rope holding my gallebeya closed, but it wouldn't support the weight of the tank, so I just carried it in my hands. We started walking across the barren, boulder-studded surface of Mars toward a collection of buildings in the far distance that I recognized as the international Martian colony.

"The atmosphere on this floor only approximates that of Mars," said il-Qurawi. "That was part of the group's consensus agreement. Still, if you're outside and not wearing the mask, you're liable to develop a rather serious condition they call 'Mars throat.' Affects your sinuses, your inner ears, your throat, and so forth."

"Let me see if I can guess, O Sir," I said, huffing a little as I made my way over the extremely rough terrain. "Group of people in the colony, all would-be Martian colonists, and they've voted on how they wanted the place to look." I gazed up at a pink peach-colored sky.

"Exactly. And they voted on how they wanted it to feel and smell and sound. Actually, it approximates the reports we get from the true Mars Project rather closely. CRCorp supplies the area, for which we charge what we feel is a fair price. We also supply the software that maintains the illusion, too."

I kicked a boulder. No illusion. "How much of this is real?" I said. Even using the tank, I was already short of breath and eager to get inside one of the buildings.

"The boulders, as you've just discovered, are artificial but real. The buildings are real. The carefully maintained atmosphere is also our responsibility. Everything else you might experience is computer or holo generated. It can be quite deadly out here, but that's the way this group wanted it. We haven't left anything out, down to the toxin-laden lichen, which is part of the illusion. For all intents and purposes, this is the surface of Mars. Group 26 has always seemed to be very pleased with it. We've gotten very few complaints or suggestions for improvement."

"Naturally, O Sir," I said, "I'm looking forward to interviewing a few of the residents."

"Of course," said il-Qurawi. "That's why I brought you here. We're very proud of Group 26, and justly so, I think."

"Praise Allah," I said. No echo from my client.

After more time and hiking than I'd been prepared for, we arrived at the colony itself. I felt like a physical wreck; the executive with me was not suffering at all. He looked like he'd just taken a leisurely stroll through the repro of the Tiger Gardens in the city's entertainment quarter.

"This way," he said, pointing to an airlock into the long main building. It appeared to have been constructed of some material derived from the reddish sand all around, but I wasn't interested enough to find out for sure if that were true or part of the holographic illusion.

We cycled through the airlock. Inside, we found ourselves in a corridor that had been painted in institutional colors: dark green to waist-level, a kind of maddening tan above that. I was absolutely sure that I would quickly come to hate those colors; soon it proved that they dominated the color scheme of most of the hallways and meeting rooms. The people of Group 26 must have had a very different aesthetic sense than I did. It didn't give me great hopes for them.

Il-Qurawi glanced at his wristwatch, a European product like the rest of his outfit. It was thin and sleek and made of gold. "The majority of them will be in the refectory module now," he said. "Good. You'll have the opportunity to meet as many of Group 26 as you like. Ask whatever you like, but we are under a little time pressure. I'd like to take you to floor seven within the next half hour."

"I give thanks to the Maker of Worlds," I said. Il-Qurawi gave me a sidelong glance to see if I were serious. I was doing my best to give that impression.

The refectory was down the entire length of the main building and through a low, narrow, windowless passageway. I felt a touch of claustrophobia, as if I were down deep beneath the surface; I had to remind myself that I was actually on the twenty-sixth floor of an office tower.

The refectory was at the other end of the passageway. It was a large room, filled with orderly rows of tables. Men, women, and children sat at the tables, eating food from trays that were dispensed from a large and intricate machine on one side of the front of the room. I stared at it for a while, watching people go up to it, press colored panels, and receive their trays within fifteen or twenty seconds each.

"Catering," said il-Qurawi with an audible sigh. "Major part of our overhead."

"Question, O Sir," I said. "Who's actually paying for all this?"

He looked at me as if I were a total fool. "All these people in Group 26, of course. They've signed over varying amounts of cash and property, depending on how long they intend to stay. Some come for a week, but the greater portion of the group has paid in advance for ten- or twenty-year leases."

My eyes narrowed as I thought and did a little multiplication in my head. "Then, depending on the populations of the other thirty-some floors," I said slowly, "CRCorp ought to be making a very tidy bundle."

His head jerked around to look at me directly. "I've already mentioned the high overhead. The expenses we incur to maintain all this—and the CRs on the other floors—is staggering. Our profits are not so great as you might think."

"I ask a thousand pardons, O Sir," I said. "I truly had no intention to give offense. I'm still trying to get an idea of how large an operation this is. Maybe now's the time to speak to one or two of these 'Martian colonists.' "

He relaxed a little. He was hiding something, I'd bet my wives and kids on it. "Of course," he said smoothly. I thought back on it and couldn't recall a single time he'd actually called me by name. In any event, he directed me to one of the tables where there was an empty seat beside an elderly man with short-cropped white hair. He wore a pale-blue jumpsuit. Hell, everyone there wore a pale-blue jumpsuit. I wondered if that was the official uniform on the real Mars colony, or just a group decision of this particular CR.

"Salâm alêkom," I said to the elderly man.

"Alêkom-os-salâm," he said mechanically. "Outsider, huh?"

"Just came in to get a quick look."

He leaned over and whispered in my ear. "Now, some of us really hate outsiders. Spoils the group consensus."

"I'll be out of here before you know it, inshallah."

The white-haired man took a forkful of some brown, smooth substance on his tray, chewed it thoughtfully, then said, "Could've at least gotten into a goddamn jumpsuit, hayawaan. Too much trouble?"

I ignored the insult. Il-Qurawi should've thought of the jumpsuit. "How long you been part of Group 26?" I asked.

"We don't call ourselves 'Group 26,' " said the man, evidently disliking me even more. "We're the Mars colony."

Well, the real Mars colony was a combined project of the Federated New England States of America, the new Fifth Reich, and the Fragrant Heavenly Empire of True Cathay.

There were no—or very few—Arabs on the real Mars.

Someone delivered a tray of food to me: molded food without texture slapped onto a molded plastic tray; the brown stuff, some green stuff that I took to be some form of vegetable material—as nondescript and unidentifiable as anything else on the tray—a small portion of dark red, chewy stuff that might have been a meat substitute, and the almost obligatory serving of gelatin salad with chopped carrots, celery, and canned fruit in it. There were also slices of dark bread and disposable cups of camel's milk.

I turned again to the white-haired gentleman. "Milk, huh?" I asked.

His bushy eyebrows went up. "Milk is the best thing for you. If you want to live forever."

I murmured "Bismillah," which means "in the name of God," and I began eating my meal, not knowing what some of the dishes were even after I'd tasted and chewed and swallowed them. I ate out of social obligation, and I did pretty well, too. When some of the others were finished, they took their trays and utensils to a machine very much like the one that dispensed the meals in the first place. The hard items disappeared into a long, wide slot, and I felt certain that leftover food was recycled in one form or another. CRCorp prided itself on efficiency, and this was one way to keep the operating costs down.

I still had my doubts about the limited choices in the refectory —including the compulsory camel's milk, which was served in four-ounce cups. As I ate, il-Qurawi turned toward me again. "Are you enjoying the meal?" he asked.

"Praise God for His beneficence," I said.

"God, God—," il-Qurawi shook his head. "It's permissible if you really believe in that sort of thing. But the people here are not all Muslim—some belong to no organized religion at all—and they're using whatever agricultural training they had on 'Earth,' and they're applying it here on 'Mars.' They grew a small portion of these delicious meats and vegetables themselves—it came from their skill, their dedication, their determination. They receive no aid or interference from CRCorp."

"Yeah, you right," I said, and decided I'd had enough of il-Qurawi, too. I hadn't tasted anything the least bit palatable except possibly the bread and milk, and how wildly enthusiastic could I get about them? I didn't mention anything about CRCorp's inability to reproduce the noticeably lower gravity of the true Mars, or certain other aspects of the interplanetary milieu.

I spoke some more to the white-haired man, and then one of the plainly clothed women farther down the table leaned over and interrupted us. Her hair was cut just above shoulder-length, dull from not having been washed for a very long time. I suppose that while there was plenty of water in the thirty-six-story office building, in the headquarters of the CRCorp, and on some of the other consensus-reality floors, there was extremely little water available on floor twenty-six—the Mars for the sort of folks who yearned for danger, but no danger more threatening than the elevator ride from the main lobby.

"Has he told you everything?" asked the filthy woman. Her voice was clearly intended to be a whisper, but I'm sure she was overheard several rows of tables away on either side of us.

"There's so much more I want you to see," said il-Qurawi, even going so far as to grab my arm. That just made me determined to hear the woman out.

"I have not finished my meal, O fellah," I said, somewhat irritably. I'd called him a peasant. I shouldn't have, but it felt good. "What is your blessed name, O Lady?" I asked her.

She looked blank for a few seconds, then confused. Finally she said, "Marjory Mulcher. Yeah, that's me now. Sometimes I'm Marjory Tiller, depending on the season and how badly they need me and how many people are willing to work with me."

I nodded, figuring I understood what she meant. "Everything that passes in this world," I said, "—or any other world—" I interpolated, "is naught but the expression of the Will of God."

Marjory's eyes grew larger and she smiled. "I'm a Roman Catholic," she said. "Lapsed, maybe, but what does that do to you, camel jockey?"

I couldn't think of a safely irrelevant reply.

In her mind, the CRCorp probably had nothing to do with her present situation. Perhaps in her own mind she was on Mars. That may have been the great and ultimate victory of CRCorp.

"I asked you," said Marjory with a frown, "are they showing you everything? Are they telling you everything?"

"Don't know," I said. "I just got here."

Marjory moved down a few places and sat beside me, on the other side from the white-haired man. I looked around and saw that only she and I were still eating. Everyone else had disposed of his tray and was sitting, almost expectantly, in his molded plastic seat, politely and quietly.

The woman smelled terrible. She leaned toward me and whispered, "You know the corporation is just about ready to unleash a devastating CR. Something we won't be able to manage at all. Death on every floor, I imagine. And then, when they've tested this horrible CR on us, may their religion be cursed, they'll unleash it on you and what you casually prefer to call the rest of the world. Earth, I mean. I grew up on Earth, you know. Still have some relatives there."

By the holy sacred beard of the Prophet, may the blessings of Allah be on him and peace, I've never felt so relieved as when she discovered a sudden interest in the gelatin salad. "Raisins. Rejoicing and celebrations," she said to no one in particular. "Consensual raisins."

I slowly closed my eyes and tightened my lips. My right hand dropped its piece of bread and raised up tiredly to cover my tightly shut eyelids, at the same time massaging my forehead. We didn't have enough facilities for mentals and nutsos in the city; we just let the ones with the wealthier families shut 'em away in places like Group 26 in the CRCorp building. Yaa Allah, you never knew when you were going to run into one of these bereft cookies.

Still with my eyes covered, I could feel the man with the close-cropped white hair lean toward me on the other side. I knew that son of a biscuit hadn't liked me from the get-go. "Get Marjory to tell you all about her raisins sometime. It's a fascinating story in its own right."

"Be sure to," I murmured. In the spring with the apricots, I would. I picked up the bread with my eating hand again and opened my eyes. Everyone within hollering range was staring at me with rapt attention. I don't know why; I didn't want to know why then, and I still don't want to know why. I hoped it was just that I was an oddity, a welcome interruption in the daily routine, like a visit from one of Prince Shaykh Mahali's wives or children.

I'd had enough to eat, and so I'd picked up the tray—I'm quick on the uptake, and I'd figured out the disposal drill from observation. It wasn't that difficult to begin with, and, jeez, I'm a trained

professional, mush hayk? Yeah, you right. I slid the tray into the
proper slot in the proper machine. Then il-Qurawi, having nothing
immediate to do, chose to be nowhere in sight. I slumped back
down between Marjory and the old, white-haired man. Fortunately,
Marjory was still enchanted by her gelatin salad—the al-Qaddani
moddy, a Palestinian fictional hardboiled-detective piece of hardware I was wearing, let me have the impression that Marjory was
like this at every meal, whatever was served—and the old gentleman
gave me a disapproving look, stood up, and moved away, toward
what real people did to compensate society for their daily sustenance. For a few moments I had utter peace and utter silence, but
I did not expect them to last very long. I was correct as usual in this
sort of discouraging speculation.

Almost directly across from me was a woman with extremely
large breasts, which were trapped in an undergarment which must
have been painfully confining for them. I really wasn't interested
enough to read if they were genuine—God-given—or not; she
must've thought she had, you know, the most devastating figure on
all of Mars, and of course we understand what we mean when we
speak of Mars. She wore a long, flowing, print shift of a drabness
that directed all one's attention elsewhere and upwards; bare feet;
and a live, medium-sized, suffering lizard on one shoulder that
was there only to extort yet another sort of response from you. As if
her grotesque mamelons weren't enough.

Oh, you were supposed to say, *you have a live, medium-sized
lizard on your shoulder.* Now, when someone has gone to that
amount of labor to pry a reaction from me, my innate obstinacy sets
in. I will not look more than two or three times at the tits, casually,
as after the first encounter they don't exist for me. I won't even
glance furtively at her various other vulgar accoutrements. I won't
remark at all on the lizard. The lizard and I will never have a relationship; the woman and I barely had one, and *that* only through
courtesy.

She spoke in a voice intended to be heard by the nearby portion
of mankind: "I think Marjory means well." She looked around
herself to find agreement, and there wasn't a single person still in
the refectory who would contradict her. I got the feeling that would
be true whatever she said. "I know for a fact that Marjory never goes
beyond the buildings of the Mars colony. She never sees Allah's
holy miracle of creation. Does it not say in the Book, the noble
Qur'ân, 'Frequently you see the ground dry and barren: but no
sooner do We send down rain to moisten it than it begins to trem-
ble and magnify, putting forth each and every kind of blossoming

life. That is because Allah is Truth: He gives life to the dead and has power over all things.' She sat back, evidently very self-satisfied. "That was from the sûrah called 'Pilgrimage,' in the holy Qur'ân."

"May the Creator of heaven and earth bless this recitation of His holy words," said one man softly.

"May Allah give His blessing," said a woman quietly.

I had several things I might have mentioned; the first was that the imitation surface of Mars I'd crossed was not, in point of fact, covered with every variety of blooming plant. Yet maybe to some of these people that was worth reporting to the authorities. Before I could say anything, a young, sparsely bearded man sat beside me in the old, white-haired resident's seat, and addressed the elderly woman. The young man said, "You know, Umm Sulaiman, that you shouldn't hold up Marjory as a typical resident of the Mars colony."

Umm Sulaiman frowned. "I have further scripture that I could recite which supports my words and actions."

The young man shuddered. "No, my mother-in-law"—clearly an honorific and a title not to be taken seriously—"all is as Allah wills." He turned to me and murmured, "I wish the both of them—the two old women, Marjory and Umm Sulaiman—would stop behaving in their ways. I admit it, I'm superstitious, and it frightens me."

"Seems a shame to pay all this money to CRCorp just to be frightened."

The young man looked to either side, then leaned even closer. "I've heard a story, O Sir," he murmured. "Actually, I've heard several stories, some as wild as Marjory's, some even crazier. But, by the beard of the Prophet – "

"May the blessings of Allah be on him and peace," I said.

"—there's one story that won't go away, a story that's repeated often by the most sane and reliable of our team." Team: as if they really were part of some kind of international extraterrestrial project.

I pursed my lips and tried to show that I was rabidly eager to hear his bit of gossip. "And what is this persistent story, O Wise One?"

He looked to either side again, took my arm, and together we left the table and the others. We walked slowly toward the exit. "Now, O Sir," he said, "I've heard this directly from Bin el-Fadawin, who is CRCorp and Shaykh il-Qurawi's highest representative here in the Mars colony."

"Group 26, you mean," I said.

"Yeah, if you insist on it, Group 26." It was obvious that he didn't like his illusion broken, even for a moment. It cast some preliminary doubt on what he was about to tell me. "Listen, O Sir," he said. "Bin el-Fadawin and others drop hints now and again that CRCorp has better uses for these premises, that they're even now working on ways to turn away and run off the very people who've paid them for long-term care."

I shrugged. "If CRCorp wanted to evict all of you, O Young Man, I'm sure they could do it without too much difficulty. I mean, they got the lawyers and you got, what, rocks and lichen? Still, you and all the others have handed over—and continue to hand over— truly exorbitant amounts of cash and property; and all they've really done is decorate to your specifications a large, empty space in a restored office tower."

"They've created our consensual reality, please, O Shaykh."

"Yeah, you right," I said, amazed that this somewhat intelligent young man could be so easily taken in. "So you're telling me that the CRs—which the corporation has worked so hard to create, and for which it's being richly rewarded—will start disappearing, one by one?"

"Begin disappearing!" cried the young man. "Have Shaykh il-Qurawi – "

"Did I hear my name mentioned, O Most Gracious Ones?" asked my client, appearing silently enough through the door of the refectory room. "In a pleasant context, I hope."

"I was commenting, O Sir," I said, covering quickly, "on the truly spectacular job CRCorp has done here, inside the buildings and out. That little lizard Umm Sulaiman wears on her shoulder— is that a genuine Martian life form?"

"No," he said, frowning slightly. "There aren't any native lizards on Mars. We've tried to discourage her from wearing it—it creates a disharmony with what we're trying to accomplish here. Still, the choice is her own."

"Ah," I said. I'd figured all that before; I was just easing the young man out of the conversation. "I believe I've seen enough here, O Sir. Next I'd like to see some of the vandalism you spoke of."

"Of course," said il-Qurawi, moving a hand to almost touch me, almost grasp my elbow and lead me from the refectory. He gave me no time at all for the typically effusive Muslim farewells. We left the building the way we'd come, and once again I used the mask and bottled air. However, we didn't make the long trek across the make-believe Martian landscape; il-Qurawi knew of a nearer exit. I guess he had just wanted me to come the long way before, to sample the handiwork of CRCorp.

We ducked through a nearly invisible airlock near the colony buildings, and took an elevator down to floor seven. When we stepped in, I removed the mask and air tank. The air pressure and oxygen content of the atmosphere was Earth-normal.

I saw immediately il-Qurawi's problem. Floor seven was entirely abandoned. In fact, except for some living quarters and outbuildings in the distance, and the barren and artificially landscaped "hills" and "valleys" built into the area, floor seven was nothing but a large and vacant loft a few stories above street level.

"What happened here, O Sir?" I asked.

Il-Qurawi turned around and casually indicated the entire floor. "This used to be a re-creation of Egypt at the time of the Ptolemies. I personally never saw the need for a consensual reality set in pre-Islamic times, but I was assured that certain academic experts wanted to reestablish the Library of Alexandria, which was destroyed by the Romans before the birth of the Prophet."

"May the blessings of Allah be on him and peace," I murmured.

Il-Qurawi shrugged. "It was functioning quite well, at least as well as the Martian colony, if not better, until one day it just . . . went away. The holographic images vanished, the specially created computer effects went offline, and nothing our creative staff did restored them. After a week or ten days of living in this emptiness, the people of Group 7 demanded a refund and departed."

I rubbed my dyed beard. "O Sir, where are the controlling mechanisms, and how hard is it to achieve access to them?"

Il-Qurawi led me toward the northern wall. We had a good distance to hike. I saw that the floor was some molded synthetic material; it was probably the same as on floor twenty-six. All the rest was the result of the electronic magic of CRCorp—what they got paid for. I could imagine the puzzlement, then the chagrin, finally the wrath of the residents of floor seven.

We reached the northern wall, and il-Qurawi led me to a small metal door built into the wall about eye-level. He opened the door, and I saw some familiar computer controls while others were completely baffling to me; there were slots for bubble-plate memory units, hardcopy readout devices, a keyboard data-entry device, a voice-recognition entry device, and other things that were to some degree strange and unrecognizable to me. I never claimed to be a computer expert. I'm not. I just didn't think it was profitable to let il-Qurawi know it.

"Wiped clean," he said, indicating the hardware inside the door. "Someone got in—someone knowing where to look for the control mechanisms—and deleted all the vital programs, routines, and local effects."

"All right," I said, beginning to turn the problem over in my mind. It had the look of a simple crime. "Any recently discharged employee with a reason for revenge?"

Il-Qurawi swore under his breath. I admit it, I was a little shocked. That's how much I'd changed since the old days. "Don't you think we checked out all the simple solutions ourselves?" he grumbled. "Before we came to you? By the life of my children, I'm positive it wasn't a disgruntled former employee, or a current one with plans for extortion, or any of the other easy answers that will occur to you at first. We're faced with a genuine disaster: Someone is destroying consensual realities for no apparent reason."

I blinked at him for a few seconds, thinking over what he'd just told me. I was standing in what had once been a replica of a strip of ancient civilization along the banks of the Nile River in pre-Muslim Egypt. Now I could look across the unfurnished space toward the other walls, seeing only the textured, generally flat floor in between. "You used the plural, O Sir," I said at last. "How many other consensual realities have been ruined like this one?"

"Out of thirty rented floors," he said quietly, "eighteen have been rendered inactive."

I just stared. CRCorp didn't just have a serious problem—it was facing extinction. I was surprised that the company hadn't come to me sooner. Of course, il-Qurawi was the Chief of Security, and he probably figured that he could solve the mess himself. Finally, with no small degree of humiliation, I'm sure, he sought outside help. And he knew that I knew it. It was a good thing I wasn't in a mood to rub it in, because I had all the ammunition I needed.

Il-Qurawi showed me a few other consensual realities, working ones and empty ones, because I asked him to. He didn't seem eager for me to get too familiar with the CRCorp operation, yet if he wanted me to help with his difficulty, he had to give me a certain amount of access. He and his corporation were backed against the wall, and he recognized the truth of the matter. So I saw a vigorous CR based on an Eritrean-written fantasy-novel series almost a century old; and a successful CR that re-created a strict Sunni Islamic way of life that had never truly existed; and two more floors that were lifeless and unfurnished.

I decided that I'd seen enough for the present. Il-Qurawi thanked me for my time, wished me luck in my quest for the culprit, and hoped it wouldn't take me too long to complete the assignment.

I said, "It shouldn't be more than a day or two, inshallah. I already have some possibilities to investigate." That was a lie. I was as lost as Qabeel's spare mule.

He didn't think it was necessary to accompany me back to my office. He just put me in the limousine with his driver. I didn't care.

I got a scare when I got back to my office. During the time while I'd visited the CRCorp building, someone had defeated my expensive, elaborate security system, entered, and wiped my own CR hardware and software. The shabbiness had disappeared, replaced by the true polished floors and freshly painted walls of the office in the building. I'd worked diligently to reproduce the run-down office of Lufty Gad's detective, al-Qaddani; but now the rooms were clean and new and sleek and modern. I was really furious. On my desk, under a Venetian glass paperweight, was a sheet of my notepaper with two handwritten words on it: A *warning*.

In the name of Allah, the Beneficent, the Merciful. I took out my prayer rug from the closet, spread it carefully on the floor, faced toward Makkah, and prayed. Then, my thoughts on higher things than CRCorp, I returned the rug to the closet. I sprawled in my chair behind the desk and stared at the notepaper. A *warning*. Hell, some guy was good at B & E, as well as cleaning out CRs, large and small. He hadn't made me afraid, only so angry that my stomach hurt.

I didn't want to look at my office space in its true, elegantly modern, fashionable form. Changing everything back the way it had been would be simple enough — I'd been wise enough to buy backups of everything from the small consensual-reality shop that had done up al-Qaddani's office for me in the first place. It would take me half an hour to restore the slovenly look I preferred.

I was certain that Shaykh il-Qurawi had backups to his dysfunctional floors as well; it was only that CRCorp had tried to pass along the costs of the replacement to the residents, and they had balked, perhaps unanimously. I recalled an old proverb I'd learned from my mother, may Allah grant her peace: "Greed lessens what is gathered." It was something CRCorp had yet to learn.

It also meant that everything that il-Qurawi had mentioned to me seemed to be close to its final resolution. I tipped a little from the office bottle into a tumbler and glanced at the setting sun through it. The true meaning — the actual one, the one that counted — had nothing to do with resolutions, however. I knew as well as I knew my childhood pet goat's name that things were never this easy. Mark this down, it's a free tip from an experienced operative (that means street punk): Things are never this easy. I'd known it before I started messing around on the street; then I'd learned it the simple way, from more experienced punks; and finally I'd had to learn it the hard way, too many times. Things are never this easy.

What I'm saying is that Simple Shaykh il-Qurawi knew perfectly well that he could do the same as I had, by way of chunking in the backup tapes, programs, and mechanisms. His echoing, forlorn floors would all quickly return to their fantasy factualities, and they'd probably be repopulated within days. CRCorp would then lose just a minimum of cash, and all the evil time could be filed away as just one of those bad experiences that had to be weathered by every corporation now and then.

Begging the question: Why, then, didn't CRCorp use the backups immediately rather than suffer the angry defection of so many of its clients? And did il-Qurawi really think I was that stupid, that it all wouldn't occur to me pretty damn fast?

Don't ask me. I didn't have a clue.

As the days went by, and the weeks, I learned through Bin el-Fadawin—CRCorp's spy on floor twenty-six—that in fact some of the other floors had been restored, and some of their tenants had returned. Great, wonderful, I told myself, expecting il-Qurawi himself to show up with the rest of my money and possibly even a thank-you, although I don't really believe in miracles.

Three weeks later I get a visitor from floor three. This was a floor that had been changed into a consensual-reality replica of a generation ship—a starship that would take generation upon generation to reach its goal, a planet merely called Home, circling a star named in the catalog simply as Wolf 359. They had years, decades, even longer to name the planet more cheerfully, and the same with their star, Wolf 359. However, the electronics had failed brutally, turning their generation ship into the sort of empty loft I'd witnessed in the CRCorp building. The crew had gotten disgusted and resigned, feeling cheated and threatening lawsuits.

After CRCorp instituted repairs, and when the science-fiction-oriented customers heard that floor three had returned to its generation-ship environment, many of the crew reenlisted at the agreed-upon huge rates. I got another visit, from Bin el-Fadawin this time.

"CRCorp and Shaykh il-Qurawi are more grateful than they can properly express," he said, putting a moderately fat envelope on my desk. "Your work on this case has shown the corporation which techniques it needs to restore for each and every consensual reality."

"Please convey my thanks to both the shaykh and the corporation. I'm just glad everything worked out well at the end," I said. "If Allah wills, the residents of the CRCorp building will once again be happy with their shared worlds." I knew I hadn't done anything but check their security systems; but if they were happy, it had been worth investigating just for the fun I'd had.

Bin el-Fadawin touched his heart, his lips, and his forehead. "Inshallah. You have earned the acknowledged gratitude of CRCorp," he said, bowing low. "This is a mighty though intangible thing to have to your credit."

"I'll mark that down in my book," I said, through a thin smile. I'd had enough of il-Qurawi's lackey. The money in the envelope looked to be adequate reward and certainly spendable. The gratitude of CRCorp, though, was something as invisible and nonexistent as a dream djinn. I paid it the same attention—which is to say, none.

"Thank you again, O Wise One, and I speak as a representative of both CRCorp and Shaykh il-Qurawi."

"No thanks are necessary," I said. "He asked of me a favor, and I did my best to fulfill it."

"May Allah shower you with blessings," he said, sidling toward the inner door.

"May God grant your wishes, my brother," I said, watching him sidle and doing nothing to stop him. I heard the outer door open and shut, and I was sure that I was alone. I picked up the envelope, opened it, and counted the take. There were three thousand kiam there, which included a sizable bonus. I felt extravagantly well paid-off, but not the least bit satisfied. I had this feeling, you see, one I'd had before. . . .

It was a familiar feeling that everything wasn't as picture-perfect as il-Qurawi's hopfrog had led me to suppose. The feeling was borne out quite some time later, when I'd almost forgotten it. My typically long, slow afternoon was interrupted by, of all people, the white-haired old gentleman from floor twenty-six. His name was Uzair ibn Yaqoub. He seemed extremely nervous, even in my office, which had been rendered shabby and comfortable again. He sat in the red-leather chair opposite me and fidgeted for a little while. I gave him a few minutes.

"It's the Terran oxygen level and the air pressure," he said in explanation.

I nodded. It sure as hell was something, to get him to leave his "Martian colony," even for an hour or two.

"Take your time, O Shaykh ibn Yaqoub," I said. I offered him water and some fruit, that's all I had around the office. That and the bottle in the drawer, which had less than a slug left in it.

"You know, of course," said ibn Yaqoub, "that after your visit, the same trouble that had plagued other consensual realities struck us. Fortunately for floor twenty-six, the CRCorp technicians found out what was wrong on Mars, and they fixed it. We're all back there living just as before."

I nodded. That was chiefly my job at this stage of the interview.

"Well," said ibn Yaqoub, "I'm certain—and some of the others, even those who never agreed with me before—that something wrong and devious and possibly criminal is happening."

I thought, what could be more criminal than the destruction— the theft—of consensual realities? But I merely said, "What do you mean, O Wise One?"

"I mean that somehow, someone is stealing from us."

"Stealing what?" I asked, remembering that they produced little: some vegetables, maybe, some authentic lichen. . . .

"Stealing," insisted ibn Yaqoub. "You know the Mars colony pays each of us flight pay and hazardous-duty pay during our stay."

No, I hadn't heard that before. All I'd known was that the money went the other way, from the colonist to the corporation. This was suddenly becoming very interesting.

"And that's in addition to our regular low wages," said the white-haired old man. "We didn't sign up to make money. It was the Martian experience we longed for."

I nodded a third time. "And you think, O Shaykh, that somehow you're being cheated?"

He made a fist and struck my desk. "I know it!" he cried. "I figured in advance how much money to expect for a four-week period, because I had to send some to my grandchildren. When the pay voucher arrived, it was barely more than half the kiam I expected. I tried to have someone in the colony explain it to me— I admit that I'm not as good with mathematics as I used to be—and even Bin el-Fadawin assured me that I must have made an error in calculation. I don't particularly trust Bin el-Fadawin, but everyone else seemed to agree with him. Then, as time passed, more and more people noticed tax rates too high, payroll deductions too large, miscellaneous costs showing up here and there. Now we're all generally agreed that something needs to be done. You've helped us greatly before. We beg you to help us again."

I stood up behind my desk and paced, as I usually did when I was thinking over a new case. Was this a new case, however, or just an extension of the old one? It was difficult for me to believe il-Qurawi and CRCorp needed every last fiq and kiam of these poor people, who were already paying the majority of their wealth for the privilege of living in the "Mars colony." Cheating them like this seemed to me to be too trivial and too cruel, even for CRCorp.

I told ibn Yaqoub I'd look into the matter. I accepted no retainer, and I quoted him a vanishingly small fee. I liked him, and I liked most of the others in Group 26.

I returned first to the twenty-sixth floor, not telling anyone I was coming—particularly not il-Qurawi or Bin el-Fadawin. I knew where to get a mask, oxygen tank, and blue coveralls. Now I also knew where the control box was hidden on the "Martian" wall, and I checked it. I made several interesting discoveries: Someone was indeed bleeding off funds from the internal operation of the consensus reality.

I returned to my office, desperate to know who the culprit was. I was not terribly surprised to see my outer office filled with three waiting clients—all of them from other consensus realities. One, from the harsh Sunni floor, threatened to start taking off hands and arms if I didn't come up with an acceptable alternative. The other two were nowhere as bloodthirsty, but every bit as outraged.

I assured and mollified and talked them back down to something like peacefulness. I waited until they left, and I opened the bottom drawer and withdrew the office bottle. I felt I'd earned the final slug. A voice behind me spoke: "Got a gift for ya," the young man said. I turned. I saw a youth in his mid-twenties, wearing a gallebeya that seemed to shift colors from green to blue as he changed positions.

"For you," he said, coming toward me, setting a fresh bottle of gin on my desk. "On account of you're so damn smart."

"Bismillah," I said. "I am in your debt."

"We'll see," said the young man, with a quirky smile.

I built us two quick white deaths. He sat in the red-leather chair and sipped his, enjoying the taste. I gulped the first half of mine, then slowed to his speed just to show that I could do it.

I waited. I could gain much by waiting—information perhaps, and at least the other half of the white death.

"You don't know me," said the young man. "Call me Firon." That was Arabic for Pharaoh. "It's as phony a name as Musa. Or your own name."

The mention of Musa made me sit up straight. I was sore that he'd broken his way into my inner office, eavesdropped on my clients, and knew that I was out of gin on top of everything else. I started to say something, but he stopped me with a raised hand. "There's a lot you don't know, O Sir," he said, rather sadly I thought. "You used to run the streets the way we run them, but it's been too long, and you rose too high, and now you're trapped over here on this side of the canal. So you've lost touch in some ways."

"Lost touch, yes, but I still have connections—"

Firon laughed. "Connections! Musa and I and our friends now decide who gets what and how much and when. And then we slip back into our carefully built alternate personalities. Some of us make use of your antique moddy-and-daddy technology. Some of us make a valuable practice of entering and exiting certain consensual realities. The rest of us—well, how many ways are there of hiding?"

"One," I said. "Just one good way. The rest is merely waiting until you're caught."

Firon laughed brightly and pointed a finger. "Exactly! Exactly so! And what are you doing? Or I? Can we tell?"

I sat back down wearily. I didn't want another white death, which I interpreted as a bad sign. "What do you want then from me?" I asked.

Firon stood and towered over me. "Just this, and listen well to me: We know who you are, we know how vulnerable you are. You must let us continue to make our small, almost inconsequential financial transactions, or we'll simply reveal your identity. We'll reveal it generally, if you take my meaning."

"I take it precisely," I said, feeling old and slow. Firon and his associates were threatening to expose me to my large number of enemies. I did feel old and slow, but not too old and slow. Firon, this young would-be tyrant, was so certain of his power over me that he wasn't paying very close attention. He was a victim of his own pride, his own self-delusions. I took the nearly full bottle of gin and put it in the bottom drawer. At the same time, I took a small but extremely serviceable seizure gun—the one that used to belong to my second wife—from my ankle holster and I showed it to him. "Old ways are sometimes the best," I said with a wry smile.

He sank slowly into the red-leather chair, a wide and wobbly grin on his face. "In the name of Allah, the Beneficent, the Merciful," he said.

"Praise Allah," I said.

"Now what?" asked Firon. "We're at one of those famous impasses."

I thought for a moment or two. "Here," I said at last, "how's this as a solution? You're ripping off people in the CRCorp building who've become my friends, at least some of them have. I don't like that. Still, I don't have a goddamn problem with you and Musa and whomever else works with you pulling this gimmick all over town. You don't turn my name over to Shaykh Reda, and I let you guys alone, unless you take on my few remaining friends. You do that wrong thing, and I'll hand you right to the civil authorities, and you know—Musa sure as hell knows—what the penalties are."

"We can trust you?"

"Can you?"

Firon took a deep breath, let it out, and nodded. "We can live with that. We can surely live with that! You're a kind of legend among us. A small legend, an ignoble kind of legend, but if you were younger, our age. . . ."

"Thanks a hell of a lot," I said, still holding the seizure gun on him.

Firon got up and headed for my inner door. "You know, CRCorp knew about us from the beginning, and let us be. Shaykh il-Qurawi and the others just wanted to test out their security measures and their alarm programs. You care more about those people in that building than they do."

"Somebody's got to," I said wearily.

"Peoples' lives are their own, and there are no corporations, man!" He made some sort of sign with his hand in the gloomy outer office. I recalled what it had been like to be his age and youthfully idealistic.

Then he was gone.

Introduction to
The City on the Sand

In some ways, this is the ultimate tale of Budayeen Nights.

In every other tale of the Budayeen, while the action is going on, the presence of Ernst Weinraub is more or less implied, sitting at his café table, watching what goes on without the faintest idea of what's actually going on. You can almost see him out of the corner of your eye.

This is another one printed here from George's file copy, not the version actually published in F&SF—*and this story was later expanded upon to make up George's novel* Relatives. *It was the first appearance of the Budayeen, and one of the few works in which it, and the nameless City, are described: the Chinese quarter; the canal with its restaurants, bars, casinos (i.e. Canal Street in New Orleans, which was named after a canal that was never dug); the marketplace and miniature golf facilities; and the bizarre replica of Singapore built by a crazed millionaire. (On St. Charles Avenue in New Orleans stands a 1960s copy of the mansion "Tara" from the film* Gone with the Wind.*)*

"The city was the final hope of those who truly needed to hide."

As was—and is—New Orleans.

The hiding place to which George fled from the noise and stress of New York in the early seventies; the place where he returned after the final disaster of his last marriage in Los Angeles.

We see a day in the life of the Budayeen, through the eyes of lost, shabby, and hopeless expatriate Ernst Weinraub (or Weintraub). We meet, for the first time, Monsieur Gargotier, proprietor of the Fée Blanche; see Sandor Courane in one of his few nonfatal roles; hear tell of Marîd's favorite hangouts, the Solace and Chiriga's. We see the ubiquitous Arab boy, here called Kebap ("Roast Beef"), though he has other names in other tales, coming and going like a troublesome little ghost.

Weinraub himself, like Sandor Courane, was one of George's generic recurring heroes, appearing in a number of early stories before he was supplanted by Courane. In most of them, Ernst is the ultimate square-jawed hero, but without Courane's doomed and hapless charm; maybe that was Ernst's point. In this tale he has been sawed and filed down to being a legend in his own mind: aloof in his self-conscious dreams, mocked at by the street folk, losing himself deeper and deeper into his alcoholic fantasies. He wants to be a writer and wants desperately to be noticed, but he only pretends to write—a fate that befalls and befell many writers who get seduced by the "New Orleans lifestyle."

I suspect George had met a number of Ernsts in New Orleans—I know he was friends with Tennessee Williams's houseboy, to whom he lived next door for many years. (I still have the smudged and blotted napkins bearing the outlines of trilogies never written, in George's spiky block-print hand, including the outline of the fourth Budayeen novel, Word of Night.*)*

Weinraub has tried—as George tried for so many years—"to write . . . short, terse essays about the city . . ." But "he couldn't seem to capture the true emotions he experienced . . . the pervasive sense of isolation, of eternal uncleanness, of a soul-deep loss of personality. . . ."

But where poor Ernst failed, George succeeded dazzlingly. This is very much a Budayeen night: a night on which nothing in particular takes place. The nameless city simply winds its accustomed way through another turning of the sterile Earth. Everyone in it goes about their own obscure business like the characters in the Dylan song "Mr. Tambourine Man," observed by a failed poet who has nowhere left to go.

—Barbara Hambly

✢ ✢ ✢

The City on the Sand

IN EUROPE, THERE WERE ONLY MEMORIES OF GREAT cultures. Spain, Portugal, Italy, France, England, Carbba, and Germany had all seized control of the world's course and the imagination of the human race at one time or another. But now these great powers of the past were drifting into a cynical old age, where decadence and momentary pleasures replaced the drive for dominance and national superiority. In Asia, the situation was even worse. The Russias struggled pettily among themselves, expending the last energies of a once-proud nation in puerile bickerings. China showed signs of total degeneration, having lost its immensely rich heritage of art and philosophy while clinging to a ruthless creed that crushed its hopeless people beneath a burden of mock-patriotism. Breulandy was the only vibrant force east of the Caucasus Mountains; still, no observer could tell what that guarded land might do. Perhaps a Breulen storm would spill out across the continent, at least instilling a new life force in the decaying states. But from Breulandy itself came no word, no hint, as though the country had bypassed its time of ascendancy to settle for a weary and bitter mediocrity.

Of the rest of the world there was nothing to be said. The Americas still rested as they had in the few centuries since their discovery: huge parklike land masses, populated by savages, too distant, too worthless, too impractical to bother about. None of the crumbling

191

European governments could summon either the leadership or the
financial support to exploit the New World. The Scandinavian
lands were inhabited by skin-clad brutes scarcely more civilized
than the American cannibals. Farther east, beyond the teeming
Chinese shores, between Asia and the unexplored western reaches
of the Americas, no one was quite certain just what existed and
what was only myth. Perhaps the island continent of Lemarry
waited with its untold riches and beautiful copper spires.

And then, lastly, there was Africa. One city sat alone on its fiery
sands. One city, filled with refugees and a strange mongrel population, guarded that massive continent. Beyond that single city, built
in some forgotten age by an unknown people for unimaginable
purposes, beyond the high wooden gates that shut in the crazy heat
and locked in the citizens, there was only death. Without water, the
continent was death. Without shade, the parching sharaq winds
were death. Without human habitation, the vast three thousand
miles of whispering sands were death for anyone mad enough to
venture across them. Only in the city was there a hollow travesty of
life.

Ernst Weinraub sat at a table on the patio of the Café de la Fée
Blanche. A light rain fell on him, but he did not seem to notice. He
sipped his anisette, regretting that the proprietor had served it to
him in such an ugly tumbler. The liqueur suffered. M. Gargotier
often made such disconcerting lapses, but today especially Ernst
needed all the delicacy, all the refinement that he could buy to hold
off his growing melancholy. Perhaps the Fée Blanche had been a
mistake. It was early, lacking some thirty minutes of noon, and if
it seemed to him that the flood of tears was rising too quickly, he
could move on to the Café Solace or Chiriga's. But as yet there was
no need to hurry.

The raindrops fell heavily, spatting on the small metal table.
Ernst turned in his chair, looking for M. Gargotier. Was the man
going to let his customer get drenched? The proprietor had disappeared into the black interior of his establishment. Ernst thought
of lowering the striped canopy himself, but the shopkeeper-image
of himself that the idea brought to mind was too absurd. Instead,
he closed his eyes and listened to the water. There was music when
the drops hit the furnishings on the patio, a duller sound when
the rain struck the pavement. Then, more frequently, there was the
irritating noise of the drops hitting his forehead. Ernst opened his
eyes. His newspaper was a sodden mess and the puddle on his table
was about to overflow onto his lap.

Ernst considered the best way to deal with the accumulating water. He could merely cup his hand and swipe the puddle sideways. He dismissed that plan, knowing that his hand would be soaked; then he would sit, frustrated, without anything on which to dry it. He would end up having to seek out M. Gargotier. The confrontation then, with the proprietor standing bored, perhaps annoyed, would be too unpleasant. Anyway, the round metal top of the table was easily removed. Ernst tipped it, revealing the edges of the white metal legs, which were sharp with crystal rust. The water splashed to the paved floor of the patio, loudly, inelegantly. Ernst sighed; he had made another compromise with his manner. He had sacrificed style for comfort. In the city, it was an easy bargain.

"It is a matter of bodies," he said to himself, as though rehearsing bons mots for a cocktail party. "We have grown too aware of bodies. Because we must carry them always from place to place, is that any reason to accord our bodies a special honor or affection? No, they are sacks only. Rather large, unpleasant, undisciplined containers for meager charges of emotion. We should all stop paying attention to our bodies' demands. I don't know how. . . ." He paused. The idea was stupid. He sipped the anisette.

There were not more than twenty small tables on the Fée Blanche's patio. Ernst was the only patron, as he was every day until lunchtime. He and M. Gargotier had become close friends. At least, so Ernst believed. It was so comforting to have a place where one could sit and watch, where the management didn't eternally trouble about another drink or more coffee. Bien sûr, the old man never sat with Ernst to observe the city's idlers or offer to test Ernst's skill at chess. In fact, to be truthful, M. Gargotier had rarely addressed a full sentence to him. But Ernst was an habitué, M. Gargotier's only regular customer, and for quite different reasons they both hoped the Fée Blanche might become a favorite meeting place for the city's literate and wealthy few. Ernst had invested too many months of sitting at that same table to move elsewhere now.

"A good way to remove a measure of the body's influence is to concentrate on the mind," he said. He gazed at the table top, which already was refilling with rainwater. "When I review my own psychological history, I must admit to a distressing lack of moral sense. I have standards gleaned from romantic novels and magistral decrees, standards which stick out awkwardly among my intellectual baggage like the frantic wings of a tethered pigeon. I can examine those flashes of morality whenever I choose, though I rarely bother. They are all so familiar. But all around them in my mind are the heavy, dense shadows of events and petty crimes."

With a quick motion, Ernst emptied the table top once more. He sighed. "There was Eugenie. I loved her for a time, I believe. A perfect name, a lesser woman. When the romance began, I was well aware of my moral sense. Indeed, I cherished it, worshiped it with an adolescent lover's fervor. I needed the constraints of society, of law and honor. I could only prove my worth and value within their severe limits. Our love would grow, I believed, fed by the bitter springs of righteousness. Ah, Eugenie! You taught me so much. I loved you for it then, even as my notion of purity changed, bit by bit, hour by hour. Then, when I fell at long last to my ardent ruin, I hated you. For so many years I hated you for your joy in my dismay, for the ease of your robbery and betrayal, for the entertainment I provided in my youthful terror. Now, Eugenie, I am at peace with your memory. I would not have understood in those days, but I am at last revenged upon you: I have achieved indifference.

"How sad, I think, for poor Marie, who came after. I loved her from a distance, not wishing ever again to be wounded on the treacherous point of my own affection. I was still foolish." Ernst leaned back in his chair, turning his head to stare across the small expanse of vacant tables. He glanced around; no one else had entered the café. "What could I have learned from Eugenie? Pain? No. Discomfort, then? Yes, but so? These evaluations, I hasten to add, I make from the safety of my greater experience and sophistication. Nevertheless, even in my yearling days I recognized that la belle E. had prepared me well to deal not only with her successors but with all people in general. I had learned to pray for another's ill fortune. This was the first great stain on the bright emblem of virtue that, at the time, still resided in my imagination.

"Marie, I loved you from whatever distance seemed appropriate. I was still not skillful in these matters, and it appears now that I judged those distances poorly. Finally, you gave your heart to another, one whose management of proximity was far cleverer than mine. I could not rejoice in your good fortune. I prayed fervently for the destruction of your happiness. I wished you and him the most total of all disasters, but I was denied. You left my life as you entered it—a cold, distant dream. Yet before you left, you rehearsed me in the exercise of spite."

He took a sip of the liqueur and swirled it against his palate. "I've grown since then, of course," he said. "I've grown and changed, but you're still there, an ugly spatter against the cleanness of what I wanted to be." With a sad expression he set the tumbler on the small table. Rain fell into the anisette, but Ernst was not concerned. This morning he was playing the bored expatriate. He smoked only imported cigarettes, his boxed filters conspicuous among the packs of Impers and Les Bourdes. He studied the strollers closely, staring with affected weariness into the eyes of the younger women, refusing to look away. He scribbled on the backs of envelopes that he found in his coat pockets or on scraps of paper from the ground. He waited for someone to show some interest and ask him what he did. "I am just jotting notes for the novel," he would say, or "Merely a sketch, a small poem. Nothing important. A transient joy mingled with regret." He watched the hotel across the square with a carefully sensitive expression, as if the view were really from the wind-swept cliffs of the English coast or the history-burdened martial plains of France. Anyone could see that he was an artist. Ernst promised fascinating stories and secret romantic insights, but some-how the passersby missed it all.

Only thoughts of the rewards for success kept him at M. Gar-gotier's table. Several months previously, a poet named Courane had been discovered while sitting at the wicker bar of the Blue Parrot. Since then, Courane had become the favorite of the city's idle elite. Already he had purchased his own café and held court in its several dank rooms. Stories circulated about Courane and his admirers. Exciting, licentious rumors grew up around the young man, and Ernst was envious. Ernst had lived in the city much longer than Courane. He had even read some of Courane's alleged poetry, and he thought it was terrible. But Courane's excesses were notorious. It was this that no doubt had recommended him to the city's weary nobility.

Something about the city attracted the failed poets of the world. Like the excavation of Troy, which discovered layer upon layer, settlement built upon ancient settlement, the recent history of the civilized world might be read in the bitter eyes of the lonely men waiting in the city's countless cafés. Only rarely could Ernst spare the time to visit with his fellows, and then the men just stared silently past each other. They all understood; it was a horrible thing for Ernst to know that they all knew everything about him. So he sat in the Fée Blanche, hiding from them, hoping for luck.

Ernst's city sat like a blister on the fringe of a great equatorial desert. The metropolitan centers of the more sophisticated nations were much too far away to allow Ernst to feel completely at ease. He built for himself a life in exile, pretending that it made no differ-ence. But the provinciality of these people! The mountains and the narrow fertile plain that separated the city from the northern sea effectively divided him from every familiar landmark of his past. He could only think and remember. And who was there to decide if his recollections might have blurred and altered with repetition?

"Now, Eugenie. You had red hair. You had hair like the embers of a dying fire. How easy it was to kindle the blaze afresh. In the morning, how easy. The fuel was there, the embers burned hotly within; all that was needed was a little wind, a little stirring. Eugenie, you had red hair. I've always been weakened by red hair.

"Marie, poor Marie, your hair was black, and I loved it, too, for a time. And I'll never know what deftnesses and craft were necessary to fire your blood. Eugenie, the creature of flame, and Marie, the gem of ice. I confuse your faces. I can't recall your voices. Good luck to you, my lost loves, and may God bless."

The city was an oven, a prison, an asylum, a veritable zoo of human aberration. Perhaps this worked in Ernst's favor; those people who did not have to hire themselves and their children for food spent their empty hours searching for diversion. The laws of probability suggested that it was likely that someday one of the patricians would offer a word to Ernst. That was all that he would need. He had the scene carefully rehearsed; he, too, had nothing else to do.

The rain was falling harder. Through the drops, which made a dense curtain that obscured the buildings across the square, Ernst saw outlines of people hurrying. Sometimes he pretended that the men and, especially, the women were familiar, remnants of his abandoned life come by chance to call on him in his exile. Today, though, his head hurt and he had no patience with the game, particularly the disappointment at its inevitable conclusion.

He finished the last of the anisette. Ernst rapped on the table and held the tumbler above his head. He did not look around; he supported his aching head with his other hand and waited. M. Gargotier came and took the tumbler from him. The rain fell harder. Ernst's hair was soaked and tiny rivulets ran down his forehead and into his eyes. The proprietor returned with the tumbler filled. Ernst wanted to think seriously, but his head hurt too much. The day before, he had devised a neat argument against the traditional contrast of city and Arcadian life in literature. Shakespeare had used it to great effect: the regulated behavior of his characters in town opposed to their irrational, comedic entanglements outside the city's gates. Somehow the present circumstance destroyed those myths. Somehow Ernst knew that he didn't want them destroyed, and he had his headache and the everlasting morning rain to preserve them another day.

As the clock moved on toward midday, the rain stopped. Ernst leaned back in his chair and waited for the sun to draw pedestrians from their shelters. He signaled to M. Gargotier, and the proprietor brought a rag from the bar to mop the table. Ernst left his seat to check his appearance in the Fée Blanche's huge, cracked mirror. His clothes were still soaked, of course, and in the sudden afternoon heat they clung to him unpleasantly. He ran his hand through his hair, trying to give it a more raffish, rumpled look, but it was far too wet. M. Gargotier returned to his place behind the bar, ignoring Ernst. There were voices from the patio. Ernst sighed and gave up the bar's muggy darkness.

Outside, the sun made Ernst squint. His headache began to throb angrily. He went back to his usual table, noticing the crowd that had collected beyond the café's rusty iron railing. A few people had come into the Fée Blanche, preferring no doubt to witness the unknown spectacle from a more comfortable vantage. It was nearly time for Ernst to change from anisette to bingara, his afternoon refreshment, but M. Gargotier was busily serving the newcomers. Ernst waited impatiently, his tumbler of anisette once again empty. He stared at the backs of the people lining the sidewalk, unable for the moment to guess what had attracted them.

"Now," thought Ernst, "if I look closely enough, I will be able to recognize the backsides of every person I've ever known. How tedious the world becomes, once one realizes that everyone in it can be divided into a dozen or so groups. That young woman there, ah, a fairly interesting knot of black hair, attractive legs, a thick waist. If she were to turn around, her face would be no surprise. Heavy eyebrows, no doubt, full lips, her upper front teeth protruding just a little. Large breasts hanging, her shirt cut to expose them, but it is ten years too late for that. It is too boring. I have no interest even in seeing if I'm correct."

Ernst smiled, realizing that he was deliberately avoiding any real observation. It was nonsense, of course, to think that twelve physical types might be enough to catalogue the shabby mass of people that filled the city. He had exhausted that particular entertainment, and rather quickly; what remained was the more tiresome prospect of actually describing the crowd. Perhaps M. Gargotier would arrive soon, interrupting the intellectual effort, scattering the energy, mercifully introducing a tiny but vital novelty.

"An interesting point," Ernst said aloud, imagining himself a lecturer before dozing students in some stifling European hall, "a genuine philosophical point that we can all grasp and taste for truth, is that there is nothing in the world quite like the opportunity of seeing someone make an ass of himself. Free entertainment is, after all, the Great Leveler, not death, as we have often been told. In the case of death, the rich are often able to regulate its moment of victory, staving off the final instant for months, even years, with purchased miracles of medicine. The poor take what they are given. But free entertainment is democratic! No one may say when a spectacle may arise, may explode, may stumble. And then, when that moment comes, every man, rich or poor, must take advantage as best he can, elbowing aside the crowds all together at the same time. So, by sitting here, I have conquered them all, diversion and audience alike. And I can delude myself with my own analogies, considering death a lesser antagonist, and applaud my own immortality."

In a while, Ernst heard a ragged ruffle of drums, and a high-pitched voice shouting orders. Only the Jaish, thought Ernst with disappointment. It was only the new Citizens' Army; there would be little chance here to advance his position. He did not care for the local folk and their sudden and silly politics, and his own sort of people would not be long entertained by the fools' parade. He called M. Gargotier in a loud, rude voice. "Bring me some of that ugly Arab drink," he said. "It's noon, isn't it?" There was not a word from the proprietor, not a smile or a nod.

The people on the sidewalk, however, were having a wonderful time. Ernst could hear the rattling of the snare drums playing a syncopated, unmilitary cadence. The several drummers had evidently not had much practice together; the strokes rarely fell in unison, and with a little attention one could identify the different styles of each man. The slapping of the marching feet against the rough stones of the pavement was likewise without precision. Ernst frowned, looking at his own frayed, stained suit. If things could be arranged according to merit, then certainly he would be granted a better situation than this. He remembered the white linen suit he had owned when he first came to the city. He had worn it proudly, contemptuous of the city's natives and their hanging, shapeless garments, all darkly sweat-marked, torn, and foul. That suit had not lasted long. It, along with the white, wide-brimmed hat and his new boots, had been stolen within a week, while he indulged himself at the Sourour baths. He had never returned to that establishment, nor any other in the Arab quarter. Now he looked much like those he had disdained on his arrival, and, strangely, that brought him a certain pleasure as well. At least he didn't seem to be a mere newcomer. He had been initiated. He belonged, as all the cityful of mongrels belonged.

So the time passed with Ernst trying mightily to ignore the

exhibition in the street. Often the movements of the crowd opened spaces and he could see the garishly outfitted militia. The workmen and slaves of the city cheered them, and this made Ernst even more cheerless. He swallowed some of the local liquor in a gulp, holding the small wooden bowl on the flat of one palm. What good is that army? he wondered. The Jaish had no weapons. An army of no threats. And, beyond that, thought Ernst as he waved once more to M. Gargotier, they have no enemies. There is nothing on all of this damned sand but this single city. Just bread and circuses, he thought, observing the crowd's excitement. Just an entertainment for the groundlings. He had other, more important things to consider.

"Eugenie," he thought, "magnificent horror of my youth, I would trade my eternal portion to have you with me now. How old you must be! How like these cheap dorsal identities I see before me, without personality, without more than the instantaneous appetites, without the barest knowledge of me. They, who have drifted here from the living world, have been charred slowly to that condition. They have greedily accepted their lot, their badge of grime, their aristo suppuration, their plebeian filth. They left Europe as I did, to change slowly and by degrees of privation, like a slow sunset of amnesia, into this life of utter exhaustion. Never again will my eyes, my nose and mouth, the wet hairs of my body be free of grit and sand. The wealthy and I have had to labor to attain such an existence. But you, Eugenie, you had it with you all the time. You would be queen here, Eugenie, but you would be as ugly as the rest."

Ernst sipped more of the liqueur. He dipped three fingertips into it, and flicked the dark fluid at the backs of the people crowding against the railing. Spots formed on the clothing of a man and a girl. Ernst laughed; the too-loud noise sobered him for a moment. "You'd be ugly, Eugenie," he said, "and I'd be drunk." The heat of the African noon enveloped him, and the stillness made it difficult to breathe. Ernst struggled out of his old worn jacket, throwing it onto the chair across the small metal table from him.

"Marie, you don't matter. Not now. Not here. Africa would be perfect for Eugenie, but you, Marie, I picture your destruction among the million mirror shards of Paris or Vienna. So forget it, I'm talking to Eugenie. She would come right across that square, scattering the pigeons, the pedestrians, the damned army just the same, marching right across the square, right up to this café, to my table, and stare down at me as if she had walked the Mediterranean knowing where I was all the time. But it won't work again. She wouldn't have thought that I could catch up to her laughing crime, that I'd still be the same rhyming idiot I always was. And she'd be old, older than I, lined and wrinkled, leaning, tucked in, shaking just a bit in the limbs, aching just a bit in the joints, showing patches and patterns of incorrect color, purples on the legs, brown maculae on the arms, swirls and masses on the face beneath the surgery and appliances. Then what would I do? I would buy her a drink and introduce her to everyone I know. That would destroy her surely enough, speedily enough, satisfyingly enough, permanently enough. Oh, the hell with indifference. I really can't maintain it." Ernst laughed again and hoped some patrician in the Jaish's audience would turn around, bored by the mock military show, and ask Ernst what amused him. No one did. Ernst sat in glum silence and drank.

He had been in the Fée Blanche all morning and no one, not even the most casual early strollers, had paused to wish him a good day. Should he move on? Gather "material" in another café? Have a sordid experience in a disorderly house, get beaten up by a jealous *gavroche?*

"So, Sidi Weinraub! You sit out under all skies, eh?"

Ernst started, blinking and rapidly trying to recover his tattered image. "Yes, Ieneth, you must if you want to be a poet. What is climate, to interfere with the creative process?"

The girl was young, perhaps not as old as seventeen. She was one of the city's very poor, gaunt with years of hunger and dressed in foul old clothes. But she was not a slave — she would have looked better if she had been. She earned a trivial living as a knife sharpener. Behind her she pulled a two-wheeled cart, dilapidated and peeling, filled with tools and pieces of equipment. "How does it go?" she asked.

"Badly," admitted Ernst, smiling sadly and pulling a soggy bit of scrap paper from his pocket. "My poem of yesterday lies still unfinished."

The girl laughed. "*Chi ama assai parla poco,*" she said. "'He who loves much says little.' You spend too much time chasing the pretty ones, no? You do not fool me, yaa Sidi, sitting there with your solemn long face. Your poem will have to be finished while you catch your breath, and then off after another of my city's sweet daughters."

"You've seen right through me, Ieneth," said Ernst with a tired shrug. "You're right, of course. One can't spend one's entire life chasing the Muse. Wooing the Muse, I mean. If you chase the Muse, you gain nothing. Wooing becomes a chief business. It's like anything else—you get better with practice." He smiled, though he was dreadfully weary of the conversation already. The necessity of keeping up the pretense of sexual metaphor annoyed him.

"You are lucky, in a way," said the girl. "Pity the poor butcher. What has he in his daily employment to aid him in the wooing? You must understand your advantage."

"Is there a Muse of Butchery?" asked Ernst with a solemn expression.

"You are very clever, yaa Sidi. I meant, of course, in the wooing of a pretty girl. Were a butcher to approach me, a blood sausage in his hands, I would only laugh. That is not technique, yaa Sidi. That is uninspired. But these poems of yours are the product, as you say, of one kind of wooing, and moreover the weaponry of another sort."

"So poems still work their magic?" asked Ernst, wondering if this meeting were, after all, better than simple boredom.

"For some young girls, I suppose. Do you favor many young girls with them?"

A sudden cry from the crowd on the sidewalk prevented Ernst's reply. He shook his head in disgust. Ieneth interpreted his expression correctly, looking over her shoulder for a few seconds. She turned back to him, leaning on the railing near his table. He, of course, could not invite her to join him. There were only two classes of people in the city, besides the slaves: the wealthy and those like Ieneth. She was forbidden by custom to intrude on her betters, and Ernst was certainly not the crusading sort to sweep aside the laws of delicacy. Anyway, he thought, her people had their own dives, and he surely wouldn't be made welcome in them.

"Ah, I see you disapprove of the Jaish," said Ieneth. "At least your expression shows contempt, and its object must be either our army or myself."

"No, no, don't worry, I have nothing but affection for you," said Ernst. He was amazed by his facile speech; generally he would have been reduced to unpleasant sarcasm long before this. In point of fact, he felt even less than mere affection for the girl. He felt only recognition; he knew her as another resident of the city, with little to recommend her in any way. He didn't even feel lust for her. He rather wished that she'd go away.

"Then it's the Jaish. That's a shame, really. There are several very nice gentlemen involved with it." She smiled broadly. Ernst felt certain that she would wink, slowly. She did.

Ernst smiled briefly in return. "I'm sure there are," he said. "It's just that I'm not one of them, and I have no interest at all in making the acquaintance of any, and I wish they'd stop spoiling my afternoons with their juvenile tin-soldiery."

"You should see the larger story," said Ieneth. "As long as they spend their time marching and carrying broom rifles, you will have no competition for the company of their mothers and daughters."

"You mistake me," said Ernst, "though you flatter me unduly. Surely it is hopeless for such a one as I, with such, ah, cosmopolitan tastes."

"I would not agree," she whispered. Ernst became aware that he had been staring at her. She reached across the railing and touched him confidentially on the shoulder. The motion exposed her wonderful breasts completely.

Ernst took a deep breath, forcing himself to look into her eyes. "Do you know what I mean then?"

"Certainly," she said, with an amused smile. She indicated her little wagon. "I know that sometimes men want their scissors sharpened, and sometimes their appetites. And anyone may have a lucrative avocation, no?"

"When I was young, there was an old man who ground scissors and sharpened knives. He had a cart very much like your own."

"There, you see? I am of the acquaintance of a—what shall I say?—an organ grinder."

"I don't understand."

Ieneth shook her head, laughing at his obtuseness. She motioned for him to come closer. He slid his chair nearer to the railing. She touched his arm at the elbow, trailing her fingers down his sleeve, across his hip, and, most lightly of all, over the bunched material at his crotch. "I will meet you here in an hour?" she asked softly.

Ernst's throat was suddenly dry. "I will be here," he said.

"A poem," thought Ernst. "I need a poem. Nothing impresses the uneducated mind quite like rhymes. But it must be the right sort, or it will bring nothing but ruin and humiliation. How the women used to laugh at my romantic verses! How dismayed I was, left alone on the darkened balcony, holding the flimsy product of my innocent wit. The sonnet on the arch of her brow. Good God, how could I have done it? I wish I could return, go back to those iron moments, stand behind a curtain and listen to myself. I wonder if I would be amused. I cannot understand why those brainless princesses so easily dismissed me; they couldn't have been so plagued with clowns. I ought to have been kept as a refreshing antidote to dawning maturity."

He took out a pen and began to compose on the back of a soiled napkin. The atmosphere of the Fée Blanche was not the best for the generation of poetry, he realized. But he also understood that the unknown recipient of his craft would be more awed by the simple fact of the poem than by any singular verbal charm. Surely no friend of Ieneth's could be sophisticated enough to appreciate anything but the grossest of street chants. In that case, all that was required was a quick collection of lines, without attention to musical values, arranged visually in a recognizably poetic way. The ink from the fountain pen blotted on the napkin, spreading rapidly and obscuring each letter, obliterating all sense and intention. Ernst cursed and crushed the paper into a ball, tossing it to the floor.

"My life would have been greatly different, Eugenie, if this had happened while I loved you. If I had only known enough to keep my mouth closed, to express myself only in abstract looks and gestures, so that it all might be disowned quickly as worldly nonsense. Wisdom does not necessarily come with age, only silence. And that is the greatest treasure of all." He returned his pen to his pocket and called for M. Gargotier.

In the time it took for Ernst to drink two more bowls of bingara, the parade had ended. The crowd broke up, shouting new slogans which Ernst could not understand. The other patrons finished their drinks and departed, and the café was again empty except for its single poet. The sun had marked noon and now, hotter still, moved down the sky just enough to hurt his eyes as he looked westward, across the street.

"West," thought Ernst, rocking restlessly in his chair. "What absurd, empty thoughts does that bring to mind, to help pass this hour? One day after another. It gets to be so tedious. I should begin walking through this blighted city, through the wealthy sections clustered near this quarter, through the more populated tradesmen's quarter, through the filthy paupers' streets, past the noisy, dangerous rim of utter human refuse just within the walls, beyond the city's gates and across the dunes. Then what? Then I would die in about twelve hours, burned by the noonday sun, chiseled by the windborne sand, frozen by Barid, the cold wind of night. Westward, toward the Atlantic, toward England and her debauched civilities. West, the direction of death, decay, finality, and poetic conclusions. Into Avalon. Perhaps if it weren't for Ieneth and her sly, snickering hints, I would wander off that way. Pack a picnic lunch, perhaps, and bake myself dead upon a hill of sand. I always dreamed of a heroic death, defending Eugenie's intermittent honor, or fighting for Marie's bemused favor. Gasping, I would lie upon the specified lap and the lady would weep. Her tears would restore my fleeing mortality. Then I would smile, as would Eugenie or Marie in her proper turn, amazed and joyful. A signal that would be for me to begin the dream anew. Another way of getting through the hours, though much too unfulfilling for my present needs."

Ernst watched the clock on the hotel impatiently. The pedestrians moved by in their aimless courses, and each ticked off a few seconds on the yellow clock face. Yet the traffic was too sluggish to move the clock's iron hands quickly enough to suit Ernst, and thus could not beguile his furious anticipation.

It was while Ernst was silent in thought, staring at the damned clock, lost in his own strange expectant horror, that someone moved a chair to his table and joined him. He looked up, startled. The intruder was a tall, thin Polish man named Czerny, a wealthy man who had come to the city a political refugee and who had made his fortune by teaching the city's hungry inhabitants to require the luxuries of Europe. Ernst had been introduced to Czerny a few times, but neither had been overly taken with the other's company.

"Good afternoon, M. Weintraub," said Czerny. "Although there are a number of tables free, I have preferred to join you. I hope you will forgive my rather forward behavior."

Ernst waved away the apology, more curious about Czerny's motives. He did realize that the blond man was the founder of the Jaish, the Citizens' Army, and its principal financial support. His appearance after its show was not mere happenstance.

"I'd like to speak with you for a moment, if I may, M. Weintraub," said Czerny.

"That's Weinraub, without the *t*. Certainly. Would you care for a drink?"

Czerny smiled his commercial smile. "No, thank you. This new religion of mine doesn't allow it. But look, M. Weinraub, I wonder if you realize the service you could render, in the time you spend idly here?"

Ernst was slightly annoyed. Surely Czerny wanted something, and his patronizing attitude wasn't going to help him get it. "What service do you mean, Monsieur Czerny? I doubt if I have anything that you might envy."

"It is your talent. As you know, the Jaish is still small in numbers, even smaller in resources. I have been doing my limited best to help, but for our purposes even all my savings would be too little."

Ernst finished half a bowl of the liquor in one swallow. He raised his hand for M. Gargotier. "What are these purposes?" he asked.

"Why, liberty for all, of course," said Czerny, disappointed that Ernst had need to ask. "We distribute leaflets at all parades. Surely you've seen them."

"Yes," said Ernst, "but not read them."

"Ah, well. Perhaps if they were composed in a better style. . . ."

"Might I ask who has the task now?"

"A young man of great promise," said Czerny proudly. "Sandor Courane."

Ernst leaned back, lifting the front two legs of his chair off the pavement. "M. Czerny," he said slowly, "that is very interesting, but I must embarrassedly admit that you have chosen an inopportune time for this interview. This afternoon I have something of an assignation, and so. . . ." Ernst settled his chair, smiled drunkenly, and shrugged.

Czerny looked angry. He rose from his seat. "M. Weintraub, I will return later. I believe it is time that you considered such matters as duty and honor. Perhaps this evening you will be more of a mind to discuss this. Good day, and have a gratifying . . . assignation."

"Weinraub," whispered Ernst, as Czerny strode away. "Without the *t*."

Czerny walked swiftly along the eastern edge of the square until he came to a parked limousine. It was one of the very few automobiles in the city; Ernst did not doubt that it was Czerny's private car. The driver got out and handed Czerny a gray uniform coat, taking the wealthy man's more expensively cut jacket in return. "Ah," thought Ernst, "at least I rated a change of clothing. We shall see whether or not the same thing happens this evening. It is sad that so frequently the scheme of great men may be deciphered by such paltry tokens." Czerny put on his uniform coat and waited until the driver opened the rear door of the limousine for him. Then he entered; the driver walked around the car and disappeared inside. In a moment the vehicle moved slowly away from the curb, its siren crying shrilly and the pennants of the Jaish whipping in the breeze. The car drove down the length of the square, turned along the north side, and went on for a short distance. Then it stopped again, and Czerny spoke with two figures on the sidewalk. From that distance Ernst could not recognize them.

"If I were you, Czerny," he thought, "I would not involve myself too deeply with the people of this city. There is always the danger that you may find people to like or, most deadly of all, to love. What should you do, having fallen in love with some rare woman, and then find yourself betrayed? Ah, I anticipate your outraged reply.

We are both too far along to have that happen to us again. Perhaps you are right, though one can never be too careful. But what if you are not betrayed, eh, Czerny? What then? No final demarcations, however painful. You have forgotten that. Nothing to chop it off before weariness sets in. Lifetimes go by that way, Czerny. Boredom and angry frustration are only the first symptoms. No mistresses for you, no other men's wives, no playful daughters of police commissioners. We find that we need them, sooner or later. And that is the first of the body's spasms of death. Years, years, years in this city, with the same faces, yours and hers. Years, years, years. Do not stop for them, Czerny. Tend to your army."

Czerny's car drove away, and after a few moments Ernst saw that one of the two people walking toward him was the girl, Ieneth, without her knife-sharpening equipment. With her was another girl, taller and darker. Ernst rose from his chair by the railing, and the two girls joined him at his table. M. Gargotier, evidently expecting that Ernst would soon depart, did not come to take an order. He stood glaring in the bar's doorway, obviously resenting the presence of the two lower-class women. Ernst made a flamboyant gesture to summon the proprietor. He switched his drinking to absinthe, and the girls ordered wine.

"What is her name, Ieneth?" he asked, staring at the new girl. She looked shyly at the table.

"She is called Ua. In her language it means 'flower.' She does not understand our speech."

"How charming she is, and how lovely her name. Truly a flower. Convey to her my sincerest compliments." Ieneth did so. "What language is that?" asked Ernst.

"It is a strange dialect, spoken by the black people beyond the desert and the mountains. It is called Swahili."

"Black people? How interesting. I have only heard stories. They actually exist?"

"Yes, yaa Sidi," said Ieneth.

"And how did she learn the tongue? And you, also, for that matter?"

Ieneth closed her eyes, fluttering her painted lashes, and smiled.

Ernst turned to Ua. "What is this called?" he said, pointing to her foot. Ieneth translated, and Ua replied.

"*Mguu*," she said.

"And this?" said Ernst, pointing now to her ankle.

"*Kifundo cha mguu.*"

"What is this?"

"*Jicho.*" Eye.

"How do you say 'mouth'?"

"*Kinywa.*"

Ernst sipped his drink nervously, although he labored to seem casual and urbane. "This?" he asked.

"*Mkono.*" Arm.

"This?" Ernst's fingers lingered on her breast, feeling the rough material of the brassiere beneath the cotton blouse.

Ua blushed. "*Ziwa,*" she whispered.

"She is indeed very lovely," Ernst said.

"And worthy of reward for her, ah, agent?" asked Ieneth.

"Certainly," said Ernst absently, as he moved his hand down past Ua's stomach, stopping at the juncture of her thighs. "Now, my love, what could this be?"

Ua said nothing, staring at the table. She blushed fiercely while she played with the base of her wineglass.

"Ask her what the word for this is," he said. Ieneth did so.

"*Mkunga,*" Ua said at last, removing Ernst's hand.

Ieneth laughed shrilly, clapping her hands. Tears ran down her cheeks as she rose from her seat. "Ah, your cosmopolitan tastes!" she said.

"What is so amusing?" asked Ernst.

"*Mkunga!*" said Ieneth. "*Mkunga* is the word for 'eel.' Oh, enjoy your hour together, yaa Sidi. You and she will have much to discuss!" And she went out of the café, laughing as she walked away from Ernst's disconcerted and savage glare.

It was late afternoon, and already the sun was melting behind the hotel across the street. Ernst sipped wine now, for he appreciated the effect of the slanting sun's rays on the rich, dark liquid. He had discovered this by accident when he had first come to the city, strolling along the walled quarter's single, huge avenue. He had seen the red shimmers reflecting on the impassive face of a shopworn working girl. How much better, he had thought then, how much better it would be to have that singularly fortunate play of light grace a true poet.

"It may be a bit naive of me, nonetheless," he thought. "After all, if these loiterers of the city lack the verbal sophistication to appreciate the verses themselves, how can I expect them to have any greater regard for the wielder of the pen? But I must defeat that argument by ignoring it if by no more rigorous means. I cannot allow myself to be pulled down into the intellectual miasma of these Afric prisoners. The sun must burn out all wonder and delight at an early age; it is only we unlucky travelers who can deplore their sand-worn ignorance." He took some more of the wine and held it in his mouth until he began to feel foolish. He swallowed it and pushed the glass away.

While Ernst sat there, sucking the taste of the wine from his teeth, a young boy walked by on the sidewalk. He was small, nearly hairless, and quite obviously had strayed from the neighborhood of his parents. He stopped when he saw Ernst. "Are you not Weinraub the wanderer, from Europe?"

"I am," said Ernst. "I have been, for some time. Has my fame then spread as far as your unwashed ears?"

"I have heard much about you, yaa Sidi," said the boy. "I never believed that I'd really see you."

"And are your dreams confirmed?"

"Not yet," said the boy, shaking his head. "Do you really kiss other men?"

Ernst spat at the boy, and the dark boy laughed, dancing into the street, hopping back on the sidewalk. "Come here," said Ernst, "and I'll wrap this chair around your skinny neck."

"It was only a joke, yaa Sidi," said the boy, not the least afraid.

"A joke. How old are you?"

"I am nine, yaa Sidi."

"Then you should know the danger of mocking your betters. I have the power to do you great harm: I may draw a picture of you. I may touch you with my left hand. Your mother will beat you dead when she hears."

"You are wrong," said the boy, laughing again. "You are a Nazarene, yes, or a Jew. But I am no rug-squatter. Touch me with your left hand, yaa Sidi, and I will gnaw it off. Do you wish me to fetch your supper? I will not charge you this time."

"I tend to doubt your offer. In any event, I have a regular boy who brings my food. What is your name, you young criminal?"

"I am Kebap," said the boy. "It means 'roast beef' in the language of Turkey."

"I can see why," said Ernst dryly. "You will have to work hard to take the place of my regular boy, if you want this job."

"I am sorry," said Kebap. "I have no wish to perform that kind of service." Then he ran away, shouting insults over his shoulder.

Ernst stared after him, his fists clenching. "Ieneth will pay for her joke," he thought. "If only I could find a vulnerable spot in these people. Without possessions, inured against discomfort, hoping for nothing, they are difficult indeed to punish. Perhaps that is the reason I have stayed in this capital of lice so long. No other reason comes quickly to mind."

He sipped his wine and stared at the smudged handwriting on a scrap of paper: an *ebauche* of his trilogy of novels. He had done the rough outline so long ago that he had forgotten its point. But he was certain that the reflected light from the wineglass shifted to good effect on the yellowed paper, too.

"This was the trilogy that was going to make my reputation," thought Ernst sadly. "I remember how I had planned to dedicate the first volume to Eugenie, the second to Marie, and the third. . . ? I can't remember, after all. It has been a long time. I cannot even recall the characters. Ah, yes, here. I had stolen that outstanding, virtuous fool, d'Aubont, put a chevalier's outfit on him, taken off his mustache, and renamed him Gerhardt Friedlos. How the fluttering feminine hearts of Germany, Carbba, France, and England were to embrace him, if hearts are capable of such a dexterous feat. Friedlos. Now I remember. And there is no further mystery as to why I can't recall the plot. It was nothing. Mere slashings of rapier, mere wooings of maid, mere tauntings of coward. One thousand pages of adolescent dreams, just to restore my manly figure. Beyond the dedications, did I not also represent Eugenie and Marie with fictional characters? I cannot read this scrawl. Ah, yes. Eugenie is disguised in volume one as the red-haired Marchioness Fajra. She is consumed in a horrible holocaust as her outraged tenants wreak their just revenge. Friedlos observes the distressing scene with mixed emotions. In volume two, he consoles himself with the contrasting charms of Marie, known in my novel as the maid Malvarma, who pitiably froze to death on the great plain of Breulandy rather than acknowledge her secret love. Friedlos comes upon her blue and twisted corpse and grieves. I am happy, I am very, very happy that I never wrote that trash."

Ernst took his short, fat pencil and wrote in the narrow spaces left to him on the scrap. *My scalp itches,* he wrote. *When I scratch it, I break open half-healed sores. I have a headache; behind my right eye my brain throbs. My ears are blocked, and the canals are swollen deep inside, as though large pegs had been hammered into them. My nostrils drip constantly, and the front of my face feels as if it has been filled with sand. My gums bleed, and my teeth communicate with stabbing pains. My tongue is still scalded from the morning tea. My throat is dry and sore.* This catalogue continued down the margins of the paper, and down his body, to end with, *My arches cramp up at regular intervals, whenever I think about them. My toes are cut and painful on the bottom and fungused and itching between. And now I believe that it pains me to piss. But this last symptom bears watching; it is not confirmed.*

On a napkin ringed with stains of chocolate and coffee, Ernst began another list, parallel to the first. *The very continents shudder with the fever chills of war. Europe, my first home so far away, cringes in the dark sickroom between the ocean and the Urals. Asia teeters into the false adolescence of senility, and is the more dangerous for it. Breulandy rises in the north and east, and who can tell of her goals and motives? South of the city, Africa slumbers, hungry and sterile, under the cauterizing sun. The Americas? Far too large to control, too broken to aid us now.*

Oh, and whom do I mean by "us"? The world is fractured so that we no longer know anything but self. My self finds symptoms everywhere, a political hypochondriac in exile. Perhaps if I were still in the numbing academic life of old, I would see none of this; l'ozio é la sepoltura dell'uomo vivo—"inactivity is the tomb of the vital man." I have time to make lists now.

Of course he found sad significance in the two inventories when he completed them. He shook his head sorrowfully and stared meditatively at his wineglass, but no one noticed.

Ernst folded the paper with his trilogy synopsis and the first list, and returned it to his pocket. He skimmed through the second list again, though. " 'I have time to make lists now,' " he read. "What does that mean? Who am I trying to distress?" Just beyond the railing, on the sidewalk bordering the Fée Blanche, sat Kebap, the little boy named "roast beef." The boy was grinning.

"Allo, Sidi Weinraub. I'm back. I've come to haunt you, you know."

"You're doing a fine job," said Ernst. "Do you know anything of poetry?"

"I know poetry," said the boy. "I know what Sidi Courane writes. That's poetry. That's what everyone says. Do you write poetry, too?"

"I did," said Ernst, "in my youth."

"It is lucky, then, that I cannot read," said Kebap. He grinned again at Ernst, evilly. "I see that your usual boy hasn't yet brought your supper."

"Why are you called 'roast beef'? I doubt if you've ever seen any in your whole life."

"One of my uncles called me that," said the boy. "He said that's what I looked like when I was born."

"Do you have a lot of uncles?" asked Ernst maliciously.

Kebap's eyes opened very wide. "Oh, certainly," he said solemnly. "Sometimes a new one every day. My mother is very beautiful, very wise, and often very silent. Would you like to meet her, yaa Sidi?"

"Not today, you little thief." Ernst held up the annotated napkin. "I'm very busy."

Kebap snorted. "Certainly, yaa Sidi. Of course." Then he ran away.

"Good evening, M. Weinraub." It was Czerny, still dressed in his gray uniform of the Citizens' Army. Ernst saw that the tunic was without decoration or indication of rank. Perhaps the Jaish was still so small that the men had only a handful of officers in the whole organization. And here was the man again, to persuade him that the whole situation was not foolish, after all.

"You are a man of your word, M. Czerny," said Ernst. "Will you join me again? Have a drink?"

"No, I'll pass that up," said Czerny as he seated himself at Ernst's table. "I trust your appointment concluded satisfactorily?"

Ernst grunted. It became evident that he would say nothing more. Czerny cursed softly. "Look," he said, "I don't want to have to go through all these stupid contests of yours. This isn't amusing any longer. You're going to have to choose sides. If you're not with us, you're against us."

Perhaps it was the heat of the afternoon, or the amount of liquor he had already consumed, or the annoying events of the day, but Ernst refused to allow Czerny the chance to make a single argumentative point. It was not often that someone came to Ernst with a request, and he was certainly going to enjoy it fully. That in doing so he would have to disappoint and even antagonize Czerny made little difference. If Czerny wanted Ernst's help badly enough, Czerny would return. And if Czerny didn't mean what he said, then, well, he deserved everything Ernst could devise.

Ernst was amused by the man's grave talk. He couldn't understand the urgency at all. "Who are you going to fight? I don't see it. Maybe if you paid them enough, you could hire some nomad tribe. But it's still a good distance to ask them to ride just for a battle. Or maybe if you split your tiny bunch in half, one part could start a civil uprising and the other part could put it down. But I really just want to watch."

"We will get nowhere, Monsieur," said Czerny in a tight, controlled voice, "until you cease treating my army as a toy and our cause as a tilting at windmills."

"My good Czerny," said Ernst slowly, "you reveal quite a lot when you say 'my army.' You reveal yourself, if you understand me. You divulge yourself. You display yourself, do you see? You expose yourself. There, I see that I must say it plainly. You expose yourself, but in this locality, at this time, that seems to be a most commendable form of expression."

"Damn it, you *are* an idiot! I'm not asking you to be a dirty *goundi*. We can get plenty of infantry just by putting up notices. If we could afford to pay them. If we could afford the notices. But intelligence is at a premium in this city. We need you and the others like you. I promise you, you'll never have to carry a rifle or face one. But you have to be man enough to cast your lot with us, or we'll sweep you aside with the rest of the old ways."

"Rhetoric, Czerny, rhetoric!" said Ernst, giggling. "I came here to get away from all that. Leave me alone, will you? I sit here and get drunk. I don't mess with *you* while you play soldiers. I'm not any more useful than you, but at least I don't bother anybody." He looked around, hoping that some diversion might arise to rescue him. There was nothing. Perhaps he might cause enough of a row with Czerny that M. Gargotier would ask that they both leave; the danger with that plan was that Czerny would be sure to invite Ernst somewhere, some place where Czerny and his Jaish held an edge. Well, then, something simpler was necessary. Perhaps the young nuisance would return. With any luck, the boy would change his target; Czerny would be in no mood to ignore Kebap. Still, that didn't seem likely either.

Czerny banged the little table with his fist. The table's metal top flipped off its three legs, dumping Ernst's wineglass to the ground. Czerny didn't appear to notice. He talked on through the crashing of the table and the breaking of the glass. "Useful? You want to talk about useful? Have you ever read anything about politics? Economics? You know what keeps a culture alive?"

"Yes," said Ernst sullenly, while M. Gargotier cleaned up the mess. "People not bothering other people."

"A good war every generation or so," said Czerny, ignoring Ernst, seeing him now as an enemy. "We've got authorities. Machiavelli – he said that the first cause of unrest in a nation is idleness and peace. That's all this city has ever known, and you can see the results out there." Czerny waved in the direction of the street. All that Ernst could see was a young woman in a short leather skirt, naked from the waist up. She met his glance and waved.

"Ah," thought Ernst, "it has been a long time since I've been able just to sit and watch those lovely girls. It seems that one should have thought to do that, without fear of interruption. But there is always war, disease, jealousies, business, and hunger. I have asked for little in my life. Indeed, all that I would have now is a quiet place in the Faubourg St. Honoré to watch the Parisian girls. Instead, here I am. Observing that single distant brown woman is infinitely preferable to listening to Czerny's ranting." Ernst smiled at the half-naked woman; she turned away for a moment. A small boy was standing behind her. The woman whispered in the boy's ear. Ernst recognized the boy, of course; the boy laughed. It would not be long before Kebap learned that even industry and enterprise would avail him nothing in that damned city.

"You cannot afford silence," Czerny was saying loudly.

"I hadn't realized your concerns had gotten this involved," said Ernst. "I really thought you fellows were just showing off, but it's a great deal worse than that. Well, I won't disturb you, if that's what you're worried about. I still don't see why you're so anxious to have me. I haven't held a rifle since my partridge-shooting days in Madrid."

"You aren't even listening," said Czerny, his voice shrill with outrage.

"No, I guess I'm not. What is it again that you want?"

"We want you to join us."

Ernst smiled sadly, looking down at his new glass of wine. "I'm sorry," he said, "I don't make decisions anymore."

Czerny stood up. He kicked a shard of the broken wineglass into the street. "You're wrong," he said. "You've just made a very bad one."

Dusk settled in on the shoulders of the city. The poor of the city happily gave up their occupations and hurried to their homes to join their families for the evening meal. Along the city's avenues, merchants closed their shops and locked gated shutters over display windows. The wealthy few considered the entertainments and casually made their choices. The noises of the busy day stilled, until Ernst could hear the bugle calls and shouted orders of the Jaish as it drilled beyond the city's walled quarter. The day's liquor had had its desired effect on him, and so the sounds failed to remind him of Czerny's anger.

"There seem to be no birds in this city," thought Ernst. "That is reasonable. For them to abide in this vat of cultural horrors, they must first fly over that great, empty, dead world beyond the gates. Sand. What a perfect device to excise us from all hope of reentering the world. We are shut up like lepers, in a colony across the sand, and easily, gratefully forgotten. The process of forgetting is readily learned. First we are forgotten by our families, our nations. Then we are forgotten by those we've hated, our enemies in contiguous countries. At last, when we have alighted here in our final condition, we forget ourselves. Children must be hired to walk the streets of this city, reminding us of our names and our natures, otherwise we should disappear entirely, as we have dreamed and prayed for so many years. But that, after all, is not the reason we have been sent here. We have come not to die, but to exist painfully apart. Death would be a cleansing for us, a discourtesy to our former friends."

Ernst looked around him. The twilight made pleasant shadows on the stone-paved street surrounding the square. Some of the shadows moved. "Hey!" shouted Ernst experimentally. The shadows burst, flew up, flapped away in many directions. "Pigeons," thought Ernst. "I forgot pigeons. But that hardly ruins my thesis. Pigeons are a necessity in a city. They were sitting here, asleep on the sand, when the first parched exiles arrived on the spot. The abundantly foolish idea of building a town must have occurred to those unwanted knaves only after seeing the pigeons."

The city was certainly one of immigrants, Ernst thought. As he had escaped from a crazy Europe, so had Czerny. So had Sandor Courane. Ieneth and her false flower, Ua, had fled from some mysterious wild empire. Could it be that every person sheltered within the city's granite walls had been born elsewhere? No, of course not; there must be a large native population. These must be the ones most stirred by the absurd wrath of the Jaish, for who else had enough interest? Ernst lived in the city only because he had nowhere else to go. He had stopped briefly in Gelnhausen and the nearby village of Frachtdorf. From Bremen he had sailed to the Scandinavian settlements that bordered the northern sea. He had resided for short times in England and France, but those nations' murderous nationalism made him run once more. Each time he settled down, it was in a less comfortable situation. Here on the very lip of Africa, the city was the final hope of those who truly needed to hide.

Ernst had often tried to write poems or short, terse essays about the city, but each time he had given up in failure. He couldn't seem to capture the true emotions he experienced, feelings different in subtle, unpoetic ways from the vaguely similar emotions he had known while living in Europe. The poems could not reflect the pervasive sense of isolation, of eternal uncleanness, of a soul-deep loss of personality; these things descended upon a European, only hours after arriving at the dune-guarded gates of the city.

He had early on made the mistake of showing some of these frustrated scribblings to M. Gargotier. The proprietor had read them politely, muttering the words under his breath as he traced his progress down the page with a grimy finger. When he finished, he had handed the paper back to Ernst without a word, and stood silently, evidently uncomfortable but unwilling to make a final judgment. Soon Ernst stopped asking M. Gargotier to read them, and both men seemed happier for it.

A small voice whispered behind Ernst. It was Kebap, the young fraud. "I know of another city like this one," said the boy. "It was in Armenia. Of course, there wasn't sand all around to keep us in. This town was imprisoned by its own lack of identity. There were perhaps five thousand Turks living there, of which several may have been my true father. Indeed, 'several' hardly does justice to the whiteness of my mother's eyes, or the perfection of her skin, at least in those days of a decade past. But I must be modest in all accounts, so that later claims may be made with greater hope of acceptance."

"You are wise beyond your years, Kebap," said Ernst sadly.

"That is not difficult at the age of nine," said the boy. "Nevertheless, I continue. There were perhaps half again as many Armenians, and some Greeks. Persians passed through often, bearing objects which they could not sell. These men rode on the backs of bad-smelling horses and camels of a worse reputation, and we always deviled them continuously until they departed again.

"The houses in this Armenian wonder had flat roofs above stone walls, and it was the custom to grow grass upon the roofs. Naturally, with the best fodder in the neighborhood up there, our sheep and calves grazed above our heads. When we stood on the hillsides not far from this town, the houses were invisible against the surrounding plain. I forget what the name of this city was. One day my mother and several of my uncles took me on a long walk; we packed a lunch of cold meat and water, for the Persians had arrived early that morning and we wanted to escape their presence. We climbed far into the hills so that it was almost time for evening wagib when we stopped. I was asleep, carried by an uncle, on the return journey. I was told the next day that our city could not be found. Every time a herd of sheep was investigated, it was discovered to be firmly on the ground, not upon our familiar rooftops. We wandered the hills and the nearby country for weeks, searching for that disguised city. At last, we arrived here."

"Your strategy was shrewd, Kebap," said Ernst. "That is very difficult to believe."

"It is fully documented."

"I shall have to examine your records someday." Ernst turned to see the boy, but there was no one there. "He is a quick monster indeed," thought Ernst.

Night crept westward, sweeping more of Africa under her concealing shroud. Ernst sat at his table with his bits of paper and his little supper of cheese and apples. Around him the city prepared for night but he didn't care. Customarily each evening after dinner he declared the day productive; arriving at this point, he ordered Scotch whisky and water.

"It is time to relax now," thought Ernst. "It is time to pack away for the day the tedious, essential hatreds and hopes. It is time to sit back and bring out my informal thoughts. How I am growing to despise these memories even more than I despise their subjects. The very issue of my thoughts is soiled by this city, so that had I known the dearest saint of Rome in my youth, I could not think on her now with anything but scorn and malice. I am not interested by my musings, and their temper is becoming too acid for my dispassionate self.

"Eugenie, you seem to be suffering the most, though even now, at this unofficial time of day, I can still summon up nothing but a tepid dislike. You must hold a special position of disfavor in my heart; that is your fate, grow used to it. Marie, you look lovely tonight. A constellation of false memories enriches you. If I do not look at them too closely, I can successfully pretend a few moments of joy. Permit me this indulgence, Marie. I will do the same for you, if ever I'm given the opportunity."

The people on the sidewalk were rushing by now, their faces marked by an intensity of purpose that was never apparent during the day's business hours. Despite Ernst's glum appraisal, the city held many sorts of wonderful things, nonetheless, things rare in Europe and prized by the slaves and the poor. For instance, there was a large colony of artists, and their pottery and sculpture had a certain reputation beyond the walls of the city, though not so great that it attracted either merchants or collectors. Ernst was bored by clay pots, and he had little enough of his own art to offer in trade. At this time of day, the craftsmen of the city would be heading for the bars with their day's earnings, eager for the less tangible beauties of wine and poetry.

The citizens of this place of oblivion chased amusement relentlessly, as a plague victim might follow a hapless doctor in hope of miracles. At night, with only the cold cosmetic of moonlight, the city slipped on a shabby mask of gaiety, but no one criticized. Ernst smiled to himself, nodded to the grim-faced celebrants, observed in a clinical fashion the desperate pursuit of diversion.

It was a dangerous thing to pray that a lasting release might be had from the day's troubles. Each day was so like the previous day that the pleasures pilfered during the night cheapened with the sun's rising. It was as hopeless a thing as the Bridge of the Mad

Berber, who cried for many years to the people of the city that a bridge be built—a gigantic bridge, the world's largest suspension bridge, an engineering marvel to catch the imagination of all civilized peoples. It would rise from the north gate of the city, span the immense waste of sand, cross the distant range of mountains, the narrow strip of coastal plain, the rolling leagues of the sea, to end at last, abruptly, curiously, on the island of Malta. It would be a hardship, indeed, for anyone traveling along that bridge. The Mad Berber chose Malta as the terminus evidently only because that island had been the birthplace of his mother.

Many of the people hurried along the street to the south, toward the Chinese quarter, where another eccentric resident of the city, a weary, stranded Breulen duke, had long ago built a fantastic parody of various memorable sections of Singapore. Like many things in the city, this dollop of Asia seemed romantic at first, but soon distressed the observer with a richness of unwholesome detail. The Breulen nobleman had loved Singapore, the story went, or, at least according to other accounts, had been fascinated by written descriptions and never actually visited the island at all. In any event, he, like so many others of his class, at last took up residence in the lonely African city. His project to reproduce the more spectacular attributes of Singapore was no less insane than the Mad Berber's bridge, but in this case the duke had the wealth to accomplish his goal.

That had been many years ago, and now the false Singapore wore the decaying garments that clothed all the rest of the city. The imitation Tiger Balm Gardens were uncared for—a tangle of brittle growths perverted from their natural forms by the arid climate, the heat, and the genius of the city itself. There was a tumbling-down replica of the Raffles Hotel, but there was no mystery there, merely the scorpions scuttling across the littered parquet. Street dining stalls after the Singapore fashion once dominated a narrow alley, which was now used as a public open-air toilet. The Breulen duke died during the construction of a likeness of Singapore's Happy World; he was to have been buried beneath the joget platform, but his corpse was lost and never found again.

Following the street to the north, the strollers would reach the city's quarter, where replicas of more familiar scenes from other lands dug at their buried homesickness. Ernst could see the brightly colored strings of lights go on, shining through the gaps between trees and buildings, diffused by mist and distance.

A canal ran parallel to the avenue toward the northern gates of the city. On its west bank were restaurants, bars, and casinos.

Women danced naked in all of them. Diamonds were sold by old men in tents, and every building had a few young whores in the front window. There were areas set aside for dozens of different sports: bocci, tennis, and miniature golf facilities were the most popular. The large marketplace was lit by torches. All goods available within the city were also on sale here, at higher prices: fine leather goods; lace; gold and silverware; expensive woods made into furniture, alone or in combination with steel or plastic; perfumes; silks; rugs; every sort of luxury.

Floodlights went on, illuminating models of the ruins of Rome Staeca and Athens. The replica of the Schloss Brühl opened its gates, complete with exact representations of the ceiling paintings of Nicholas Stüber, and the furnishings in white and gold of the dining room, music room, and state bedroom upstairs. Other European landmarks were reproduced in bewildering combinations, but Ernst had only heard stories. He had never seen any of this. He preferred rather to spend his evenings dedicated to serious drinking.

"Allo again, Sidi Weinraub, man of mysterious desires," whispered a thin voice.

"Allo to you, Kebap, youngest scoundrel, apprentice felon. My desires are not so hidden after all. It is only that you will not open your eyes to them. My most supreme desire, at this particular unpleasant moment, is to have you sunken to your lice-ridden ears in that vast ocean of sand."

"That will happen to me, no doubt," said the boy. "That is the sort of thing that occurs to people like me, who have chosen the life of the shadow, the way of the murmured delights. I shall probably pass a good portion of my life bound to creaking wooden racks; or with right wrist chained to left ankle I shall languish forgotten in damp cells beneath this municipal fantasy; or perhaps someone such as yourself will capture me on an aristocratic whim and compel me to violate my principles."

Ernst laughed. "You are doubtless in error," he said loudly, drunkenly. "You shall not be the violator of those principles. You will be the violatee."

"Ah, yaa Sidi, I must take exception. One cannot make such forthright statements as that. One cannot anticipate the odd pleasures of the leisured class. You, yourself, are an example of that."

"I was merely deceived," said Ernst angrily.

"Of course, yaa Sidi."

"And if you do not cease exaggerating the incident, I shall grab you by your scruffy neck and imprison you on a rooftop of grass, where you can munch your life away like the mythical sheep of your babyhood."

Kebap sighed. "Were you then so impressed by my tale?"

"No, but it gave me some interesting glimpses of the shiny new cogwheels of your intellect."

"Then I will tell you of another town," said the young boy. "This place will wipe all memory of the Armenian village from your thoughts."

"A not overly difficult feat."

"There is a town in Nearer Hindoostan," said Kebap in a low, monotonous voice, "which has only one remarkable feature. The area around the city is infested with wild beasts of all kinds. Tigers roam the plains, fearing neither animal rivals nor human guile. Huge beasts somewhat like elephants browse the lower branches of the slender dey trees. There are other curious things about that plain, but my story does not concern them other than to say they caused the citizens of the village to erect a large gray wall. This mud-brick barrier is supposed to be for protection. It does serve to keep out the beasts at night, of course. It also reminds the towns-people of the dangers beyond, and jails them in their city as surely as if the gates were permanently locked."

"How curious," said Ernst scornfully. "Do you know, I don't care at all."

"The principal occupation of the people of this city, in light of their self-imposed imprisonment, is to build and change their town, to provide entertainment both in the labor and in the enjoyment thereafter. And the model they have chosen to follow is our city, here. It was the wall that inspired them. You must know that the mayor's office here receives a letter from this village perhaps eight times yearly, asking for instructions on how they may reproduce the newest alterations in our city. I have seen their version, and it is so exact a rendering that it would give you the nervous ailment peculiar to white Europeans. You would lose all sense of reality and orientation. This café has been built, table by table, tile by tile, bottle by bottle. The very crack in the mirror inside has been recon-structed perfectly, attention having been paid to angularity, width, depth, and character. A man owns the café, from whom Monsieur Gargotier could not be differentiated, even by M. Gargotier him-self. And, do you think, there is a dejected drunkard sitting at this table, many thousands of miles away, whose eyes have the same expression as yours, whose hands flutter just as yours, whose parts smell as foul as yours. What do you think he is doing?"

"He is wishing that you would go away."

"That is mildly put," said Kebap. "I wish I could know what you really thought to say."

"You may find out easily enough. Ask that solitary winesop in Nearer Hindoostan." Ernst had been observing a dimly lighted tower across the square. He turned to look at Kebap, to fix the teasing boy with a venomous stare, perhaps to frighten him away at last, but Kebap was not there. Ernst sighed; he would ask the proprietor to do something about the annoyance.

Every quarter hour a clock tower chimed more of the night away. Sitting alone in the Café de la Fée Blanche, he could hear the distant carnival noises: sirens, the flat clanging of cheap metal chimes, the music of small silver bells, shrill organ melodies, gunshots, voices singing, voices laughing. In the immediate area of the café, however, there were few people about—only those who had exhausted their money or their curiosity and were returning home. Occasionally, the wind brought tenuous hints of strange smells and noises. Still, Ernst had no desire to discover what they might be. Over the years, his route to the city had been long, and these days he was tired.

"I have returned," said Kebap. He leaned casually over the iron rail of the café. Ernst regarded him with some boredom, realizing that this was the first time in quite a while that he had actually seen the boy, though their conversation had been growing increasingly bizarre for several hours.

"There is no such town in Nearer Hindoostan," said Ernst. "There is no such perfect imitation of this corrupted city. The Lord of Heaven would not allow two pits of damnation in one world."

"Of course not," said Kebap with a wink. "Wherever did you get the idea that there might be another?"

"From the pigeons, of course," said Ernst, greatly irritated. "The pigeons have to come from somewhere."

"Why?"

"Have you ever seen a baby pigeon?" asked Ernst. "I don't believe I ever have. I always wondered where the fledgling pigeons were. We see numbers of adult birds around every day; there must be a proportionate mass of immature young. It is a great mystery. And one never sees a dead or dying bird, unless it has been the victim of some accident, generally caused by cruel or careless human agency. I theorize that pigeons are immortal, and the actual carriers and disseminators of all human knowledge. This town of yours in Hindoostan is the product of unimaginative pigeons."

"You ask dangerous questions, yaa Sidi," said Kebap, his

expression fearful. "We had wrens in Armenia, I recall. There were many newly hatched chicks, chirping pleasantly before dusk. But here, concerning the pigeons, you must learn to keep silent."

"I believe I know who your mother might be. At least, if she is not, Eugenie would be proud to call you her son."

"My mother stands over there," said Kebap. "She has not clothed her breasts, as she should in the evening, only because she hopes to beguile you. She is a very energetic person, yaa Sidi, and even though the hour grows late, she still reserves a place in her heart for you."

Ernst shook his head. The liquor had made him sick. "No, I am sorry. I have ceased hunting after hearts. Indeed, I thought no one followed that fruitless sport any longer."

"Then there is my older sister. That is her, on the far side of the square, pretending that she is an armless beggar."

"No, you tactless procurer. You still have much to learn."

"I am sorry again," said Kebap with a cruel grin. "My own body will not be available for perhaps another three years. These are the days of my carefree childhood."

Ernst stood up and screamed at the boy. Kebap laughed and ran toward his mother.

There were few customers in the Fée Blanche after dark. Ernst did not mind. His nights were entrusted to solitude; he actually looked forward to night, when he ceased performing for the benefit of the passersby. Now his only audience was himself. His thoughts grew confused, and he mistook that quality for complexity. By this time, he was taking his whiskey straight.

There had been a woman, Ernst thought, later in his life than either of his juvenescent calamities. This woman had brought a great settling of his rampant doubts, a satisfaction of his many needs. There had been a time of happiness, he thought. The idea seemed to fit, though the entire memory was clouded in the haze of years and of deliberate forgetfulness. There was a large open space, an asphalt field with painted lines running in all directions. Ernst was dressed differently, was speaking another language, was frantically trying to hide somewhere. He couldn't see the picture any more clearly. He couldn't decide whether or not he was alone.

Somehow it now seemed as if it hadn't even been his own experience, as though he were recalling the past of another person. He had forgotten very well indeed.

"Your passport, sir?" he whispered, remembering more.

"Yes, here it is," he answered himself. "I'm sure you'll find it all in order." He spoke aloud in German, and the words sounded odd in the hot desert night.

"You are Ernst Weinraub?"

"With a *t*. My name is Weintraub. A rather commonplace German name."

"Yes. So. Herr Weintraub. Please step over here. Have a seat."

"Is something wrong?"

"No, this is purely formality. It won't take but a moment to clear it up."

Ernst recalled how he had taken a chair against the gray and green wall. The official had disappeared for a short time. When he returned, he was accompanied by another man. The two spoke quietly in their own language, and quickly enough so that Ernst understood little. He heard his name mentioned several times, each time mispronounced as "Weinraub."

Ernst shook his head sadly. He had never gone through such a scene with any border officials, and he had never spelled his name with a "t." He stared at the hotel across the avenue and took a long swallow of whiskey. Now the Fée Blanche was empty again except for himself and M. Gargotier, who sat listening to a large radio inside the dark cave of the bar.

"Monsieur Weinraub?" It was Czerny, his gray uniform soiled, his tunic hanging unbuttoned on his thin frame. "You're certainly dependable. Always here, eh? What an outpost you'd make." Czerny staggered drunkenly. He supported a drunken woman with the aid of another uniformed man. Ernst's own eyes were not clear, but he recognized Ieneth. He did not answer.

"Don't be so moody," said the woman. "You don't have any more secrets, do you, Sidi Weinraub?" Czerny and the other man laughed.

Ernst looked at her as she swayed on the sidewalk. "No," he said. He took some more of his liquor and waved her away. She paid no attention.

"Here," said Czerny, "try some of this. From the amusement quarter. A little stand by the Pantheon. The man makes the best stuffed crab I've ever had. Do you know Lisbon? The Tavares has a name for stuffed crab. Our local man should steal that honor."

"Alfama," said Ernst.

"What is that?" asked Ieneth.

"Alfama," said Ernst. "Lisbon. The old quarter."

"Yes," said Czerny. They were all silent for a few seconds. "Oh, forgive me, M. Weinraub. You are acquainted with my companion, are you not?"

Ernst shook his head and raised his hand for M. Gargotier, forgetting that the proprietor had retired inside his bar and could not see.

"We have met before," said the stranger in the uniform of the Jaish. "Perhaps M. Weinraub does not recall the occasion. It was at a party at the home of Safety Director Chanzir." Ernst smiled politely but said nothing.

"Then may I present my friend?" said Czerny. "M. Weinraub, I am honored to introduce Colonel Sandor Courane."

Czerny grinned, waiting to see how Ernst would react. Courane reached over the railing to shake hands, but Ernst pretended not to see. "Ah, yes," he said. "Forgive me for not recognizing you. You write verses, do you not?"

Czerny's grin vanished. "Do not be more of a fool, M. Weinraub. You see very little from your seat here, you know. You cannot understand what we have done. Tonight the city is ours!"

Ernst drained the last drop of whiskey from his glass. "To whom did it belong previously?" he said softly.

"M. Weinraub," said Ieneth, "we've had some pleasant talks. I like you, you know. I don't want you to be hurt."

"How can I be hurt?" asked Ernst. "I'm carefully not taking sides. I'm not going to offend anyone."

"You offend *me*," said Czerny, beckoning to Ieneth and Courane. The woman and the two uniformed men tottered away down the sidewalk. Ernst got up and took his glass into the bar for more whiskey.

The lonely night passed. It was very late. Ernst drank, and his thoughts became more incoherent and his voice more strident; but there was only M. Gargotier to observe him now. He sang to himself, and thought sadly about the past, and, though he gestured energetically to the proprietor, even that patient audience remained silent. Finally, driven further into his own solitude, he drew out his most dangerous thoughts. He reviewed his life honestly, as he did every night. He took each incident in order, or at least in the special order that this particular night demanded. "The events of the day," he thought, "considered with my customary objectivity. A trivial today, a handful of smoke."

Only the bright, unwinking lights of the amusement quarter still pierced the darkness. The last celebrants had all straggled back up the street, past the Café de la Fée Blanche. Now there was only Ernst and the nervous, sleepy barkeep.

When was the last time Ernst had seen Gretchen? He recalled the characteristic thrill he got whenever he saw his wife's comfortable shape, recognized her familiar pace. What crime had he committed, that he was left to decay alone? Had he grown old? He examined the backs of his hands, the rough, yellowed skin where the brown spots merged into a fog. He tried to focus on the knife ridges of tendon and vein. No, he decided, he wasn't old. It wasn't *that*.

Ernst listened. There were no sounds now. It had been a while since Kebap had last sauntered past with his vicious words and his degenerate notions. It was so like the city, that one as young as the boy could already possess the bankrupt moral character of a Vandal warlord. The festivals in the other quarters of the city had long ago come to an end. The pigeons in the square did not stir; there wasn't even the amazed flutter of their sluggish wings, lifting the birds away from some imagined danger, settling them back asleep before their mottled feet touched the ground again. They wouldn't move even if he threw his table into their sculpted flock.

There was no Kebap, no Czerny, no Ieneth. There was only Ernst, and the darkness. "This is the time for art," he said. "There can't be such silence anywhere else in the world, except perhaps at the frozen ends. And even there, why, you have whales and bears splashing into the black water. The sun never sinks, does it? There's always some daylight. Or else I have it wrong, and it is dark all the time. In any event, there will be creatures of one sort or another to disturb the stillness. Here I am, the one creature, and I've decided that it is a grand misuse of silence just to sit here and drink. The night is this city's single resource. Well, that and disease."

He tried to stand, to gesture broadly and include the entire city in a momentary act of drama, but he lost his balance and sat heavily again in his chair. "This is the time for art," he muttered. "I shall make of the city either a living statue or a very boring play. Whichever, I shall present it before the restless audiences of my former home. Then won't I be welcomed back! I'll let the others worry about what to do with these mean people, these most malodorous buildings, and all this sand. I'll drop it all down in the middle of Lausanne, I think, and let the proper authorities attempt to deal with it. I shall get my praise, and they shall get another city."

He fretted with his clothing for a few moments, fumbling in drunken incompetence with the buttons of his shirt. He gave up at last. "It is the time for art, as I said. Now I must make good on that claim, or else these gentlefolk will be right in calling me an idiot. The concept of presenting this city as a work of art, a serious offering, had a certain value as amusement, but not enough of enchantment to carry the idea beyond whimsy. So, instead I shall recite the final chapter of my fine trilogy of novels. The third volume, you may recall, is entitled *The Suprina of the Maze*. It concerns the suprine of Carbba, Wreylan III, who lived about the time of the

Protestant Reformation, and his wife, the mysterious Suprina With-out A Name. The suprina has been variously identified on many occasions by students of political history, but each such 'authoritative account' differs, and it is unlikely that we shall ever know her true background."

Ernst looked up suddenly, as if he had heard a woman calling his name. He closed his eyes tightly and continued. "This enigmatic suprina," he said, "is a very important character in the trilogy. At least I shall make her so, even though she does not appear until the final book. She has certain powers, almost supernatural. And at the same time, she is possessed of an evil nature that battles with her conscience. Frequently, the reader will stop his progress through the book to wonder at the complications of her personality.

"She is to be loved and hated. I do not wish the reader to form but a single attitude toward her. That is for Friedlos, my protagonist. He will come riding across the vast wooded miles, leaving behind in the second volume the bleak, gelid corpse of Marie, lying stiff upon the frontier marches of Breulandy. Friedlos will pass through Poland, I suppose, in order to hear from the president there a tale of the Queen Without a Name. I must consider how best to get Friedlos from Breulandy to Poland. Perhaps a rapid transition: 'A few weeks later, still aggrieved by the death of his second love, Friedlos crossed the somber limits of Poland.' Bien. Then off he starts for Carbba, intrigued by the president's second-hand information. Ah, Friedlos, you are so much like your creator that I blush to put my name on the book's spine."

Ernst dug in his pockets, looking again for his outline. He could not find it, and shrugged carelessly. "Gretchen, will you ever learn that it is you he seeks? I have put you on a throne, Gretchen. I have made you suprina of all Carbba, but I have given you my own life."

He longed to see Steven, his son. It had been years; that, too, wasn't fair. Governments and powers must have their way, but certainly it wouldn't upset their dynastic realms to allow the fulfilling of one man's sentiments. How old was the boy now? Old enough to have children of his own? Perhaps, amazingly, grandchildren for Ernst? Steven might have a son; he might be named Ernst, after his funny, old grandfather.

"How unusual it would be, to bounce a grandchild upon this palsied knee," he thought. "I doubt if ever a grandchild has been cuddled in all the history of this city. Surely Kebap could not accurately identify his own grandparents. Would they be anxious to claim him? He is, after all, somewhat of an objectionable child. And he has had only nine years to develop so remarkably offensive a manner. It is truly an accomplishment—all emotional considerations aside, one must give the wretched boy his due.

"There is something about him, though, that obsesses me. If there were not, I should without hesitation inflict some kind of permanent injury upon him, to induce him to leave my peace unspoiled. I detect an affinity. I cannot dispute the possibility that I, myself, may be the lad's own father. What a droll entertainment that would be. I shall have to explore the possibility with him tomorrow. Indeed, the more I consider it, the better the idea becomes. I hope I can remember it."

He heard the rattling of M. Gargotier drawing the steel gate across the door and windows of the small café. The sound was loud and harsh, and it made Ernst feel peculiarly abandoned, as it did every night. Suddenly, he was aware that he sat alone in a neglected city, a colony despised by the rest of the world, alone on the insane edge of Africa, and no one cared. He heard the click of a switch, and knew that the Fée Blanche's own sad strings of lights had been extinguished. He heard M. Gargotier's slow, heavy steps.

"M. Weinraub?" said the proprietor softly. "I will go now. It is nearly dawn. Everything is locked up. Maybe you should go, too, eh?" Ernst nodded, staring across the avenue. The proprietor made some meaningless grunt and hurried home, down the street.

The last of the whiskey went down Ernst's throat. Its abrupt end shocked him. So soon? He remembered M. Gargotier's last words, and tears formed in the corners of his eyes. He struggled to order his thoughts.

"Is that the whiskey? I need some more whiskey," he said aloud. There was an unnatural, cracked quality to his voice that alarmed him. Perhaps he was contracting some disgusting rot of the city. "There had better be some more whiskey," he thought. "It isn't a matter of courtesy any longer. I require a certain quantity of the stuff to proceed through this. Gretchen would get it for me, but I cannot find Gretchen anywhere. Steven would get it for me, but I haven't seen Steven in years. One would think that someone in my position would command a bit more devotion."

He wondered about his sanity for a moment. Perhaps the day's excitement, perhaps the liquor, had introduced a painful madness into his recollections. He realized that, in point of fact, he had never been married. Gretchen, again? Where had that name come from? Who could she be? Steven, the fantasy son? Ernst's father's name had been Stefan, perhaps there was some connection.

He called to M. Gargotier. "More whiskey, straight, no water." He wanted to believe that there was still some darkness left, but he could already make out the lines of the hotel across the street, just beginning to edge clearly into view from the mask of nighttime.

"I have never traveled *anywhere*," he admitted in a whisper. "I did not come from anywhere." He sat silently for a few seconds, his confession hanging in the warm morning air, echoing in his sorrowing mind. *Will that do?* he wondered. He looked in vain for M. Gargotier.

He could almost read the face of the clock across the street. He picked up his glass, but it was still empty. Angrily, he threw it toward the clock. It crashed into pieces in the middle of the street, startling a small flock of pigeons. So it was morning. Perhaps now he could go home. He rose from his creaking latticed chair. He stood, wavering drunkenly. Wherever he turned, it seemed to him that an invisible wall held him. His eyes grew misty. He could not move.

"No escape," he said, sobbing. "It's Courane that's done this. Courane and Czerny. He *said* they'd get me, the bastards, but not *now*. Please." He could not move.

He sat again at the table. "They're the only ones who know what's going on. They're the ones with all the facts," he said, searching tiredly for M. Gargotier. He held his head in his hands. "It's for my own good, I suppose. They know what they're doing."

His head bowed over the table. Soon he would be able to hear the morning sounds of the city's earliest risers. Soon the day's business would begin. Not so very long from now, M. Gargotier would arrive again, greet him cheerfully as he did every day, roll back the steel shutters and bring out two fingers of anisette. Now, though, tears dropped from Ernst's eyes onto the table's rusting circular surface. They formed little convex puddles, and in the center of each reflected the last of the new morning's stars.

Introduction to
The Plastic Pasha

This is what George had to say about "The Plastic Pasha":
"It's about Marîd Audran's kid brother (I've mentioned in the books that their mother sold the younger brother when they were young). He's grown up now and become the ruler of Algeria. I don't think Marîd ever meets him, though. The story's about the official acceptance of the brain-wiring technology in the Islamic world . . . Somebody comes up with a personality module of the perfect Islamic governor, and that leads to a battle over who is qualified to wear it. . . ."

George had also told me that the personality moddy was that of Thomas Jefferson—one of George's personal heroes—thus leaving the reader with the rather puzzling question of who's really in charge here?

George's relationship with his own brother was stormy and difficult, and they finally became estranged about three years before George's death. I don't know how, or if, that would have translated into this story, or which of the characters we've met so far, in the few pages that he wrote, is the protagonist, if any.

George finally began work on this story the week of April 15, 2002; I got this fragment off his computer's hard drive after he died.

—Barbara Hambly

The Plastic Pasha

TO THE NORTH OF THE CITY OF BEKHAOUT WAS A narrow pass through the mountains to the coastal lowlands and the sea. Around the city to the east, west, and south was a wide hardscrabble plain, and not far from the ancient fortified walls flocks of sheep foraged where sun-scorched grass still grew. They grazed unaware of the day's significance, although some would be selected as sacrifices to mark the Great Feast, celebrated throughout the Islamic world as the culmination of the year's pilgrimage to Makkah.

A fresh wind blew fine grit and sand first from one direction, then another. Two men in khaki uniforms held a struggling black ram, while a third man hobbled it with ropes. A fourth man, much older than the others, watched with shrewd eyes. In his youth he had stood tall and straight, but now he was bent over, leaning on a stout wooden staff. He wore a clean white shirt buttoned to the neck, with its shirttails flapping over black trousers, a white robe over them, leather sandals on his feet, and on his head the turban of a scholar of the Qur'ân. "This is a good animal," the old man said in a dry, hoarse voice.

"It's the finest ram on the plain of Bekhaout, Imam Abbas," one of the uniformed men said. He and his fellows had begun to decorate the animal with long satin ribbons of scarlet, blue, yellow, and green.

"Soon the ulema will choose a new leader for our country," the imam said thoughtfully. "Then next year, Allah willing, that man will relieve me of this privilege."

The three soldiers were startled. "But, Wise One," one of them said, "it's a holy tradition."

"Yes," the imam said, sighing, "and when I perform it, I recall the faith of Father Abraham when the Lord directed him to sacrifice his son, Ishmael. Yet of all my duties, it's the least pleasant. Now, hold this beautiful animal still. His head must be turned toward Makkah—that way." The old man pointed across the plain with one long, bony forefinger.

"The sword, Wise One," said the third man, who wore a sergeant's uniform. He drew a magnificent gold-hilted ceremonial blade from its jeweled scabbard and passed it to the imam.

Imam Abbas took the sword in his right hand. "In the name of Allah," he said in a loud, clear voice. He slashed the helpless ram's throat and said, "God is most great." Then, without turning his head, he handed the bloody sword back to the sergeant who held the scabbard.

"I'll take the ram to the qadi," the second man said. He was younger than the others, and his face was flushed with excitement.

"Ride quickly," Imam Abbas said. "If the ram is still alive when you arrive at the house of the qadi, then there will be peace and good fortune in Bekhaout for the next year."

The young man grinned. "That's why I'm using the jeep and not my horse," he said. The three soldiers wrapped the terror-stricken ram in a blanket and threw it into the back of the open jeep.

"Go with God, Salim!" shouted one of the other men. They watched as he got behind the steering wheel and roared off across the stony plain toward the gates of the city, raising a thick, choking cloud of dust behind him.

"Superstition," the imam muttered. The two soldiers overheard, and exchanged glances.

"Imam Abbas," the sergeant said, "you have no horse."

"No," the old man said, "I walked here from the city."

"May I offer you my own horse to return, Wise One?"

The imam smiled but shook his head. "Thank you, sergeant, but I wish to go back on foot as well. For me, the most pleasant part of this day's observance is to be left alone to meditate, here beyond the ramparts of the city. I enjoy the exercise."

"As you wish, Wise One," said the sergeant. "I return to you the Sword of the Sharif."

The imam took the ceremonial weapon and watched the

sergeant and his companion mount their horses. They saluted the old man, then wheeled their mounts and set off after the jeep at an easy trot.

Imam Abbas choked on the dust in the air, and unwound his turban a bit to serve as a mask over his mouth and nose. He looked about himself for a moment, seeing the northern mountains pink as crystal quartz in the summer sun, the dry, barren beauty of the plain, and the proud aspect of the city itself, which had witnessed too much history ever to admit that it was becoming a forgotten ruin. Here, where another man might have seen only desolation and poverty, Imam Abbas felt an inexplicable flush of happiness. "God is most great," he murmured, and he prayed that Salim would, indeed, deliver the ram still alive to the qadi of Bekhaout.

The army private felt a similar joy as he bounced along in the jeep on the rocky track that led to the Bab es-Sayf, the Gate of Summer. Salim felt that bringing the ram sacrificed for the city was the most important event in his young life, and for a time the world seemed unnaturally vivid. The intensity of the colors, the smells, and the sounds exhilarated him. As soon as he rattled through the city's gate and up the Avenue Colonel Boushaar, Salim pressed the jeep's horn with the palm of his right hand and did not let it up again, sounding a shrill warning to the old women and donkeys beyond the sudden turns of the cobblestone street.

There were men and boys squatting in the meager shade of whitewashed walls, their heads covered with blue turbans or red felt tarbooshes. Their eyes turned to follow as Salim rocketed by, though none of them was curious enough in the heat of the day to stand and run after the jeep. Salim grinned as he wrenched the steering wheel once hard to the right, and then immediately back to the left, and finally stamped his foot on the brake to come to a halt before the house of the qadi on the north side of 10 January Square.

"This must be the sacrificial animal," said the qadi to a young man in a gray business suit and white knit skullcap.

Salim jumped out and ran to the back of the jeep. "Look, Your Honor," he said, pulling away the bloodstained blanket, "the ram is still alive!"

The man in the business suit turned his face away. The qadi came nearer to the jeep and glanced at the dying animal. "The butcher will attend to it now, soldier," he said.

"Yes, Your Honor," said Salim. "Good fortune to you, and to the city of Bekhaout!"

The qadi paid no further attention to him, but gestured to his companion. "My cooks will roast the animal," he said, "and we'll

dine on it later, but I always distribute most of the meat to my
neighbors for their festival. The streets will be filled with their
singing all day long." The qadi shrugged. "So this one day out of the
year I feed their hunger, and all the rest of the year they call me
Father of Generosity."

"That is the art of politics, Taalab," said the young man in the
business suit.

The qadi smiled. "An art you've studied and learned well,
Hussain Abdul-Qahhar," he said. "Now, come with me. Let's make
ourselves comfortable. We have much to discuss before your meeting tonight."

They entered the qadi's home and climbed the stairs to a large,
low-ceilinged room overlooking a tidy courtyard and splashing
fountain. The warbling of caged songbirds came in through screens
made of narrow strips of wood, and there was the delicate perfume of cultivated flowering shrubs on the warm breeze. The qadi
indicated that Hussain Abdul-Qahhar should make himself comfortable, and he himself reclined on one of two lacquered divans,
both upholstered in green brocade.

A servant girl brought a tray and set it on a low table between
the two divans. "Coffee, Hussain?" asked the qadi.

"May your table last forever, Taalab."

The qadi nodded, and the servant girl poured two cups of
coffee. She handed one to Abdul-Qahhar and one to her master.

"Bismillah," said Taalab. In the name of God.

"Bismillah," murmured Abdul-Qahhar. He sipped the coffee.
"Always! It is excellent."

"May God lengthen your life," said Taalab. He drained all the
coffee in his cup and put it aside. "If we may, I'd prefer to dispense
with the social niceties and get right to the immediate problem."

"As you wish, Taalab. I'm at your disposal."

The qadi regarded his guest in silence for a moment. "I'm
too battle-hardened to take your meaning literally, my young friend.
I wish to know if you think you have enough support among the
ulema to be elected."

Abdul-Qahhar sipped more coffee as he thought. He wondered
if he dared be entirely truthful. "I admit that there's been some
doubt," he said finally. "You haven't attended the meetings of the
Consultation, so you haven't heard the arguments."

Taalab yawned lazily. "The same old bickering, I expect. The
conservatives fighting the young hotheads pushing for reform, am
I right?"

Abdul-Qahhar shrugged. "Only now it's complicated by the

Berbers, who are demanding a higher standard of living. They claim that the Arab majority in the cities is holding them down."

"It's true enough, isn't it?" The qadi was beginning to look bored.

"That's beside the point," said the younger man. "No, the issues are not new, but the matter of Unification is causing conflict even between long-time allies. The ulema will choose our new leader today or perhaps tomorrow, but he may not be the most qualified man. He may only be best at soothing tempers and making empty promises."

"The best politician, you mean," said Taalab. He poured himself another cup of coffee.

"Yes. I've come to despise politicians."

"Then if you aren't elected, who'll be the next president?"

"Yahya ben Sadiq," said Abdul-Qahhar with a grimace, as if he'd bitten into a rotten fruit.

"Ben Sadiq is a pirate, all right," said the qadi, "but he has charisma. He knows how to make you smile while he robs you."

The man in the business suit nodded agreement. "I wish I had some of that skill," he said. "He's masquerading as a liberal this session, pleading for tolerance and aid for Arabs and Berbers alike, arguing that Western science can't be entirely evil if it feeds our Muslim brothers."

Taalab leaned back against his cushions and tapped a thumbnail thoughtfully against his strong white teeth. "Is it true that he's had his brain wired?"

Abdul-Qahhar took a deep breath and let it out heavily. "Yes, and he flaunts the implant before everyone. He has arrived bareheaded to every session of the Consultation."

The qadi nodded knowingly. "Watch him, Abdul-Qahhar. I'll bet he'll find a way to make the neurosurgery seem a gift from Allah. You must undermine his strategy at every opportunity."

"I've tried, but the radical delegates have been swayed by his talk of reviving the Islamic brotherhoods. He clamors for spiritual politics, but he carefully avoids talking about practical goals and methods. When he begins to speak, the council chamber fills immediately with wispy, warm clouds of optimism."

Taalab laughed. "And you can't pin him down to how he intends to make those marvelous changes, or administer them, or pay for them. You'd hardly believe that Ben Sadiq was the most ruthlessly conservative member of the ulema not so long ago. Now he's a radical. At the next session, who knows what his politics will be?"

They talked for a while longer, until the qadi's servants brought in platters of couscous and vegetables and roast mutton. They had a leisurely meal, during which they spoke no more of the Consultation, but inquired instead into the health of each one's family and friends. Finally, just after the evening prayers, the qadi walked with his guest down to Abdul-Qahhar's small electric automobile.

"I wish you luck, my friend," said the qadi. "I'd offer you advice, but it is your hand in the fire, while mine is in the water."

"I thank you for your good wishes," said Abdul-Qahhar.

"Go with safety, then, and protect the future of our nation."

Abdul-Qahhar got into his car and shut the door. "Allah yisallimak," he said. God bless you. He started the car and drove to the meeting hall of the Consultation of the Two Peoples.

The evening session had not yet been called to order, and the council chamber was a riotous madhouse of noise and confusion. The ulema, the scholars and experts in Islamic law who had convened in Bekhaout, were gathered in many small groups, all loudly arguing over their interpretations of Islamic tradition that governed their individual political outlooks. Hussain Abdul-Qahhar paused at the entrance to the meeting hall and smiled ruefully, watching the wildly gesturing Arabs and Berbers. It had been a long time since such a convention had been called, and Abdul-Qahhar prayed briefly that it wouldn't explode into violence—at least not until the necessary work of choosing a national leader had been finished.

He saw a young man wearing a black turban waving to him from a desk near the front of the assembly. It was Muhammad Timgadi, who had been his classmate at religious college in Oran. Abdul-Qahhar pushed his way through the crowded aisles and took a seat beside his old friend.

"Did you have a pleasant day?" asked Timgadi.

Abdul-Qahhar shrugged. "Pleasant enough."

"And where did you go? Your absence this afternoon was widely noted."

"I had business elsewhere. Besides, there were no important debates scheduled for this afternoon."

Timgadi pretended to study his fingernails. "And how is the health of Taalab the qadi?"

Abdul-Qahhar turned and glared. "What, am I being followed?"

Timgadi laughed at his friend's reaction. "Hussain, you don't need to be followed. No one in this hall needed to have your absence explained. It was quite obvious that you were out trying to consolidate support for your candidacy."

"Yes, I suppose so. Forgive me, my friend." Abdul-Qahhar frowned. "I wonder if I accomplished anything."

"For your sake and ours, I hope so," said Timgadi, turning to stare back toward the great double doors. "Your rival, Ben Sadiq, spent the noon hours engaged in the same business."

Abdul-Qahhar's eyebrows went up. "Is that true? Taalab mentioned nothing of a visit from Ben Sadiq. Where did he—"

Timgadi laid a hand on his friend's arm. "Quiet," he said, "the imam is making his entrance."

*   *   *

Three thousand copies of this book have been printed by the Maple-Vail Book Manufacturing Group, Binghamton, NY, for Golden Gryphon Press, Urbana, IL. The typeset is Electra, printed on 55# Sebago. Typesetting by The Composing Room, Inc., Kimberly, WI.